TERROR IN THE
Kingdom

Jeff Dixon

Courtney
Enjoy the Adventure
i Whats Kight
Bless! [signature]

Deep River
B O O K S

THIS BOOK IS BUILT upon the following facts:

Fall 1942—Walt Disney, his wife, Lillian; her sister Hazel; and Hazel's husband, Bill Cottrell, paid a surprise visit to the home of legendary American artist Norman Rockwell while the Disneys were traveling in Arlington, Vermont. This started a long and enduring friendship between Norman and Walt.

Spring 1943—Walt Disney was given a gift by Norman Rockwell. The legendary artist gifted Walt with the original art of a *Saturday Evening Post* cover entitled *Girl Reading the Post*. The oil painting was inscribed, "To Walt Disney, one of the really great artists, from an admirer, Norman Rockwell."

August 1943—Walt Disney sent a print of his animated film *Victory Through Air Power* to the Quebec Conference. President Roosevelt and British Prime Minister Churchill were both in attendance, and both would watch the film. This easy-to-understand adaptation of a book explained some revolutionary approaches on how to win a war, along with introducing technologies and methods that were not yet developed.

Spring 1954—Walt Disney visited with Dr. Wernher von Braun, chief of the Guided Missile Development Operation Division at Army Ballistic Missile Agency (ABMA) in Redstone Arsenal, Alabama. Von Braun worked with the Disney Studios as a technical director, making critically acclaimed films about space exploration for television.

April 12, 1965—The Disney brothers, Walt and Roy, were invited guests at the Marshall Space Flight Center in Huntsville, Alabama. The following day, *The Huntsville Times* featured the headline, "Walt Disney Makes Pledge to Space."

November 15, 1965—Walt and Roy Disney held a press conference at the Cherry Plaza Hotel in Orlando, Florida. They announced to the public their plans to build a new Disney theme park in Central Florida.

January 1966—Walt Disney and an assortment of Disney team members traveled to Pittsburg, Pennsylvania. The purpose of their visit was to visit with executives from the Westinghouse Company. Walt gave them a detailed presentation about Epcot, inviting them to be a part of it. Disney was given a behind-the-scenes tour and had several cutting-edge technologies presented and explained to him. Several days later, Walt made an appearance at General Electric offices for the same purpose.

December 15, 1966—Walter Elias Disney passed away at the age of sixty-five in St. Joseph's Hospital in Burbank, California.

December 16, 1966—A private memorial ceremony was held at the Little Church of the Flowers at Forest Lawn Cemetery in Glendale, California. No announcement of the funeral was made until after it had taken place. Only members of the immediate family were in attendance. Forest Lawn officials refused to disclose any details of the funeral or disposition of the body, stating only that "Mr. Disney's wishes were very specific and had been spelled out in great detail."

January 1967—Disney department heads were invited to a screening room at the Disney Studios. Sitting in assigned seats, they viewed a film featuring Walt Disney sitting behind his desk and addressing them as individuals, gesturing toward them as he spoke, and laying out future plans. Roy Disney postponed his retirement to complete the Florida project.

February 2, 1967—Roy Disney was the host at Wometco's Park Theatre in Central Florida for Project Florida. This invitation-only event screened the film *Walt Disney World Resort: Phase 1,* followed by a press conference. The film included portions of the documentary *EPCOT,* featuring Walt Disney and filmed just months before his death.

October 1, 1971—The Walt Disney World Resort opened the gates to the Magic Kingdom theme park.

October 23, 1971—Roy Disney dedicated the Magic Kingdom theme park based upon the philosophies and vision of his brother, Walt Disney. Roy passed away less than two months later.

November 2010—A novel, *The Key to the Kingdom,* a work of factual fiction, is released for the first time.

October 2012—A sequel, *Unlocking the Kingdom,* is released. This work of factual fiction, now known as "faction," continues the story started in *The Key to the Kingdom.*

November 2014—Another installment of the Kingdom series, *Storming the Kingdom*, is released. This third work of "faction" continues to unfold the saga started in the previous two novels.

Today—The lives and legacy of Walt and Roy Disney continue to touch the lives of people around the world.

CHAPTER 1

Under Attack

METALLIC DOORS CLOSED with a slight click as the elevator began its short three-story ascent to the top of the Astro Orbiter. The ride up to the loading platform would only take a few moments, but as the doors shut and the passenger car began to vibrate, Grayson Hawkes knew he had made an error.

The attraction was the visual centerpiece of Tomorrowland. The highly stylized ironwork tower surrounded by various planets created the illusion of the rocket ride's vehicles weaving through the galaxy. In recent years, Hawk had the attraction refurbished so that not only did the twelve rockets rotate around the tower, but the planets also swirled about the outside of the attraction. The twirling planets and moons spinning around the rockets as they rotated in the opposite direction created the illusion of speed in the open-air starship—and all at a dizzying height. Guests could control their space flight eighty feet into the Tomorrowland sky, gaining a unique and thrilling view of the Magic Kingdom.

On a normal night in Walt Disney World's Magic Kingdom, guests would climb aboard one of the two elevators that climbed the gantry to deposit guests in the boarding area of the Astro Orbiter. The genesis of Hawk's mistake was in assuming this night was normal.

He had stepped inside the lift marked "Lift B to Rocket Platform" and pushed the button to rise to the top of Rocket Tower Plaza. The hitch of the elevator as it moved upward gave way to a sudden jerk as the lift car squeaked to a halt between the second and third levels. The ride had lasted just a few moments, but it was long enough for Hawk to realize that he had stepped into a trap.

Hawk's eyes darted from side to side in the empty, darkened car. The unplanned stop could have been a random malfunction, but somehow he knew it wasn't. The simple design of the lift car gave him very few choices.

While the buttons on the control panel gave daytime passengers a chance to make their selection to move the lift, their choices could also be controlled by attraction operators, who could override their selections if need be. As he had rushed through the deserted Tomorrowland, he hadn't take the time to calculate the risk of being here alone and the possibilities of all that could go wrong. In his rushed attempt to get to the top of the Astro Orbiter he had ignored what should have been obvious to him. He had ignored the danger he might have to face to get there.

Reflexively, he pressed the control buttons in an attempt to get the elevator to move. The lights inside the passenger car flickered and then went to black. For a few brief seconds he was swallowed by darkness before an emergency light fought dimly through the inkiness to cast an eerie jade glow across the interior of the cabin. Hawk took advantage of the illumination to start looking for a way out of the car. The sensation of being trapped inside the closed box crept in from the corners of his thoughts, threatening to cloud his clarity as he searched for an escape. With the car caught between floors and the safety grate covering the elevator doors, opening the doors was not an option and wouldn't provide a way out. He glanced up and saw a small escape hatch on the roof. It appeared to be his only means of breaking out of his confinement.

An explosion jarred the elevator car violently, and the gantry shuddered, driving Hawk against the floor. The ringing in his ears, clanging in behind the blast, was deafening, and he placed a hand along the wall to steady himself and will himself back to his feet. The elevator car swayed, and through the ringing he heard what sounded like a hiss of steam. A tsunami of smoke filled the cabin of the elevator, and waves of overheated air burrowed into his lungs. He gasped and choked for air. The temperature inside the elevator had risen instantly, and he widened his eyes, attempting to somehow see through the smoke.

Through the heat and smoke, his brain was screaming at him to find a way out. Now on his feet, he mentally replayed the loop of memory he had created moments before. There was an escape hatch on the roof of the elevator. He had seen it. All he had to do was find it, punch it open, and pull himself out and crawl through the roof. He had been in more dangerous situations than this; he just had to orient himself and get out while he was still able to think through the fog of smoke that threatened to smother him. He would have to find the hatch and then use the handrails along the side of the elevator to give him the height he would need to launch himself through the opening.

Stretching out his arms, he jumped up off the elevator floor and hit the roof. He felt it partially retract at his touch. The hatch had moved but not enough to open. He had guessed correctly. This would have to be his way out. Through the blinding haze, he felt his way along the wall and grasped the handrail. Lifting up his foot and using it as a launching pad, he blasted his fists through the escape panel. He grabbed one side of the panel and gripped it tightly, swinging his body away from the wall so he could pull himself up through the opening.

Smoke raced upward through the opening hungrily, looking for an escape, and Hawk attempted to crawl up and through it toward safety. Gripping both hands along the edge of the opened hatch, he pulled his body up in the billowing smoke. He held his breath as he began to move through the hole.

The second explosion ripped through the elevator shaft, lifted the car, and tossed it back and forth like a pinball trapped between two bumpers. The violent movement tore his hands away from their precious grip on hope, and he was flung like a rag doll against the floor. His body, now covered in slick sweat, thundered onto the bottom of the car. The four-sided metallic fist that had trapped him retightened its grip.

Looking up through stinging eyes, he saw glowing orange flames peeking through the crawling smoke. Hot sparks rained down through the opening, and the back of his throat hurt with a searing, scratchy pain that prevented him from crying out for help.

He'd known the moment he pressed the button on the elevator that he had miscalculated. The mistake was his, and this was his fault. He had failed, and this time they had finally beaten him.

His chest felt heavy, and he struggled to find his next breath. He closed his eyes as the heat inside the oven he was trapped in engulfed him.

CHAPTER 2

Seven days ago
Morning

HAWK TIGHTENED HIS GRIP and pulled himself upward through the black hole of space. Arms quivering slightly, he kicked his dangling legs until they found a foothold on the steel beam beneath him. Now able to shift his weight to his legs, he traversed the monstrous metal playset he found himself perilously perched upon. Reaching another junction where the steel formed an intersection, he tried to focus through the darkness to mentally map where he was going next. Pushing against the structure with his legs to propel himself higher, he found another handhold, and the stretching and pulling of his interstellar climb continued.

Screams pierced the onyx sky above him, and the tremor of the racing rocket ship reverberated through the steel lifelines he clung to. The noise and vibration were par for the course; he had been hearing them from the moment he began his unplanned attempt to scale Space Mountain.

The iconic Tomorrowland attraction had been scaled by others—over the exterior. Regularly scheduled maintenance allowed for cast members to clean, paint, refurbish, and repair the easily recognizable outside of the attraction, traversing the exterior using a variety of methods that allowed for safety. As Hawk clung to his perch, he wondered if anyone had ever climbed it like he was trying now, from the inside out, using the infrastructure of the roller coaster ride as an oversized playground climbing set.

If they had, they'd forgotten to ensure the "safety" part.

All of the elements that made the attraction one of the most popular ever created by the Disney Imagineers now had to be conquered as he climbed through the dangerous darkness of man-made deep space.

Walt Disney had originally dreamed up an idea for an indoor roller coaster that would hurtle guests through space for his Disneyland theme park. Years of development and planning went into the concept before the first Space Mountain became a reality at Walt Disney World in 1975. Eight years of planning and an additional three years of construction had unveiled the structure, which reached a stunning 183 feet above the ground. It was a mountain in every sense of the word. As impressive as the gleaming exterior was to see as it glistened against the Florida sky, the interior was a massive monument to the creativity of Disney designers. The roller coaster had been constructed over a 72,500 square-foot area, made to be ridden in the dark, with special effects creating a feast for the senses. Projections of asteroids tumbling through space, mirror-ball-like reflections of stars stretching out across the infinite span of the cosmos, and the coasters racing along two tracks in and out of all of the surprises that space might contain created the illusion of space travel filled with thrills.

More screams and rumbling overhead caused Hawk to pause a moment, holding his position with every muscle tensed. Space Mountain had been ridden by astronauts and dignitaries from all over the world. The most notable VIP to give her approval of the attraction was one most had never heard of. Edna Disney, the widow of Walt's brother Roy, came to visit the Magic Kingdom and insisted on riding the rocket coaster. She was eighty-four years old, and Disney officials cautioned her against riding due to the turbulent nature of the attraction. Edna pushed back against the warnings and insisted on traveling through space. When she got to the end of the ride, as she was assisted out of the vehicle, she was asked if she was all right. With a wry smile and bit of pride she responded, "My sister and I used to ride all the roller coasters!" She then added, "Of course, that was sixty years ago."

That moment had given Space Mountain the official Disney seal of approval.

Hawk once again pulled himself up and secured another place to grip the structure, using his arms and legs to distribute his weight. He looked through the dimly illuminated sections of the attraction in an attempt to find what he was searching for. As he often did when he faced stressful situations, he talked to himself quietly under his breath.

"What are you doing up here? You've lost your mind. This is insane, you are never going to find what you are . . ."

The blinking light had blended into the background of other special effects so well he had almost missed it.

He stared and tried to focus his eyes through space. There it was—he had seen it again. The red light was periodically flashing on and off below the steel track twenty feet above his head. Now all he had to do was figure out how to get there from where he was.

He turned his head to see if there was a clear way to climb higher. He was disappointed but not surprised that there was not. Twisting about slightly and shifting his weight, he battled to keep his balance and waited through another rush of a rocket over the tracks that sent all the metal trembling beneath him. Seeing no other option or way to get there, he knew that he was going to have to jump to the next metallic beam above his head.

It was only about six feet away. He would leap out toward it, and he could grab it with both arms if he did it correctly. If he didn't, the result would be disastrous. He tried not to imagine his body bouncing off the steel supports that pierced the darkness between him and the concrete floor one hundred feet below. In trying not to imagine it, he realized he'd actually pondered it for a moment.

Shaking his head and scolding himself, he muttered, "So much for trying not to worry about what might happen. Concentrate on what you are about to do."

Leaping into the outer space of Space Mountain, for one breathtaking heartbeat he felt motionless. That sensation gave way to the beam meeting him midflight, and he wrapped his arms around it. It wasn't a graceful transition, and he didn't care. Hugging the metal support to himself, he inhaled and exhaled deeply, making sure he had a good grip. Satisfied he was secure, he swung his legs up to catch the beam and pulled his body around it until he was nestled safely on top. He was going to have to stand up in order to reach the next beam and make his way up to the blinking light.

Slowly rising to his feet and wobbling a bit as he tried to keep his balance, he was now standing on the support. Another rocket full of passengers went screaming past overhead, and the vibration of the beam below his feet caused him to battle for his balance even more.

"You can do this, you can do this, you can do this . . ."

Steadying himself, he reached up and grabbed the next beam. Tightening his grip, he flexed his arm and again pulled himself up higher toward the track.

Space Mountain was the first rollercoaster ever to be placed inside a darkened building. The attraction had captured the spirit of an era in history as the race for space had ignited imaginations all over the world. Space Mountain dared to suggest that the future might feature a casual trip across the universe that was available just by finding the nearest spaceport. Hawk was sure that in none of the designers' imaginations had they ever considered traveling to the top of Space Mountain like he was doing now.

Reaching the source of the blinking light, he pulled himself into a resting position so he could inspect it more closely. The light blinked a brilliant crimson and then darkened. It was positioned on a rectangular box with a switch, similar to what one might find inside an electrical breaker box, and another light, which was not illuminated. The brick-shaped box was connected to another brick of a substance that looked like some type of modeling clay. Hawk assumed it was some type of explosive.

He held his breath and reached out for the switch. Grabbing it between his fingers, he gently tried to flip it down into what he hoped was the off position.

"You have no idea what you are doing—or even if this is going to work. But you are the only one here, and if what you were told was correct, you don't have time to waste."

Great, now he was arguing with himself.

He flipped the switch down into the off position. A scream came from directly above his head as the roar of the roller-coaster rocket rolled past. Instinctively he had ducked as the ride car whizzed past him. The passengers were oblivious to the activity taking place just a few feet below them.

And then it happened: the green light illuminated and glowed like an otherworldly shamrock, a beacon signaling that good fortune was not only his but belonged to every passenger and guest in the attraction. Exhaling and freeing up one of his hands, he found his watch, flicked his finger across its face, and tapped it. The watch, connected to his cell phone, placed a call. The voice on the other end said, "Hello?"

"Close down the attraction and clear the area. I think we are safe now."

Instantly the lights began to flicker on throughout the attraction, chasing away outer space and revealing a very this-worldly interior. Hawk pulled himself up to the coaster track level and sat down on the track near the top of the ride. Getting his bearings, he saw an emergency stairway used to get passengers off the ride in case the computer that managed it had to brake and shut off a zone. It could happen for any number of reasons. Hawk smiled. It was going to be easier to get down than it had been to get up here. Footsteps clanked on the metal steps, and security and law enforcement officers raced up toward him.

Impressive and perhaps even more frightening with the lights on, Space Mountain looked like a mangled maze of metal scaffolding, winding in and through itself, covered in track and surrounded by props that looked like they had been designed for a space exploration film. The glow of the lights revealed a structure that looked more like a warehouse than a spaceport, but that was part of the genius of the storytelling tricks used in the attraction.

Two officers wearing backpacks and vests arrived first.

"Bomb squad," the one man identified himself as he surveyed the situation.

Hawk pointed down, over the side of the track toward the brick with the glowing green light below.

"Down there, about six feet. It had one switch in the middle. I threw it like a breaker, and the red light went out and the green light came on." Hawk rose to his feet.

"Are you sure it's a bomb?" The officer asked.

"I have no idea." Hawk shrugged. "It was dark, I was climbing, and I saw this mechanism that doesn't belong in Space Mountain. I turned it off. I'll let you figure out what it was."

Disney security surrounded Hawk to escort him down the stairway, but he waved them off. He was fine, and he didn't need help.

One of the security guards was looking at the mountain of metal below them. He looked back up toward Hawk.

"Did you really climb all the way up here?" The guard looked back down over the side, and then back toward Hawk. "From all the way down there?"

Hawk paused and allowed his gaze to look over the edge toward the ground. The height made him dizzy. "I did, but I'm glad the lights were off." He smiled at the security team. "If they had been on, I never would have tried it. It looks too scary. I would have been terrified."

"Sir, you put yourself in some kind of danger doing what you just did." The guard, whose name tag identified him as Mac, smiled. "I'm not sure many people would have ever tried to do it. That was pretty heroic, sir. I'll bet you're glad that's over."

"Mac," Hawk shook his head, "there is a very fine line between heroic and crazy. Some people would vote this was a little bit crazy."

Mac nodded at the chief creative architect of the Walt Disney Company, and Hawk descended the long metal stairwell. The attraction was filling with more people as he got closer to the ground level. Pausing on the steps, he looked back up to the top of the structure, where he could see the bomb squad detaching the device from the roller coaster. Hawk had no idea whether it was dangerous or not. It could have been nothing but a box with blinking lights and a switch attached. If it was indeed an explosive device, whoever had placed it there had made it far too easy for him to deactivate.

He let out a sigh and closed his eyes. If what he was thinking was right, this wasn't over as Mac had suggested; it was only just beginning. And that was terrifying.

CHAPTER 3

Seven days ago
Morning

HAWK EMERGED FROM STARPORT Seven-Five, the entrance of Space Mountain, into the bright Florida morning. The golden sphere of the morning sun brilliantly illuminated Tomorrowland like a glistening glimpse of the future—a future, that is, as it might have been envisioned by people in the past. The struggle of Tomorrowland was best summarized by Walt Disney himself when he said, "The only problem with anything of tomorrow is that at the pace we're going right now, tomorrow would catch up with us before we got it built." That had only grown more true since Walt's day.

The gnawing concern consuming Hawk's thinking now was that he was getting ready to face some people from his past who had their own vision for *his* future. Well, he wasn't going down easy. He had refused to let them write the story of his future on other occasions; he wasn't about to give them the chance to write his tomorrows today.

Blinking into the sunlight, Hawk took in what was unfolding before him. Immediately after he had placed his phone call, a number of predetermined security procedures were implemented. The gleaming streets were empty of guests. Each attraction in Tomorrowland was closed and evacuated. Walt Disney World cast members moved through the area and formed a human chain that walked through the streets and effectively herded each guest out, pushing them back to other regions of the park. Tomorrowland was now temporarily was off limits. This method of evacuating an area had only been used a few times before, yet once again it appeared to be effective. Hawk stepped into a Tomorrowland that no longer brimmed with tourists exploring the retro-future of the Intergalactic Space Port Disney Imagineers had created. They had been replaced by what seemed like an ever-increasing army of law enforcement and security teams.

For a moment the sight made him feel wistful. The sudden transformation of Tomorrowland mirrored that of his own life.

Six years ago Hawk had been given a key that changed the trajectory of his life forever. His friendship with an Imagineering legend, Farren Rales, opened up a world he never knew existed. Walt Disney and his brother, Roy, had devised a plan to preserve, protect, and propel the company they had created into the future. They chose three people to help them develop and implement this unbelievable plan. Years later, Rales selected Hawk to become the person entrusted with the responsibility of making Walt's plan a reality. Within a matter of months, Grayson Hawkes, a former pastor who desired to become a better storyteller, was named the chief creative architect of the Walt Disney Company.

Hawk's role as CCA had been exciting and challenging as he discovered that the secrets of the Disney brothers were far different than most might imagine. He also discovered that in the realm of Disney, the villains were very real, and they were not animated. They played a high-stakes game where every move mattered, and the cost, both to Hawk and those he loved, was devastatingly high. He discovered that there were secrets worth dying for, and those close to him had already paid that price. Being close to him involved putting yourself at risk, and Hawk had constantly worried about how to best shield the people, the places, and the things he loved from coming to harm.

A familiar voice called his name, and he turned to see Shep Albert jogging toward him. Shep was one of Hawk's longtime friends who had been drawn into the web of danger. He made some bad choices, and although his intentions were noble, those choices resulted in catastrophic circumstances. Hawk forgave him, but rebuilding trust was slow and at times painful for both. Shep worked on special projects for the company. Hawk extended opportunities for those closest to him to join him at Disney. Hawk needed them: they were his family. At the same time, trying to protect them had proven extremely difficult.

Shep reached Hawk in front of the Star Port.

"You okay, boss?" Shep huffed, and ran a hand through his wiry, tousled hair.

"I am, thanks." Hawk cringed slightly as Shep patted him on the shoulder. Pain stabbed across his shoulder and ran down his back. Perhaps he had not come through his climb in Space Mountain as healthy as he had first thought. He wasn't as young as he used to be. He shook his head and ignored the ache he was sure he would feel in the morning. "Did we get everyone where they needed to be?"

"Just like you asked me to do." Shep waved in front of them. He drew deep breaths into his husky frame, clearly not accustomed to running. "All of the guests were evacuated as soon as you gave the word to go. I contacted Juliette, who sounded the alarm and got both security and the sheriff's department activated."

"You did good, Shep . . . you got everything taken care of." Hawk smiled to reassure him. It felt good to be friends again, even if they were still working on it.

Both men turned when Juliette Keaton arrived. Her slender form moved effortlessly toward them. Blonde, shoulder-length hair surrounded her fresh, pleasant face, which had become the face that stood before the cameras to make media announcements. As the head of communications for the Walt Disney Company, her role involved so many different areas that she had emerged as one of the most powerful voices and individuals within the organization. Like Shep, she had known Hawk for many years. She served alongside him on their ministry staff during the years that Hawk was a pastor. Juliette was perhaps the one person in the world who knew Hawk better than anyone else. Juliette, her husband, Tim, and their children considered Hawk part of their family.

"Hawk, are you hurt?" Juliette rushed her words with concern.

"I'm fine."

"Are you sure?" Disbelief gave way to relief.

"I'll probably be sore tomorrow, but I'm not hurt." Hawk appreciated both of them caring about his well-being.

Juliette clenched her fist and threw a jab, connecting with Hawk's already-sore shoulder. He recoiled at the punch, but it didn't hurt as much as it surprised him.

"Have you lost your mind?" Juliette's relief seemed to melt into the fire of frustration. "You could have been killed! What made you think it was smart to climb up and through the infrastructure of a roller coaster in the dark, looking for a bomb?" She wagged her finger in front of his face. "What if the bomb had gone off? What if you had fallen? What if—"

Hawk reached out and caught the finger she was waving, then gripped her hand with both of his. She shook her head and then looked him directly in the eyes.

"I'm okay, Juliette. Really . . . I am fine." He released her hand and rubbed his shoulder where she had punched him. "Or I was fine, until you hit me."

Juliette smiled and patted Hawk on the shoulder, then gave him a hug. She was careful not to hug his shoulder too tightly.

"I'm just glad you're safe." Then she dropped her voice to a whisper. "Tell me this is not what I'm afraid it is."

Before Hawk could answer, another voice interrupted. "Yes, we are *all* glad you're safe." Cal McManus stepped up to join the three friends.

McManus was the highly respected and regarded Orange County sheriff. Their relationship had changed three years ago when an assassination attempt on Hawk's life, the murder of Hawk's girlfriend, and a series of accidents had plunged the pastor into a world of danger that nearly destroyed him. McManus knew that Hawk held secrets passed down to him from Walt Disney. He didn't like it that Hawk refused to share those secrets with him, but he understood and respected the Disney executive's tenacity.

"My team tells me you just disarmed a bomb placed on a roller coaster. If it had gone off, it would have killed everyone inside the building, injured anyone close to the building, and blown a hole in your Magic Kingdom. Why don't you tell me what's going on."

It wasn't really a request. It was an order.

McManus stared at Hawk, waiting for his answer. Hawk nodded and pointed toward a seating area located to the right of their group. He didn't want to talk here, in the middle of the beehive of activity around the entrance as investigators moved in and the scene was being secured.

The four of them took a seat around the table, and Hawk slid a folded map across the surface toward Cal. The sheriff picked it up and cocked his head.

"This is a map of the Magic Kingdom." He unfolded it. "The same one any guest can pick up when they enter the theme park." His eyes glanced across the map, and then Hawk saw his gaze come to rest on the center.

"That is how I got here. That is how we got here. That is why we are all here now." Hawk allowed his eyes to move from the map to each person seated around the table.

The full-color map was a park guide, available at the entrance of the Magic Kingdom, in multiple shops inside the park, and at each of the resort hotel locations. What set *this* map apart were the words written in black marker across the center.

In the dark you are powerless
What began six years after the death explodes today
Tell no one or it happens even sooner
It is the beginning of the end

"Let's walk this back a little bit for me and explain what it means, so I can understand how this—" McManus stabbed his finger toward the writing on the map— "got us all sitting here outside of Space Mountain talking about bombs and theme parks blowing up."

Hawk took a deep breath and allowed himself a moment to retrace the past hour. He chose a place in his personal timeline to begin the tale, leaned forward in his seat, and rested his arms on the table.

"A little over an hour ago I was at home," Hawk spoke loud enough to be heard by Cal, Juliette, and Shep—but just too low to be heard by anyone close enough to eavesdrop.

McManus interrupted. "At the fire station?"

Hawk lived on Main Street, U.S.A. in the firehouse on the corner of Town Square. "Engine Co. 71" was displayed over a series of second-story windows that in actuality were the windows of the CCA's apartment. After being given the key to the kingdom, he had become a permanent resident of the Magic Kingdom. The second-story space was converted into a living area for him and then expanded over the past few years to give him more room. Just as Walt had done by keeping an apartment over the firehouse in Disneyland, Hawk moved into the firehouse in Walt Disney World. Now park guests would often look toward the windows to see if there was a light on or any indication Hawk was home. Hawk also kept an expansive executive office in the Bay Lake Towers connected to the Contemporary Resort, which included its own living area. McManus knew all of this, so Hawk understood why he might want clarification about where the story began.

"Yes, I was in my apartment." Hawk watched McManus nod and then continued. "Shep was coming to meet me, and we were going over to the Studios for a meeting. He knocked on the door and handed me the map when he came in."

"That would be this map, the one with the message written on it?" The sheriff looked toward Shep suspiciously.

"Yes." Shep cleared his throat. He knew that McManus had been bothered by the decisions Shep made a few years ago which had got him involved with some criminals in the resort. Had it not been for Hawk, the sheriff might have pushed to bring accessory charges against him. "I had just come up the steps and found the map taped to the door of Hawk's apartment. So I just grabbed it and handed it to Hawk when he opened the door."

"So there was just a map randomly stuck to Hawk's door?"

"Like I said." Shep scraped a hand through his hair. "It was just stuck there, right above the doorknob. So I plucked it off the door and handed it to the boss."

Hawk sighed a little at Shep's obvious nerves and McManus's glower. "Sheriff," he said, "people who visit the Magic Kingdom and are big Disney fans know that I live in Town Square. It's not unusual for someone to come up the stairs and knock on the door. Sometimes they'll leave notes under the doormat, or like in this case, stick them right on the door. Usually they are addressed to Hawk at Main Street, U.S.A. or something like that." Hawk leaned back in his chair. "Sometimes we put security at the bottom of the staircase, but when we do that it's a giveaway that I'm home. It's easier to keep security close by. Most people are respectful and just look up to my windows at times. I guess people just want to see if I'm there."

McManus pursed his lips as he listened, nodding. "So there was no security there today, someone stuck a map on your door, and Mr. Albert here found it and gave it to you."

"Yes." Hawk waited to see if McManus was going to ask anything else before he continued. The sheriff was silent, so Hawk launched in to the next chapter. "I opened up the map and saw the note." He spun the map on the table so the words were turned in his own direction. Like they had when he first saw them, the words seemed to darken the whole map with menace. "It took me a moment, but I realized it was a warning and a clue."

McManus rubbed his chin and leaned in closer. "I can't wait to hear how you figured it out."

Hawk shrugged and pointed to the first line written across the map. "In the dark you are powerless." Hawk tapped his finger on the word *powerless*. This line didn't help me until I connected it to the line below it. 'What began six years after the death explodes today.' Construction began on Space Mountain on December 15, 1972 . . . six years to the day after the death of Walt Disney. That's when I was able to understand the first line: 'In the dark you are powerless.' We closed the Tomorrowland Light and Power Company in 2015." Hawk pointed to the large building space at the exit of Space

Mountain. "So the note was referring to Space Mountain in Tomorrowland. The obvious part was that it was going to explode today."

"Overall the clue is pretty vague." McManus shook his head lightly.

"True. But more than enough to figure out what it meant." Hawk swept his hand and gestured across the expanse of Tomorrowland that surrounded them. "Whoever wrote the clue on the map knows the story, the backstory of this area, which most people don't. A metropolis the size of the Tomorrowland community needs power. Tomorrowland is the home of the League of Planets, the Tomorrowland Expo Center, and even a Galactic Federation Teleportation Center, all woven into a storyline that attempts to unpack the story of what Tomorrowland really is. A guest who's just trying to cram in all the attractions they can into one day would never really notice or care about that kind of stuff. But the real fan, the real Disney buff, doesn't just notice; but the storyline matters to them."

"And that tells me what about being in the dark and powerless?"

"Look over there at that mechanical-looking metal palm tree." Hawk pointed to one in a series of metallic trees rising up out of the landscape around them. "That is a power palm. When the metal palm fronds are extended, they capture the energy from the sun and store it in those coconut-shaped globes all around the top of the trunk. The more energy they collect, the more they glow. At night they provide light for this area. When the globes are full, they're removed from the tree. Just like harvesting: the energy is taken out of the globe, it's emptied, and then replaced on the tree again."

Hawk redirected their gaze to another tree nearby. "See that tree? The fronds are drooping and the globes are gone. That's supposed to convey a tree that was loaded with energy and is now currently being harvested. That's why it was left that way, different from all the rest."

Hawk pointed to the building at the exit of Space Mountain. "The harvesting was done, the power was stored, and then it was redistributed from the Tomorrowland Light and Power Company."

"And this was closed in 2015?" McManus followed.

"Yes, so according to the Disney Imagineering storyline, the area would no longer have had a power and light company. Leaving us in the dark with no power."

Hawk paused, then continued. "Connecting that to the clue that said 'six years after the death,' I was able to figure out the location."

"How do you know all of that kind of information?"

"I just do . . . it's about the story. It is always about the story."

"Then why did you make the decision to close the Tomorrowland Light and Power Company?"

"Because we weren't telling the story very well in this area anymore. Most people thought it was a gift shop and video arcade. Our storyline had just fallen apart, and it wasn't being useful anymore, so we decided to close it so we could revamp it, fix it, and tell a better story. If you have a great story, you need to tell it and tell it well. No one cared or knew the story anymore."

"Whoever left you the clue and planted the bomb knew the story." Juliette jarred Hawk back into the moment, stating the obvious.

"And they knew you would know it." McManus said. "They wanted to get you to look for the explosive device. You, personally."

Hawk nodded. "When I read that I was to 'tell no one or it happens even sooner,' I was afraid that whoever was doing this was somehow watching. So if we had shut down Tomorrowland or emptied the attraction, they would've detonated whatever they had put in there." Hawk turned toward Juliette. "So I called Juliette on my watch and told her what was going on as I headed over here. I told her to call you, put the teams on standby to clear the area, and wait until I told them to go. Shep made sure we were ready, but I decided to see if I could find the bomb myself."

"But by creating no observable activity, if there was someone watching they would believe you hadn't said anything." McManus inhaled deeply. "You were taking a dangerous risk."

"Dangerous, yes." Hawk paused. "But I calculated the danger. When I read the last line of the clue, 'It is the beginning of the end,' I realized they had told me not only the location but details about where the device was hidden."

"In the last line?" McManus folded his arms across his chest.

"The beginning of the end. There are two tracks inside Space Mountain, the alpha and the omega. The bomb was hidden on the alpha track, near the top of the ride, near the . . ."

"Beginning."

"Exactly." Hawk nodded, glad McManus understood. "The meaning of the Greek word *alpha*—the beginning."

"And so," McManus opened his hands, "when the clue said this is the 'beginning of the end,' did it mean they were trying to blow up an attraction, that they wanted to kill you, or that there's something else starting here?"

Hawk could see that McManus was already as suspicious as he was. Having lived through the events of a few years ago, McManus was all too familiar with the extremes some would go to in an attempt to take the secrets Grayson Hawkes now held.

"I think whoever did this wanted you to find the bomb—if it was a bomb." Juliette sighed. "They knew you would know the backstory and figure out the clue in time to stop it."

"Do you agree?" McManus looked toward Hawk.

"Yes." Hawk knew Juliette was right. "Whoever did this knew I would find it."

"So our perpetrator is trying to draw you into their game. If you hadn't found it, they would have killed countless others. Do you know what they want, Hawk?"

Hawk groaned inwardly. "Secrets."

"Why? Why now after years of waiting?" McManus leaned in.

"The clue told us why." Hawk pointed again to the map. He tapped the last line with his finger. "It is the beginning of the end."

CHAPTER 4

Seven days ago
Early afternoon

THE MUGGY MIDDAY FLORIDA SUN stretched its warmth down Main Street, U.S.A. as Juliette and Hawk moved through the flow of people. Morning had melted into afternoon while Hawk gave his account of the day's events to three different detectives following his conversation with the sheriff. After much discussion, the decision had been made to reopen portions of Tomorrowland, although Space Mountain would remain closed as law enforcement continued to investigate its interior.

Juliette had drained the battery on her phone acting as a one-woman command center, giving instructions to various departments as she coordinated maintenance, operations, security, and guest relations. The walk back from Tomorrowland to Main Street, U.S.A was the first chance she and Hawk got to talk since the initial chat with Cal McManus. Although guests recognized and acknowledged them as they walked down the street, most resort visitors didn't notice the army of security personnel, all dressed as tourists, moving along with the pair.

"Hawk, what is this about . . ." Juliette asked, ". . . this time?"

Her brow was wrinkled in worry. Juliette had been part of Hawk's Disney adventure from the start. Along with some of their closest friends, it had been her adventure as well. A few years earlier, when Hawk had first come to understand that there were enemies who wanted to seize control of the company from him, Juliette was the first victim of the plot when she was kidnapped. Hawk's love and admiration for both Juliette and Tim Keaton grew even more, because instead of distancing themselves from him through the ordeal, they chose to stand with him and face his enemies. They had become closer than ever.

"I'm not sure," Hawk admitted. "Yet."

He stopped moving and turned toward her. A balloon vendor bumped into him as he handed a helium-filled, mouse-eared balloon to a family. Hawk moved a step or two away, rubbed the middle of his forehead with his fingers, and closed his eyes for a moment. Juliette was clearly as worried as he was, and he desperately wanted to say something to reassure her.

He just didn't know what.

"If their plan really was to hurt park guests, they wouldn't have left a clue as to how to stop them." Hawk kept his voice low. The normal sounds of the Magic Kingdom swirled around them, providing a wall of sound to keep their conversation private while surrounded by thousands of people.

"But what if you hadn't gotten there in time? Do you think the threat was a fake?"

"No."

"So then . . ."

"Then a lot of people would have been hurt."

"Or killed."

"Or killed. And the damage would have been unthinkable. But whoever did this didn't really want that as badly as they wanted *me* to find the . . . device." Although Hawk was sure no one was listening, he wasn't going to use the word *bomb* or *explosive* as a precaution. "This is the next wave in someone's plan to hurt or stop me. Everyone and anyone else who might be hurt by it are just collateral damage to whoever is doing this."

A sudden explosive pop came from behind Hawk. Juliette quickly ducked as Hawk reflexively wrapped his arm around her and moved his own body between her and the sound. A sudden surge of security people moved toward the pair. Eyes dancing across the landscape, Hawk relaxed his protective grasp on Juliette, then waved off the incoming security team. The sound had only been a balloon popping. The cries of a child who had been startled by the bursting souvenir filled the air in its wake.

A nervous smile crossed Juliette's face, and Hawk was snatched back to a time two years earlier in their journey, when an assassin had tried on multiple occasions to shoot them. The proximity of the popping balloon brought those moments back once again, and he flinched. We shouldn't be out here right now, he decided.

"Let's get off the street." Hawk pointed in the direction of the firehouse, which was still a good distance away, and they began moving once again. "The question you asked earlier is the most important one: what is this about? If whoever did this wanted me dead, they could have made that happen in Space Mountain. So, do they want control of the company, or do they want . . ."

"The secrets of Walt Disney you keep?" Juliette stated the question with conviction. They both dreaded the possibility, but based on previous experiences, their fears seemed founded.

"Of course, they want the secrets . . . and this is their end game," Hawk said flatly.

"Or, as the clue said, it's the beginning of the end."

As they rounded the corner of the Emporium, they stepped across the street toward the building marked Engine Co. 71. They were headed toward the stairs that led up to Hawk's apartment when Juliette slowed next to him. As he turned to look at her, he saw her focused on something above them, on the building.

"Hawk, what is that on your window?" Juliette pointed to the second-story window of his apartment that gave him a view of Town Square.

He followed her gaze and saw it. Flat against the window was a rectangular piece of paper. The colors and the shape created a sinking feeling in his chest. Even from the distance between them and the window, he knew what it was.

Another theme park map.

Juliette recognized it at the same time and picked up her pace to match his. Hawk threw open the door of his apartment, then ran the remaining few steps across the room and peered closely at the window.

Taped to the inside of the glass was another theme-park resort map. But this one wasn't a map of the Magic Kingdom. This was a map of Disney's Animal Kingdom. He hesitated for a moment, as if afraid to touch it, then pried it off the window. He placed it on the table below the window, and then they both leaned in as he unfolded it. There had been a message scrawled in marker in the center of the Magic Kingdom map from earlier; he was hoping this new map contained no such message.

That hope was short-lived.

Written in the same handwriting across the center of the map, with the same black ink, was another message. He read out loud.

Go fishing along the 498 and try to stop it
If you can!

To make it fair—Walt did what they did with a magic skyway
Tell no one—or their extinction will happen today.

The muscles in Hawk's shoulders tightened as he began to untangle the meaning of the words. Juliette exhaled. She too must have been holding her breath as he read the words.

"We are looking for something in Animal Kingdom," Juliette said.

"Whatever it is, it's in Dinoland U.S.A." Hawk focused on that section of the map.

"How do you know that?" Juliette found the section.

"We have to go fishing, or looking for something, along the 498. The road signs the Imagineers placed in Dinoland say "US Highway 498," because Animal Kingdom opened in the fourth month, April, of 1998. And 'extinct' . . . extinction has already happened there."

"What about the rest of the clue?" Juliette looked relieved that Hawk had figured out the meaning so quickly. "Where in Dinoland are we looking?"

"I don't know." Hawk shook his head and started folding up the map. "I'm on my way to Animal Kingdom. I'll figure it out there."

"I'm going with you." Juliette headed toward the door.

"No, stay away." Hawk's voice turned sharp. She stopped and turned back to face him.

"Not now, Hawk." Juliette placed her hands on her hips defiantly. "We don't have time for this discussion right now. You need help, I'm going, let's go." She turned toward the door and headed out without waiting. Hawk had seen that look before, heard that tone, and knew she was right—about not having time for discussion. She was wrong about wanting to go, and whether he needed help, well . . . that was probably a matter of opinion. But she was going with him, and he was clearly not going to dissuade her.

As he reached the apartment door, she was already halfway down the stairs. His phone went off and he fumbled to answer it as he moved down the stairs. The call was from Shep, short and sweet, confirming that it had indeed been a bomb inside Space Mountain. He and Juliette disappeared behind an unmarked door to the cast-member-only area behind Town Square. They both headed for the gleaming red-white-and-blue Harley Davidson parked in the exclusive covered parking spot reserved for Hawk alone. Hawk's classic red Mustang had been the previous occupant, until it was blown up in an attempt to scare the CCA a few years earlier. He replaced it with the classic Harley Davidson Sportster XR750, a vintage collector's bike once owned by American daredevil Evil Knievel. It was an enthusiast's dream, not only fast, but screaming "Don't try this at home!" because of the notoriety the legendary daredevil had bestowed on the bike.

Hawk kicked the motorcycle to life, and the engine's whine echoed off the walls. Juliette climbed on behind him. On any other day, he would have taken time to make sure they both had helmets. As reckless as some believed him to be, he was a safety advocate for riders. But this was not any other day.

"Hang on," Hawk shouted over his shoulder. He twisted the accelerator and the engine clanked into first gear.

The Harley roared as they cornered onto the access road surrounding the Magic Kingdom. Beyond the sight line of guests, an intricate network of roadways and access streets allowed for the theme park's day-to-day operation. Narrow, well-taken-care-of asphalt passageways carried scores of service vehicles safely each day.

Moments later, the pair was racing along Floridian Drive, weaving in and out of the other passenger cars that traveled within the Walt Disney World Resort. Hawk calculated the fastest way to get there and decided on Buena Vista Drive. That would keep him out of the path of guests, and he could use one of the access points meant for cast members entering Animal Kingdom. Over the noise of the bike and the breeze, Hawk felt Juliette lean in closer.

"Where are we going in Dinoland?" She spoke in his ear.

"I don't know, exactly. But it has to be there somewhere." His mind was racing faster than the motorcycle.

Hawk replayed the history of Dinoland U.S.A. in his head as he tried to concentrate on the road. The story went that along US Highway 498, in Diggs County, in the heartland of America, the discovery of a fossil had forever changed the area. A small, local lodge was purchased by a research group, and eventually the Dino Institute was created.

Cars slowed up in front of them as they approached an exit. Leaning slightly, Hawk moved left and then cut back to the right to avoid the traffic. His turn was just ahead. Decelerating, he swung the bike wide to make sure he wasn't going too quickly into the tight series of curves ahead.

There had to be a clue in the backstory of Dinoland. According to the story, Chester and Hester were an older couple who owned a local gas station, the only building besides the lodge that existed in the area before the fossil discovery. Their little gas station eventually became a gift shop, and the couple opened up a roadside attraction patterned after the tourist spots that used to dot American highways in a bygone era.

Pulling the motorcycle through the security checkpoint, Hawk and Juliette were recognized by the guard and waved on through. Hawk parked the bike next to the gate that would carry them into the guest portion of the theme park. Hawk helped Juliette get safely off the seat, and they pushed their way through the gate. In a matter of steps they were surrounded by rich, colorful vegetation, the smells of vendor carts offering tasty morsels of food, and the sounds of conversations as people moved around them.

"Juliette, call McManus, call Al Gann, and call Shep. We need to be ready to clear out this area just like we did Tomorrowland." Hawk scanned the wide pathways surrounded by bamboo and lush palms. The crowds were a bit lighter than normal in this area. Good. This was the first break they'd caught so far on this crazy day.

"Hawk, my phone is dead." Juliette held out her hand as they ran. "I drained my battery this morning working the Magic Kingdom site. Give me yours."

Hawk handed her his phone as they rounded the corner into Dinoland U.S.A., and he heard both carnival sounds and screams from guests on thrill rides from Chester and Hester's Dino-Rama filling the air. The miniland within the bigger Dinoland area was loaded with rides, games, and fun. Next to it was Chester and Hester's Dinosaur Treasures, the massive gift shop that was built after the elderly couple expanded the gas station when the fossil exploration boom began. Juliette began making the calls and put distance between them, while Hawk searched for the clue that had brought him to this place.

Suddenly, he thought he knew where it was.

Hawk ran around the side of the building, and saw it. Smiling, he dropped to his knees and searched for another black box. Nestled alongside the building and unnoticed by most, the rusted old gas pump was a bit of history hidden in plain sight. The circular logo of Sinclair Dino Gasoline featured the iconic dinosaur that was the trademark of the very real company. Hawk had noticed this pump years earlier, but it was so long ago that he hadn't been sure it would still be there. Relief flooded him.

But now, as he searched around it, his heart sank. There was nothing out of the ordinary.

Juliette arrived and looked over his shoulder as he pulled back metal cans near the pump, sliding unattached props to the side, turning up nothing. Her face registered concern as Hawk looked up at her.

"What is it?" Her eyes widened.

"There's nothing here." Hawk stood and began looking across Dinoland U.S.A. for something that might catch his attention. "I've missed something. I don't know where it is."

CHAPTER 5

Seven days ago
Afternoon

JULIETTE STARED AT HAWK as he stood looking about. He clenched and unclenched his fists as he scanned the landscape for anything that might spark a thought for what to do next. Surrounded by so much detailed décor, it was easy to be blinded to its uniqueness. Hawk stood in an area that could have been snatched out of a roadside tourist trap along a country road anywhere in the Midwest. Rusted signs; weathered, hand-painted markers; dusty but gaudy decorations; all screamed out to tourists to hand over their money and time.

"Okay, talk me through what you're thinking." Juliette exhaled slowly. "Maybe I can help you figure it out."

Hawk quit his aimless looking around and focused on Juliette. He nervously pulled the Animal Kingdom map out of his pocket and opened it so they could both see the clue.

"Go fishing along the 498 and try to stop it—if you can." Hawk looked back toward her. "The 498 is the highway the Imagineers created to commemorate the date the park opened. Their backstory said that a fossil discovery was made along the 498 in Diggs County. It started a rush of bone hunters coming to this area. Chester and Hester owned a gas station next to the old lodge that was here before the area exploded with researchers, students, and tourists."

"And we are here, right here . . . why?"

Hawk pointed to the gas pump. "This is a Sinclair gas pump. The next line, 'to make it fair, Walt did what they did with a magic skyway,' is what made me think of this. Sinclair is a real oil and refining company established a long time ago. This logo of the brontosaurus was on signs all over the US for years. At the 1964–65 New York World's Fair, Sinclair sponsored a dinosaur exhibit. They called it Dinoland, and it featured life-size reproductions of nine different dinosaurs." Hawk paused, thought, and then continued. "'To make it fair' . . . that references the World's Fair, because Walt Disney was also at the New York World's Fair with his own dinosaur attraction. It was called Magic Skyway, and guests rode in Ford convertibles traveling through time from the day of the dinosaur to the modern era. After the fair, the Audio-Animatronic dinosaurs were moved to Disneyland. So Walt did what they did: they both had dinosaur stuff in their attractions. The word 'extinction' is the rest of the dinosaur reference."

They both grew silent. Juliette looked from the map to Hawk and then glanced back to the gas pump. Tilting her head, she looked back toward her boss. "Is this the only reference to Sinclair hidden around here?"

Hawk snapped his gaze to meet her eyes. "There has to be another. But where?"

He ran his hand through the mop of hair on his head, messily coiffured by the windy motorcycle ride. He smiled and motioned for Juliette to follow him.

"The first line of the clue is what I missed. 'Go fishing along the 498.' We're in the wrong place. We have to go to Restaurantosaurus."

They ran toward the large, guest dining facility, which looked like a cross between an old storage shed and a campground general store. They quickly crossed the concrete path to get there. "Most people have never really noticed that this dining area is an attraction in and of itself. I'd forgotten that in the backstory this used to be an old fishing lodge."

They arrived at the entrance door and hesitated. After a quick glance around, Hawk moved inside as he continued to tell Juliette the story.

"After dinosaur bones were found, this building was no longer used as a fishing lodge; it became just a lodge. Professors and grad students moved in and created a dormitory. They needed a place to eat, so a cafeteria was added. Since research programs are always looking for funding and grants, the students decided to open their cafeteria to the public and make a few extra bucks to underwrite the cost of their digs. Not being too particular about what to call their eatery, they simply erected a large sign on the roof that said RESTAURANT."

Hawk surveyed the room, looking for inspiration. The décor, a mix of student clutter and dusty artifacts, offered a thousand possibilities—but nothing stood out. "College students being college students, it didn't take long before adding the suffix 'osaurus' to signs everywhere became the fad.

One ambitious young man decided to add a huge 'OSAURUS' to the 'RES-TAURANT' sign, and the name stuck."

Juliette nodded, scouring the building for anything marked with a Sinclair logo. Around them, a few diners noticed Hawk and recognized him, gawking in his direction. He pointed toward another section of the restaurant, and they moved through the doorway.

"As more and more relics were unearthed, the paleontologists displayed them on the walls and shelves of the lodge. Eventually, this was supposed to be part visitor center, part museum, part support facility. The more the operation and the digging expanded, the more infrastructure was needed. So they added this area . . . this is a Quonset hut. Built adjacent to the lodge, this would have been the maintenance bay for their field vehicles."

The interior of the hut was trimmed with old engine parts, a variety of tools, hubcaps, and car parts. The walls were decorated with greasy handprints, strategically positioned to create grease paintings of dinosaurs. Like so many other places within Walt Disney World, there were too many details to take in on any single visit.

The oil cans on a shelf across the room, for example—Hawk had never noticed those before.

With his heart leaping, he raced toward the shelf. He grabbed a nearby chair, stepped on top of it, and reached toward the cans.

Oil cans with the same distinctive brontosaurus logo. The logo on the cans was Sinclair. The same brand of gasoline Chester and Hester sold at their service station.

As he pulled back the cans gently, papers fell from the shelf and floated to the floor. Ignoring them, he kept searching—and then he saw it. A black, brick-shaped box, nearly identical to the one he'd found in Space Mountain, attached to the same clay-like substance. The crimson light on the box blinked steadily at him, and he sucked in his breath. He reached out to flip the switch on the box. It had worked before; surely it would work again.

A click sounded as he moved the miniature lever. The red light cut off, and the glow of the green light on the box began to shine. He exhaled loudly and glanced upward, uttering a silent prayer of thanks.

Hawk turned, still standing on the chair. Some of the diners in the room were looking at him through the viewfinders of their cell phones. They were taking pictures and filming what was taking place. This would be a disaster in the social media world that Juliette was going to have to unravel in the days ahead. But for now, the immediate crisis was averted—he hoped.

Juliette was holding the papers that had fallen to the ground. Her hunched posture and drooping head sent a chill through Hawk. Something was wrong. He would learn what it a moment.

First, he needed to do a little damage control. While still positioned on the chair, he spoke to the diners around him.

"I am very sorry to interrupt your lunch and your visit." He managed to smile. "We have an unexpected situation that has come up, and I need you to do me a favor and move into another area of the restaurant. I am so sorry to inconvenience you. To make it up to you, lunch is on me." Surprised smiles crossed the faces of the guests.

Pointing to one of the Restaurantosaurus managers, who had just entered the space to find out what was going on, Hawk continued, "This is one of our great cast members. He is in charge here today, and he and our other cast members are going to pass out a food voucher that you can use at any Disney location. I need you to follow him out of this room, where he will take care of you."

The cast member looked at Hawk with confusion. Hawk nodded, confirming the manager had heard him correctly. "Give them all vouchers; send the report to my office. Thanks."

Chairs slid and scraped across the floor as guests got up, and the manager quickly gave them directions to follow. In less than a minute the room was clearing as Hawk stepped off the chair to stand next to Juliette.

"What's wrong?" He followed her gaze.

In her hands she held another theme-park map. It had fallen off the shelf when Hawk moved the oil cans. This one was a map of Disney's Hollywood Studios. Written in the same black ink across the center of the map were the words

> *On the road of cowards you must travel*
> *If you dare*
> *Destruction is found between the letters*
> *What you fear is found in what most will never see*

"I have to get to the Studios." Hawk's voice came in a low whisper.

"I know." Juliette looked at him. "But why are they doing this? If you don't get there in time, are they really going to allow a bomb to go off?"

"The first explosive device was real." He cocked his head toward the shelf. "I have to assume the one we just found is as well. I can't risk not getting to the next one in time, can I?"

"No, you can't." Juliette's voice quivered. Hawk knew she was battling the same jumbled thoughts he was.

The enemies he had faced before had never resorted to this type of attack on the Walt Disney World Resort. The potential for widespread carnage and damage was greater than ever before. Was this a new enemy making a first appearance? Hawk began to move toward the door as she placed a hand on his arm above his elbow. He slowed and turned back to face her.

"What about the explosive device you just found?" She nodded toward the shelf. "We can't just leave it sitting there."

Hawk smacked his forehead. In his haste to get to the Studios, he hadn't even considered what to do about the device he had disarmed. Hearing a voice call his name, his attention turned to the doorway. Shep entered with members of the bomb squad, a look of concern and relief across his face.

"You weren't where Juliette said you were." Shep shrugged. "I saw the people streaming out of the restaurant and figured you had to be here."

"I didn't have time to call," Juliette said.

"I miscalculated where it would be hidden," Hawk added.

Shep stopped in his tracks. "You found another one?"

Hawk motioned to the shelf as the highly trained members of the sheriff's department rushed past him. The three friends moved out of the way.

"There is another, I think." Hawk raised the map folded in his hand. "I've got to get to Hollywood Studios. Tell McManus and his team I'm headed to the Great Movie Ride."

"You've figured out the next clue already." Juliette smiled and turned toward the door.

"What are you doing?" Hawk stopped her.

"I'm going with you." Juliette paused and pointed at the shelf. "You can find them, but you apparently don't know what to do when you are done." She leaned in and whispered. "You can't leave things that will blow up just lying around. Somebody has to clean up behind you."

Concern cracked into a slight smile as Hawk acknowledged her point. He turned back toward Shep and placed a hand on his shoulder. "Call the sheriff. Tell him we think there is another, and we're on our way."

This clue, at least, he was sure about. Hawk and Juliette raced back through the streets of Animal Kingdom, toward the road of cowards.

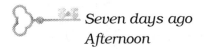 *Seven days ago
Afternoon*

THE VINTAGE HARLEY THUNDERED along World Drive toward a back-lot cast-member entrance to the Studios. Security had already been alerted, and as the bike slowed near the security gate, the guard opened the barricades and waved them in. Hawk glided the motorcycle through the backstage area, determined to get as close as possible to their destination. He brought the bike to a stop and hopped off. He and Juliette would cover the last part of their journey on foot.

Disney's Hollywood Studios had changed radically from the days when Hawk first became accustomed to navigating the backstage areas. The park had opened in 1989 during a race to get the first studio theme park built in Orlando. Michael Eisner was at the helm of Disney in that era, and he managed to beat the opening of rival Universal Studios by one year. Although there was little film production happening in Orlando during that time, a few live-action shows and some animation moved into the new Florida production home. The goal of the theme park was to create the Hollywood that never was but had always been imagined. In many ways, the theme park was always a work in progress. When Hawk arrived, he noticed that even though the theme park was the fifth-most-visited in the United States, it was the least attended at Walt Disney World.

Building off the valuable Disney-owned properties of Pixar and Lucas-film, the theme park had recently gone through a major overhaul and redesign and now was home to Toy Story Land and Star Wars Land. In order to make room, a number of popular original attractions were gone.

Juliette and Hawk emerged from the backstage area into the streets of Toy Story Land. With the whole area now scaled to make guests feel the size of a toy, guests could explore Andy's backyard from the films. A gigantic Buzz Lightyear stood enticing guests to enter this place with a toy's-eye view of the world. Green army men, each standing over six-feet tall, waddled past in a single-file line, their feet firmly attached to flat toy bases as if they had just come out of the toy box. Walking beneath a bridge held up by colorful, oversized dog bones, Hawk and Juliette raced past a crowd of people waiting to ride the Slinky Dog roller-coaster and then turned toward the back entrance of the Great Movie Ride housed inside the Chinese Theater.

After stepping inside the theater's expansive, old-Hollywood interior, they found the manager on duty and gave the word to momentarily stop placing new passengers on the ride. Hawk hesitated a moment, then said, "Those currently on the ride can finish and then exit." Although this time the clue had not warned against letting others know, Hawk decided he needed to proceed cautiously and try not to draw more attention to the potential danger. A public relations nightmare wasn't the only thing he wanted to avoid; panic of any kind could endanger guests all by itself.

They navigated to the track area where the ride cars carried guests through scenes of classic and popular movies. Cutting through a series of stage doors, Hawk remembered the passageways that interconnected each scene and stepped out into a scene inspired by the Wizard of Oz.

"We're here," Hawk announced.

The last riders were already through, and there were no longer passenger cars moving through Munchkin Land. Small houses, colorfully and magically decorated, allowed each guest to find themselves in the action of the classic film. As the soundtrack played behind them, it felt as if they were standing in a world snatched right off the silver screen.

"In Oz?" Juliette looked around. She had never viewed the scene from this perspective.

"One of the subdivisions of Oz. We're in Munchkin Land." Hawk pointed toward a house to their right. "See, Dorothy's house has landed on the witch, and we are getting ready to walk down the yellow brick road to get to the wonderful Wizard of Oz. He resides in the Emerald City, the epicenter of Oz."

Juliette stared at Hawk waiting for him to finish. "And that matters . . . why?"

"The clue." Hawk moved onto the yellow brick road that covered the floor of the attraction. He motioned toward the road, then pointed toward both ends of the road. Juliette looked to where he was directing, but the look on her face said she didn't understand.

"The clue said, 'On the road of cowards you must travel.' Cowards are often said to be 'yellow.' So it is a yellow road. Or in this case, the yellow brick road."

Juliette had taken the map from Hawk with the clue written on it. She frowned. "It says, 'Destruction is found between the letters.' Does that mean letters that someone has written? If so, I don't see them."

"Actually, that's what gave the clue away for me. Whoever is doing this knows a lot more about Disney detail than most. And because of the way they are putting together these clues, they know that *I* know a lot about the details as well." Hawk again pointed to where the ride vehicles enter. "A detail that most never notice is that the yellow brick road begins here, and the road forms an oval . . . an O. Now, follow the yellow brick pathway as it leaves this scene and moves toward the other end. You remember what's there?"

"Yes, it's where Dorothy and friends are looking toward the Emerald City or the epicenter of Oz."

"Exactly. When you reach the end of the yellow brick road, the designers have the road zig and zag, and it forms . . ."

"The letter Z." Juliette understood.

"Yes, so between the letters O and Z is where we find destruction. Or the threat of destruction—in the Wicked Witch." Hawk pointed to where the Wicked Witch would emerge and threaten the guests riding through the scene. "The secret of the clue was understanding what 'between the letters' meant. A detail that most have never even considered or noticed."

Juliette moved to the area where the Wicked Witch would emerge on cue as the show unfolded. "And what we fear is found in a detail that most will never see." She looked back toward Hawk. "But you can't enter this part of the ride without seeing the witch. What is the detail?"

Hawk's expression darkened. "That is what is so scary about whoever is doing this. They know so many details."

"No, it's not scary that they know details, it's scary that they've planted two bombs, maybe three. It's scary that they are willing to play some silly game with you and put us all at risk. That's what's scary."

Hawk sighed. "Juliette, you're right, but the scary stuff is found in the details. They have some other agenda, or they would have just planted the bombs and been done. They also know where to hide them, and they are doing it by understanding the details. That is very scary."

She nodded in agreement. Juliette watched Hawk jump up onto the set pieces and walk to where the witch would emerge. The soundtrack of singing munchkins that had been continuously blaring around them stopped all at once, and smoke began to rise from the platform next to Hawk. The lights flickered, dimmed, and went to red below it as the Wicked Witch rose. One of the most lifelike Audio-Animatronics ever created, she moved with a frightening realism. Children and adults cringed as she predicted the destruction of the guests and demanded to know who killed her sister.

"This has got to be it." Hawk reached toward the Wicked Witch as she spoke.

"Who killed my sister? Who killed the Witch of the East?" She wagged a crooked finger toward Hawk, who just happened to be standing in the right place to make it look like she was personally addressing him. "Was it you?"

"I think she's talking to you," Juliette said. "This is surreal."

"Well, my little pretty, I can cause accidents too!" The witch continued her dialogue as Hawk ignored the Audio-Animatronic witch and spoke to Juliette instead.

"The Imagineers wanted this to be so realistic that they included every detail they possibly could. In the film, the witch had a purse she always wore. Most of us have watched the film over and over and yet never seen it. But the Imagineers did, and they included it—'What you fear is found in what most never see.'"

"Very well. I'll bide my time. But just try and stay out of my way. Just try! I'll get you, my pretty. And your little dog too!" The witch finished her scene with a cackle and then a wall of smoke came up from the base of the platform.

Hawk grabbed the purse at the moving witch's side and pulled it open just as the platform lowered and she disappeared from the scene. As he had hoped, inside was another black box attached to the explosive material. This time, he flipped the switch without hesitation. The signal light began to glow a steady green. Exhaling loudly, Hawk turned to Juliette with the explosive brick in his hand.

"Is that it?" Juliette smiled with relief.

"That's it. Disarmed just like the others." Hawk smiled back at her.

"So we are done?" She closed her eyes as she offered up a quick prayer of thanks.

Hawk cringed at her question. In focusing on finding the explosive, he hadn't paid attention until this moment to something else. When he had placed his hand in the purse to extract the bomb, he'd felt something else. Paper.

He swallowed hard and turned back as the show sequence began to play again. The witch rose up on the platform and restarted her dialogue. As she did, he reached back into the purse one more time.

Juliette's eyes widened as Hawk pulled out a bright, colorful folded brochure. He let it unfold in front of him. Holding the disarmed explosive in one hand, Hawk raised the map of Epcot and then slowly turned it so Juliette could see.

Just as on the other maps, black writing was scrawled across the middle. Another warning, another clue. And that meant . . . another bomb.

CHAPTER 7

Seven days ago
Evening

HAWK AND JULIETTE EXITED The Great Movie Ride through a back entrance as the attraction was shut down and guests were evacuated. Once again the sheriff's department moved in to investigate. The police were now in three of the four theme parks, but one more was in jeopardy. Cal McManus arrived with a contingent of officers. One dressed in black and wearing body armor took the explosive brick from Hawk.

"You just carried the bomb out with you?" McManus asked.

"I didn't want to leave it inside." Hawk watched as the bomb squad placed it inside a reinforced container.

McManus huffed. "If it matters to you, the one you found in Animal Kingdom was just as real as the one you found in the Magic Kingdom. I am certain that the latest addition to your collection will be real as well."

"What did you want me to do with it?" Hawk knew the sheriff was frustrated. He also knew the irritation was not at him but at the dangerous situation unfolding. Hawk was convinced that, although their unknown enemy was much more aggressive this time, whoever was doing this was doing it to draw him into some sort of scenario. He didn't know the reason why . . . yet. But whoever was planting these bombs had to be monitoring what he was doing somehow. He feared that if he created a mass exodus from the parks, the enemy would respond by detonating whatever explosive devices he might have planted. The result would be cataclysmic.

Keeping the parks open was a high-stakes, calculated risk involving such a huge number of people it overwhelmed and terrified Hawk. If he didn't follow the scenario that was being placed in front of him, the results could be far worse.

"I did turn it off."

McManus rolled his eyes, unimpressed. "What is that?" He nodded toward what Juliette held in her hand.

She unfolded the map without answering. The full-color Epcot map was marred by words marked across the center.

If you do not hurry it will be gone.
The end rises above what protects it as it flows.
Step beyond the eight guards to find
Life or death.

McManus growled. "Let's head to Epcot. Do you know what it means?"

"Not yet," Hawk's mind was firing through endless possibilities of where the fourth bomb might be.

"I'll drive us. We can take my car." McManus began moving in the other direction.

Hawk paused and spoke thoughtfully. "I can get there faster without you."

McManus turned on him as he spoke. "Really?"

"I know the backroads and entrances better than you, and my motorcycle will navigate traffic quicker than you can." Hawk smiled. "And I'm parked a lot closer than you are, I imagine."

"I suppose you are. Where are we going in Epcot?"

"I'm not sure yet. I've gotta figure that out." Hawk was already moving away from McManus. Juliette fell in step with him. "I'll have Juliette call you when I know exactly where it is."

Hawk knew McManus did not want to handle it this way, but they had no options. As they ran toward where the Harley was waiting, Hawk tried to figure out the clue.

"If you do not hurry it will be gone," Hawk said aloud.

"It will be gone," Juliette echoed. "That sounds like it means time."

"That's what I'm thinking as well."

"So what tells time?" Juliette asked and then answered herself. "A clock. So the bomb is near one of the clocks in Epcot?"

They arrived at the XR-750, and it roared to life once again. As they began to move, Hawk finally answered Juliette over his shoulder.

"It could be a clock, but that seems too easy." Hawk grew quiet as he leaned left and took the corner a little faster than he should have. The bike wobbled slightly; Hawk had to correct and shift his weight, and the motorcycle again leveled out. "Sorry about that. Maybe it isn't something that tells time but instead something that keeps time."

"Wouldn't that still be a clock or some kind of watch?" Juliette spoke into his ear over the whine of the engine.

Hawk had been right about being able to get to Epcot quicker on the Harley. He briefly steered along Buena Vista Drive before taking an unmarked access road that would steer him toward Epcot. He planned to travel behind the theme park and circle the exterior of the World Showcase section of the park. He turned the clue over in his mind as the wheels of the bike rolled over the asphalt drive that opened into a massive parking area. Hitting the brakes, he slowed the motorcycle and then braced their balance by placing both feet on the ground. Juliette remained silent as the engine idled and the pieces of the clue continued to swirl in Hawk's mind.

Evening had fallen across Central Florida, and the glow of lights from Epcot cast shadows across the parking area. The lights in this backstage area were just beginning to flicker to life. Tilting his head, he looked off in the distance and allowed his mind to visualize the World Showcase. As the lights came on, a thought lit in his brain.

"Time flows . . ." Hawk spoke so Juliette could hear him.

"If we don't hurry, it will be gone." She played with the clue. "The end rises above what protects it as it flows. Time flows . . . what protects it?"

Hawk kicked the bike back into gear and churned over the pavement, pulling up behind a series of concrete-block buildings. On the other side was an entrance that would take them into the World Showcase. Parking and dropping the kickstand, he got off their ride and then helped Juliette off as well. As he did, he took the map from her and glanced once more at the clue.

"You just said it, I think." Hawk smiled and began walking briskly toward the back entrance. "You just asked what protects where time flows. If I am right, then we are close."

"Time flows . . . like a river," Juliette summarized. Her face lit up. "We're going to Mexico."

"Yes, we are!" Hawk started to fill in the gaps for her as they hit the streets of the World Showcase. Each step through the Showcase was a sensory delight. The plants, the architecture, the smells of food transported you to a different country and swept you along on an immersive tour. "El Rio del Tiempo is the river inside the Mexico pavilion."

"The River of Time," Juliette added. "So time will be gone, we are running out of it, it flows, and something protects it?" Now she was bogged down in the meaning.

"It has to be the pyramid." Hawk hoped he was correct.

The pyramid in the Mexican pavilion was modeled after an Aztec Temple and climbed high into the Epcot skyline. The size and construction of the area was unique in the World Showcase, because it was a single show building, unlike the open plazas and multiple structures that formed the other nation's pavilions around the Showcase. Inside, it housed an attraction, shops, a restaurant—and a river. They were all protected under the roof.

When the pair arrived at the base of the pavilion, someone in the crowd recognized Hawk. He pushed in and asked for an autograph, which caught the attention of other guests standing close by. Absently, Hawk signed the map that was thrust in front of him, but he was studying the pyramid as he wrote. As others began to ask for his signature, he moved away and ignored them and walked up the stairs toward the entrance of the pavilion. Juliette said a few apologies as she followed him, but the crowd kept pressing in.

Hawk had become a celebrity, the face of the company, although he had been reluctant to let it happen. His meteoric rise to the top had created many questions, rumors, and stories. His romance with Kate Young, who was one of the most recognizable journalists in the world, had only increased his visibility and popularity, and her untimely and tragic death in Walt Disney World had kept Hawk in the public spotlight for far more than just being the new king of Walt Disney's kingdom.

"Hawk." Juliette motioned to the crowd of people surrounding them. "There are a lot of people here."

Hawk snapped his attention back to the guests gathered around the pavilion. He understood what Juliette was concerned about, but he could find no alternative but to continue with what he was planning on doing. He shrugged toward her, smiled, and tried to reassure her with a look, then turned and jumped over the entrance sign to the pavilion. He could sense people pulling out their cell phones and cameras as he began to do the unthinkable—climb the very narrow steps to the Aztec Temple, ascending three stories to the top.

Halfway up, Hawk glanced back at Juliette. She stood surrounded by crowds. From the look on her face he knew she didn't like it—if they did manage to save these people, there was going to be a lot to explain and a whole lot of damage control.

She had managed to get through the crowd enough to stand at the base of the steps and was watching Hawk climb. He turned to his left, looked down, and saw a wave of security cast members running toward the pyramid. He also saw a small group of law enforcement from the sheriff's department pressing in. They began to move the crowds away from the pyramid, but as Hawk climbed higher, the spectacle of what was happening in Mexico was now viewed by guests all around the World Showcase. He heard a swell of shouts and chatter mingling with the sounds of music from other parts of the Showcase.

Hawk paused his climb and turned toward the ornate decoration that looked like a serpent head on his right and then on his left. He reread the clue written on the map in his mind as he closed his eyes for a moment. *If you do not hurry it will be gone*—this was clearly a reference to time, as they had figured out. *The end*, he believed, meant another explosive device. *Rises above what it protects as it flows*—this pyramid, this Aztec Temple, protected the river of time. He might not like it, but this was definitely the right place.

He reopened his eyes, again glanced toward the serpent heads, and kept climbing. There were eight of the heads between him and the top. *Step beyond the eight guards*—he had to go beyond, or in this case above, the eight guards. The serpent heads represented, as best he could remember, the ancient gods of learning, knowledge, priesthood, and life. *To find life or death*—At the top of the stairs, there was a representation of a temple for high priests. That had to be where the explosive device was located.

Higher and higher Hawk climbed. He used his hands on the cool rock steps above him to steady himself. He had risen too high to be comfortable looking back down. He crested the top step and pulled himself up. The sounds from below grew softer and more distant as he gazed across the water and saw the lights of the world ripple across the liquid surface. This was a view very few would ever see, but he did not have time to sightsee. Breathing heavily, he rose to his feet and did not slow down. He moved into the area that was supposed to be the temple but was actually a control center for Illuminations, the evening show spectacular at Epcot.

With his heart pounding from the climb, he looked about quickly. He had no idea how much time he had or didn't have. Then he saw it: mounted to the side of one of the faux stone walls, a brick-shaped explosive device just like the other three. In one motion he moved to it and flipped the switch. The blinking red light went dark, and the green safety light began to glow. He dropped to his knees, put his head in his hands, and ran his fingers through his hair as he became aware of how much he was sweating and how frightened he had been.

That made four out of four theme parks. Surely this job was done.

He reached down to pull the explosive away from the wall. A note was attached to it. This time it was not a park map, just letters written on a white piece of paper, fastened on the side of the control mechanism of the lethal brick. He drew in a short breath and then read the words written by the same hand that had placed the messages on the maps.

You saved the world today
What will you do tomorrow?
The end has begun.

Hawk rose to his feet with purpose. Standing atop the Aztec pyramid, he looked out across Epcot. The lights of the park twinkled and reflected off the waters of the lagoon. This place embodied in many ways what Walt Disney had dreamed of—the hope and future of tomorrow.

A wave of exhaustion splashed over Hawk as he reflected on what had brought him to this moment. He glanced at the note again. Today he had saved the world, or at least his little corner of it. As far as tomorrow was concerned, he understood that you had to face life in real time, one day at a time.

But if he had to save the world again tomorrow, he would do it.

He was once again fighting to save a kingdom.

CHAPTER 8

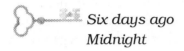 *Six days ago*
Midnight

THE ADRENALINE SURGE that had fueled him all day had now receded. Wearily Hawk climbed the steps to Engine Co. 71. He loved seeing the Magic Kingdom at night, after the guests had gone home. The lights, the music, the almost perfect surroundings that somehow managed to create magical moments for anyone who visited—he never tired of taking it all in. It filled him with an overwhelming sense of wonder . . . usually. But arriving at his apartment door tonight, he slouched as he put the key into the lock. He was so tired it felt like turning the key took all the energy he had left.

Yawning, he stretched his arms to relax his muscles and then slumped into his favorite chair. The plush recliner sat near the window where he could look out over Town Square. Tonight he didn't even glance in that direction. He closed his eyes, was vaguely aware of his head slumping downward, and then . . . music.

Music? He heard music. Blinking back to consciousness, he realized his cell phone was ringing. Bleary eyes focused on the screen. Juliette was calling. Sluggishly, he slid his finger across the touch screen and leaned his head against the phone.

"Hello, Juliette." He let her name trail off as he spoke.

Her voice was strangely sharp. "Where are you?"

"I'm home. I just got here . . . I think. What time is it?"

"Close to one o'clock in the morning." Her tone was subdued.

"I just dozed off."

"I need you to come to my office." Juliette paused for a moment. "Now, Hawk."

The adrenaline that had moved and exhausted him earlier in the day returned. He felt himself jolt with the realization that something else was wrong. He was on his feet, and with each step his mind moved back into high alert.

"What's wrong?" Hawk asked as he descended the steps.

"Not over the phone. Just get here. Okay?" Juliette's voice was tired and clouded with concern.

"I'm on my way." He ended the call as he threw a leg over the seat of the Harley. In one fluid motion the bike was moving. The maintenance crew had already started the extensive nightly cleanup to ready the world's most popular place for the next day's crowds. Since the park closed so late at night, it would take the cleanup crews until daybreak to ready the park for the next operating day. But having only cast members at work in the park, without the thousands of guests crowding the streets, made the usually packed resort seem isolated. The absence of crowds allowed him to maneuver the motorcycle through Town Square and under the train station. The sound of the engine reverberated off the concrete walls of the tunnels beneath the depot. A security guard recognized Hawk on board his ride; the CCA frequently took late-night rides through the streets of the Magic Kingdom. With a wave, the guard swung open a security gate, giving Hawk room to glide through it. Leaning to his left, he guided the bike toward the Contemporary Resort.

The resort was closest in proximity to the Magic Kingdom of any resort in Walt Disney World. Juliette occupied an office space inside the Bay Lake Towers, created especially for her. A few years before, Hawk had a two-story guestroom converted into a private office for himself to use. In the aftermath of the devastating events and the death of Kate Young, he had spent a little over six months away from Central Florida. During that period, Juliette worked behind the scenes to keep his absence from being noticed, kept things moving forward, and preserved the leadership guidance the company required during his badly needed hiatus. At Hawk's urging, she had a guest area remodeled as her boss had done. It was right next door to his. For years before that, she had managed not to have an official office location. She had been able to work most effectively by using temporary spaces created near whatever project or situation she was involved in. But as all of their roles expanded and the bigness of operating the world's most recognized entertainment brand settled in, she had agreed that it was time to settle into a permanent work space as well.

Hawk wheeled into the parking lot. Law enforcement vehicles were parked along the sidewalk, blocking the entrance to the front door. He jumped off the bike, and an officer motioned for him to go inside as he swiped his identification card. Running through the lobby, he pushed through an unmarked set of doors that opened into another lobby where a private elevator would carry him up to their office floor. As soon as the door to the elevator opened, Hawk looked down the hallway. Juliette's office suite door was open, and a uniformed sheriff's officer stood guard in front of it.

Stepping into the reception area of the suite, he paused. It was a mess. Blinking, he looked about at a floor littered with papers, desks overturned, computer monitors tossed carelessly onto the ground. The chairs in the waiting area had been slit, and padding and stuffing strewn about coated the room in a layer of white fluff.

"Hawk." A strong voice spoke.

Hawk turned as Al Gann came down the stairway to greet him. Al was the head liaison between Disney Security and the Orange County Sheriff's Department. Hawk had met Al years before when Al joined the Celebration Community Church. When Hawk was given the key to Walt Disney's kingdom, Al became a firewall between Hawk and local law enforcement as he unraveled that very first puzzle. It seemed so much simpler then. Hawk had a key and had to figure out what it was supposed to open. He had discovered that was only the beginning.

After Hawk was named CCA of the company, he expanded Al's role. On a personal level, as a good friend to Hawk and his staff, Gann often stepped in to make sure Hawk was not only safe, but he had the freedom to skirt the rules or expectations of the sheriff's department if need be to preserve and protect Walt Disney's legacy and secrets. On a number of occasions Hawk had been tempted to share all of the things he had discovered with Al, but for the protection of both of them, he had not. Although Al did not know what the secrets were, he realized how dangerous Hawk's world had become since he was now the keeper of the key to the kingdom.

"Al, what's going on?" Hawk moved to meet him at the stairs.

"As you can see, Juliette has had some visitors." Al motioned to the chaos Hawk had just come through. The room buzzed with activity as officers and crime scene technicians moved about. "But if you think this is bad, wait until you see Juliette's private office."

They ascended a set of stairs and turned toward an open doorway that led to Juliette's office. The upstairs of her office suite had been designed very like Hawk's. A private office was located here, and across from it was a large conference and meeting room. Both the office and meeting room were oversized. The massiveness of the space was something they had joked about as being a perk of the job. Both the office and meeting room featured floor-to-ceiling windows with a view of the Magic Kingdom—another perk.

Hawk paused in the door leading to her office. If the downstairs was a mess, the usually neat and orderly office was absolute chaos. Not one shelf, counter space, chair, or desk drawer had not been trashed. It was a malicious mess—confusing rubble that law enforcement was now forced to sift through.

Hawk felt Al pull him back from the doorway as another officer breezed past him, going inside. Wordlessly, Al guided him toward the meeting room. Juliette stood next to the window, looking out over the Magic Kingdom. The castle towers rose from the center, glowing white in the darkness of early morning. Al nodded as Hawk moved inside and the door closed behind him. Juliette and Hawk were alone in the massive meeting room.

"You all right?" Hawk moved toward the window.

Juliette turned and smiled. "Fine."

She motioned for Hawk to take a seat. He did, and she sat down in the chair opposite him.

"What happened?"

"After we left Epcot, I decided to come back here before I went home." Juliette leaned her head back, closed her eyes for a moment, and then returned her focus to her friend. "I'm not sure why I came back here. Like you, I am exhausted. It has been a horrible day. I guess I was just trying to make sanity out of the insanity of it." She laughed. "Believe it or not, I came by to see if my team had left a report on the new 'Walt Disney—The Artist' exhibit we are getting ready to unveil."

"Why in the world would that have been important today?" Hawk allowed himself to laugh with her for a brief moment.

"Because I guess I am just a little bit crazy after our day." She pointed at him. "*You* make me a little bit crazy. This insane life you have dragged us all into sometimes is a little bit too much. You know?"

"Yes, I know." He was no longer smiling. The world he had pulled everyone into was an adventure that had come at a high cost. Although it was exhilarating, they had all been forced to change. Because of his friends' loyalty to him, they had never really had the chance to have any input into the direction of their lives. He felt responsible for that. He knew he couldn't undo it, and deep down he knew they didn't want him to. But there were days, like this one, where he recognized the sacrifices they all had made over the past few years.

Leaning forward, he spoke softly. "I'm sorry. As long as you're okay, go home, grab Tim and the kids, and go away for a while. Get as far from here as you can, and come back when it's safer."

"And leave you here . . . in charge . . . alone?" Juliette rolled her eyes. "That's a great plan."

"Juliette, we don't even know what is going on right now. All we know is someone decided to attack the parks, the guests, and us today. Why or what they want, well . . ."

"Oh, just stop it. We both know what they want, Hawk." Juliette's eyes tightened as she looked at him. "This is about the secrets Walt Disney left for you. The day Farren Rales gave you that key and all of the mystery that goes with it, everything changed. There are people who live out on the fringes of sanity, lurking and waiting for their moment to sweep in and steal those secrets. They are ruthless, they are blinded with greed, ambition, or hatred. I'm not sure what drives them. But they have driven off the road of reality and like the darkness of destruction. These enemies, your enemies, are never going to stop until you are dead . . . or . . ."

"Or . . . what?"

"Or . . . until you beat them once and for all." Juliette's eyes flashed with flecks of anger and intensity that caused Hawk to lean back slightly in his chair. "This time, whatever this is, let's end it, once and for all, and find a real Disney *happily ever after*. For a change." She sighed the last few words.

Hawk let her words sink into his tired mind. Looking out the window at Cinderella Castle, he realized she was right. She usually was. It was time to end this battle forever.

He closed his eyes and breathed out a prayer. They had tried to stop them before. These were very bad people, and for some reason they always seemed to stay one step ahead of Hawk and his friends. But with each attack, each attempt to steal the secrets, they had ramped up the intensity, the danger, the recklessness. As a result, everyone close to Hawk was in danger, and now people who knew nothing of this battle unfolding behind the veil of Walt's world were in harm's way as well.

"Hawk." Juliette brought him back from his thoughts. "There is something else."

Hawk tilted his head and waited for her to continue.

She waved her hand toward the door, indicating the carnage in the office space. "The only thing I've noticed so far that is missing is the footage."

"Footage?"

"The footage." Juliette waited and then told him the rest. "The footage from *Total Access.*"

For a moment he thought his heart had stopped. Hawk's first encounter with journalist Kate Young had been less than spectacular. Juliette had set up an opportunity for her to get an exclusive scoop about Grayson Hawkes and his amazing rise to power in the Walt Disney Company. Although reluctant to participate, Hawk had trusted Juliette's instincts enough to agree. When Kate and her production team from *Total Access* arrived to spend time at the resort and get to know Hawk, his enemies had made another attempt to steal the secrets of Disney from the CCA.

Kate had eventually discovered a great deal about Hawk's new life. She knew that Walt and Roy Disney had developed an elaborate plan for a new leader to one day be chosen to secure the future of the company. The Disney brothers had selected a very small handful of trusted friends within the company—an inner circle charged with carefully choosing the right person to whom their legacy should be passed.. Farren Rales had been given the task, by Walt himself, of choosing the visionary to become that new leader. Years later, Rales had developed a close friendship with Hawk. He had learned to respect him as a storyteller, as a man with a deep conviction to follow God, and as a person who valued the importance of the Disney brand and legacy. Rales had given Hawk a key, the key to the kingdom, along with a series of puzzles to unravel that would ultimately unlock the future of the Walt Disney Company.

But the plan was much more elaborate than even Farren had understood. Walt and Roy's select friends who were tasked with the responsibility of moving into the future had each been given a different piece of the puzzle, and the ultimate prize was something far bigger and more important than just sitting atop an entertainment empire.

While Kate worked on her documentary about Hawk, a second Imagineer, George Colmes, had sent Hawk on another treasure hunt to discover another layer of the Disney secret. It had placed him in the unwinnable position of trying to entertain and give *Total Access* journalist Kate Young her exclusive while at the same time unraveling a new mystery . . . even while trying to preserve the secrets he had already been entrusted with.

Kate had managed to capture footage of Hawk searching and digging up a clue in an old cemetery in the middle of the night during a driving rainstorm. He had been attacked, fought off that attacker, and had to rescue one of the production crew who managed to fall into an open grave. Kate caught it all on film. In a one-on-one interview, she had managed to peel back some unknown layers of Hawk's past and found some very unflattering stories about the death of his family and his own condition the night of the horrible accident.

Hawk had convinced her not to run the documentary until she knew the entire story and promised her an exclusive that would be better than what she already had. She agreed. Their relationship had been tense at times, and they had clashed on a number of occasions, but there was also an attraction that blossomed into so much more. Eventually they had become a very visible celebrity couple, and Hawk had willingly opened his heart and chosen to love. They had planned a future together. But the enemies of Walt Disney had now become his enemies, and they had progressively become more of a threat. They had murdered Kate and George Colmes, they had kidnapped Juliette, and they had attempted to assassinate Farren Rales and himself. Now they had escalated their brand of terror to an even more dangerous level: they were willing to attack unsuspecting guests in the resort.

All of that was a part of Hawk's history in the most magical place in all of the world . . . Walt Disney World. With Juliette's mention of the footage from *Total Access*, his rewinding of events from the past few years spooled out into thoughts he had carefully tried to lock away and categorize.

"I didn't realize you had the footage from *Total Access*," he stated flatly.

Juliette winced with empathy. She knew how painful this would all be for Hawk. Not because of the footage itself but because of his love for Kate Young. "Kate gave it to me after you two became a couple." She waited for Hawk to respond. He did not. "She approached me and wanted a place to keep it safe, to protect you, and because she never had any intention of running it. She also wanted to make sure no one from any other production company ever got a hold of it. She was hiding it here from the production team of *Total Access*, to protect you."

Hawk listened and then asked what he believed to be an obvious question. "Why didn't she just destroy it?"

"Because of what it contained," Juliette said calmly.

"So you watched it?"

"All of it." Juliette nodded. "Kate and I spent an evening where she went through all of it with me, showing me the documentary she never aired. And more importantly . . . all of the additional footage she had managed to secure."

"What additional footage?" Hawk felt himself growing warm.

"There was a lot. She was so good at what she did." Juliette smiled. "She loved you so much."

Hawk felt his eyes begin to burn. He nodded. Juliette's understanding was strangely comforting.

"There was the footage you knew about. The stuff they captured in the cemetery with you digging up a clue at Walt Disney's grandparents' grave. There was the interview you did with her where she talked with you about your family, the accident, and what happened."

Hawk lowered his head. He felt Juliette's hand reach over and squeeze his shoulder tightly. He looked at her through watery eyes.

"I told her she didn't have the story of the accident quite right."

He felt a pang—of gratitude or pain, he wasn't sure. Only Hawk's closest friends—Juliette, Tim, Shep, and Jonathan Carlson—knew what had really happened the night of the accident.

"I also told her to give you time and that one day you would tell her yourself. I just wanted her to know it wasn't your fault."

Hawk nodded slightly but said nothing.

"She also had footage you didn't know about. She had interviewed Farren Rales. He told her the story about Walt and Roy, how they chose him and how he had chosen you."

"And?" Hawk wanted to know.

"And he told her about the key, what it opened, the plan they had and how you were on a quest to not only discover but also protect something far more important than a theme park or a film studio. Farren gave her a lot of details. He didn't tell her everything, but he decided she was someone who could be trusted with the story. I think he was afraid if he didn't tell her the truth, she might do some sensational slander piece on you. As always, he was protecting you by telling her just enough without telling her everything."

"Kate knew a lot more than I . . . " Hawk bit his lip lightly. "She never mentioned any of it."

Quiet fell across the room for a few moments.

"I think she was waiting for you to tell her one day," Juliette said in almost a whisper.

Hawk breathed in deeply and then slowly exhaled. It had been a long and emotional day already. He hadn't gotten very much sleep and now the emotion was almost overwhelming.

"But I still don't understand. Since she knew it all, and she wasn't going to ever use the footage," Hawk looked to Juliette for answers, "why didn't she just destroy it?"

"I asked her that." Juliette nodded. "I suggested it was too explosive to keep a copy of. But you know Kate. She said it was too important to destroy. That there would be a day when we would want to pass it down to continue the legacy of Walt, Roy, Farren, George, the Disney company, and of course . . . you." Juliette sighed. "That's why she gave it to me and made sure I knew what it contained. Because she trusted that I cared enough about both of you to know what to do with it."

"Who knew we would become the keepers of so many secrets?" Hawk hoarsely whispered.

"Who knew," Juliette softly agreed and watched as Hawk surveyed the magical world that stretched out in front of him through the window. For a guest, it was a dream destination, a once-in-a-lifetime escape where everything was as close to perfect as possible. Very few understood how difficult it was to create and protect the place they loved so dearly. "So again . . . if this is the beginning of the end, end it this time. Let's tell these enemies good-bye once and for all."

"The beginning of the end." Hawk nodded slightly.

She was right.

CHAPTER 9

Six days ago
2 a.m.

"THE BEGINNING OF THE END." The voice interrupted Juliette and Hawk. "I believe that is the same line from the clue we read earlier."

Hawk and Juliette turned toward the door and the direction of the sound. Sheriff Cal McManus had entered the room along with Al Gann. The deep lines on his face revealed he was just as weary as Hawk was; it had been an extremely long day for all of them. Juliette waved toward a nearby chair, and Cal took the seat closest to them. Al remained standing. Even though the door was closed once again, he stood sentry between the cluster of chairs by the window and anyone who might enter the room uninvited.

"You don't mind me joining you, do you?" The sheriff managed a slight smile as he relaxed for a brief moment in the softness of the chair. "It has been a long day."

He closed his eyes and rubbed them with his fingers. Repositioning himself, he returned from the few seconds of relaxation to reengage the situation at hand. "Tell me what you think is going on here."

Hawk allowed his eyes to move from McManus toward Al, standing across the room, to Juliette and then back to the sheriff. He cleared his throat. He hadn't had time to process it all, but now that McManus asked, he thought he *did* know what was going on. "I uh . . . believe that the four explosive devices today were planted to keep all of us busy so whoever was responsible had time, all day actually, to ransack Juliette's office."

McManus nodded and looked toward Juliette. "Do you agree?" Juliette affirmed the conclusion. "So Mrs. Keaton, what have you discovered to be missing?"

"A briefcase. It was locked away in the closet of my private office."

"That is the only thing you have found missing?"

"Yes, so far."

McManus looked down toward the ground. His frustration seemed close to surfacing. The day had been long, the hour of the morning was early, and he was trying to solve a puzzle without all of the pieces. "Both floors of your office suite look like a hurricane has blown through them. And in the midst of all of the disheveled destruction, all that you have found missing is a briefcase?"

"Like I said, so far," Juliette repeated.

"And when you came into the office and saw the mess, you were able to move through it and decided to go looking for the briefcase, which is why you know it is missing—because it contains something so valuable it was worth attempting to detonate bombs in four theme parks to attain?"

"Yes." Juliette sighed as she slumped back in her chair.

"Okay, you two." Cal breathed deeply. "What is in the case, and why is it the most valuable thing in your office?"

Hawk cleared his throat. "It's a long story."

McManus crossed his legs and got more comfortable in his seat. "How could it not be?"

Over the next thirty minutes, Hawk and Juliette unpacked the story of Kate and the *Total Access* footage. They shared some of the information Farren had chosen to give Kate in the interviews. Hawk carefully kept some details to himself. There were things he possessed that were a part of this elaborate Disney story created by Walt and Roy that only he knew—that only he *should* know. While the original key Farren gave him had started the adventure, there were other discoveries that were far more valuable—discoveries that were the real secrets others desperately wanted. These secrets, he couldn't tell McManus.

Hawk realized how valuable these secrets were. He also knew no one else understood. Even his enemies, although they wanted to possess them, really had no concept of just how much they were worth. The real secrets were knowledge. Hawk had not only been given a key, he'd been given access to an elaborate bunker that contained secrets beyond anything known in the Disney archives, an iconic ring that opened locks most would never notice, and the Disney diary. The notebook Walt had written in was loaded with directions, plans, personal thoughts, and ideas that were still being mulled over in his visionary brain. But the complexity of what Walt had been involved in hadn't really set in for Hawk until he found the journal

Wernher von Braun had given Walt shortly before Disney passed away. The more Hawk had studied it, the more frightened he had become about how far people might go to attain this knowledge.

He had not shared this with even his closest friends. They only knew he was the keeper of Walt Disney's secrets. The great entertainer had chosen not even to share these secrets with his family and closest friends, to protect their lives, and now Hawk was doing the same.

The events of the day warranted more explanation than Hawk had offered in the past, and he gladly gave it. At the same time, he protected the most private and precious secrets.

"So now there is an explosive story about Walt, Roy, some Imagineers, and me that adversaries have control of," Hawk summarized.

"So, Preacher." McManus leaned forward. He still referred to Hawk as a preacher although he rarely spoke at the Celebration Community Church these days. "What do you think your foes will do with this *Total Access* treasure chest?"

"Use it to blackmail me, try to manipulate me to do what they want," Hawk said.

"What do they want?" McManus volleyed. "Do they want control of the company? Do they want you to step down and give them the key? What are they after? How do they win?"

"All of those things." Hawk shrugged.

"And what else?" McManus asked.

The room grew quiet as Hawk looked at the sheriff. He knew this was a defining moment. He had to make a choice as to whether he would trust McManus with the rest of the story or keep protecting the secrets entrusted to him.

"I can't tell you," Hawk said.

"You mean you *won't* tell me."

"Yes." Hawk did not break his gaze on McManus. "I won't tell you."

"Why?"

"Because of what the secrets I know are. They are important enough that people have been killed over them. I have lost people I love trying to protect them."

"A great number of people could have died today because of you keeping these secrets."

"And if I tell you what they are, it doesn't change anything." Hawk's voice grew darker. "If you know the secrets, it won't do one thing to stop the people who want them. It just means you know what they are, which puts you at risk."

"Risk is part of my job," McManus retorted.

"Not like this. You have no idea how big these secrets are." Hawk paused and thought back. "You asked me one time if the secrets were worth dying for. I told you they are now. Others died so I could find, keep, and protect them. That hasn't changed. The missing *Total Access* footage gives our enemies information that will fan the flames on their intensity . . . but the secrets are still safe."

The cloud of tension lay heavy over the room. No one spoke for a few moments. It was obvious to Hawk there was nowhere else the conversation could go.

Clearing his throat, it was Sheriff McManus who decided to push through the cloudiness first.

"So, what are you supposed to do with these secrets, besides keep them?" McManus raised his palms slightly before continuing. "Right now, based on what I know, this is an endless cycle. There is no end in sight. That is unacceptable, you understand?"

"I do," Hawk agreed. "Sheriff, I don't know what to do with the secrets, because I don't think I have all of them yet. There was a third Imagineer who was supposed to have another part of the Disney brothers' plan, and I haven't found him yet."

"This is the third Imagineer Kiran Roberts supposedly had kidnapped a few years back?" Kiran had simply disappeared. She was on a list of people who were actively being sought in connection to the mayhem they had created in Walt Disney World during the last attack on Hawk and company.

"Yes."

"Do you have a plan to find the last Imagineer?"

"Not yet."

"Then you better figure one out." McManus abruptly stood. "Juliette, how many people knew about the *Total Access* footage you had?"

"Three."

"Three? Who knew about this when I didn't?" Hawk asked.

"I can keep secrets too." Juliette turned her attention from Hawk to the sheriff. "Farren Rales knows, Al knows." She gestured toward Gann, who still was standing guard. "He went with Kate and me to pick up the briefcase when she gave it to me. He was our protection. I knew it was that important." Gann nodded and affirmed what she was saying. "And myself. That's it. No one else knew it was here."

"And who else saw the footage besides you?" McManus asked.

"Just me. I watched it with Kate in private. Then it all was locked back up in the briefcase along with all of her notes and research."

McManus turned and began moving toward the door. He paused and spoke with Al Gann. "Al, take a team and have Kate show you where the briefcase was hidden. Let's let our investigators see if they can find any trace of evidence from that spot. I am having my doubts about finding anything else that will be helpful in the rest of this mess." Al nodded. He moved out and across the hall to Juliette's office.

McManus turned back to Hawk and Juliette. There were just the three of them in the room now.

"Hawk, let me tell you something I heard a preacher say at a funeral a while back. I think he said something like, 'You did not choose this path for yourself. It is the path chosen for you. That is the way life works at times. However, the choices you make as you travel the path are always yours, and you must make them wisely.' I think that's how it went." McManus waited, and Hawk closed his eyes. Those were his own words—he'd spoken them when he officiated the funeral for Kate Young. Hawk nodded, confirming he remembered.

McManus continued. "You need to take your own advice. We are on some very dangerous ground. There are lives at stake now, and what you do is going to matter more than ever before. Be wise. We'll talk soon."

McManus turned and exited the room into the hallway. The heavy door closed behind him.

Juliette and Hawk looked toward the closed door for a few extended moments before Juliette broke the silence.

"So today was all about getting the *Total Access* footage?" She tilted her head. "That was an extreme way to go about it, don't you think?"

"They were also sending a message. To me, to you, to all of us." Hawk looked back toward Juliette. "I'm not convinced they knew what they would find in your office. They just needed time to look when they knew they wouldn't be interrupted. There was no chance of that today; we had a crisis of epic proportions we were dealing with."

Hawk replayed the events of the day in his mind as he continued. "They created clues that kept us moving and law enforcement following us. They were looking for something that would allow them to exert some type of control, they hope, over me. They hit the gold mine with the briefcase."

"I'm sorry I didn't tell you about it," Juliette said. "I could have let you help me hide it away."

"No, you didn't do anything wrong," Hawk assured her. "Whoever is doing this doesn't play by our rules. You were doing the right things for the right reasons."

"So what happens now?"

"Exactly what you asked." Hawk smiled. "I'm going to end this once and for all."

"How? You have a plan?" Juliette's eyes opened wider.

"No, sorry." Hawk deflated her momentary excitement. "But I'll come up with one."

"Where do you start?"

"I start with the person who started all of this for me. Farren Rales."

CHAPTER 10

Six days ago
Noon

THE BLISTERING HEAT of the Central Florida sun pounced off the pavement and across Hawk's body as he skillfully zigzagged through the heavy traffic on Interstate 4, which connects Central Florida from Daytona Beach to Tampa. Along the route you can easily access Orlando and the Walt Disney World Resort area.

Hawk leaned and skillfully guided the Harley through the always-crowded Florida roadway and exited at Princeton Street, just northeast of the downtown Orlando area. Taking a left, he accelerated the motorcycle into College Park and the main thoroughfare of the community, Edgewater Drive. Yale, Harvard, Vassar, and Dartmouth: all were streets that ran through the neighborhood, a popular place for seniors and young professionals due to its proximity to the downtown area. College Park had a small-town community feel adjacent to major city. His first introduction to this amazing community had been through Farren. Rales had allowed his home to become Hawk's home away from home. Spending time in College Park had allowed Hawk to feel a connection to the place. The more time he spent there, the clearer it became why Farren Rales had chosen to call it home when he moved to Orlando prior to the opening of Walt Disney World.

Rales was an Imagineer hired by Walt Disney himself on Rales's thirtieth birthday. Originally he had been hired as an animator, but he quickly became a part of that exclusive creative team at Disney that Walt had hand-picked. WED was the company name Walt gave the group before it was changed to Imagineering.

Farren's friendship with both Walt and Roy had grown deeper through the years, and eventually, he had become one of the three point people selected by the Disney brothers to keep the most important secrets of the organization and eventually pass them along to someone else. Farren had chosen Hawk as that "someone else," and the cost to both of them had been tremendous.

Hawk pulled his motorcycle up in front of an old-fashioned soda fountain and removed his sunglasses, squinting in the bright sun. Farren had been shot in an ambush in the streets of Orlando. Had Hawk not helped create a myth that he had passed away, Farren might not have lived to see another day. But Hawk had helped hide him away, and after months of recovery, the old Imagineer had rallied and survived. He remained one of Hawk's most beloved friends.

As usual, Farren had set the parameters of where and when they would meet. When Farren first arrived in this area of Orlando, "the Drive" had been lined with distinct shops and businesses. Toy Parade. JoAnn's Chili Bordello. Gabriel's Sub Shop. Vorhees Gulf Station. Pickerill's Sporting Goods. Johns Hardware. Royal Castle. Long's Christian Books. And not just one, but two 7-Elevens anchored both ends of the street. The years had seen most of those places disappear, but Rales was loaded with stories about each of them as well as the new places that had emerged, giving the community its unique vibe.

The whir of a blender greeted Hawk as he entered the soda fountain Rales had chosen for their conversation. The vintage-styled ice cream parlor sat nestled on the corner of Bryn Mawr Street and Edgewater Drive. The cheery décor invited patrons back to a simpler time when families would gather at the local ice cream shop for frosty treats to push back the hot summer afternoon. He glanced across the little shop and saw Rales sitting at a corner table in the back of the room. He greeted Hawk with a raised spoon and motioned for him to step up to the counter and place an order. The CCA smiled as Rales dove his spoon back into the ice cream float on the table, and he moved toward the counter to order.

The ice cream shop was busy, and it took a few moments for Hawk to make his way to the table to join Farren. Carrying his two scoops of ice cream in a cup, he slid out the chair and sat down across from his friend.

"Glad you could come." Rales continued to make the ice cream float disappear at a remarkable pace.

"Thanks for making time to see me." Hawk chased the words with his first spoonful of the rich, homemade ice cream. It was very good, he thought, as he savored the first cool bite.

"Rough day yesterday." Rales allowed his spoon to clank into the cup, and he pushed it aside, ready to get into the conversation.

"Yes, it was bad." Hawk was a bit surprised Farren so quickly dispensed with the small talk. For Farren, the story, the setting, and the details were always important. He usually told a story slowly and allowed Hawk to fill in the gaps, so it was rare for Farren to act rushed. Hawk sensed today was different.

"Catch me up." Rales spoke quietly and leaned in closer across the table.

The sounds of children laughing, parents talking, and the tap of the ice cream scoops being cleaned created enough ambient noise for them to talk without being overheard. Over the next few minutes, Hawk gave the old Imagineer a rundown of the previous day. Occasionally the old man would nod, at times closing his eyes as Hawk described the placement of the bombs and how much damage they could have done. Then his eyes bore into the preacher as he described the scene in Juliette's office.

When Hawk was finished, he waited for Rales to take in all he had just heard. He turned his attention back to his ice cream cup. The sugary cold cream reminded him of eating homemade ice cream right out the churn as a child at family events.

"And no one was hurt?" Farren shook his head in disbelief.

"No." Hawk nodded. "Amazingly enough, no one was hurt."

"So what are you going to do?" Rales searched Hawk's face for an answer.

"That's why I'm here." Hawk finished his ice cream. "I'm not sure what to do. I know that very soon, whoever is doing this is going to tell me they want all the things I have discovered. They'll try to blackmail me. But there is still another Imagineer out there. The third Imagineer, who has what I guess is the last piece of all of the things Walt and Roy wanted protected."

Rales let out a heavy sigh. The old man was feebler than when Hawk first met him. Nearly dying after the ambush had accelerated his frailness. The preacher-turned-theme-park-expert waited as Rales thought.

"I have something to tell you." Rales paused. Hawk raised an eyebrow in the long silence. "After we spoke last night, I reached out to the third Imagineer."

"You told me you didn't know who it was." Hawk sat back slightly at the news.

The smell of fresh waffle cones drifted across the room, mixed with the scent of fresh-cut strawberries. But even these friendly smells didn't relax the growing tension building inside of Hawk.

"I don't." Farren waved his hand, dismissing Hawk's misreading of what he had just said. "I never have. Walt and Roy didn't want us to know each other. If you remember, I didn't know George Colmes was a part of their plan until you told me."

The mere mention of the name sent a wave of sadness across the table. Colmes was another casualty of the Disney secrets. Hawk had wished for more time to get to know him better.

"What I never told you," Farren continued, "was that Walt gave us some vague instruction about what to do in the most extreme emergency situation. He had told me, and I assume each of the three Imagineers, 'You know, if you need each other—use my last window in my world to find each other.'"

"And you knew what he meant?"

"Well, I thought I did. But I never had to try it until last night."

"So you didn't think the other situations we have been in were bad enough to warrant trying to reach out to the other Imagineers?" Hawk was stunned.

"No." Farren reached across the table and patted Hawk's hand assuredly. "As bleak as some days have seemed, I had great confidence you would figure it all out. After all, that is why I chose you. That is the reason that Walt chose you." He smiled at his friend.

"But last night . . ."

"Last night, I decided it was time. I think we have come to a moment where we need to make sure you have the last piece of the puzzle."

Farren folded his hands as he continued. "Like you, sometimes I have to figure out what a clue might mean. Walt taught all of us to pay attention to details. So when he said to use the last window in his world to find each other, I assumed it meant his window on Main Street U.S.A."

Hawk thought about Farren's line of reasoning. Walt had been developing Walt Disney World when he passed away. The decision to build the Magic Kingdom and Epcot were already underway. The tradition of honoring people with their names on windows along Main Street, U.S.A happened at both Disneyland and Walt Disney World. However, in Florida it was Walt's world, not just his land. Hawk understood.

"And?"

"Last night, I put a Mickey Mouse balloon in the window at the end of Main Street, U.S.A. with Walt's name on it."

Hawk immediately knew why. The windows on Main Street, U.S.A. are designed to be seen like the credits of a motion picture. The first name you see as you enter the Magic Kingdom is Walt's on the Main Street Train Station. The closing credit, or in this case the last window, is above The Plaza Ice Cream Parlor. It reads "Walter E. Disney—Graduate School of Design & Master Planning."

"The Mickey Mouse balloon is the way Walt said to reach out?"

"Well, there was no detail like that. But the window is usually empty, decorated with a curtain. So last night, I put up a balloon and a light."

"And you think someone is going to see that?" Hawk did not have a lot of confidence in this simple plan.

Farren studied his friend before continuing. "Hawk, I have checked that window in the Magic Kingdom every single day since the park opened in 1971 to see if there was anything that might look like a signal, a decoration, or a beacon I needed to respond to."

"Every single day?"

"Every single day. When I haven't been in the park, I've arranged for someone to send me a picture or check for me. Always. They never knew what they were looking for. They were just looking. Then, after the technology was there, I started using a webcam. So, yes . . . every single day I have checked that window."

"So is the third Imagineer as faithful and resourceful as you?" Hawk was trying not to get his hopes up too much.

Again, Farren paused. He pursed his lips and seemed to ponder what to say next. Then he reached into his pocket and pulled out a slip of paper, folded in half, and slid it across the table. He left his hand on top of it as he spoke once again.

"I am an old man. My fear was that on the day when we might need to do this, we wouldn't all still be alive." Farren cleared his throat and looked down momentarily. "After I found out George Colmes was a part of the plan, and after his death, I feared we might not ever be able to finish what Walt and Roy started."

Farren pulled his hand back from the paper now lying on the table between them. Then: "Apparently the third Imagineer lives and has been checking the window just like I have."

Hawk felt as if his heart would skip a beat. He reached out, unfolded the note, and read the words typed on it. The letters were in black ink that had clearly been punched into the paper through an inked ribbon—an old-fashioned typewriter. Each letter created a slight indent in the paper. He read the words carefully.

In Walt's dream—
The day has arrived—
Look in the eye to see what is left in the capital.

His eyes devoured the three typed lines over and over again. The background noise of the ice cream shop faded into silence as his focus bored into the eighteen words on the paper. It was another clue. There was always another clue. But this one had been typed out by the last of the Imagineers who had been tasked with preserving the Disney dream. For the first time in a long time, he thought he might finally be able to put all of the pieces of the elaborate puzzle together.

Hawk looked up at Farren and saw his old friend smiling. He too felt the anticipation that Hawk was enjoying in the moment. The plan was still intact, and Walt Disney himself had provided the lifeline they needed to have a chance of figuring it all out.

Behind Hawk, the bell on the door jingled as a new customer entered the small shop. Hawk saw Rales tilt his head in confusion. Hawk spun in his chair to see what Rales had seen.

It was too late.

CHAPTER 11

Six days ago
1 p.m.

HAWK FELT HIMSELF BEING PULLED out of his chair. Off balance, he was hurled backward toward the long counter where customers would peer through the glass into the gallons of ice cream nestled in the frost inside. Customers scampered, parents scooped up their children, and audible gasps of surprise drowned out the background music that moments before had created an atmosphere of fun.

Hawk hit the counter, and his shoulder crashed into the glass bins loaded with chopped nuts, sprinkles, chocolate chips, crushed cookies, and mini marshmallows. Each container was now airborne and spewing out its contents on its tumbling flight off the counter. Glass shattered as the bins slammed onto the floor, and Hawk fell against the counter in a heap.

Turning his head, for the first time he saw his attacker and realized that there was more than one assailant in the shop. Dressed in black from head to foot and wearing a full-faced black mask covering all his features, the one who had thrown Hawk across the room moved back toward him.

Readying himself, Hawk lunged and met the opponent moving his direction. They clashed, and the momentum of the collision threw both men off balance. Slipping on shattered glass and escaped toppings, both lost their footing. The floor was also slick with abandoned ice cream that had been quickly discarded by patrons as the unexpected fight began. Struggling to get back on their feet, both men hit the floor with a thud.

Hawk felt the sting of broken glass biting his arm. He ignored it and zeroed in on the person who had attacked him. Instead of continuing the battle with Hawk, his aggressor had turned his attention to assist the other assailant, who had set his sights on Farren Rales. Hawk watched in horror as the fragile body of Rales was slung ruthlessly toward the window of the shop. A crack, followed by the distinct sound of breaking glass, filled the room as Hawk watched his old friend sail through the broken window, disappearing on the patio outside.

Rales's bulky accoster, also completely dressed in black, paused as he looked out the window where he had just hurtled Rales. Apparently satisfied, he slowly turned his attention to the table where they had only moments before been seated. Hawk saw him pick up the paper Farren had given him. With a quick, unified motion, both goons moved toward Hawk.

Hawk clenched his fist and waited for the first man to arrive. He threw the punch and felt his knuckles connect with the man's jaw, which snapped back at the impact. The second assaulter did the same thing to Hawk. His face grew numb the instant the punch connected; then the numbness was followed by a spreading pain. The attacker grabbed Hawk by his shirt and threw him toward the cash register. He hit the counter, and the momentum of the toss flipped him backward up and over the counter. He landed with a crash next to a young employee who had ducked behind the counter for safety. He noticed she had out her cell phone.

"Did you call 911?" His voice was raspy as he struggled to get to his feet.

"Yes," said the cashier, eyes wide with fear.

"Good. Stay down." Hawk sprang back to his feet, ready to continue the battle.

Rising up, he was shocked to see that both of the attackers were gone. Frightened customers cowered in every corner of the ice cream shop, and the floor was a mess, decorated with the ingredients of every ice cream sundae one could imagine. A man in the corner motioned that the attackers had run out of the building.

Hawk headed for the doors with a growing knot in his throat. As he burst through, he looked down the patio to the motionless body of Farren Rales. Ignoring the possibility that the assailants might be waiting for him, he rushed to Rales and gently turned him over to check on his condition. Bloodied and unconscious, Rales was limp on the sidewalk.

Hawk cradled Rales as he heard the sound of an ambulance nearby.

"Stay with me, Farren," he whispered to his friend.

CHAPTER 12

Six days ago
4 p.m.

HAWK SAT ALONE IN THE QUICKLY secured lobby of the Creation Center at Florida Hospital. From this vantage point he had a magnificent view out the window to the Walt Disney Children's Pavilion of the complex. He had visited the pavilion many times delivering gifts from the company as well as working for his favorite charity, Christmas Dreams. He found something very rewarding about sharing the hope of Christmas with children and families who were struggling through life-threatening illnesses. But where he was now was new to him. He wasn't accustomed to being isolated in this massive seating area, seeing guards at every door, and waiting.

He couldn't stand the waiting.

The events from a few hours ago were replaying in an endless loop over and over in his mind. He could still see the reaction of Farren as the men entered the room. He had known there was something wrong. How could the assailants have known where they were going to meet? Hawk had been stubborn and not told anyone about their meeting. In his life full of secrets, especially when it came to Farren Rales, he hadn't wanted to take the time to add the extra safeguard of telling anyone where he would be or what he was doing. His recklessness might have made the situation worse. Once again, he had watched as Farren had been attacked and hurt. He hated the feeling of helplessness as he waited to hear how badly.

Hawk felt like they had cheated death once before, although deep in his heart he knew that was not really possible. There was a day appointed for each person to die. The quest of life was to live the life you were created to live before that day arrived.

He shook his head, pushing back the memory of saying something like that at Kate's funeral. The muggers had taken the clue Rales brought. Had they known it would be there? How could they have known that? Hawk thought about the clue briefly, but as of yet, he had no idea what it meant or how to solve it.

All of these thoughts were exploding rapid-fire in his head when he saw a familiar face come through the door.

Mitch Renner, who was a detective for the Orlando Police Department, was also a friend. Hawk had gotten to know him a few years before, and it had been Renner who helped create the plan to keep assassins away from Farren by making the world think he had died. It had also made Hawk a target, and at some level, it had worked—just not as well as they had all hoped. But it had given Farren the opportunity to heal and recover. In some ways that had been miraculous.

Hawk stood, and Renner embraced him as they greeted each other. Hawk sat back down. Renner took the chair opposite him and looked at him with concern.

"How are you?" Mitch wrinkled his brow.

"I'm fine," Hawk quickly responded. "How's Farren?"

"Well, he's not in great shape," Renner began. "A fall through a window for a man of his age, his physical condition, is . . . well . . . not good."

Hawk had expected this report. He had been there, he had seen what had happened. He felt himself grow warm as a wave of anger flowed through him. Sensing this, Renner held up his hand to get Hawk's attention.

"But there is more." Renner looked down at his electronic tablet, which he had touched. The screen responded by showing him a page of notes. "Apparently during the attack he was infected with a poison."

Hawk thought he had misheard. "What did you say?"

"Farren was poisoned." Renner referred back to his notes. "According to the doctor he sustained cuts and lacerations from the fall through the window, he has a concussion, and there's a slight crack in his hip. But the most serious condition is that he has been poisoned." Renner looked up from his notes and now focused directly on Hawk.

"Poisoned?" Hawk had been completely unprepared for this revelation. "How?"

"Apparently, your attackers did it. Witnesses said that when the assailants left the ice cream shop, they used a syringe on Farren's neck. Then they ran away, laughing."

Mitch Renner paused to let Hawk think about what he had just said and then anticipated his next question. "The doctor called the poison torpid cyan-toxoid. It is a slow-acting variation of a cyanide-type poison."

"So they attacked us to poison Farren?" Hawk knew there was far more to the situation than just that, if that wasn't enough. Why not just kill Farren outright? None of this made sense.

"Somehow, I think this is more about you than Farren . . . again." Renner turned off his tablet. "Tell me what is going on. I know about what happened yesterday in the resort. I heard you were involved in finding all four explosive devices. What have you gotten yourself into this time?"

"Is there a cure for the poison? How do the doctors treat it?" Hawk ignored Renner's questions.

Renner sighed deeply. "They don't have a cure yet. Cyanide is a rapidly acting toxin that inhibits cellular respiration. It prevents the body from producing oxygen. Headaches, severe ones . . . lack of motor skills . . . weak pulse . . . convulsions. Eventually a coma, before . . . well, if Farren were healthy, he would face all of these and they would be enough to kill him. In his compromised condition, even though the toxin is slow acting, there is not much they can do unless they can figure out exactly what type of poison it is and if there is a specific antidote. They say that takes time."

"Time Farren does not have." Hawk rubbed the back of his neck, trying to relieve the frustration.

"Yes, time he doesn't have," Renner agreed.

The men sat quietly across from one another. Mitch Renner had previous experience with the complicated world of Grayson Hawkes and would probably never completely understand it. Once again, the magical allure and wonder-filled world of Disney had proven itself to be a world where the villains are real, the heroes are at war, and the stakes are higher than most people would ever really want to know, much less comprehend.

Hawk felt weary. "Can I go?"

"Sure, I have your statement. We will keep guards here just like we did before. Farren will be safe. You, on the other hand, I'm not so sure."

"Can you give me a ride home after I see Farren?"

"Yes. We already transported your motorcycle back for you." Renner got to his feet. "Let me get someone set up to take you back. Follow me; I'll put you in a car."

Hawk stood and shook Renner's hand. He knew his friend was concerned and had every reason to feel that way. They moved into the hallway and headed toward the exit. Renner spoke with a sergeant standing sentry and motioned for Hawk to follow. The sergeant escorted him through the now heavily guarded corridors of the hospital into the Intensive Care Unit.

The steady beep of monitors greeted Hawk as he entered the room where Rales was lying on a hospital bed. The florescent lighting made him look paler than normal, and the glow radiated off of everything in the room, giving it an eerie, almost frightening look. The IV pole holding the weight of saline bags from which fluid ran through small tubing into his friend's body caused him to pause. Farren looked so small and frail in the bed.

Hawk leaned over his friend and prayed. A doctor and nurse in the small room hung back and respectfully waited for him to be finished before returning to their work. He nodded a slight thanks and stepped back outside the unit.

Another officer took Hawk outside, opened the back door of the squad car, and closed him in. Hawk had grown accustomed to sitting in the back seats of fancy cars and being escorted various places. Kate had often told him it came with the territory once you became a celebrity. It might have come with the territory, but that didn't mean he had to like it. Being accustomed to something and being comfortable with something, for Hawk, were not the same thing.

This time as he slid into the seat it dawned on him that he had never rode in the back seat of a patrol car. It was odd, but the thought drowned in a sea of oddness he had already experienced over the last two days.

He waved at the officer who closed the door behind him, glanced through the steel cage separating him from the driver, and once again closed his eyes to think. The car moved into gear, the lights were turned on, and the car pulled out of the hospital toward Interstate 4.

Hawk slumped back into the seat, trying to clear his mind and process what to do next. Holding his head in his hands, he began to script out a course of action. A part of him just wanted to stay at the hospital and wait with Farren. But the helplessness of that was too much. If he could somehow, someway, once again unravel whatever it was he was supposed to figure out, maybe it might help.

Then the last thing he expected happened.

"Hello, Grayson. It has been a long time since we have seen each other."

The deep, resonant voice dragged Hawk back from this thinking with a frightened jolt. He raised his head, recognizing at once the massive frame before him. Reginald Cambridge was behind the wheel of the police car. Staring at Hawk's reflection in the rearview mirror, Reginald was smiling like a man without a care in the world. He was dressed sharply in an Orlando Police uniform.

Hawk knew he was in trouble. Reginald had been the head of security of the Walt Disney Company and in charge of the Walt Disney World Resort when they'd first met. As the new head of the company he had promoted Reginald, and at one time Cambridge had personally traveled with Hawk every place he went. He had become a trusted friend—until Hawk discovered Reginald was trying to steal the secrets of Walt Disney. He had positioned himself for years inside the company, used insider knowledge, and eventually got so close to Hawk that he believed it was time to steal the secrets, and if Hawk had to be killed in the process, so be it.

At one point, Cambridge had been working with Kiran Roberts. Eventually both had decided to make their own play for control of the company. However, Cambridge had been in prison during the last wave of attacks on Hawk, and up to this point, although he was highly suspect, there had been very little proof that he had been the mastermind behind the scenes—the one pulling the strings and directing the mayhem.

Now Hawk was trapped inside a car with him.

"Don't look so shocked, my old friend. Surely you expected to see me again." Cambridge clearly enjoyed the surprise on Hawk's face.

"I didn't expect to see you here, right now." Hawk clenched his fists and leaned forward to get closer to him. He pressed up against the cage keeping him from the front seat of the cruiser. He should have paid more attention when he thought it was strange that he was riding in the back of a squad car.

"The last time I saw you was on the People Mover in Tomorrowland. The finish was very unsatisfactory," Reginald said.

"I actually thought it was very satisfying." Hawk remembered their fight and how he had gotten the best of Reginald that day. Cambridge had been arrested minutes after.

"I bet you're ready for another round," Reginald said over his shoulder. "Let me explain what you should have already figured out, but somehow haven't." Cambridge snickered. "You know, Grayson, that has always been your problem. You are slow to figure things out. You are impulsive, passionate, but you make things up on the fly. You never have a real plan. I, on the other hand, always have a plan."

Cambridge turned the car and accelerated onto the interstate. Reluctantly Hawk leaned back as the car picked up speed. He glanced around the car, taking in every detail he could.

"Here is what I want you to do for me." Reginald handed Hawk a rolled-up piece of paper through a small opening in the security grate. It was the clue that had been stolen from the ice cream shop. As soon as he saw Reginald, Hawk knew it had been him in the mask. Pieces were slowly falling into place.

"I want you to find what the third Imagineer has hidden for you," Reginald said calmly. "I want you to give it to me along with all of the other goodies that Walt, Roy, Farren, and George placed out there for you to find."

"And tell me, why would I do that?" Hawk smiled, masking a growing rage.

"A number of reasons. One, because there is a cure to the toxic cocktail I gave Farren. I would imagine he has a week, maybe less before it is too late. The toxin is slow, but in his weakened condition, I'm not sure how long he'll last. After all, he did fall through a window. I would imagine he will have a harder time battling through the symptoms. It will be a slow, painful, and debilitating process. It's a shame he will have to endure it."

Reginald raised a single finger, then for dramatic effect raised another. "Two, you already know I can destroy what you love the most. Your precious Walt Disney World. I could have forever destroyed attractions, people, and anything else I wanted to. I didn't. Instead I gave you a chance to figure it out and stop me. Next time, I might not be so generous. And third," Reginald raised a third finger, "there is that amazing footage from Kate Young and *Total Access*. So many things I didn't know, but she was able to figure out. She would have been a great member of my little team. There's all sorts of things in that footage I can release and ruin you forever."

Hawk took in a sharp breath at the thought of Kate in any type of alliance with Cambridge. Reginald laughed at his reaction.

"Three reasons and three days. That is all you have, or Farren will die. Do what I ask, and I will give you the cure. I am giving you a fighting chance. I have given you the clue back so you can get started, I am giving you a chance to save Farren Rales, I didn't detonate the bombs. In some ways, you should be thanking me for this chance."

Hawk watched as Cambridge slowed the car and stopped on the side of the highway. It was rush hour in Orlando, but surprisingly the traffic was moving. On a stretch of interstate that was under construction, Reginald walked around the car and opened the door, motioning for Hawk to step out. Hawk did. Thoughts raced through his head as to what to do once he was outside of the car. He stood in front of Cambridge. Reginald was big and very strong. Hawk had discovered this painfully, firsthand.

Once again, Reginald smiled. It was not a pleasant sight.

"Most people think you are quite the hero. I, however, I am not impressed. So if you want to be a hero right now, take your best shot. But if you do, you must know that I already have a plan in place to ruin your life . . . and you will never be able to save Farren." Spreading out his arms in mock surrender, he said, "So if you want to do this now, go ahead, take your best swing."

Hawk stared into Cambridge's eyes. They were cold and intimidating. Reginald was daring him to do what he wanted to do so very badly. Everything within him screamed to take him on right here, right now, and end this nightmare. But on the side of the interstate, with the steady flashing of the lights on top of the car, Hawk did not. He had to help Farren, he had to figure out the mystery, and lives depended on him.

"I didn't think so." Cambridge reached out and shoved Hawk backward, causing him to bump into the retaining wall of the interstate. Without another word, Reginald Cambridge climbed back into the police car, closed the door, and drove off into the Central Florida afternoon. Hawk watched as the car slowly disappeared into the traffic. Standing on an overpass, he pulled out his cell phone to call his office.

Heather Gilbert, who ran his office for him, answered on the first ring.

"Heather, I need you to send me a car. I need a ride," Hawk informed her.

"Sure, where do you want the car sent?" she asked.

Hawk had not informed anyone at Disney of what had happened. The afternoon had become a blur, and he knew he would have to catch everyone up later on the events of the day. He looked about for a landmark. He had been so focused on Cambridge and their encounter that he hadn't noticed where he was.

"I'm at the Holy Land Experience." Hawk looked to his right and saw the local religious theme park at this exit. The massive recreation of an ancient temple, a large boat built to resemble an ark, and a massive glass building used for filming religious television shows filled in the space adjacent to the interstate. Many people saw it as a rival for area tourist dollars. Hawk did not. He knew it was a very different experience than one could find at Walt Disney World. This was much more a destination for folks looking for something different. It had an amazing history and eventually had been purchased by the Trinity Broadcasting Network.

"Seriously? The Holy Land Experience?"

"Well, I'm not visiting the place. I will be at the front gate."

"Sir?"

"Heather, just send me a car." He decided not to explain.

"It's on the way."

The call ended, and Hawk placed another call, this one to Al Gann so he could begin to figure out how Reginald Cambridge had managed to arrive back in their world as he had done. Cambridge had served notice, and Hawk agreed. This *was* the beginning of the end.

CHAPTER 13

Six days ago
11 p.m.

HAWK'S ARRIVAL AT BAY LAKE TOWERS ushered in another flurry of activity. Al Gann had sounded the alarm, and as the afternoon progressed, a steady stream of law enforcement personnel moved in and out of his office suite. He made multiple statements about the events that had occurred as he left Florida Hospital. There was obvious deep concern about how an OPD officer had managed to put Hawk into a police cruiser with Reginald Cambridge, who had managed not only to be in one of their uniforms but had secured a car. That car was now nowhere to be found.

Hawk had been quick enough to get not only the tag number but the car number as well, when Cambridge stranded him on the interstate. Not that the information would help or change their present circumstances, but Hawk could sense OPD's embarrassment and the frustration that he had been in essence kidnapped, even if only a short amount of time.

The mayor of Orlando came to the office to offer an apology on behalf of the city for the unfortunate incident. The police chief did the same. Mitch Renner had been there for hours trying to recreate and figure out how Cambridge had infiltrated their ranks. For Hawk, the how was not important. Cambridge had proven himself to be a master puppeteer. He was well connected, he operated on his own agenda, and he would do whatever it took to achieve his purpose. Hawk imagined that the how was much simpler than anyone thought it was. He was much more concerned that there was a plan at all, and that once again, he was the flash point.

Cal McManus came to the office as well. He had managed to discover that Cambridge had turned up missing from prison in the last forty-eight hours. News of that event had not yet filtered its way down to the sheriff's department. A mistake, a breakdown, and probably something there would never be a satisfying reason for ... yet all things law enforcement was forced

79

to deal with. For Hawk, those issues meant little. The situation he was now faced with was far more pressing.

Eventually, the activity swirling within the office slowed, and finally it emptied out. A massive amount of security had been stationed through-out the resort. The entire company was on heightened alert. Outside of his office suite were two officers wearing body armor and at the ready with automatic weapons. He looked out across the nighttime sky toward the Magic Kingdom. The dazzling array of colored twinkling lights created the atmosphere it was intended to create—that of a magical place where all is well and dreams come true.

But all was far from well, and the dream was a nightmare. At least for right now.

His attention turned to the door as Juliette and Shep joined him.

"Everybody is gone." Juliette motioned toward the door. "Except of course for most of the Orange County Sheriff's Department, the Orlando Police Department, Disney Security, and I'm told there are federal agents on the way. But other than those people, everyone is gone."

Hawk smiled briefly at the attempt to lighten the moment and turned to face his friends.

"Shep, what did you think about the clue?"

"Well, I think you were right in your initial take on it. It was typed on a typewriter, old-school, so I would guess our third Imagineer is a throwback to days gone by . . . no surprise, really. Farren and George had a little bit of that in them."

Shep took a seat and crossed his arms. "The clue itself is vague, but I think like so often happens, once we find the first bit of the trail, the rest will fall into place."

"Agreed." Hawk nodded. He pretended not to notice that Shep had referred to Farren in the past tense. "So break the clue down with me." He pointed to the desk where the typed clue had been placed.

Juliette moved to the desk and picked the clue up. She read the first line aloud. "In Walt's dream . . ."

"What was Walt's dream?" Shep wondered aloud.

"Which one?" Juliette shrugged. "Walt Disney was a dreamer, and he chased most of them."

"He dreamed of the Florida Project," Hawk said flatly.

"Walt Disney World?" Shep was working to figure it out.

"That was the dream. But it has to be more specific. Right?" Juliette looked to Hawk for confirmation.

"Yes. What part of the Florida Project was Walt's all-encompassing dream?" Hawk's eyes widened, waiting for them to catch up with what he was thinking.

"Epcot." Juliette got there first.

"Epcot," Shep echoed.

"I just said that." Juliette shook her head.

"So the first part of the clue is Epcot," Shep confirmed again for all of them.

"I believe so." Hawk thought out loud. "If the third Imagineer is anything like Farren and George, he or she is going to use clues that wrap around the resort and see how well I know my way around."

"The day has arrived." Juliette read off the next line of the clue. "Does that mean the day to find the next piece of the puzzle? The day to begin the search? Or does it have something to do with finding a particular date?"

"Yes," Hawk slowly paced the room as he thought.

"Yes what?" Shep scratched his head.

"Yes, it could mean all of those things or none of those things." Hawk's mind explored the recesses of his knowledge about Epcot. "Where can you find a day in Epcot?"

"Hey, I know!" Juliette snapped her fingers. "You can find a day on a calendar. You can get a calendar in some of the gift shops in Epcot."

"Right, and you can probably find calendars in the countries around the World Showcase gift shops as well," Shep added.

Hawk abruptly stopped. "What did you say?"

Shep looked surprised for a moment and repeated his thought. "Uh, I said you can get a calendar in the World Showcase gift shops."

"Exactly." Hawk smiled.

"I'm not keeping up with you on this, Hawk." Juliette pulled a strand of hair back over her ear. "What have you figured out?"

"Where to start. Or maybe nothing." Hawk admitted. "Isn't there a calendar in the Mexico pavilion in the World Showcase?"

The three let the question linger for a moment. Then Shep pulled out his always present electronic tablet and began punching in information for a search engine. While he searched, Juliette remembered what Hawk was talking about.

"It's in the main lobby entrance area, if we're thinking the same thing. An ancient stone calendar of some sort." Juliette looked to Hawk. "Right? Is that what you're thinking?"

"That's what I'm thinking." Hawk nodded and turned back to Shep, who gave the information on cue.

"It's an ancient Aztec calendar. It's a replica, an exact replica of the original, which is located in Mexico City." Shep smiled. "You can find a day on a calendar. That must be it."

"It's a great place to start." Hawk began moving toward the door. "And it's the only plan we have right now to start with."

The decision was made that Shep would remain in Hawk's office where he could do research if needed. This type of teamwork had served them well in the past. Juliette insisted on going with Hawk. He knew she was worried about him, frightened and shaken by the events unfolding, and that the inactivity of waiting could be overwhelming. So for once, he didn't argue.

Once again, they climbed aboard the Harley and headed toward Epcot. It only took a few moments, and they were able to weave their way through traffic and find the service road into the theme park. Since the park had closed and there were no longer guests in the World Showcase, Hawk and Juliette rode the motorcycle right into the streets of the resort area. The plan for this part of Epcot had been inspired by the early World's Fairs. It was intended to be a place where people and nations from around the globe would gather to interact with one another. Creating a bond built through common experiences, it would secure a better future and create unity among all people.

The dream was ambitious, but Walt Disney World was a place where dreams could come true. In many ways the World Showcase captured and embodied the power of all such big dreams.

After parking the bike in front of the pyramid that encompassed the Mexico pavilion, they quickly headed up the steps into the lobby area. Refreshing, cool air blew through the door as they entered. They strode across the dark stone floor into the dimly lit gallery that surrounded them in a showcase of Mexican arts and crafts. Spotlights glowed, highlighting each exhibit. In the center of the room, the focal point was the Sun Stone, or the Aztec calendar they were looking for.

"Wow." Juliette's voice echoed in the massive room. "When there are no other people moving around, you see how impressive this area really is."

"There is a lot of history on display in here," Hawk answered, stepping in front of the massive round stone. The ancient calendar was carved with concentric circles. Each circle contained carvings in the shape of letters or objects. They all radiated out from the center of the stone, which featured a face.

"The day has arrived. Look in the eye to see what is left in the capital." Juliette read the clue for Hawk. She had picked the paper up and brought it with them. Although Hawk was usually able to remember what he read, most often word for word, she did not have that skill.

Hawk moved in closer and studied the face in the center of the calendar. He peered into the eyes of the face, doing as the clue had instructed—looking in the eye.

Hawk gave a low whistle. "See what's left in the capital." He spun in the direction where Juliette was standing, facing her with the stone face over his shoulder. "The left eye of the face looks toward the capital."

"Huh?" Juliette frowned. She didn't understand what Hawk was trying to get her to see.

He pointed to his left toward a massive map visible through an oval-shaped glass window. Highly detailed stonework surrounded it, as it did all of the displays in this area. Silently, he moved to the display and gazed at the massive map lit up in front of him.

"This is the capital." Hawk smiled as Juliette joined him in front of it. "This is a map of Tenochtitlan, the capital of the Aztec empire. It was created in 1524 by Hernán Cortés. This map, or at least the original, was the first look most people ever had at the city. It also served notice that Cortés had made another conquest and that it was Spain's discovery." He laughed. "The clue was referring to the left eye on the stone calendar, the direction to the left of the calendar, and it says that something is left in the capital. This is a map of the capital."

As Hawk uttered the word *capital* again, the lighting in the display changed, and the map disappeared, showing a partial model of the Aztec city. The change was dramatic, and Hawk caught his breath. The map had been created and displayed on a scrim: when the lighting shifted and came on behind it, the map would disappear and the city could be seen. In all the years Hawk had visited the resort, he had never noticed this. He assumed it ran on a timer and did this all day. There was no way it could have happened for his benefit alone. Or at least, he didn't think there was.

Both of them pressed up against the glass and looked at the city. Juliette pointed at the same time Hawk noticed it: secured at the top of a miniature pyramid, resting almost unnoticeably across the top of the model in the center at the back, was what appeared to be another note.

"That has to be it." Juliette tapped on the glass for emphasis.

"You're right, or in this case left." Juliette shook her head and let him know the joke really wasn't that clever. Hawk quickly moved to find a way in. "Notice I am again moving to the left."

On the left side of the display case there was a faux rock wall. Tucked inside of the rock wall, cleverly hidden out of an easy sight line, was a door that opened into the city display. Reaching into his pocket, he took out the kingdom key, the amazing master key that usually opened any door he needed it to open on these mystery adventures the Imagineers had created. Stepping to the door, he turned the handle and discovered it was locked. Searching along the line of the doorjamb, he found a keyhole, inserted the key, and felt the click as the lock mechanism released. The door swung open.

Stepping inside a small alcove, he moved to a second door, unlocked it, and took a gentle step up and into the display area. He looked through the glass and saw Juliette smiling as he moved to the pyramid at the rear of the display. They had been correct. It was a note, and at first glance, it seemed to be typed in the same style as the note Farren had found.

Hawk freed the note and held it up for Juliette to see. Through the glass he saw her become distracted, and she answered her cell phone. He glanced at his watch and saw it was now one o'clock in the morning. Early morning phone calls were rarely good news. Her face became a mask of concern, and Hawk moved to exit the display. His heart sank. Was something wrong? Perhaps with her kids, perhaps it was Tim, or . . . He rounded the corner as she ended the call.

"What's wrong?" he asked.

"Do you have your phone with you?" She looked at him gravely.

"Yes." He reached in his pocket and pulled it out.

"You must not have been getting a signal in the display then."

"Why?"

"Um . . . that was Mitch Renner. He said he tried to reach you, couldn't, then called me. It's Farren." She lowered her gaze toward the stone floor.

Hawk's whole body went still. "He's not . . .?"

"No, no, no . . . he's not dead." She realized what Hawk had thought. "I'm sorry. He has lapsed into a coma. The doctors are having no luck finding an antidote. They're trying, but it doesn't look like he is going to make it."

"He's going to make it." Hawk curtly nodded his head as he spoke. "He is going to make it."

"Okay," Juliette patted his arm gently. "But he may not have the week Reginald told you he would have. It sounds like he has far less."

"We'll get the antidote in time." Hawk opened up the paper he'd taken from the display.

"Hawk, are you really going to give Reginald all the things you've found over these past years?" Her voice softened. "Do you really believe he will give you the cure for the poison if he even has it?"

"What else do you want me to do? " Hawk voice was low and measured. "What else can I do?"

Silence filled the massive room as the words disappeared, lost in the history surrounding them. Juliette again patted his arm gently as she nodded thoughtfully. Hawk knew she was getting ready to say something, so he waited.

"What would Farren want you to do, Hawk? Do you think he would want you to get this far, discover all the things you have discovered, only to hand it over to Reginald?"

Juliette's eyes brimmed with tears ready to flow from memories. "After all that's happened. The violence, the battles, the death . . . would Farren want you to hand it over to Reginald? If you do, then all of this has been for nothing, and the bad guys win. Right?"

Hawk felt trapped. His breath caught in his chest. Juliette was right. The Disney secrets had come at an incredibly high price. Not only for him, not only for Farren, but for Juliette and her family. She had every right to call him out on this and challenge him about what he was thinking about doing. He hadn't even really realized he was considering it until now—but he didn't know else he could do. Not only did the uncertainty fluster him, but desperation was smothering him as well.

"What do you think I should do?"

It was a heartfelt request for help.

Hawk was resilient, he was bold, and he was a risk-taker. His strong leadership skills usually carried him through every situation. But at this moment he felt hollow, unsure, and not his usual steady self. He was running on autopilot, waiting for something to click or fall into place that might give him an answer to the quandary trapping him.

"I don't know," Juliette sighed. "You don't have a plan yet, do you? You're making this up as you go, right?"

Hawk nodded and offered her a slight smile.

"Then let's figure out the next clue. You'll know what to do when the time is right." She shook her head as she said it. "Won't you?"

"Of course I will." Hawk smirked as he opened the clue. It was a weak attempt to sound confident. At this moment he had no idea what was going to happen next, much less what he was going to do, but at least he was doing *something*, and he was sure he was moving in the right direction. He taught, believed, and lived by the idea that direction, not intention, gets you to your destination. He wasn't sure where he would end up; all he knew was that he was going in the only direction he had in front of him. He would keep moving forward.

They looked at the next clue.

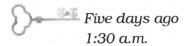 *Five days ago*
1:30 a.m.

UNDER THE LIGHTS OF THE LOBBY, the pair examined the clue. Juliette read it aloud. She kept her voice soft, but in the emptiness of the room, her voice bounced off the stone floor and walls. Just like the initial clue, this one was punched out on an old-style typewriter.

Where the Dragon Slayer protects—
Maximilian is missing—
One of the other three can help.

Hawk read the words as she spoke them. He worked what he considered to be the main hooks in the clue. A dragon slayer and a missing Maximilian. Standing quietly he played with the words, waiting for some type of image or mental picture to emerge. Without realizing it he began to slowly pace the room. Each step slogged his brain forward, prompted it to keep exploring, to keep remembering what he had tucked away in the recesses of his mind. Juliette watched as he walked, saying nothing. He made his way around the lobby once, then twice, and then on the third loop of the display area pulled up suddenly.

"Well?" Juliette broke the silence. She had seen him move through this process of figuring things out before. She had often told him that his mind and the way it worked was not only incredibly fascinating but a little bit scary. Tonight, he knew she hoped it was firing on all cylinders and that the answers they were looking for would be there.

"I know where to find a dragon slayer." He smiled.

"Serious? There is a dragon slayer in Epcot? Seems like more of a Magic Kingdom thing."

"Right here in Epcot." He began moving toward the exit.

They bounded down the steps of the Mexico pavilion and jumped on the motorcycle. The engine fired to life, and he put it in gear and let out the clutch. They moved back toward the center of the World Show-case. They rode past the Norway pavilion, which after the success of the animated film *Frozen* had gone through an extensive remodel. Although some naysayers did not like that the cultural pavilion had been reimagined to highlight a cartoon, the reality was that it invigorated the area, drew families into the showcase with a more compelling reason to come. Hawk understood there would be more of this type of approach taken in the years ahead. The goal would have to be finding the right balance to keep the original intent of the World Showcase while creating new, fresh, and exciting guest experiences.

As Norway faded over their shoulder, they passed the China pavilion next. One of the most spectacular and beautiful of the pavilions, China was Hawk's favorite place to walk and gaze at all of the history and detail the Imagineers had managed to find a home for. The detail and heritage were rich, and if you were a history buff, as Hawk was, then you loved to look. The Outpost appeared next, and Hawk slowed the bike just a bit. He thought he had seen someone move and duck behind a wall as they drew closer. It could have been a shadow, and he was not really worried about someone seeing them, but the movement was there—he was certain. Yet, as he moved at a slower speed he saw no one.

Although most never realize it, there was much to see in this little area that was originally designed to be another pavilion. As those plans never came to be, the area was now themed as an outpost in the middle of the jungle. It provided travelers with food, drink, supplies, and a place to rest before they continued on their journeys, with a snack bar, shops, and a place to find a seat and relax. Crates and old soda dispensers provided much of the décor, but the little area also included African drums and a supply of canoes used to move goods to other villages from the Outpost. All provided decorations for the little area—and also could be a place for someone to hide.

"What is it?" Juliette asked over his shoulder.

"I thought I saw someone."

Now they both looked. The area was not overly inky, since the lights of the theme park were always turned on. Still, he saw nothing. For an instant, the thought struck him to get off the Harley and go look. Instead, he decided it was more important to solve the puzzle at hand. With a turn of his wrist, the bike jerked forward, and they continued speeding away from the Outpost.

He veered to his left, and they pulled into the Germany pavilion. Moving into the *platz,* or plaza as most might call it, he was struck by how much the area resembled an American town square. Like so many things in Disney theme parks, this was a version of what someplace might look like in the mind's eye—a place that exists in the mind or memory but never really was quite that way in real life. It was created to be a classic German township, somewhere in history between the thirteenth and seventeenth centuries, with architecture from those periods.

As they dismounted the motorcycle, Hawk motioned to the area surrounding them.

"The highlight of this area was originally supposed to be an attraction known as the Rhine River Cruise. Guests would have climbed aboard a tour boat for a ride down the Rhine and Isar rivers, plus a couple of others as I remember it. The scenery was going to be miniatures of the sights along the countryside you might have seen as you traveled. The plans never came together, so the new plan was to create a continuous Oktoberfest in the pavilion."

"They succeeded." Juliette followed Hawk toward the center of the town square.

He stopped at the fountain and pointed up. A massive column rose from the center of the fountain. On the top of the pillar, a statue of a man seated atop a rearing horse was doing battle with a dragon. Juliette shook her head. "Son of a gun," she said.

"This is Epcot's dragon slayer. St. George, the patron saint of soldiers in Germany. According to legend, St. George killed a dragon with a magical sword when the king's daughter was about to be sacrificed to the creature. Almost every village in Germany has a statue of St. George somewhere within its township. He is a symbol of protection for the village."

"So this is what the clue was talking about?" Juliette stood looking around to see if something else might catch her eye and connect to the clue.

"Yes . . . at least I think so." Hawk shrugged, and like Juliette, began looking around the plaza. "There *is* another dragon slayer in the World Showcase; the statue of St. Theodore in Italy. It's on a pillar where they have recreated St. Mark's Square. But it doesn't really stand alone like this one does. If we can't find anything here, we can always go check there."

"So now we are looking for the missing Maximilian?"

"Yep," Hawk said, advancing across the plaza in his search. "Look for something or someone that isn't here."

"That makes no sense." Juliette continued to search. She moved along the front of the building closest to the dragon slayer, peering in the windows for anything that might catch her eye.

"It never does." Hawk smiled to himself. "Until it does."

"What?" Juliette turned to see that Hawk had stopped and was standing still in front of a shop in the pavilion. "Did you find him? Or not find him, as the case might be?"

He didn't answer. She stepped across the plaza to join him and looked up at the building.

"This is Das Kaufhaus, which was inspired by the very real Kaufhaus in Freiburg, Germany." He pointed up to the second-floor balcony. As she followed his gaze, he pointed his finger toward the three figures positioned between the windows on the second floor. "The original has four figures on it. The Epcot version only has three."

"The missing one is Maximilian?" Juliette was impressed.

"I'm not sure," Hawk admitted. "I'm guessing so. Let's call Shep."

Juliette already had her cell phone out, and Shep answered instantly. Passing the phone to Hawk, he laid out what he was thinking. He explained what the clue had said and that he was looking for the name of the statue that was not included here. He waited for Shep to do some quick research and then listened intently. He ended the call and handed the phone back to Juliette.

"Well?"

"On the original there are indeed four statues. They represent the first four emperors of Hapsburg. Because this version was smaller and scaled back, only three of the princes were placed on display. Philip the First, Charles the Fifth, and Ferdinand the First are on the building. There was no room for . . ."

"Come on and get on with it." Juliette sighed in exasperation.

"There was no room for Maximilian the First." Hawk smiled at their success. "Like the clue said, Maximilian is missing. One of the other three . . ."

". . . can help." Juliette completed the clue as Hawk moved to the doors of the building.

They were locked, and he once again removed his kingdom master key. To his surprise, it did not fit any of the locks on the front doors of the building. Shuffling back a few steps, he surveyed the front of the building and wandered off to the side of the structure. It was then that he saw it: a door used by cast members to enter and exit and move merchandise in and out of the area. He again tried the key. This time it slid into the lock, the lock mechanism released, and the door swung open.

Hawk wasted no time moving inside the shop and finding an interior door that opened up, giving him access to the second-floor balcony. Not intended to be used or accessed as a real balcony, it was narrow, and there was not much room to move. He worked his way down toward the bearded statue in the middle. At first glance he saw nothing out of the ordinary. Then he looked up toward the statue's face. On the top of its was a crown. Peeking out from the front of the crown was what looked like the corner of a piece of paper.

Without hesitation he reached up and found on top of the crown a folded piece of paper he knew immediately had been placed there as a clue. Grabbing it, he looked over the balcony to Juliette, who had been watching him intently. He waved the paper at her, letting her know it was what they were looking for, and he retraced his steps to head back to the plaza.

Carefully closing and locking the doors he had used to enter, he returned to the plaza. Stepping across to where Juliette was standing, he noticed she was looking back out into the World Showcase.

"What's wrong?" Hawk attempted to follow her line of sight.

"I'm not sure." She continued to look out into the empty space. "Nothing, I guess. I thought I heard something."

"Something . . . like what?"

"Footsteps. I thought I heard someone walking, but when I turned to look, there was nothing there." She turned back to Hawk. "I'm probably just being paranoid."

"You might be." He continued to look toward where she had heard the footsteps. "But like I told you, I thought I saw someone move in the Outpost and disappear. With what we are doing, with what is going on, I think being cautious is wise."

Juliette laughed softly. "Seriously? You, Grayson Hawkes, just told me that being cautious is wise? You haven't been cautious since . . . well, since I met you."

He turned and walked away from her as she completed her sentence. Going back toward the Harley, she followed him, and he heard her voice over his shoulder.

"I didn't just offend you, did I?" Her voice was mystified.

"Of course not. Because you're right. Caution is not usually one of my chosen companions in life." He grabbed the motorcycle and started to move it. "However, since you are being paranoid, maybe it's best if we don't ride a motorcycle through the streets and leave it out where it can be easily spotted. I am going to stash it out of the way so we're not so easy to track. Just in case."

He moved the bike behind the building. Juliette followed. Now they were hidden from any easy lines of sight by the corner of the structure. Once he was satisfied that the motorcycle was hidden, he pulled the clue he had found out of his pocket. He unfolded it and read it silently.

Don't let the path to romance
Get you off track.
You find the power you need if it keeps moving.

Hawk read and reread the clue, saying nothing. Juliette did the same. He felt a heaviness and noticed he was clutching the paper extremely tightly. His hands shook slightly.

"Hey." Juliette's voice drew him back to the moment. "You've been staring at the clue a little longer than you should have. Where'd you go? You all right?"

"Yes." He snapped back and suppressed the wave of sadness that washed over him. "I know where we are supposed to look. Sorry, I just got lost in a thought."

"What kind of thought?"

"Nothing, really." Hawk motioned for her to follow. He began traveling and noticed she had not moved with him.

He turned back to look at her. She stood with her feet planted firmly and hands on both hips, shaking her head. Hawk went back to where she waited.

"No way, no sir." Her voice was soft and compassionate. "We have known each other too long and been through too many tough spots for you to think that you can just . . ."

"I was thinking of Kate," Hawk said. "Again."

Juliette reached out and placed a hand softly on Hawk's shoulder. "That's understandable. I am so sorry. But why right here, right now?"

"The clue."

"The line about romance?"

"Sort of." He again motioned for her to follow him. As they moved this time, he explained. "The clue is going to take us to one of the favorite spots Kate had here in Epcot. We would come and walk around at night, and we always ended up in the same place. When I read the clue, I knew immediately where to go." Hawk breathed deeply. "I don't know exactly where to look, but I do know where we are going."

They had not gone far from the Germany pavilion when they came upon a massive garden area. Filled with trees, plants, and lush scenery, with a small stream running through it, the landscape featured an elaborate outdoor miniature garden train that ran across it. It featured a population of townspeople figurines, lighted buildings, and sights that were miniature versions of a very real, amazingly detailed German countryside.

Hawk pointed to the street sign sitting on the corner of the paved walkway that allowed guests to walk over the train scene and through the garden. The sign read, "The Romantic Road." They stopped.

"Kate and I used to walk along this sidewalk on every trip we made here. It is called the Romantic Road. It carries us over the model train layout. The clue says, 'Don't let the path to romance—the Romantic Road—get you off track.'" He stretched out his arm and pointed to the miniature village surrounding them. "Somewhere, along the track . . . the train track is what we are looking for."

"Hawk, I know I have told you this before, but Kate was great." Juliette's voice broke just a bit. "I am so heartbroken for you."

"Stop." Hawk held up his hand. He turned to face his friend in the semidarkness. "I know, we have talked through this before. I miss her too, I just had a moment." He smiled weakly. "I have them from time to time. But I don't have time to have one right now, so don't enable me, please."

Juliette nodded in understanding. "Then quit goofing around. We need to figure out what the rest of the clue means. 'You find the power you need if it keeps moving.' We need to keep moving." And with that she gave him a gentle shove and nudged him deeper into the model train village to figure out the clue.

CHAPTER 15

Five days ago
2:45 a.m.

SCANNING THE MINIATURE GERMAN COUNTRYSIDE, the pair looked for something that might connect to the line in the clue about finding power. Lush green thickets of shrubs surrounded the railroad. Even in the early morning hours, the fresh smell of flowers wafted across the railroad lines, and in the dimly lit area they explored the details of the small buildings along the railway landscape.

Moving off along the concrete path, Hawk went toward one end of the area while Juliette moved to the other. *You find the power you need if it keeps moving.* The last line of the clue rolled over and over in his thoughts. As he looked, he was reminded afresh how beautiful this area of the World Showcase was. Disney had a reputation of doing things better than anyone else, and this train setup was no exception. Hawk remembered one of the cast members telling him that before they powered up the trains each day, they had to check the tunnels positioned along the railroad line. Those tunnels became the favorite nighttime homes for bunnies and squirrels to sleep in. In the morning they would have to clear the track line before they sent the trains through. The little creatures would scurry off for the day and return to their garden homes each night.

Stepping over the rail, he carefully took a step into the display itself. Careful not to hit the track or step on a miniature display, he moved up toward the hedge line cautiously. It was as he moved into the display that he caught the building out of the corner of his eye. He looked closely and saw it was a miniature mill. On the side was a detailed waterwheel. The small stream running beside it and through the display would turn the wheel of the mill. If this were full-sized, it would be a source of power—and it would fit the criteria of the clue.

"Juliette," Hawk whispered loudly enough for her to hear. "I have something here."

He turned his attention back to the mill and began to move toward it. He heard her moving across the walkway to where he had been moments before. Reaching the mill, he reached down and place his hand on it. He traced the shape of the building to see if there was a clue attached. There was not. Kneeling down and looking closer, he rubbed his hand across his chin as he thought. Again, reaching toward the building, he spread his fingers and placed his hand across the roof of the miniature building. Tightening his grip just enough to securely hold the roof, he lifted and found the roof was not attached—it was simply sitting in place where it could be easily moved. Now that the lid of the building was off, Hawk saw that inside there was a folded note inside. He presumed it was the next clue.

In one fluid movement he removed it, replaced the roof on the building, and began to retrace his steps. Carefully avoiding any obstacle and careful not to disturb the display, he got back to the sidewalk where Juliette was waiting.

"Another clue." Her voice was edged with anticipation.

"It looks like it," Hawk said in response. "Another piece of the puzzle to unravel."

"Then let's start unraveling it."

They unfolded the paper. The typewriter-punched parchment revealed the next destination they would have to discover.

From Heaven you can hear the whispers
But very few will smile
Standing before one who kneels.

Hawk scratched his head as he looked at the words on the paper. He glanced toward Juliette to see if there was a spark of recognition in her eyes as she read. There wasn't. He again looked back at the clue. His eyes focused on what he thought the key words of the clue would be. He plucked one from each line and mentally tried to force them into a train of coherent thought. *Heaven, smile,* and *kneels* were the words he played with. Usually, taking this approach allowed him to filter through the possibilities of where something might be located. He closed his eyes and mentally moved the words around, trying to place them somewhere within the Walt Disney World Resort. "Hawk." The voice was a whisper.

"Hawk." Again another whisper.

"Hawk!" Juliette had raised her voice to a rasp, but this time she elbowed him to get his attention.

His concentration shattered as he turned to her. She shifted her weight back and forth, trying to look nonchalant as she tilted her head toward the walkway behind Hawk. "There is somebody standing there, watching us in the shadows."

Juliette stole a quick glance past Hawk and then again tilted her head so it appeared she was studying the clue. He watched her eyes and could see that she still was looking back at whoever was standing there.

"How close are they?" Hawk whispered.

"On the edge of the Germany pavilion." She quickly glanced at Hawk, then back to the shadow person. Satisfied there was still someone there, she then lowered her head back toward the clue, leaving her gaze looking toward the unknown visitor. "I noticed some movement when we were reading the clue. I looked up and saw someone in the shadows."

"A man or a woman?" Hawk resisted the urge to turn around and look.

"It's a man, I think. It's dark, and whoever is over there is trying real hard to stay in the shadows where we can't see him."

Hawk considered what they should do. He thought he had noticed someone earlier; now it was clear there was someone watching them as they gathered clues. However, whoever it was seemed content to remain out of sight and let them find whatever they were looking for.

"What do you want to do?" Juliette continued to keep her eyes casually focused on their stalker.

"I want to know who it is." Hawk took a deep breath and then slowly exhaled. He tried to evaluate the situation they were in as he saw it. The clock was ticking ever faster on Farren's life. He needed to figure out the clues to have some chance of saving him. Reginald Cambridge had been very clear about his intentions and what he would do if Hawk failed. Their window was closing, and whoever was following was trying hard to stay out of sight, and most importantly, out of their way. "But we need to track down this trail of clues from the third Imagineer."

"And?"

"And that means we're going to have to figure out who's following us while we keep going."

"You have a plan now?"

"Of course."

"A good plan?"

"Do I ever have a bad plan?" He smiled as she looked at him in disbelief before returning her gaze to the person in the shadows.

"More often than you will ever admit."

"We are going to make a run for it and try to lose him." Hawk was now mapping out his strategy. Hawk decided if they could put some distance between them, it would make it more difficult for the person to follow and keep up. In his way of thinking, that would either force them to make a mistake and expose their identity, or it might result in them losing their trail. Both were acceptable alternatives. He'd had a few moments earlier when he allowed himself to be overwhelmed by the circumstances they were facing. But he was much better when he was chasing something. As he had found so often in life, courage emerged as you climbed over the circumstances that threatened to bury you.

"I can't run in these shoes."

Hawk glanced down. Juliette was wearing her usual pair of heels.

"Then you are about to run out of those shoes. Kick them off and get ready to go."

"Where are we going?"

"China." He folded up the clue and stuffed it into his pocket.

"China?"

"Let's go." Hawk grabbed her by the hand to stabilize her until she was free of the shoes and then released her as they ran toward China. In the rumble of rushed steps, Hawk glanced back over his shoulder to see how the person in the shadows had reacted. They had scurried away so quickly and unexpectedly that he could not see if they were being chased or not. He assumed they were, and he wasn't going to lose the element of surprise by slowing down.

The pair raced past the Outpost.

Sprinting, Hawk nudged Juliette away from running right next to the Outpost, just in case more than one person might be watching them. They had no guarantee the person he'd spotted earlier in the shadows was the same person following them now. While veering away from the mini pavilion exposed them and made them easier to see, the risk was calculated, as he feared an ambush.

They cleared the area without incident and darted along the edge of the massive China pavilion. Another glance over his shoulder didn't reveal whether they were being followed, and he didn't slow down to take a better look. Satisfied that they had a lead over whoever might be behind them, he motioned to his right, and they headed into the Gate of the Golden Sun. The entire pavilion was modeled after a palace in Beijing. They slowed as they entered a world inspired by ancient China.

Running down the pathway, they moved through the park area to the pavilion's most dominant structure. The temple area in front of them was modeled after the Hall of Prayer for a Good Harvest. Hitting the entrance at a full sprint, the pair stopped instantly. Juliette instinctively tried the door handle, which was locked. Hawk had anticipated this and had pulled out the kingdom key. It unlocked the set of doors and allowed them to disappear inside. He pulled the doors closed and relocked them, and they stepped into the massive domed temple.

Even under these circumstances, Hawk found himself impressed once again with the building as they stepped inside. Its vivid colors accented the four columns inside the temple that represented the four seasons. The twelve pillars around the room represented the twelve months of the Chinese year, and the twelve outer pillars the twelve-hour division of day and night. The floor was decorated in bright concentric circles that drew visitors inward toward the middle of the room. Hawk was struck anew with the beauty of the temple and found himself looking upward to the domed roof. He walked to the center of the floor and motioned for Juliette to join him.

As she stood next to him, he whispered, "We should be safe for a few moments."

The stunned look on her face was the expression he was expecting.

"How did you do that?" she asked.

He smiled. He pointed upward. "The room under the dome is acoustically perfect. When you stand in the center of the circle on the floor and speak, your voice, even if it is a whisper, vibrates directly back into your ears." The effect was startling and compelling. Juliette had discovered it for the first time.

"I didn't know this room sounded like that." She smiled.

"Most don't. Very cool detail." Hawk went back to the door, listening for the sound of anyone moving outside. As he did, his eyes danced across the colorful temple, and he stepped backward away from the door and slowly scanned the interior with more purpose.

"Do you know where we are?" he asked.

"A temple in the China pavilion?" Juliette responded.

"Good answer, but do you know what it is called?"

"No, I don't."

"This is the Hall of Prayer for a Good Harvest," Hawk told her. "The original is part of a bigger temple complex. This one is much smaller than the real one, but this is a half-scale version of the Temple of Heaven."

"The what?" Juliette knew what he was thinking.

"The Temple of Heaven." Hawk shrugged. "I forgot what it was called for a moment. It wasn't even on my radar. But this might be what the clue was talking about."

"From heaven you can hear the whispers." Juliette repeated the first line of the clue. "I just heard a whisper in the center of the room. Is that it?"

"Could be. Partially. 'From heaven you can hear the whispers' . . ." he repeated the line. "There has to be more to it than that. I'm just not as familiar with some of the details here as I am in other places."

"You mean there is something about Walt Disney World you don't know?" Juliette feigned mock surprise. "I am speechless."

"No, you're not. You were just talking." He smirked. "I didn't say I didn't know something; I said I am not as familiar with some of the details here." He pointed toward the wall.

Hawk had chosen the China pavilion to hide because of its layout. Only once he stepped inside had it begun to dawn on him that this might be part of the next puzzle piece. He offered a silent prayer of thanks. Walt Disney had once written about faith, "It helps immeasurably to meet the storm and stress of life and keep you attuned to the Divine inspiration." Hawk not only believed that but had spent his adult life trying to get people to live their lives that way. He didn't believe in luck; he believed in the guiding hand of God, and this time he realized that in the storm and stress of the moment, he had been divinely inspired.

On the left side of the temple was a gallery. The sign on the gallery read, "Whispering Willows Gallery."

"From heaven you can hear the whispers." Juliette shook her head in wonder as the first pieces of the clue fell into place. "Here in this room, the whispers can be heard. Where better than the Whispering Willows Gallery?"

"I think we are on to something here." Hawk was already moving into the gallery and repeating the next line of the clue. "But very few will smile."

"Those guys are definitely not smiling." Juliette stood next to him and pointed at the huge display in front of them.

"The terracotta army of Qin Shi Huan." Hawk stepped closer. "These are the tomb warriors: guardian spirits of ancient China. It's a one-third-scale miniature replica exhibit of the famed terracotta army of Qin Shi Huan. In the Lintong district of China, back in the mid-1970s, the original terracotta sculptures were found. The discovery featured eight thousand soldiers, horses, and chariots. It is estimated they were created in 210–209 BCE as a form of funerary art to protect the emperor in his afterlife. In real life, the army is huge. And this small version is pretty impressive as well."

"And like I said, they are definitely not smiling." Juliette was commenting on the ferocious expressions on the neatly aligned army of nearly three hundred soldiers stretched out across the room in front of them.

"You're right . . . but are *any* of them smiling?" Hawk began to look more closely into their faces.

"That one is." Juliette pointed toward a solider.

"So is that one." Hawk saw a different one with a smiling expression at about the same time. "So some of them do smile! Not many, but a few."

"Then one of them might be what we are looking for." Juliette looked even closer into their faces.

"No, it can't be just any of them. It has to be one of these." Hawk motioned to a line of sculpted soldiers that stood sentry in front of horse-drawn carts and rows of warriors kneeling. "'But very few will smile standing before one who kneels.' It has to be someone in the row of soldiers in front of the kneeling warriors.

"Like that one." Juliette leaned in and pointed toward the face of a statue that was almost grinning, standing directly in front of a soldier kneeling on one knee.

The warrior was standing nearly in the middle of the display, and Hawk realized he was going to have to carefully step into the rows to see if there might be a clue hidden there. Navigating the tightly spaced rows of soldiers was not easy. He did his best not to disrupt or damage the display as he closed in on the smiling warrior. The closer he got, the more the smile resembled an exaggerated grimace—but compared to the other warriors around it, he figured it counted.

Working his body next to the soldier, he grabbed the statue with both hands and lifted it upward. The weight of the miniature surprised him, but there, below the base, was another folded piece of paper. He gently reached down and picked it up. Stashing it in his pocket, he took the extra few moments to return the statue to the place he had found it. By the time he was finished, no one would be able to tell that the exhibit had been disturbed in any way.

Now he began the slow journey of carefully retracing his steps to where Juliette was waiting.

"I just wish these Imagineers who have all this important information to share with you would just come out and give it to you." Juliette sighed as she waited for Hawk to return.

"Aw, but where would be the fun in that?" Hawk chided as he stepped carefully between the rows of standing warriors.

"It stopped being fun when it became so dangerous," she said with conviction.

"True," Hawk quickly agreed with her. "But if you think about it, the secrets Walt left these men to keep, protect, and share are the secrets of a lifetime. The detail, the search for them, the story behind them—it's all part of the bigger mystery. Every clue is another layer of protection."

"And what happens if you can't figure the next clue out?"

"Then I am not good enough or worthy enough to unravel and discover the secrets."

Juliette grew silent, and Hawk stepped over the exhibit barrier to join her. He watched her as she thought about what he had just said. Every challenge to this point, no matter how big or difficult, he had been able to conquer. He tried not to overanalyze the journey to this point, but instead, as he always did, he focused on moving forward. He had always taught and lived with the idea that you would never discover the unexpected if you always stuck with the familiar. This entire Walt Disney adventure had taken him away from the familiar into unexpected lands loaded with mystery.

He handed Juliette the note. She glanced at him, smiled, and then unfolded it.

CHAPTER 16

Five days ago
4 a.m.

THE TYPEWRITTEN NOTE GAVE them the information they would have to figure out next.

> **Evil be to him who evil thinks**
> **Always shining before this**
> **You find what you need to illuminate your path.**

"What do you think?" Juliette read the paper, then looked toward Hawk.

"I think we shouldn't have left the Harley in Germany." He stepped toward the doors, rubbing his chin as he walked, lost in thought.

"You already know what the clue means?"

"Sure, part of it." Hawk turned back to her. "It's the easiest clue we have been given yet."

"I'm glad you know what it means, because . . ."

"Our bigger problem is getting there." He spoke softly, cutting her off, but in a non-combative way. "We have to get to the other side of the World Showcase. Whoever is out there watching us is still going to be there. We managed to hide here, but now we have a long way to go."

Hawk was painfully aware they were on the far side of the World Showcase from where they were going next. The decision to leave the motorcycle had seemed smart at the time, but now he wished he had brought it with him. He was also more comfortable with searching without the watching eyes of the person following them, but now they had to run the risk of being seen again. The alternative was to stop looking, and that was something they just couldn't afford to do.

"Where are we going?" Juliette brought him back to the clue.

"The United Kingdom," Hawk told her.

Juliette was an expert on the Walt Disney World Resort. Although Hawk was loaded with details, hidden secrets, and little-known or unknown facts about the world Walt had dreamed up, she was an expert on how the resort was laid out, how operations took place, and how people and cast members moved most efficiently on any given day. The United Kingdom was directly on the opposite side of the World Showcase Lagoon from China. There were no shortcuts, no behind-the-scenes pathways, and no easy way to get there from where they were. Immediately she understood the reason for Hawk's concern.

"There is no way whoever is watching us was able to figure out where we went." Hawk moved to the temple door. "But once we move outside, any protection or privacy we had will be gone."

He cracked the door open and looked through the sliver into the pavilion. Through the small opening, he scanned the landscape and saw nothing. Resigning himself to the reality that they were going to have to go back into the streets, he glanced over his shoulder toward Juliette. "We will move along the edges of whatever we pass, try to stay in the shadows, and not run . . . unless we have to. But no matter what, let's try to keep moving. Okay?"

She placed a hand on his back and shoved him forward. Her answer was unspoken but clear. It was time to start moving.

As they stepped back into the serenity of the China pavilion, the shadows stretched across the pathway, providing the shade of protection for them as they made their way to the edge of the street. Clinging to the edge of the walkway, they slowly moved to their right toward Norway. The lush trees and landscaping provided some visual cover for them, and quickly they moved back into Mexico. The ground was wet, a change from earlier in the evening. That meant the cleaning crews were moving through the World Showcase. They crossed the path to move to the water side of the showcase, silently agreeing to travel along the lagoon wall since there were no more pavilions for them to use as cover. They moved behind the small food stands, the carts, and the shops as they headed into the Showcase Plaza. This was where most guests would make their way from the entrance of Epcot through Future World and then make a decision as to whether to go left or right to make their walk around the world. The two large gift areas here provided Hawk and Juliette places to stay out of sight, but they constantly had to zig and zag, changing directions and trying to find a clear lane to travel as they relentlessly moved forward.

They approached the Canada pavilion in silence. The challenge in all of the areas in the World Showcase was to find a way to highlight the expanse, history, and culture of each country. The approach in Canada was to go coast to coast. Eastern Canada featured brick architecture, while the rough-hewn wooden look was the familiar style of Western Canada.

As soon as they entered the area and moved past the gardens, Hawk saw something moving through the shadows in front of them. Grabbing Juliette by the hand, he pulled her to their right, and they quietly moved down a winding path through the impressive sunken gardens at the base of the re-creation of the Canadian Rocky Mountains. The garden path took them away from the main passageway and carried them off the route where Hawk had seen movement. Now they stopped and crouched behind some massive boulders. Heart pounding, Hawk listened through the darkness and heard distinctive voices.

"Where do you think they went?" came the first voice.

"I don't know. They could be anywhere," the second voice responded.

"And why are we looking for them?"

"Because we were told to look for them." A third voice was added to the mix. This one was female, unlike the other two. "Less talking and more looking would be nice."

Then the voices fell silent. Hawk shifted and caught a glimpse of the outline of one of the people moving past them. He leaned back against the rock and waited until he could no longer hear footsteps or voices. The wait felt like an eternity but in reality was just a few minutes.

"Did you recognize any of those voices?" Juliette whispered to him, her voice was almost inaudible.

"No, and I didn't get a good look at any of them either. I counted three that I heard. There might have been more in the group."

"Are they gone?" Juliette asked, knowing Hawk did not have that answer.

He shrugged. The pathway they were on was a normally isolated path that carried guests to a restaurant and shopping area. You would have to exit using the same path. But now that they were on the other side of the World Showcase, they had some options they didn't have before. Hawk motioned for Juliette to follow him, and once again they moved down the pathway, deeper through the gardens, toward the entrance of the buildings ahead. They could move through the building and step into a backstage area. It only took a few moments, and they had done just that.

Alone in the backstage area, they remained diligent in keeping an eye open for others who might be looking for them. They walked through to an events pavilion, which was opened periodically and used for a variety of functions. Most guests had never been inside of it. It was usually closed off by massive doors and fencing that you could not see through. To the casual observer it looked like an undeveloped future pavilion between Canada and the United Kingdom. The truth was it was a fully functioning, frequently used showcase for private parties. It was also extremely helpful at the moment, because it connected to the pavilions on either side through backstage passageways.

A few moments later, Hawk and Juliette emerged back on the streets of Epcot in the United Kingdom.

Like so many other areas in the resort, a trip through the United Kingdom pavilion was a trip through time. The thatched roof and half-timbered walls of the Tea Caddy captured the 1500s. The Queen's Table encapsulated the 1600s, with gable barge boards and diamond-shaped wood moldings, until one moved into its Queen Anne Room and the 1700s. Lords and Ladies was modeled upon the styles of the 1800s, and once you stepped into the interior of the streets of the pavilion, you were pushed back in time again as you discovered the Toy Soldier, the Crown & Crest, and the Sportsman's Shoppe.

Hawk knew where they were headed. He'd known the moment he read the clue.

"You know where we are going to look, right?" Juliette's hushed voice came over his shoulder.

"Yes," Hawk said as they moved in front of the Crown & Crest shop. Pointing up at the sign, he said, "We're here."

"The Crown & Crest?"

"Look at the stained glass windows to the left. They represent the three flags that make up the Union Jack. England, Scotland, and Wales."

As Juliette looked at the three distinct designs embedded in the glass, Hawk continued to whisper.

"*Honi soit qui mal y pense*—the motto on the England crest." Hawk read the words, having no idea if he had pronounced them correctly—but at least he knew what they meant. "They translate to the same line of the clue—'evil be to him who evil thinks.'"

"What does it mean? Why are we here?"

"Well, I don't know why we are here, but I know what it means. It is the motto of the Order of the Garter. Some think it's the motto of England itself."

"The Order of the what?"

"You heard me." Hawk smiled as he continued to speak quietly. They moved into the doorway as he explained. He decided he didn't want to tell her the story standing out on the sidewalk where they could be easily seen. He felt it was wiser to step back into the shadows as they spoke.

"The countess of Salisbury had an unfortunate and embarrassing moment at an event with King Edward. As she was dancing, the garter she was wearing slipped down her leg and ended up around her ankle. As you might imagine it was quite the scandal, and then as now, tongues started to wag. The unkind laughter that began to bubble about the room came to a halt when King Edward uttered the line, 'Shamed be the person who thinks evil of it,' and as you can imagine things got quiet after that."

"I would imagine," Juliette agreed.

"That line, that incident, became the inspiration for the order and eventually the motto. It really isn't the motto for the country as much as it is a historical reference point for an era of history. However, the Imagineers liked the story, and here it is." Hawk finished his explanation and moved back onto the sidewalk to study the motto. An idea had dimly emerged as they stood in the doorway, and now he was more confident he was thinking correctly. He turned toward the street and pointed at the streetlamp that stood along the roadway. "The motto is evil be to him who evil thinks, and we are looking for something always shining before it. The streetlamp is always shining in front of the motto."

"The rest of the clue is that you will find what you need to illuminate your path," Juliette finished it.

"So what we need next has to be in the streetlamp, right?" Hawk looked back toward her with a satisfied smile. "Like I told you earlier, this is the easiest clue yet."

"Why don't we see what's in the streetlamp?"

He was already on his way. "Okay, let's take a look."

The streetlamp flickered as Hawk climbed the lamppost and began looking for something inside the glass cover protecting the light. He searched for a panel that might be loose, or move, or perhaps slide—and found nothing. He pulled himself upward again and repositioned himself as he tried to remove the top of the lamp fixture. With a twist and a series of turns, the fastener released and he was able to take off the cover. Inside of it, he could see the note neatly folded and tucked up into a tight square. Hawk looked down at Juliette and then softly tossed the cap piece of the light fixture down to her. She reached inside, removed the note, and threw the piece back up to Hawk so he could replace it before climbing down.

Shinnying down the lamppost to the sidewalk, Hawk joined Juliette where she had once again retreated into the alcove of the doorway. Standing there in the dimly lit entrance, they were out of the line of sight of anyone who might be passing by.

"Eventually we are going to get to the end of these clues." She handed him the note so he could open it.

"I would hope so." Hawk unfolded the square of paper carefully. "The Imagineers are thorough. Think about it. If you were to accidently stumble onto one of their clues, you couldn't accidently discover anything you shouldn't. Without the right order and the right sequence, the clues mean nothing."

"We are finding them in the right order and sequence and to us they *still* mean nothing." Juliette shook her head. "They will mean nothing until we find the last one and figure it all out."

"True." Hawk nodded in agreement. "But we are getting close. We have to be."

"I know, I'm sure we are." Juliette sighed. "Read the clue."

The clue followed the same style and pattern as the previous discoveries.

I can sense your sighs.
Where you cross the bridge beyond them
You can voice your complaint.

"You shouldn't have been sighing." Hawk smugly said, enjoying the moment more than he should.

"How did the clue know I would be sighing?" Juliette said defensively.

"Oh, this isn't just any clue giver; it is the third Imagineer."

"I don't care if it's—"

"Or perhaps," Hawk smiled, "the person who created the clues knew we would be getting tired and anxious to finish the search. So they decided to work that into the clue."

"Do you have a clue what the clue means?" Juliette's tone relented to his teasing, but he realized she was getting overly tired. They had been under incredible pressure, and the fatigue was starting to show.

"Not a clue," Hawk answered with no other explanation.

They stood in the doorway silently. Pensively Hawk refolded the clue back into a tight square. He tried to think through what to do next, but fatigue was starting to bury the adrenaline he had been running on all night.

The ringing of the cell phone startled both of them, and Hawk retrieved his phone from his pocket.

"Hey," he said as he slid his finger across the screen and placed it to his ear.

Hawk listened intently and then tipped his head back as if looking toward heaven, then let it flop forward, letting his mop of hair fall across his face. Still listening, he pinched his eyebrows together as he prepared to end the call.

"Thanks. Don't give up." Hawk ended the call without saying good-bye.

Juliette blinked and waited for him to say something to her about the call. Curiosity finally got the best of her and she said, "Bad news?"

"Not good news, that's for sure." Hawk shook his head.

"Care to let me in on it? Is there something I need to know?"

"No, nothing you need to know. It's better if you don't know." Hawk smiled, trying to reassure her. "Yet."

"Okay." Juliette grabbed him by the arm. "Whatever you are doing, I don't have a good feeling about it."

"Then it's a good thing you don't live your life based on feelings," Hawk retorted.

Juliette grimaced. He knew she had heard him say that numerous times as a preacher, as a teacher, and as a leader. Sometimes they laughed about how he was not a big "feelings" kind of guy, but right now it was not humorous at all.

"I will tell you when you need to know. I promise." Hawk motioned for her to follow him.

They moved back into the streets, where the sun was starting to kiss the darkness away. They had a new clue but no place to go with it.

"Let's give Shep a call." Hawk aimlessly walked to his right, carrying him out of the United Kingdom. "Maybe he can give us some help or direction."

Juliette placed the call.

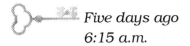 *Five days ago*
6:15 a.m.

CAST MEMBERS WERE BEGINNING to move about, making all of the preopening checklists needed each day at Epcot disappear as they readied the World Showcase for guests to arrive. Hours away from opening, the working crew was still sparse, yet the privacy found in the wee hours of the morning as Juliette and Hawk had moved through the pavilions was now lost. Together they moved into Italy. Much of the area was based upon the city of Venice. The pavilion itself was created to be a replica of Saint Mark's Square. Guests who were accomplished world travelers recognized that the Disney version was backward—a mirror image of the real thing. According to legend, the square was backward because the blueprints Disney designers used were taken from a photograph that was transposed as it was developed. There was a more reasoned response given when designers were pressed, but at the end of the day, Hawk had always believed this was one of those rare times when the company's attention to detail hadn't been thorough enough. To him, it served as a cautionary reminder that no matter how good you think you are or really are, you are not always going to be right.

From Shep Albert's command center had run multiple Internet searches in an attempt to help them unravel the clue. The Italy pavilion was the best answer they could come up with, so Hawk and Juliette arrived to search as a new day dawned in the Walt Disney World Resort.

The pink palace that served as the major structure in the pavilion was a replica of the Doge's Palace. Shep had filled them in on the details of the original in Venice. Although beautiful, the history of the place revealed a darker side. Deep within the walls of the real Doge's Palace was a prison and torture chamber where enemies were sent to be incarcerated.

They cleared the corner of the building where an alley opened up on the left. The early morning sun cast long shadows that made it look gloomy.

Hawk motioned to Juliette, and they headed across the alley to the staircase on the right-hand side. Moving briskly to the top, they found themselves at the point they were to begin their search.

They now stood on a bridge. According to history, the Bridge of Sighs was a passage all convicts would have crossed on their way into the palace prison. The prisoners had little hope for survival as they made their way into the depths of the castle. The name came from the sounds of hopelessness from all who crossed it. The Disney designers had recreated their own version of the historic bridge. The sad history was not often shared, but the beautiful detail again made the Disney experience better than other places could offer.

Juliette and Hawk stood on the bridge as Hawk repeated the clue.

"I can sense your sighs," Hawk gripped the handhold tighter. "This is the Bridge of Sighs. So the clue says you can cross the bridge beyond them."

"Actually," Juliette said, "the clue says that where you can cross the bridge beyond them, you can voice your complaint. I take it to mean the bridge is not the end of the line but merely a landmark."

"You're right. Shep may have been on to something by getting us here, but . . ." Hawk trailed off.

Juliette watched as he pointed back down to the end of the alley where they had entered. Something was affixed to the wall.

"That is kind of creepy looking," she said.

She was right. What Hawk had seen was a face, carved into concrete and mounted to the wall. It was not a great work of art, nor did it look like it was intended to be. With an open mouth, exaggerated eyes and features, it had a frightening look.

"I remember hearing about this now."

"The face?"

"Yes, the face." Hawk stayed put on the stairwell. He was amazed at how much a bit of perspective helped at times. The elevated view, the help Shep had given them to get them unstuck in their search, and now he was remembering some details he had heard long ago. "The face with the wide-open mouth fits the description of our clue."

"It will? You mean you can voice your complaint there?" Juliette followed him as he finally moved across the alley.

"Exactly. The face with the open mouth is not just a decorative element the Imagineers added to the alley. Faces like this in old historic Italy were like mail slots. People in each town were encouraged to slip notes in the mouth reporting the mistakes, transgressions, and mischief of their neighbors."

"So they would report on each other by sticking notes in the mouth of the face?"

"They were voicing complaints and disagreements. Just like the clue said we could do. You can voice your complaint."

Juliette smiled at hearing the words of the clue, and her hope began to rise at this new discovery.

"I also remember that if there was a complaint filed and it was to be taken seriously, it had to be signed to be valid. If not, it was ignored or discarded."

They reached the face on the wall, and as they got closer, they saw a white piece of paper, tightly folded and wedged inside the mouth. In some ways it appeared the gray concrete face was mocking them with a stuck-out tongue. Undeterred, Hawk grabbed the paper, freed it, and then pulled it back for Juliette to see.

A group of cast members passed through the pavilion and noticed Hawk and Juliette. Excited and surprised to see the pair of Disney executives, they walked over to greet them and say good morning. After a few moments of conversation the team members moved on into their day with an unexpected encounter to talk about.

"It's going to start getting busy in the World Showcase before too long," Juliette reminded Hawk as they moved back down the alley and ascended the stairs to the bridge again. After they got there, way off the traffic pattern for cast members beginning their workday, they unfolded the clue.

Once again, the same typewritten note greeted them—with one exception.

This time it was signed.

Go fishing and catch the lock keeper
Ain't it grand!
Press

The first two lines of the clue were typewritten as the others had been. The indentation on the paper had been created by the key strikes of an old manual typewriter. But the final line was a signature. Scrawled in legible black ink, the oversized capital *P* served as a canopy for the remaining letters, which had been created with a flourish. It was an autograph, and it set this clue apart from all of the others.

"Why is this one signed?" Juliette wondered aloud.

"Because it's personal." Hawk thought. "And because it fits the rules."

"Say that again."

"The rules in Italy for putting notes or complaints in the mouth. To be taken seriously, the note has to be signed. If it is not signed it is not valid. The person who put this clue here—Press—wanted us to know it was from him. And he also knew we would know and understand the rules. He kept them with this particular clue." Hawk smiled at the detail but wished the clue had more content.

Silence filled the air on the Bridge of Sighs as he thought about the clue. His first impression was that it was different from the other clues. Perhaps this was the last one, and it wouldn't lead to another clue but instead to what they were looking for.

"The line reads 'catch the lock keeper' . . . so there is someone out there with a lock you have to open. Maybe with the kingdom key?"

"That might be it." Hawk rubbed his chin. "But that is an interesting phrase. A lock keeper . . . the keeper of a lock. Is there some deeper meaning in the phrase?"

The cell phone in his pocket alerted him to an incoming call. Breaking his line of thinking for a moment, he did not recognize the number as he answered it. Juliette studied his face as he flinched at what he was being told. His eyes searched for hers, and he told her in a glance that what he was hearing was not good news.

"I understand. Yes, thank you. I am on my way." He ended the call.

"What?" She waited for him to tell her what was happening.

"It's Farren." Hawk swallowed hard. "His vitals are dropping. The nurse said he is continuing to fade, and we might want to come and . . ."

"Say good-bye?"

"Yes," Hawk resolutely said as he turned to descend the stairs and exit the bridge. "We left the Harley in the next pavilion over. We can leave from there."

Juliette followed him down the stairs, through the alley, and back into the World Showcase. The traffic of cast members had picked up considerably. On a normal day, Future World and the front portion of the Epcot theme park would open earlier than the World Showcase. Although the attractions in the showcase did not open until later, people could move about, and as a result everything had to be ready when they opened the gates. The park was not open yet but it would be soon.

The Germany pavilion was next to Italy, and Hawk quickly retrieved the bike from where he had hidden it out of sight hours before. He kicked it to life, and Juliette climbed on behind him. With a turn of the wrist, he accelerated around the World Showcase Lagoon, down the main entrance of the showcase into Future World. He increased their speed as they rode beneath the shadow of Spaceship Earth. As they did, Hawk remembered his encounter with Reginald Cambridge on the top of the massive globed attraction years before.

He had to stop Cambridge again. For good this time.

Hawk aimed the bike straight out the main entrance to Epcot. A very surprised security team recognized him and threw open the gate for him to ride through. Nodding his thanks, Hawk asked the motorcycle for more power as he increased his speed through the parking lot and toward Interstate 4. On any ordinary day, he would have tried to avoid the morning rush hour into downtown Orlando, but today, like many of his days, was not destined to be ordinary. Juliette held on tightly as he swerved into the morning traffic.

He was racing against time, and time was something he could not control. He needed more of it, and he could not afford to waste a minute now.

CHAPTER 18

Five days ago
4 p.m.

HOSPITALS OPERATE IN THEIR OWN unique time zones. At least, that's how it seems to those who have ever spent any time inside of one. It isn't that things are not done with a sense of urgency or in a timely manner; it's just that hospitals are their own encapsulated world, where decisions and situations unfold on a time schedule all their own. Once you step inside a hospital, the things going on in the world outside can easily become lost in the intense focus and nature of what is taking place on the inside. That is how the afternoon had disappeared for Grayson Hawkes.

Juliette and Hawk had arrived at the hospital early in the morning and were immediately ushered into the Intensive Care Unit where Farren Rales lay comatose. His vital signs had dipped deathly low, and Hawk noticed that the conversations happening around him were being spoken in the hushed tones of gravely concerned caretakers. They did not foresee a scenario where his condition would change.

The doctors allowed Hawk to spend an extensive amount of time at Farren's bedside and then eventually asked him to leave the room so they could continue their work. Now seated inside a waiting room, he sat across from Juliette and her husband, Tim. There were armed security guards at the entrance of the waiting room along with officers from the Orlando Police Department. The waiting area was private, and they had been there for a long time. Shep had joined them a few hours ago, and they anxiously awaited some word from the medical staff.

Dr. Briggs Kuhn breezed past the security at the entrance and came inside, taking a seat across from Hawk, Tim, Juliette, and Shep. The four gathered around and formed a huddle close to the doctor as he gave them an update.

To all of their surprise, the doctor smiled. "Well, I have better news now than we had earlier. Farren has stabilized some. As much as he can with the toxin he is battling." He nodded toward Hawk. "Whatever you did or said to him seemed to really help. You were the medicine he needed to slow down the rapid decline that prompted our call to you."

"I'm just glad he's stabilized." Hawk felt a wave of relief wash over him.

"That being said, Farren is still extremely sick, and we still have nothing to neutralize the poison. Being stable for now is good, but it's only slowing the inevitable if we don't come up with some solution for the torpid cyantoxoid. We are working on it, but if we introduce an experimental antidote that is wrong, it can accelerate the speed at which the toxin works. We're working with extremely sensitive substances here."

"Thanks for all you are doing, Doctor." Juliette bowed her head and closed her eyes as she said it.

"We will keep working. But like I said, he is stable for now. Thanks for coming down so quickly earlier. There were a few minutes when it didn't appear we were going to keep him with us today. And again, Dr. Hawkes, thank you for whatever you did in there."

Kuhn got up and shook hands with each of them. He turned and exited the room just as quickly as he had entered. The group fell into silence for a few moments. Each person quietly offered his or her own silent prayers of thanks for the news they had just been given. It was Tim who broke the silence.

"So what is it that you did in there with Farren?" He smiled at his friend. "It sounds like it must have been miraculous. Dr. Kuhn said you were the medicine he needed. Give it up; what did you do?"

Hawk shrugged. "Nothing, really."

"Not only are you the Chief Creative Architect of the Walt Disney Company, you preach, you solve mysteries, and now you are a doctor or medical professional?"

"Well, I needed something to occupy my free time." Hawk laughed along with the rest of the friends.

"Serious, boss . . . what did you do?" Shep repeated the question.

"Really, I didn't do anything." Hawk paused and thought back over the hours he had spent with Farren. "I did what all of you did. I told Farren that I loved him and was praying for him. I'm sure I told him that I needed him and to hang in there."

"Okay," Juliette said. "We did all of that, that's true. But what did you do or say that all of a sudden caused him to rally and stabilize? I think that's what the good doctor was talking about."

"The only other thing I did was tell him—" Hawk hesitated. It wasn't that he didn't trust his friends; he was just worried and wanted to protect them as always. "I told him I wasn't going to let him die just yet. So he needed to stay strong and let me work my plan."

"And your plan is to get the antidote from Reginald Cambridge?" Juliette uttered the name, knowing they all knew what had been going on.

"I don't think you can trust Cambridge." Tim offered his opinion even though he had not been asked. "I know you want to think the best and believe that he'll really give it to you if you cooperate with him, but the truth is he's a hardhearted hater, and a liar on top of that. And he hates you and all of us because of you."

"I know." Hawk nodded in agreement.

"So you just told Farren you had a plan, even though it's not a good one?" Shep asked.

"No, I told him to let me work *my* plan, because I am working on a plan."

"You have a different plan?" Juliette had been with Hawk for hours, and he had not mentioned anything.

"Yes," Hawk smiled weakly. "I have a different plan. It may not be a good plan, and it may not work. But I am working another plan." He turned his head and looked suspiciously around the empty room. It wasn't necessary, but he wanted to be careful. "Because you are right; we can't trust Reginald, and I *don't* trust him."

"What is your plan?" Juliette seized the silence to ask.

"I'm not going to tell you." Hawk knew she wouldn't like that answer. "It is safer for all of us if I don't tell you . . . yet. But if it starts to come together, I will, I promise."

"And when you told Farren that, he started to stabilize," Tim said. "Because he trusts you, and you gave him something to hold on to."

"There was something else."

Hawk read surprise on their faces. They all leaned in even closer. Their chairs were so close and they were gathered so tightly their knees almost touched.

Hawk whispered. "I told Farren to hold on because I knew the third Imagineer. I mentioned his name. I told him I was going to find Press. When I said that, it was right then that his heart started to beat stronger and then . . . well, he seemed to stabilize or start stabilizing."

"You gave him hope." Juliette smiled at her boss.

"Yes, I gave him hope. Sometimes a little hope can go a long way. Hope, not hurts, can shape our future. I believe that. I wanted to give him a little more future." Hawk looked at his friends. "Maybe it will give him a little more time. For now, it's all I can give him."

Juliette leaned back and closed her eyes, weariness showing in every line of her face. They were tired. Not only did hospitals seem to operate outside of normal time, they also seemed to be able to drain the energy and endurance from those who waited in them. All of them had been up all night, and now the reserves they were running on were depleted. Shep closed his eyes and actually drifted off to sleep for a moment as the group once again fell silent.

"You need to go home and get some rest," Juliette said to Hawk. "We all do. It has been a long few days, and they are going to get even longer."

"How can we help?" Tim reached over and put his arm around Hawk's shoulder.

"Take Juliette home." Hawk gestured toward her. "Keep her out of my hair for a while."

"Hey," she objected.

They all laughed. Hawk continued to answer the question. "Seriously, go home and get some rest. Make sure the kids are safe, and let's tackle this again after we've all had a chance to rest a few hours."

"About the kids . . ." Tim said. "We've been talking, and we're going to take the kids up to the panhandle to visit Juliette's sister for a few days. Keep them safe and not so easy to find."

"So that means I will be out of pocket for tomorrow," Juliette added. "Will you be okay while I'm gone? Can you stay out of trouble? If not, Tim can run them up there."

"No, no . . . you take them and spend some time together." Hawk raised his eyebrows. "I will just sit around and watch people walk up and down Main Street, U.S.A. while you're gone."

Juliette scoffed. "Liar. You don't have time to people-watch. We will hustle so we can get back fast. You have another clue to work on and a mystery to solve, right?"

"Right." Hawk raised his hand. "And before you say it, I will be careful, I promise." .

"Again, you're lying," Juliette fired back. "That is why we can't leave you alone."

Hawk burst into laughter as he stood. "Tim, take her home. She's so tired she's delirious." He hugged Juliette and Tim.

"Seriously Hawk, be careful. Don't do anything dumb," Juliette whispered in his ear as they embraced.

"You know me, I'm the model of careful," he reassured her.

"What do you want me to do, boss?" Shep said.

"The same as the rest of us. Get some sleep."

Hawk waited until they were all moving toward the exit doors. He noticed that the security team at the door was shadowing them at a very respectful distance, providing them an escort. He was glad for his friends' sake.

Emerging into the warmth of the afternoon, a blast of heat hit them as they stepped out of the air-conditioned buffer into the sun. Hawk grabbed Shep by the elbow and turned to face him.

"Start helping me figure out what the lock keeper is and what it has to do with fishing and something grand," Hawk said. "Call me later."

"Will do," Shep confirmed as he left.

Hawk stood on the sidewalk in front of the hospital. He had parked the motorcycle in a reserved space very close to the door. The police officers had waived him in when he arrived and escorted him and Juliette through the facility with fast efficiency. He glanced back over his shoulder to see three security officers watching him. He waved, and they did the same. Another officer was stationed near his bike. He nodded toward him as he made his way to the Harley. Although he was weary, his senses were on high alert.

The engine sputtered once, then roared to life and the Sportster began the trek back to the Magic Kingdom—the kingdom that once again, Hawk was battling to save.

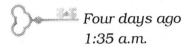 *Four days ago*
1:35 a.m.

HAWK HAD LUMBERED up the metal steps to his Fire Station apartment on Main Street, U.S.A. and collapsed in a heap on his couch. Telling himself he would only take a short nap, he closed his eyes and now, a blink later, discovered that shadows had ushered in the midnight darkness throughout his apartment. The only light glistening through the window was the sparkling glimmer of shine from the Magic Kingdom's Town Square.

Hawk stretched his body to allow the muscles to recover from his fatigued sleep. Slowly he sat up and rubbed his eyes as thoughts began to organize. Once they were aligned, he was pulled back to the present and got to his feet. He made his way to the compact kitchen and rummaged through the wooden cabinet for a coffee mug.

The rich aroma of coffee brewing soon filled the room, and Hawk leaned on the counter as he waited for the java to finish. He glanced along the countertop and pushed aside the banged-up wooden block that held three old kitchen knives, revealing the ceramic container that held the sugar behind it. Loading up a spoonful of sugar, he dumped it into the bottom of the cup. A second container held the powdered creamer, and with the same spoon he scooped a powdery heaping of flavor into the mug, which now was waiting for the coffee to finish.

Once the last few drops made it through the percolator, he poured a generous cupful and took a hot sip. He savored it. The warmth of the liquid moved through his chest, and the caffeine seemed to jolt his brain back into puzzle-solving mode.

Go fishing and catch the lock keeper. Ain't it grand—Press. Now awake, he refocused on the Mickey Mouse clock mounted to the wall. It read one forty-five. If there was a clue to be found, it was easier for him to navigate the resort at night. But he still wasn't sure where to go next. His instincts told him to head back to Epcot. That seemed to be the place Imagineer Press had chosen to create his trail of clues. Hawk sensed he was getting closer to finding what he was looking for. Or at least he hoped so.

Grabbing his cell phone, he noticed he had missed some text messages. He read the first and smiled. It was the beginning of what he hoped was good news. He scrolled to the next message, which was from Shep, sent about an hour ago. *Call me when you're awake,* it said. The third message was from Juliette. It read simply, *Whatever you are about to do or are thinking about doing, BE CAREFUL.*

He smiled and pressed the speed dial to connect with Shep.

"Hey Hawk." Shep's voice was alert for the early hour.

"Hi, did you get some sleep?"

"Not much. Been working on the clue."

"And?"

"Well, I don't have it figured out. But I have been thinking." Shep ended the line with a lift in his voice, inviting Hawk to delve into his train of thought with him.

"Okay, so what have you been thinking about?"

"I have been thinking most of the night about the word *lock.*" Shep exhaled. "To me it is the key to the clue."

"I get it. Lock and key." Hawk shook his head although Shep could not see him.

"Oh, I didn't even think about that. I'm funny."

"Yes, you are funny. Now what about the word *lock?*" Hawk sat down at his table and took another sip of coffee.

"There are a lot of things you can lock. The possibilities are endless. You can lock a door, lock a window, lock a garage, lock a safe, lock a computer, lock a bicycle, lock a diary . . . as I said, the possibilities are endless if you think about things you can lock."

"I guess so. And you think that is important because... "

"Because of the word the clue used with it. Lock *keeper.*" Shep quit talking for a moment to let Hawk think about what he'd just said. "If we were just looking for a lock, it would be about impossible. But we're not. According to the clue you are not just looking for another lock that you need to open; we are looking for a person. Someone with the responsibility of being a lock keeper, just like you're a key keeper in a sense. You with me?" Shep waited.

"Yes, I'm with you."

"Well," Shep asked, "do you know what a lock keeper is?"

Hawk shook his head, caught himself, and said, "No, I guess I don't. Someone . . . with a lock."

"A lock keeper traditionally is someone who is responsible for watching, working, and guarding a lock on a river or a canal. That is what a lock keeper is." Shep spoke with a hint of triumph.

Hawk sat up straighter. He had not even considered that the lock keeper mentioned in the clue might refer to a person's job or role instead of merely being someone who held a lock that he must open.

"Do you know what a lock keeper does?" Shep asked.

"Sure," Hawk was quick to answer. "Don't I?"

"Probably, but let me make sure." Shep wasn't being condescending; he was simply going to share more information. "A lock keeper operates and sometimes maintains the lock mechanisms that allow boats to pass from one level to another on canals and rivers. This job is mostly common to the network of rivers and canals in England, Scotland, and Wales. A lock keeper has to make sure the lock chambers and lifesaving equipment are in full working order. Their top priority is the safety of anglers, walkers, and boaters who might be in the area. Lock keepers also have to monitor the water levels and try to control them using sluice mechanisms and weirs. They rescue boaters and other visitors in trouble on the water. Basically, they are in control of everything in their little pocket of the world. Their world is their lock, and they are responsible for it. They are lock keepers."

"I guess I didn't really know all of that." Hawk admitted.

"So what do you think?"

"You said something earlier about where a lock keeper works. Say it again."

"You mean what they do on the lock?"

"No, no, no . . . where they work. Where do you find lock keepers at?" Hawk was now thinking, and he got up and began to move to the couch to put on his shoes.

"Along the waterways of England, Scotland, and Wales," Shep said.

"In other words, the United Kingdom," Hawk stated confidently.

"Yes, the United Kingdom." Shep added, "So what we are looking for is in the United Kingdom pavilion at Epcot?"

"It makes sense. Most of the clues Imagineer Press gave me have been in Epcot, so it stands to reason that it would be there. I just have to see if there is a lock keeper in the United Kingdom pavilion."

"Is there?"

"I don't know," Hawk admitted. "But I will say this series of clues has stretched me beyond some of the hidden details I have been familiar with. There has to be something there. I'll find it. I spent all of last night in Epcot; I might as well start there again tonight." Hawk headed for his front door. "Shep, you've done good work here. Keep your phone close; I will call you."

"Do you want me to come with you?"

"No." Hawk was not sure if he sensed disappointment through the phone or not. "You can be more help to me if you stay connected with information as I need it. You good with that?"

"Whatever you need, boss."

"Thanks." Hawk ended the call and bounded down the steps. Still on the stairs, he paused and looked across the street. On each corner he saw a security guard watching him. He had insisted they not stand post at the steps to his apartment. It hadn't worked well in the past, and Hawk was on a quest—he needed some degree of freedom to move about. He waved at the guards, and they acknowledged him. One spoke into his radio, and Grayson knew he was sending out word that he was on the move. Indeed, he was.

Hawk's shoes clanked against the metal landings and he turned left to exit into Town Square through a cast member door. As always, the resort seemed empty at night, although it was anything but. Guests had retreated to their hotels, and now a massive cast was prepping the guest areas for the next day. It was an endless cycle of activity that most would never see.

Climbing aboard his motorcycle, Hawk heard a noise behind him just before he started the bike. Jerking his head back in the direction of the sound, he saw someone stepping out of the shadows. In one fluid motion he was back off the bike and turned to confront whoever was coming his way.

"Whoa, sorry," a familiar voice said. "Didn't mean to startle you."

Al Gann stepped into the light where Hawk could see him. Hawk smiled at the sight of his friend and waited for him to approach.

"You did surprise me." Hawk exhaled loudly. "Don't sneak up on me like that."

"Like I said, sorry. Where are you off to?"

"Epcot," Hawk told him without hesitation. Al was his friend, and Hawk knew he made Al's job and life very difficult. He did not intend to do so, ever, but it seemed to be the nature of how he was forced to operate.

"Another mystery to solve?" Al didn't wait for Hawk to answer. Hawk sensed he already knew the answer. "Is there anything I need to know, officially or unofficially?"

"Not yet," Hawk told him. "I'll tell you when I have something definite. Any luck finding Cambridge?"

"No." Al looked down to the ground. He raised his head and met Hawk's gaze. "But we will. He is not going to get away with this, and this time . . ."

"You'll get him." Hawk reached out and patted his friend on the shoulder.

"Let me go with you to Epcot," Al said. "It's easier to keep an eye on you if I can stay with you."

"It's better if I go alone." Hawk knew he was getting close to finding something, but he had no idea what. That was why he had insisted Tim take Juliette home, why he had told Shep not to come, and why he was now telling Al the same thing. He didn't know what surprise he might be getting ready to walk into. For the sake of their safety and of his own responsibility to guard Walt Disney's secrets, he couldn't allow anyone else to be with him when he made the final discovery. "I'm not trying to make it difficult for you. I just need to do this alone."

"All right, but I have to keep you safe. So I have to make sure . . ."

"Al." Hawk stopped him midsentence. "By any chance were you in Epcot last night?" It had suddenly dawned on Hawk that Al might be watching him from a distance, trying to keep him safe. He could also have a team of people who had been tasked with that assignment. If it had been *Al* who followed him around last night he would have a thing or two to say about it, but he would be relieved too.

"No, why? Did something happen in Epcot last night?" Al leaned forward, concern masking his face.

Hawk's hopes fell. "Everything is fine. Just asking. I didn't know if you had been tagging along with me from a distance or not. Just curious." There was an awkward silence. Hawk had asked the question without being prepared to explain himself if the answer was no.

"You sure everything is fine?" Al looked skeptical. "Maybe I should go with you if you are concerned about someone following you."

"No, just wondering out loud." Hawk smiled. "I need to get moving."

"You know I'm getting ready to make a call to heighten the security at Epcot right now since you are headed there, right?"

"I expect nothing less." Hawk threw his leg across the seat of the motorcycle and kicked it to life. "Thanks, Al." Maneuvering the bike away from his friend, he began to make his way out of the Magic Kingdom backstage area toward Epcot.

CHAPTER 20

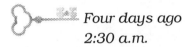 *Four days ago*
2:30 a.m.

LESS THAN AN HOUR LATER, Hawk was once again in the darkened streets of the World Showcase, standing in the United Kingdom pavilion. He didn't know what he was looking for, but he was searching, taking in everything. As he wandered the streets of England he found himself searching out every detail he could think of, noticing some he had never seen before, and trying hard to unravel the mystery of the lock keeper—mostly without success.

Striding through Britannia Square, he noticed the design of the buildings. The butterfly garden was what most people noticed in this area; what they missed was that the facades were actually created from set drawings from the original Mary Poppins film, which Walt Disney himself had supervised. Perhaps there was something in them because of their connection to Walt. He paused and looked and then realized he wasn't thinking clearly.

If a lock keeper had the responsibility of managing traffic and areas along a waterway, then there needed to be water. The only building in the United Kingdom pavilion along the water was the Rose & Crown, the traditional British pub, nestled along the edge of the World Showcase lagoon. The pub was a combination of four different styles from different areas and eras of the United Kingdom. The typical street pub that would have been familiar in Victorian England featured brick along with wood paneling, decorated with etched glass that gave it a touch of elegance. The Dickensian pub, which was modeled after the Cheshire Cheese pub in London, displayed a brick-walled flagstone terrace along with a slate roof and an Elizabethan wood design. The country pub was more of a typical suburban establishment, with stone elements creating the traditional look most associated with pubs. But the area Hawk was most interested in was the waterfront or river pub. This area had a village inn look to it, with a clay roof and a stone terrace surrounded by an iron fence.

Standing next to a red telephone booth, he observed the pub area carefully from across the walkway and scanned for anyone in the vicinity. If Al had alerted security, they were doing a great job of staying out of sight. When Hawk entered the park, he was greeted not only by security but by members of the sheriff's department. They had told him to be safe and that they would be close, but he hadn't seen a sign of them since he entered.

Adjacent to the Rose & Crown Pub was the Yorkshire County Fish Shop, a walk-up service counter for guests to get something to eat with an English flair. These two establishments together formed the area of the United Kingdom along the waterfront. Hawk took a step to cross over to the Rose & Crown and then stopped. Pausing, he stepped back to his corner of the telephone booth and once again looked to the buildings.

There was something here he had never noticed before: a building between the two eating establishments that connected them together. It was not really noticeable, and it looked like a typical cast member area . . . or was it? Its styling was that of a traditional English home. He now moved across the street at a fast pace. There was a white picket fence along the front. He opened the gate and turned the handle for the front door of the home. It did not open. Not surprised, he removed the kingdom key and tried to unlock the door. It didn't fit. He couldn't get in.

Stepping back, Hawk went back outside the gate to the other side of the fence. Maybe he could find another door. Looking up at the building, he realized he might have been right with his first thought. It might be nothing more than a cast member area. He had passed these buildings for years and had never noticed this one until tonight—perhaps that was the design and how it was supposed to be. He decided to head back to the entrance to the pub and then once again stopped.

No, details mattered in the world of Imagineering. He was looking for something hidden in the United Kingdom, along this very waterfront. Perhaps it was here somewhere.

He moved along the front of the Fish Shop, staying purposely close to the building, and when he came to the edge of it he decided to walk down behind the little house. As he did he realized that in all his years of visiting Epcot he had never walked down this path before, not once. He followed the gently sloping path toward the water and then noticed something else he had never seen before. There was a stone wall running along the edge of the waterway, creating a river or lock within the World Showcase Lagoon. He'd noticed the river before as he ate along the water's edge at the Rose & Crown Pub, but he had never really paid attention to it. Now on the backside of the buildings, he turned to look back at them.

The little house in the middle, made of red brick and surrounded by a picket fence, had a gate and walkway that rose slightly uphill to a wooden door, decorated with thick glass panels allowing light and visibility for anyone who might be at the door. Next to the door, to the left, there was a white sign.

Hawk quickly entered the gate and went up the walk to where he could get a good look at the sign. It read: *Grand Union Canal—Thomas Dudley, Lockkeeper.*

Hawk laughed out loud. He reached out and turned the doorknob. It was locked, as the door on the other side of the building had been. Undaunted, he tried the kingdom key, and once again, surprisingly this time, it did not work.

Hawk furrowed his brow and took a step back from the door, contemplating what to do next. He was looking for the lockkeeper. This *had* to be the place. He glanced down at his watch. The hands of the Mickey Mouse watch face told him it was now getting close to four o'clock in the morning. He had to get inside this door and find out what was on the other side. But how? He had a thought that he almost jettisoned as quickly as it came—but with a pause, he realized that with all the things that had happened to him and all the things he had experienced, he must never take the simple and obvious for granted.

He decided to knock.

With his knuckles, he gently rapped against the wood next to one of the window panes. Nothing happened. He understood that it was the early hours of the morning; the likelihood of someone being inside was miniscule at best. He rapped again with a knock, knock, knock, a little more forcefully. Again, nothing happened.

He shook his head. He was just thinking that he was going to have to devise another plan when startlingly, a light came on from the other side of the door.

A soft glow was visible through the curtained windows. Hawk felt his heartbeat quicken as he heard the distinctive click of a lock being opened. A shadow moved past the door, shrouded behind the sheer curtains decoratively hung up to block any visibility. There was someone inside, and they were opening the door. He held his breath as the heavy wooden door swung open.

CHAPTER 21

Four days ago
4:00 a.m.

"GOOD MORNING, DR. HAWKES." The rich, mature voice spoke with an alertness that belied the early hour of the morning. "I've been expecting you. Please come in."

The elderly gentleman stepped back from the doorway, and Hawk peered inside to a cozy room. A large area rug stretched across a hardwood floor, underlying plush chairs and a couch. A fireplace with a small fire blazing invited him to move across the threshold. He did and heard the man close the door behind him.

"You've been expecting me?" Hawk repeated.

"Why, of course." The man stood with a relaxed posture and a smile highlighting the lines of his face. His rangy frame and thinning hair revealed an aging man, but his rugged complexion and tanned, thick arms indicated he was strong and had worked throughout his lifetime.

Hawk had seen this man before. He quickly tried to connect the voice, the face, and the smile in the data processing bank in his brain. He was certain he had seen this man before and had spoken with him . . . somewhere, someplace, at some other time.

"You recognize me, but you don't know why." The man seemed to sense exactly what Hawk was thinking.

"Yes," Hawk said slowly. "But I haven't connected the dots yet."

The man laughed. It was a pleasant laugh that Hawk immediately enjoyed. He gestured toward an overstuffed chair with a quilt thrown across its massive arm. Hawk took a seat. The seat was comfy and inviting, offering instant relief to his tired body. The man sat down facing him on the couch and said nothing. The silence was broken only by the ticking of the oval clock, a Mickey Mouse clock, hanging over the fireplace.

"Well?" the man said after a minute. "Have you figured me out yet?"

"No." Hawk shook his head. Was it exhaustion or something else making it so hard to find anything beyond the familiarity of this man's face? "Are you Press? Are you an Imagineer?"

"That's not it." The man laughed. His laughter was so genuine that Hawk smiled at the sound of it. "I am not an Imagineer, and I am not Press. Let me help you. I am not an Imagineer, but I know some engineers. That is where you know me from."

Great, Hawk thought to himself. *This guy talks in puzzles and riddles.* Like he hadn't had enough of those over the past few days. But one thing Hawk did like was a challenge, and he believed he had found an important clue in this search for answers. This man was that clue. Still, Hawk was coming up with nothing that connected him to where he knew this man from.

"I don't blame you for not remembering." The man cleared his throat. "It was a long time ago, and a lot has happened since then."

Hawk leaned forward in his seat, which wasn't easy because of the oversized design of the chair. "I'm sorry, I just can't seem to place you."

"I first met you a little over six years ago. You were standing in the train station on Main Street, U.S.A. and trying to get into the ticket booth of the station. I walked up on you as you were trying to turn the handle on the door. You had a stuffed Mickey Mouse you had been holding up to your ear. You were listening to some message from it, and I asked you if I could help you."

As the man spoke, Hawk's thoughts flew back across the calendar to a moment before he was the Chief Creative Architect of the Disney Company. The stuffed Mickey Mouse had been an amped-up, one-of-a-kind version of a Disney souvenir called Pal Mickey. Farren Rales had designed it for him, and it had become an interactive tour guide that delivered messages to keep Hawk moving forward in claiming the role he had been selected for. At one point in that journey, he had found a clue hidden in the ticket booth at the train station. This man, he suddenly remembered, had scared him because he'd thought he was going to chastise him or call security. But even in that first strange moment, he had been kind, and his enthusiasm had impressed Hawk.

"You were the conductor in the train station that day." Hawk grinned at finally mining the answer from his memory.

"Yes," the man said with gusto. "That was me. I told you—"

"You told me," Hawk picked up, "that the railroad station would have been a favorite for Walt Disney if he had ever seen the park completed. Trains were a favorite pastime of Walt's."

"Exactly. That is what I told you." The man sat back and settled deeper into the cushions of the couch, grinning.

"But that was not the only time I'd seen you." With the early-morning fog of his memories clearing away, Hawk was now reliving the moments from years ago that had launched him on this dreamlike journey into the world of Disney. "You had been watching me. I think the first time I saw you was in Caribbean Plaza in the Magic Kingdom."

"Yes." The man nodded approvingly. "You were with Kiran Roberts, a very poor choice of company, by the way."

"I know." Flashes of betrayal, pain, and hurt danced through Hawk's memories. He pushed back the storm clouds, not wanting to let hurtful thoughts hide the light of recognition he was now unpacking. "And then you also showed up at Tony's Restaurant in Town Square."

"That was quite a standoff. You, Kiran, a man who held her at knife-point, and—"

"Sandy, Jim Masters, and Reginald Cambridge." Hawk remembered it all too well. It was the moment when he'd realized the people surrounding him were not always what they appeared to be. In the years that followed, the pain and the price of understanding had been very costly. Sandy was a cast member whom Hawk had misread completely. Hawk's first impression of Sandy had been that he was arrogant and brash. He had decided the young man was a nuisance only to discover later that he was committed to making sure Walt's plan for the future would be successful. He had regretted misreading him. Jim Masters had turned out to be a villain, an ally of Reginald's. Kiran herself had turned out to be an enemy.

But this man, who now sat across from Hawk in a hidden corner of Epcot, had proven to be a friend of Walt's. Like Sandy, he seemed to be committed to making sure Walt's plan happened as the Disney brothers had intended.

"A lot happens over the years, doesn't it?" the old conductor asked gently. "Yet in some ways time also stands still. I believe, if I remember correctly, the first thing I ever said to you was 'Can I help you?'" The man smiled brightly. "That is the same question I am going to ask you now—can I help you?"

Hawk pulled the folded piece of paper out of his pocket. *Go fishing and catch the Lock Keeper. Ain't it Grand! Press.*

He handed it to the conductor, who read it and reread it.

Cocking his head, he asked. "Would you mind telling me where you found this?"

"In the Italian pavilion, near the Bridge of Sighs," Hawk said.

"In the face of the wall." The man reared his head back and laughed. "That's why it's signed. Brilliant, brilliant, brilliant. What an amazing detail!"

Hawk waited for the man to finish laughing and watched as he shook his head in appreciation for the note and clue that had led Hawk to his door.

"May I ask, who exactly are you?" Hawk said once the man had refocused on him. He was disappointed not to have found Press after all, but clearly, meeting this man was no accident.

"You already know. My name is on the door."

"Thomas Dudley?"

"That's me. Thomas Dudley, lockkeeper of the Grand Union Canal. Or at least the Epcot version of the canal. That is the reference to 'Ain't it Grand?' in your clue. The real Grand Union Canal spans 137 miles from Birmingham to London with 166 locks. Our version is much shorter, with no real locks except this imagined one."

"And this is your home?"

"Yes, this is it," Thomas Dudley replied. "Welcome. I'm glad you finally arrived."

"You said you've been expecting me."

"Yes," the man said with a twinkle in his eye. "I have been expecting you since October 1, 1982."

"What?" Hawk sat up straighter. He knew the date as the opening day of Epcot. He didn't really understand what Thomas meant beyond that.

"Let me explain. When Epcot opened, this became my home. I arrived from California with a team that worked on opening Walt's dream, and I was chosen by a very dear and trusted friend of Walt's to move in right here. I was told to wait and there would come a day when someone would knock on my door, and I would know who it was and why they were here. Until then, I was to work here, live here, and do my best to preserve and protect the legacy of Walt and Roy Disney."

"So you've been living here since 1982?"

"Yep. I was starting to think you would never get here." The man laughed again. "In the meantime I have worked as a conductor, a riverboat captain, a skipper on the Jungle Cruise, and other places in the resort. I also have managed for the last six years to keep a watch out for you and some of the things you have been doing. I knew you were the chosen one, the one chosen by Walt, and of course his team of kingdom warriors, to preserve his secrets and legacy. So one day I knew it would be time and you would knock."

"So you know Press the Imagineer?" Hawk had more questions than he could organize, and he wanted answers to them all.

"Yes, although I have never heard him called that before." The man nodded. "It's accurate."

"Can you take me to where he is?" Hawk opened his eyes wide.

"No, I have never known how to find him."

Hawk let those words sink in. Although confusing, he plowed forward. "And you knew Walt Disney?"

"No, I never knew Walt. I knew Roy. When Roy passed away it was one of the saddest times in my life. I cried for days and thought there would come a day when someone would have to fight to preserve the world they worked so hard to create. I didn't know how it would play out. The beauty and genius of their plan was that everyone had a role, and we only had to know our part. Like an elaborate mosaic. Each little piece makes the entire picture. You don't know how you fit into the big picture exactly, but you do your part, find your place, and trust that when it's all done, the finished product will be a work of art. Kind of like life, isn't it, Hawk?"

"Yes, it is." Hawk fell silent. He realized that Thomas Dudley probably didn't have the answers for all of his questions. He was just another piece of the plan Disney had designed.

Thomas leaned forward on the couch. "Hawk, you are living out a story. A story designed by a master storyteller. A story so amazing that he created it, designed it, and after he put all of the pieces in place, let the story play out. Walt Disney put all this together, never knowing how it was going to work—he just had to put the right pieces in place so the story could be told. What happens next really depends on you. Because, well . . . to state the obvious, you are the main character of the story."

Thomas's voice softened. "I would imagine that the adventure to get to this moment hasn't been easy. I know it hasn't. I have been watching it play out from a distance. But let me tell you something that should encourage you. Although it hasn't been easy, each day, each month, each year you have gotten better at fulfilling your role. It might not be easy, but you make it look like it is. I'm proud of you."

Thomas Dudley stood to his feet and reached out to pat Hawk on the shoulder. "Good job," he said. Giving Hawk's shoulder a squeeze, he turned and walked into another room.

"How about some breakfast?" Dudley said over his shoulder.

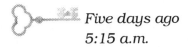 *Five days ago*
5:15 a.m.

HAWK FOLLOWED THOMAS into the kitchen and was handed a hot mug of coffee. Thomas motioned for him to have a seat on one of the two wooden chairs slid under a scarred brown wooden table. The chair scraped across the checkerboard tiled floor as Hawk seated himself facing the stove, where Thomas Dudley had gone to work fixing breakfast.

Scrambling eggs with a whisk, Thomas was a flurry of activity. He moved from the cabinet to the refrigerator and then back to the range with a grace and fluidity that reminded Hawk of the conductor of an orchestra instead of the conductor of a train. By the time Hawk had drained the last drop out of his coffee cup, a plate of scrambled eggs, sausage patties, grits, and toast was slid across the table in front of him. With a refill of his mug, both men were diving into the fluffy eggs with a fork and enjoying the meal thoroughly. They hadn't really spoken since they left the living room. The early morning dawn was beginning to sparkle against the frosted glass of the kitchen window. Hawk assumed the kitchen faced the main walkway of the World Showcase, with the frosted glass in place to keep the illusion intact for the guests and preserve a level of privacy for Thomas.

"Mmm . . . that was good." Thomas complimented his own culinary skills with a pat of his stomach. "Hope you enjoyed it."

"I did. I was hungry, and breakfast is my favorite meal. I can eat it anytime of day," Hawk said through the wisp of steam coming up from his coffee mug as he took a sip.

"I know. I know a lot about you." Thomas took a drink from his own mug before setting it down with a clank. "Now, let me give you what you came for."

"That would be great, because to be honest, I'm not sure what I'm here to get," Hawk admitted.

"You are here for the next piece of the mosaic we were talking about earlier, Hawk." Thomas cleared his throat. "Each piece fits together into a masterpiece, a true-life adventure that Walt Disney created for you to make sure that his world, his dreams, his vision, and the future of our planet were protected."

"The future of our planet?" Hawk stopped mid-sip.

"Yes, the future of our planet." Thomas smiled. "You have already figured out that Walt Disney was perhaps the most influential man of his generation. One of the most influential men in all of human history, actually."

Hawk agreed. "It's staggering, the people Walt knew. He was connected to world leaders, scientists, inventors, entertainers. The vast knowledge he was always accumulating was unprecedented."

"You know Walt's history very well," Thomas complimented him. "So I am going to give you a story. That is what you have come here for, and that is what I have been tasked to give you."

"A story?"

"Yes, a story. If you can learn the lessons of the story and figure out what to do with them, then another piece of the mosaic falls into place," Thomas said. "But understand something, Hawk, and this is very important. I don't know how the story fits into anything else. I just know what I am supposed to tell you and help you with. That is my part, my role, my task, my piece of the puzzle. I am an expert in this one thing, and this is all I can do for you. So make sure before you leave here that *you* understand it. Once we are done, my part of this adventure is over. Understand?"

"Sure, as much as I can," Hawk responded.

He took in a deep, cleansing breath. The possibility that he might get another piece of information that would allow him to make sense of all that had happened over the past few years made him cautiously optimistic. He didn't fully understand how it could impact the future of the planet, but he believed if it was something Walt Disney had discovered, then it had to be exciting, if he could protect it. At least he was getting closer to knowing what *it* finally was.

"Good." Thomas reached over and patted his hand before taking another swig from his coffee cup. He kept his eyes focused on Hawk above the mug and then replaced it on the table as he prepared to tell his story.

"You are here in the United Kingdom pavilion because of a connection Walt Disney had to Winston Churchill," he began. "It started with this."

Thomas turned in his chair and looked up toward the top of the fridge. Hawk followed his gaze and saw a row of cookbooks lined up between two square metal bookends. He watched as Thomas got up and stood inspecting the row of books. Thomas reached up and carefully selected the one he was looking for. Dragging it off the shelf, he blew the dust off the edges and returned to the table. He placed it softly on the tabletop in front of Hawk.

Hawk reached out and pulled it closer. He read the title out loud: "*Victory through Air Power* by Alexander de Seversky. That was the title of a film Walt made during World War II, right?"

"Yes, indeed it was." Thomas was pleased. "You do know your Disney history. You have been such a great choice. I am so happy to be able to help you with this."

Hawk still didn't understand the significance of the book. "So this is a book based on the movie?" Hawk asked.

"No, the movie was based on the book." Thomas feigned disappointment. "Perhaps you don't know everything about Disney after all."

"I didn't know there was a lockkeeper's home in Epcot, much less that someone had been living here since 1982." Hawk tapped the book with his fingers. "What I don't know would fill volumes of books."

"Walt read this book. He was always reading something. He had so many interests, and if a book hit his sweet spot, he would tear into the subject and read everything he could on it. This was one of those books that caught his interest."

"I've heard about Walt during the war years, but why this book?" Hawk asked.

"Walt got a telephone call the morning of the attack on Pearl Harbor that jolted him from sleep. It was a security guard at his studio. The guard told Walt that the military had just forced their way onto the studio grounds and that he needed to get there right away. As you can imagine, Walt was anxious to find out why the United States Military had invaded Walt Disney Studios."

"I would guess so!"

"Disney Studios was very near the Lockheed plant, which was going to need protection. Lockheed was one of our nation's major military defense contractors. It turned out the studio was the ideal place for the military to set up shop. We were at war, and for the duration of the war, the studio was the home base for the military. Walt didn't like it, because it meant that in many ways the studio was going to have to shut down, but at the same time, the crisis was real, Walt knew it, and he wanted to do what he could to help. It was a tough time. You do things when an enemy strikes that you don't necessarily want to do but you have to do, because it is the right thing, the best thing, the only thing to do."

Thomas looked down toward the table as he said this.

"I understand," Hawk said. Thoughts of Farren, of Kate, of his other friends invaded his mind. He knew what it meant to be under attack. He understood what it meant to protect the people and the places that you love and value. Many times in his life he had found himself at a crossroads of faith, needing to decide what to do next—especially the last few years. In some ways Walt Disney was responsible for this. But this was a part of Walt's history he was not as familiar with.

"Walt had a way of convincing people to do what he wanted, and he was able to convince the military that he would be a better helper for them if, instead of shutting down the studio for them to use, he could produce some training films and do promotional and propaganda pieces for the war effort." Thomas shrugged. "So they let Walt keep the studio operating. As a result, he could still do animation work for himself, while at the same time he did a lot of work for the military."

Thomas leaned back further in his chair. "Walt Disney loved America. He was a patriot in so many ways. He agreed to produce the films and create insignia for the military at cost or less in some cases. He created everything from designs on up. He allowed his characters to be a part of the badges, and the signs became an important symbol of the war effort. Disney went to war."

"If I remember correctly, this was an era when there was not a lot of income for the studio. The war years were tough for everyone."

"That's right." Thomas nodded. "There was no money coming in. It was a matter of survival, and Walt very quickly managed to figure out that World War II was not really a war against the Germans so much as it was a war against Nazis and their anti-individual and anti-freedom political system. So Walt was very eager to call out the enemy by name and make sure the German people knew that he was clear on the radical, extreme ideology of the Nazis and that they were the real enemy—that it was Nazi beliefs we were really at war against. Not everyone completely understood that. Sometimes in war, clarity and understanding the enemy is not always easy."

"And there are always voices eager to tell you what to think when you are not so sure," Hawk stated.

"In a vacuum, there is always someone who will speak into the silence and fill it with noise," Thomas said carefully. "That was Disney Studios during the war years. So Walt read this book, *Victory through Air Power,* and was convinced by the time he closed the last page that the ideas in the book were the keys to winning the war."

"Really?" Hawk flipped open the book with a new respect.

"Really." Thomas tapped the table. "Walt immediately contacted Seversky to see if he would let Walt produce a film based on the book and if he would appear in the film. He agreed, and Walt decided to pay for the film out of his own pocket. Fifteen months after the release of the book, on July 17, 1943, the film, which Walt had rushed through production as fast as any film he had ever worked on, was shown for the first time."

"You said this connected Walt Disney to Winston Churchill."

"Yes," Thomas folded his hands together on top of the book. "I will get to that in a moment. Remember, Hawk, you need to know the story."

Hawk nodded. He wasn't exactly sure what Thomas meant by that, but he wanted to make sure he didn't miss anything. He exhaled, forcing himself to slow down and wait for the tale to be unpacked.

"Among other things, *Victory through Air Power* promoted two main ideas. One was the need for the United States of America to create an air force as an entirely separate and unique branch of the military. Although we take it for granted now, there was no distinct branch of the service that focused on aviation power as a resource for defense and in this case, war. The second main idea of the film was that the United States should create long-range bombers, aircraft that would fly deeper into enemy airspace and destroy targets that would make it difficult if not impossible for the enemy to conduct warfare. This would also radically change the way the army and navy were used and deployed. It was in some ways revolutionary; a film by Walt Disney was laying out a major shift in how the United States should defend itself and structure its military."

Hawk tilted his head. "This is a chapter of Walt history I was completely unfamiliar with. True?"

"All of it." Thomas nodded. "Most don't know this part of Walt's story, because it has nothing to do with entertainment, cartoons, or theme parks. The public didn't exactly know how to deal with it either. After all, it was a

Disney film that was not like anything Disney had ever done before. Walt had produced it for the express purpose of convincing America to use new technology, develop new ideas, and implement new strategies to win the war. He was sharing what he believed was a vision of how to do things right, do things better, and ultimately win the war and defeat the Nazis." Thomas again paused. "During this era, this was the last full-length animated film Walt produced. Everything else he produced was short training films, informational films, and motivational media."

Hawk shook his head. He pushed back from the table a bit and rubbed his eyes, thinking about what he had just heard. Walt Disney was one of the most influential men who had ever lived, but somehow, Hawk had never realized he had *this* kind of influence.

"So as a result, the United States started the air force and developed long-range bombers . . . all because of the inspiration of an animated film?"

"Yes," Thomas sighed. "That is a simplified summary, to be sure, but in a nutshell the film was the inspiration for winning the war. Walt figured out how to tell the story that he saw as he read *Victory through Air Power* in a way people could understand it, embrace it, and internalize it. It changed their lives and thinking, it changed everything . . . it changed the world as we know it."

"That's huge."

"That's the power of a story told by a great storyteller—in this case, Walt Disney." Thomas motioned for Hawk to lean in closer. "But there is more. In the film Walt included some things that didn't even exist at the time. The technology was there in theory, but it hadn't yet been developed."

"Like what?" Hawk leaned forward.

"One example is a bomb that could be released from one of these new long-range bombers that could bust through concrete. During World War II this became a weapon that was not only developed but used very successfully. It was called and is still referred to as the Disney Bomb."

"What?"

Thomas gave a wry smile. "Seriously. Walt inspired the creation of a new weapon and gave enough details of how it could be used to influence others to do it. Again, the power of a story in the hands of a great storyteller."

"And so . . ."

"Walt finished the film and knew he had created the future. Although the public didn't know how to react to the film, the government saw how

important it was. He sent a copy of the film to the Q
August of 1943. The conference included the govern
States, Canada, and Great Britain. Their focus was on
dismantle members of the Axis powers. The range o
ing. Invasions, contingency plans, and even agreemen
weapons and the assurance that they would never be us
were all a part of this gathering. It was a significant moment of history.

"Prime Minister Churchill was attending along with President Roosevelt. The conference, at that time, was focused on the Allied invasion of
France, but Churchill decided to watch the film. After he did, he told President Roosevelt that he needed see it as well. It had impressed Churchill,
and he believed it held the key to the future. So the president watched the
film and agreed with the ideas Walt had captured from Seversky's strategy.
He fast-tracked the development of long-range bombers and the development of the concrete-busting bombs, and then he set in motion what
would be the creation of a new branch of the military, the United States
Air Force."

Hawk gave a low whistle as Thomas said the last line. "Wow. That was
some animated film."

"Most people have never seen the film," Thomas said. "But *Victory
through Air Power* is not only a part of the rich history of cinema and the
life of Walt Disney, but it holds a crucial spot in the history of the American
military. And *that* is why you are here, Hawk."

"Because of the film?"

"Yes, because of the film and the influence it had."

Hawk rubbed his chin. Sleep was still pushing at the edges of his mind,
but his body was newly adrenalized now as he tried to make sense of Thomas's words. "So Walt makes a film that inspires world leaders so much that
they change the way they fight the enemy and they win World War II." He
paused, still trying to connect the dots back to himself but failing. "He revo-
lutionizes the way we structure our military and suggests new weaponry
that was not only developed but used."

"A form of it is still used today, and the branch of the military he suggested still exists. The influence continues on." Thomas continued. "Walt
realized, maybe for the first time or maybe just in a new way, how powerful
the way you told a story really was. This was not *Snow White and the Seven
Dwarfs*, although that was a powerful story that could influence people."

Hawk smiled. "Yes, of course it was. Walt discovered that *Snow White* could give people comfort, inspiration, and even hope." Hawk flashed back to a late-night meeting he'd once had with Farren Rales, years ago inside a cottage that was created after the owners watched the film. A family had found a way to cope with grief and loss in that situation. It had been a sobering moment. It had been there, in that cottage, that Rales had given him the kingdom key.

Thomas was still speaking. "This was a battle against an enemy that was playing for keeps, an enemy that wanted world domination, that stood in opposition to American values and freedom and everything Walt believed in. He found he could fight back through the incredible power of communicating through a story, and he realized that if you did that well, you could unleash and explain to people big ideas and concepts in ways they could understand and internalize."

"The story could change the world," Hawk said.

"Yes." Thomas picked up the book from the table and returned it to the top of the fridge.

"So what do I do with the story?" Hawk asked, as the man returned to the table.

Thomas stared at him thoughtfully before answering. "I don't know." He shrugged. "Like I told you before, my job is just to tell you the story. I am a lockkeeper, and I have just given you a lock. *You* are the keeper of a key that has to unlock it."

Hawk furrowed his brow. "So I have to unlock the meaning of the story?"

"Yes, in essence." Thomas smiled. "I don't know what you do next, Hawk, but somehow I have to think you do. You are a preacher with strength, as I have listened to you in the past."

"You have heard me preach?"

"Yes, many times." Thomas waved off any further discussion about that with a twitch of his hand. "The strength of your teaching is that you always take what you are communicating and help people make application in real time, real life, in the real moment of right now. That is what you have to do."

Hawk spoke as he thought, the wheels turning in his mind, pushing away the last vestiges of exhaustion. "I have to take your story and add it to all I have found on this journey, and then I have to unlock the meaning of it."

"Exactly." With an "Oh, one more thing," Thomas once again got up from the table and retrieved the book. "I almost forgot."

Hawk watched as Thomas removed a folded piece of paper from the book. He carefully held it in his hand, then closed the book and returned it to the shelf. Taking the few steps back to the table, he handed it to Hawk. As Hawk closed his fingers on the edge of the paper, Thomas didn't release his grip on it quite yet.

"This will help you keep moving," he said. Then he released it.

Hawk stood up and placed the paper in his pocket. Their meeting was over. Hawk extended his hand. Thomas gripped it and shook it strongly.

"You can do this, Hawk."

"Thanks. I just wish I knew exactly what I was doing."

Thomas smiled. "You will, I believe . . . you will."

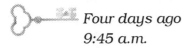 *Four days ago*
9:45 a.m.

HAWK OPENED THE DOOR of his apartment as his phone started to ring. Glancing at the screen, he saw the incoming call was from Al Gann. Touching a finger to the screen and sliding it across, he answered as he moved into his kitchen and opened the refrigerator door. He extracted a carton of orange juice and prepared to take a slug when Al stopped him mid-drink.

"I think you need to come over to Epcot," the head of security said. There was a tenseness to his voice.

"I was just at Epcot. I just got home," Hawk responded, knowing there was more coming.

"I really think you need to get over here. Now, right now."

"Where is here?" Hawk returned the carton to the fridge without ever taking a drink. "Where are you at?"

"I'm in the World Showcase, the Germany pavilion. I will send someone to bring you over."

"Not necessary." Hawk was already moving to the door. "I can get there quicker if I leave now."

"No, let me send someone over to get—"

Hawk ended the call as he bounded down the steps. The Magic Kingdom was brimming with people. As soon as he stepped into the Town Square, tourists recognized him. Several people waved cameras. He nodded and smiled as he tried to move quickly through the crowds toward the main gate of the Magic Kingdom.

Breaking into a jog, he ran through the exit as a couple of cast members greeted him, and he turned to his right and increased his speed as he ran up the ramp to get on board the monorail that had just pulled into the station. Cast members at the top of the ramp let him pass, and he made his way down the length of the monorail to the cab. He hesitated as he saw the open door. He realized in a blast of memories that he had not been in the front car of a monorail since he was there with Kate on the day she was killed.

Shoving back the flood of emotion that threatened to swallow him, he stuck his head in the door of the car and told the driver to sound the notification to "please stand clear of the doors." Taking a seat on the bench that allowed riders to look out through the observation window, he knew he would be alone up here. As a result of a fatal accident years before, no guest was allowed to ride with the driver in the front compartment. He could immediately grab another express monorail to Epcot from the Transportation and Ticket Center. Considering the size of the crowds in the park he was guessing, this was actually the fastest way to get where he wanted to be.

The doors clicked shut, and the monorail began to snake its way along the massive concrete beam around the Seven Seas Lagoon toward the Ticket and Transportation Center. It had not been that long since he had been in the very pavilion he was heading toward now. All was as it should have been. What might be different now? What was there that he had to see instead of just being told about it over the phone? Why was it so important he had to see it for himself? Lost in wondering, he realized that the driver, a young cast member, was speaking to him.

Shaking his head to refocus on what was being said, he heard the driver say, "I was so sorry to hear about your fiancé and the tragic way she . . ."

Hawk nodded and held his hand up with another shake of his head. He was not going to have this particular conversation right now. Instead he chose another one.

"When we get there, let me get out before you open the doors on the rest of the monorail, please. That will allow me to get to the Epcot express line before the guests get off of this one."

"Sure, so you're headed to Epcot?" The driver said.

"Yes, and I need to get there quickly, so if you can just help me avoid the crowd."

"Say no more. Consider it done." The young man slid the control lever forward, and Hawk felt the monorail increase in speed. He knew there was a regulator on all of the monorails and that they could only go so fast, but he appreciated the effort to get him there faster nonetheless. Hawk knew how to override the protocol, but with guests on board, he decided not to use that information now. "According to the radio, the monorail to Epcot is at the station."

"Tell them to hold it until we get there." Hawk turned to see how close they were.

As he looked, the monorail moved out of the Contemporary Resort, the morning sun causing his transport to glow as it moved toward the Ticket and Transportation Center. Gliding along the highway in the sky, they passed by breathtaking views of the Magic Kingdom across the water. The Epcot express, a monorail with a black stripe, was already in the station waiting on him to climb aboard. Guests were packed inside as Hawk's monorail arrived. As soon as the door was open, he was out and sprinting across the loading platform to make the connection.

As the monorail left the station, Hawk glanced out the window at some of the lushest green areas of natural woodlands many guests would ever see. The view was another reminder of just how rich and vast the Walt Disney World Resort really was. He was always amazed at the stark contrast between the preserved and undeveloped forests and the colorfully themed parks and hotels. He whispered a prayer of thanks for the monorail system. A train mounted in the air and powered by electric engines, the monorail was capable of reaching speeds greater than seventy miles per hour, but it was restricted for safety reasons to forty-five miles per hour. On an average day it would transport over 150,000 guests to and from the parks.

Anxious, Hawk again considered taking the regulator off right now and letting the train in the sky fly, but he knew he was still making very good time and would be at Epcot within minutes. Once there, he would exit at the station and run back into the World Showcase. It was a long, healthy run, but he was confident he could get there quickly.

The Epcot track passed into the park and looped through the Future World portion of Epcot, coming to a stop above the main entrance. Once the monorail arrived, Hawk stuck with his plan and ran. He weaved through the crowds, trying to predict the ebb and flow of the people as they moved. At times he cut across the stream of guests and at other times found that staying in the river of people was quicker.

He slowed his pace as he ran past the outdoor model railroad and approached the Germany pavilion. Security had closed it off, and a mass of guests stood behind barricades, watching whatever was happening beyond them.

Hawk's arrival brought a flurry of activity as security teams moved to create a path for him into the area. As he glanced at the crowd, he could see a number of cell phones recording his arrival and capturing the unexpected activity in the Germany pavilion. Al Gann broke away from a group of people he was speaking with when he saw Hawk approaching. He met him near the entrance of the pavilion.

"What took you so long?" Al said softly so none of the onlookers could eavesdrop.

"Seriously?" Hawk took in what was happening around him. "We have a resort full of people. There is no easy way to get anywhere fast."

"I thought you needed to see this." Al motioned for Hawk to follow him.

Hawk's eyes were like sponges soaking in his surroundings, looking for something that was out of place or not right. He saw nothing unusual. Distracted as he searched, he bumped into Al, who had stopped in front of him unexpectedly. Al glanced at him over his shoulder as Hawk moved up next to him.

"A guest brought it to our attention this morning." Al pointed upward.

Hawk followed his gesture and looked up at the statue of St. George slaying a dragon. At first glance, he saw nothing out of the ordinary. Al took him by the arm and pulled him closer to the statue so he could look up at it from a better angle.

He saw it. He drew his head back quickly and gasped in surprise.

The statue of St. George is a dramatic creation. George is seated upon a horse that is rearing up. The saint is using a spear and has shoved it into the dragon curled up below him and the horse. Caught up in the heat of the battle, the statue captured the tension of the moment . . . but now it looked very different from the sight Hawk had seen the day before. Across the chest of St. George's armor was a spray-painted swastika. An equilateral cross of four black lines that abruptly turned into ninety-degree angles, it was the well-known, much-hated symbol of Hitler's Third Reich.

The Nazis.

As a historic symbol, the swastika was forever linked to one of the most evil rulers ever to have lived and a tragic reminder of the slaughter of so many at the hands of the Nazi Party. Hawk blinked in disbelief that it had been placed here, in the World Showcase, in the Germany pavilion, inside of Epcot—here, in this place that was intended to bring the nations together in peace and mutual understanding.

"Thought you would want to see it," Al spoke again.

"How did someone do this?"

"Well, it wasn't easy. It took time, and they had to have a ladder or lift to get up there. They couldn't have been real discreet, one would assume." Al placed his hands on his hips as he looked up at it.

Hawk glanced over his shoulder and realized that guests could see what they were looking at. Once again in the world of instant communication, he was sickened to realize that the pictures they were taking would be posted instantly to social media sites and seen all over the globe.

"Let's cover it up. We'll clean it up as soon as we close," Hawk said to one of the security team standing close to him. "If we need to, let's put up a solid retaining wall for security purposes and leave the pavilion shut down today."

A manager for the pavilion made his way to where Hawk was standing at the base of the statue. Hawk called out to him as he approached. "Close it down and send your cast members home for the day. Check to see if we can cross-utilize them in other areas, and if not, pay them for the day so they don't lose their hours." Hawk moved through the Disney security team that had been assembling since the discovery. "Send a team into the guests who have been watching this. Get a sense of what they have seen, what they might know, and what they are thinking. We regret that some vandal has temporarily robbed them of the full experience we want them to have in the World Showcase. Contact your leads if there is someone who is especially upset and demanding some additional assistance."

Hawk sighed as the team dispersed. There were always a few guests who, in the midst of an inconvenience, would try to take advantage of the situation. As a leader, he strived to be proactive instead of reactive. He would do his best to get in front of whatever the fallout from this moment might be.

Juliette would be proud, he thought.

Hawk paused as the Disney team moved to take care of the necessary business. Again he turned to survey the hateful sign scrawled across the chest of the statue. He covered his mouth with his palm as he surveyed it. Someone had gone to great effort to place the vile graffiti there.

Once again, Al had moved over to stand alongside him and joined him in gazing up at the detestable work of the vandals.

"Some sort of prank?" Al asked.

Hawk continued to stare with a serious gaze. "Painting a swastika in Germany seems a little more deliberate than just a prank. And it took a great deal of planning to place it up there." Hawk jabbed his finger toward St. George for emphasis. "Or—"

Thomas Dudley.

The conversation only hours before came crashing back.

"Al, I need you to follow me." Hawk turned abruptly and began moving out of the pavilion.

Caught off-guard, Al raced to catch up with Hawk. He was already at the edge of the barricades and moving around them.

"Where are we going?" Al asked as he fell in stride with Hawk.

Hawk was not running, but his pace was uncomfortably brisk, like a child who had been told not to run. He didn't want to draw more attention to himself, but they didn't have time to lose.

"We are going to see a lockkeeper," Hawk said as he glanced at Al's puzzled expression.

The two of them began their journey around the World Showcase toward the United Kingdom pavilion.

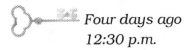 *Four days ago*
12:30 p.m.

AS THEY STEPPED UP TO THE DOORWAY of the modest stone building with its clay-tile roof behind the British pub, Hawk felt his heart beating faster with dread. He beat his fist against the door much harder than he had intended. Some curious onlookers had recognized him and decided to follow at a respectful distance, and he didn't want to alert them that something was wrong.

There was no answer, so Hawk pounded on the door again.

"Why are we here, Hawk?" Al said.

"This is the home of Thomas Dudley." Hawk pointed to the sign he had seen earlier.

"I can see that." Al cleared his throat. "But why are we at the home of Thomas Dudley?"

"Because this is where I was earlier. He told me he's been living here since the day Epcot opened. And he told me something else, something important."

"Living inside of here?" Al took a small step back and surveyed the exterior of the building once again. "This is a restaurant."

"It is on either side, but this is a residence." Hawk tried to look through the glass inside, but he couldn't see anything.

Al's voice intruded. "I guess my next question would be, why is there someone living here?"

Hawk turned to face Al. He spoke in a measured tone, making sure no one could hear what he was about to say. "Because he knew one day I would be coming by, and he had something to tell me."

Al's face registered a blend of confusion and disbelief. The disbelief dissipated quickly. Al had seen and heard enough by now to realize that most people's impossible scenarios had become commonplace for his friend.

"Okay." Al crossed his arms and waited for more to be unpacked.

"A few hours ago, Thomas Dudley told me a story about Walt Disney and how he chose to face the threat of the Nazi Party years ago. Now you're showing me their symbol scrawled across a statue in the Germany pavilion. That can't be a coincidence, can it?"

Al shook his head as Hawk began to search for a way inside. The door was locked, the windows provided no access, and the doors couldn't be opened by the kingdom key. Stepping back from the door, he considered his possibilities. The need for caution was outweighed by his concern.

"Kick it open, please," Hawk said to Al.

"What?"

"You know, kick it open, break in . . ."

"This is not a television show. We don't run around kicking doors in." Al furrowed his brow.

"We need to get in to make sure Thomas is all right."

"You can't just break in."

"I'm not breaking in. I am in charge of the company, so I have the authority to go in . . . don't I?"

"I guess, but—"

"So let's quit the talking and start breaking."

Al stepped back. Tilting his head to the side, he pointed toward the glass panel on the door. Hawk followed his train of thought instantly. The glass panel was located next to the handle of the door; it would be simple to bust out the glass, reach inside, and open the door.

Nodding, Hawk took another step back. Al took a miniature tactical baton off his belt. With a sharp turn of his wrist, the friction mechanism released, and the baton extended as he struck the glass with it. A crack formed across the pane. Al followed it with another short punch with the end of the baton, and the glass shattered and then broke away.

Using the rod to clear away the clinging shards of glass, Al reached inside and released the lock. As he grabbed the handle to open the door, he struck the baton on the door frame, and it retracted to its original size.

Allowing the door to swing open, Hawk stepped into the doorway of the darkened room. He felt Al's hand on his shoulder holding him back. Turning, Hawk moved out of the way as his friend stepped past him, flashlight illuminating the area in front of them. Hawk followed him inside and reached over, flipping on the light switch. The darkness disappeared, revealing a room that, although it contained furniture, looked as if it was no longer occupied.

"Thomas?" Hawk called out.

The house that just a few hours ago had been so warm and inviting was deserted. The comforter across the chair was gone. There were no books, no coat hanging on the door, no pictures on the walls. The fireplace was empty, cleaned out, with no remains of burned logs or cooled embers. The faint smell of a fire remained, but there was no other trace to say that a fire had been blazing just hours before. Hawk felt Al watching him, waiting for some further explanation as to what they were doing and what had happened here. Hawk moved into the kitchen and opened the refrigerator. The light came on, revealing emptiness. Closing the door, he saw the books that had been positioned on top were gone.

There was no sign of anyone having been here.

Hawk stepped back into the living room and explored the space, looking for something, anything that was a sign of life. There was nothing. From all observable signs, no one had been here in a long time.

"Do you want to go over with me what we are doing here?" Al scratched his head.

"Al, I'm telling you, I was here last night, and Thomas Dudley lived here."

"The Thomas Dudley whose name is on the sign outside the door?"

"Yes," Hawk stated.

Al didn't look convinced. "Isn't that just some name the Imagineers threw out as a detail to theme the area?"

"Sure, it would be, but in this case, Thomas Dudley was here, and he was here because he knew I was coming by one day."

"So he has just been here waiting for you?"

"Yes." Hawk shrugged. "He's been here since Epcot opened. He's worked a number of places in the resort, but his real purpose was to give me whatever I need to accomplish whatever I'm supposed to accomplish. He's part of the plan."

"Hawk . . ." Al sighed before continuing. "We have been down this road before. We have been through a lot, so I believe you. Believe me, I believe you. But what is this about? What are you into? What are you after now?"

"Al, if I knew, I would tell you. Just like every other time. I'm having to figure it out."

"Figure it out," Al repeated. "You always figure it out. But this time, the stakes seem to be higher, don't you think? Explosives in the theme parks put every guest at risk. Another attack on you and Farren, Reginald Cambridge has escaped. We never even found Kiran or her mother. Maybe they're back too." Al held up his hands. "This time I think the game may be getting away from us. We don't know what enemy we are trying to find, what the end game is this time, and how you will be able to do whatever it is you are trying to do."

"So what do you think we should do about that?" Hawk stepped back to the doorway. Meeting Thomas Dudley had given Hawk a sense of closing in on some answers. The unexpected turn of events had surprised him but not panicked him. He didn't feel fear; he felt he was getting close to what he needed, and he had a sense of rising confidence that he would solve this soon.

"Look outside, Hawk." Al motioned to the open door behind him. Outside, light sparkled on the water, and the voices of people talking and laughing in the pub drifted in. "Epcot is loaded with people, Animal Kingdom is packed, the Studios are full, and the Magic Kingdom is the same way. The resorts are full, Disney Springs is busy. These people are your guests, and now they are all targets! You have some nut out there playing a game with you, after some old secret, something they think Walt Disney has chosen you to find, and you are letting them string you along so they can take whatever it is you find when you find it."

Al waited and then added, "Did I sum it up correctly?"

"That is a summary." Hawk's voice was strained. "I may not agree with how you did it, but I understand what you are saying." He closed his eyes and tried to roll the tension from his shoulders before turning his focus back to Al.

"Hawk, there is no other way to see it." The words rushed out as his frustration rose.

"Then what else do you want me to do?"

"I think you should close Walt Disney World down. Keep people safe, let me keep you safe, and let us find and stop whoever is doing this."

Silence dropped like a sudden Florida rainstorm. The room felt hot and humid as the words hung thick in the air. Seconds ticked into a minute before Hawk spoke again.

"Let me make sure I understand what you just said." Hawk breathed in and exhaled before continuing. "You want me to shut down the Walt Disney

World Resort and send thousands and thousands of guests home from the vacations that some have been waiting a lifetime to take?"

Al set his jaw. "Don't send them home, just close the parks."

"And where will the guests go? They came for the parks and all the other things surrounding them. There aren't enough places to shop, there aren't enough pools for them to swim in, and they didn't just come to eat. They came for the whole entire experience, and the experience is anchored in our theme parks."

"What if a guest gets hurt or worse?" Al asked.

"Do you not think I worry about that all the time? Every single time this Disney mystery has surfaced I have stressed over that, lost sleep, because I know as well as you do how it puts all of us and all of our guests at risk. That's why I've done what I've done, to solve it, to protect what Walt has hidden, and to preserve it . . . while keeping people safe."

Hawk narrowed his eyes. He understood what Al was saying, but after all they had been through, he found himself shoving back his frustration that his friend couldn't understand what he was trying to do. "Al, it doesn't matter what we do, the bad guys, the villains keep coming back. We can't keep them in jail; we can't seem to find them. They keep slipping away, or when we think we have one, another one shows up. We have to take the fight to them and end this thing, once and for all."

"At what cost?" Al said with no emotion.

"Whatever it takes." Hawk leaned back against the door frame. "Because if we don't, what we will lose will be more than we can imagine or bear."

"What does that mean?" Al now took a step toward Hawk.

Hawk closed his eyes. He knew the things he had discovered were far more important than just entertainment or the dreams of a theme park. Each day he understood the importance of Walt's secrets a little bit better, at a deeper level than before. For now, he had to figure this out. He had to find whatever had been hidden for him to protect. It was the only way to preserve and help everyone else.

"You know I can't tell you what it means. I'm sorry about that. You know I can't."

"No, I *don't* know that you can't. I know you won't." Al took another step toward him. Hawk could hear the strain of frustration in his voice. "And I can't keep you safe."

Hawk opened his eyes again. They stood facing each other. Al was upset and angry. Hawk understood. The task Al Gann tackled each day was way beyond daunting. He was helping to keep an entire world safe—Walt Disney World really is a world unto itself.

Hawk straightened up in the doorway and smiled apologetically. "I'm sorry, Al." Hawk was sincere in his words. He spoke slowly, softly, and with conviction. "I have continually put you in an impossible position. I understand that. You have always gone to the wall for me, above and beyond what I could ever expect."

Hawk shook his head. "I promise you, if I ever think this has gotten away from me, I will be the first to shut the entire operation down. That is my call, not yours, and I don't expect you to understand it. In your position, I would not agree with me. But you are correct, you can't keep me safe. So quit trying. Pull back your team; tell them to quit trailing me and following me around. Do me a favor and trust me enough to see if you can find out what happened to Thomas Dudley. He is a real person, and he really was right here just a few hours ago. And while you are at it, figure out who is responsible for painting a swastika on that statue."

"We will start looking for Dudley, but leaving you unprotected is not an option."

Hawk shook his head, battling away frustration with his friend. "I am not asking you; I am telling you that's the way it's going to be. Pull back law enforcement from trailing me. I will send the mandate through Disney Security. I will be fine, and if I need you, well . . . I have you on speed dial." Hawk grinned trying to ease the tension.

"No." Al looked down toward the ground. "That is not going to work."

Hawk heard the end of the sentence as he stepped out of the doorway back into the World Showcase. He left Al standing inside Thomas's home and cut through the pub's dining area headed toward Future World. He was a man on a mission, and the mission was continuing now.

CHAPTER 25

Four days ago
3:00 p.m.

THE BRIGHT AFTERNOON SUN BEAT down across the Millennium Plaza in the heart of Epcot's Future World Central. Hawk kept a steady pace as he strategized his next set of moves. He felt bad about his conversation with Al Gann, but at the same time, he knew that what Al wanted and why he wanted it were not bad—they were just not the best ways to unravel the mystery. And if he was going to be true to his mission and protect the people around him, that mystery had to be unraveled.

He was worried about Thomas Dudley too. There was something too sudden, too quick, and too complete about his departure. Hawk feared the worst, and he wondered if the painting on St. George was a message letting him know that someone had figured out his connection to Thomas. The story of Walt's war history played in somehow too, but how it all connected together and what he had to do with it were all still puzzle pieces floating out there, refusing to blend.

He paused and stopped alongside the World Fellowship Fountain. The massive fountain was calm and blue for the moment, serene under the hot afternoon sun. Later, the dancing waters of the fountain would leap to synchronized music in one of the most unappreciated yet brilliant displays in the entire theme park. Walt's wife, Lillian, had dedicated the fountain during a ceremony as the park was opened to the public. Representatives from twenty-three countries had attended, and each brought a gallon of water from a major body of water from their homes. It was all to create a fountain that would be a gathering place representing the world community. Full of hope for the future, it was just another reminder of what Walt had intended for Epcot to be.

There were times, like this moment, when Hawk felt like he was trying to get ideas from seemingly disconnected places to blend together into something that made sense. Was there something about the fountain he was supposed to pay attention to?

"Dr. Hawkes, could I have a moment?" A female voice came from behind him.

He turned around and saw a lean, athletically built woman dressed in a jet-black professional pantsuit with a white blouse accenting the ensemble. Shoulder-length brunette hair encircled her face, and she brushed it back in a battle with the warm breeze that blew across the fountain. Her dark eyes locked on Hawk's instantly and bore into him with surprising force.

He was taken aback for a moment, not by her attractiveness, but by the intensity of her gaze.

"I'm sorry." Hawk blinked in an attempt to disconnect the seriousness of her stare. "Now is not a great time, but is there something I can do for you?"

"I'd like to talk with you a few minutes if that would be possible." Her expression was serious.

"Actually, that's not possible right now. I have a few things that are pressing."

"Like standing here looking at a fountain?"

He stiffened. "I didn't catch your name."

"I didn't offer it, so you didn't miss it." She glanced pointedly away. "It would probably be better if we went somewhere else to talk."

Hawk stepped back a half-step. She had managed to stand just a little closer than he was comfortable with and was invading his personal space. She had returned her unrelenting stare in his direction. He studied her face and once again could not read any emotion or intention. Hawk wondered who she might be. If she were a reporter, she had approached him far too confrontationally to get an interview. Most fans were much more subdued in their approach. She had to be connected to what was happening somehow, but he wasn't sure of that connection yet.

"As I told you, that is not possible right now." He smiled, trying to be cordial. "You know my name, you haven't given me yours, and you seem very . . . intense."

"I am Jillian Batterson. I'm with United States Homeland Security."

His heart sank at the announcement he was standing in front of a federal agent. This would make his already complicated life much more difficult. He immediately began to plan his exit strategy from this conversation.

"Well, that's great. You already know that I'm Grayson Hawkes, chief creative architect of the Walt Disney Company. And if you are really from Homeland Security, you can set up an appointment through my office." Hawk nodded and turned to move away.

He felt a hand grip his arm and stop him. He turned to find a set of manicured fingers clasping his arm.

"I have been at your office. Heather has done a great job of telling me that she doesn't expect you to come in and she isn't real sure what your schedule is as of late. So we can talk now."

"You've been following me?"

"I dropped by to see what the disturbance was in your Germany pavilion earlier and saw you and I believe his name is Al Gann leave." She let loose of his arm. "I decided to wait and speak with you when you were done doing whatever a chief creative architect does."

Hawk tried to read in her inflection whether she was being sincere or snide, but he couldn't infiltrate the stoic demeanor. He leaned in closer and asked, "Do you have any identification?"

"You want me to show you my badge here, in front of any guest who may be watching us because you are a Disney celebrity?" She raised a surprised eyebrow. It was the first crack in her emotionless facade.

"Here is good." Hawk smiled again. He swayed back and forth slightly as he waited. His thumping heartbeat provided a countdown to the moment he would get out of this interaction. A warning radar in his head kept sweeping the need to be wary across his mind. He would be very careful, and he wanted some proof of what she had told him.

Quickly, she produced a badge from the black jacket. The gold shield and identification were clearly marked and identified her as a US Homeland Security Agent. She waited for him to read it and then tapped it with her fingernail, impatient, as if it were taking too long.

"Satisfied?" She flipped the wallet closed and returned it to her jacket.

"Satisfied." Hawk nodded. "What do you want, Agent Batterson?"

"Seriously, you want to talk here?"

"Right here." Hawk motioned to the fountain as music began to play and the water began to shoot up into the sky.

The water splashed down, sending mist across the fountain and getting both of them wet. The water danced as the music played and shot into the air in plumes in time with the song. It was Hawk's turn to be stoic as he tried to ignore the distraction and noise of the fountain. He knew it was silly, but she had caught him off-guard, and somehow he felt like this brought the unexpected meeting back onto familiar turf. This was his home, his territory.

He wasn't the only one who felt the change. The fountain showcase seemed to have accomplished what he anticipated. Once again, Agent Batterson showed a crack in her stern demeanor and allowed her eyes to cut toward the water next to them.

"Tell me about Reginald Cambridge," she said, speaking loudly enough to be heard over the noise but not so loud as to attract the attention of anyone else.

"You are investigating Reginald?" Hawk answered with just enough volume for her to hear him.

"He is suspected of planting explosive devices in your theme parks. That is a possible act of domestic terrorism. So we are investigating." She turned an appreciative glance to the fountain. The music and falling water perfectly shielded their words from anyone who might listen.

"You think Reginald is a terrorist?"

"It is possible he might have been radicalized while in prison."

Hawk was quick to reply. "Then you should have done a better job of making sure he stayed in prison."

Hawk understood that terrorism could manifest itself in many forms. Planting bombs in tourist areas was definitely a terrorist activity. But Hawk suspected that Cambridge wasn't driven by the usual terrorist goals and motivations. He was driven by a personal desire to have the secrets Hawk guarded. He wasn't "radicalized"; it was just that terrorist activity was his chosen path to his goal—for now.

"Nice attitude. Do I detect a crack in the Disney demeanor?" Agent Batterson smiled. "Did I say something that struck a nerve?"

"I understand from Sheriff McManus that in situations like ours, Homeland Security has to be involved. That makes sense, and I am willing to help in any way I can." Hawk looked toward the water and then back to her. "You certainly understand that this has been a busy few days. I expect you can do better than suggesting that Reginald Cambridge was radicalized in prison. He is a lot of things, and he is an evil man, but he is not your run-of-the-mill terrorist bomber. I guarantee it. If you profile him like you would any other terrorist, you will never catch him or figure him out."

She looked at him and was silent for a few moments. "Can we continue this conversation somewhere else?" Jillian tilted her head toward the dancing water. "You knew the dancing water show was getting ready to start, didn't you? That's why you weren't worried about being heard right out here in front of all of these tourists, isn't it?"

"They are not tourists. They are my guests." Hawk smiled. "You might ask Heather to set up an appointment for you to speak with Juliette Keaton. She can probably fill you in on some of the background you need."

"I have an appointment with her this afternoon. I'm told she has been out of town."

"Yes, she has." Hawk frowned. He'd known she would be back from taking the kids to her sister's home very soon. He didn't know Homeland Security had contacted her. For some reason, it irked him.

Hawk felt his phone vibrate and removed it from his pocket. He looked at the screen and could hardly contain a grin. Realizing that with the explosion of water and sound going off next to them it would be difficult to hear, he eagerly answered the call anyway.

"Excuse me for a moment," he said to Agent Batterson, knowing she would hear his portion of the call over the watery extravaganza. "Hi, it's me . . . yes, I am by the fountain in Epcot and it's loud, sorry." He listened and began to smile. "You are awesome. Fantastic job. You know what to do. Go straight there; I'll meet you. And thanks."

He ended the call and turned his attention back to the agent.

"Sorry about interrupting our conversation. I've been waiting for that particular call."

"It sounded like good news."

"It was indeed." Hawk stuck out his hand. "Sorry I couldn't give you any more help. I'm sure Juliette will give you anything you might need."

"I'm not sure our conversation is over." Jillian returned the handshake. Her grip was strong. "There are a lot of things I want to discuss with you."

"As I said, my office can set up—"

"The office you are never in and never check in with?" She continued to shake his hand, her grip growing more firm by the moment.

"Yes," Hawk broke off the handshake. "That office is how you need to get in touch with me."

"Perhaps I will find a better way another time." She smiled again. This time the smile seemed more pleasant to Hawk.

"Sure, another time." Hawk smiled and turned to leave.

Once again he felt her hand on his arm. Her grip was not as strong this time, but it was still strong enough to turn him back toward her. She leaned in close to make sure she could be heard over the water.

"There is something very wrong about what is happening here. I don't know what it is, what you are up to, what you are involved in. But I am persistent, I am not going anywhere, and I will figure it out. I promise you that." She released her grip on his arm.

"I'm sure you will," Hawk said with very little conviction as he again turned to leave. This time she did not stop him, and he walked around the fountain and headed toward the front exit. If she could figure this out, he thought, then she was smarter than he was. He had no idea what was going on . . . yet. But like her, he was going to figure it out.

For now, though, there was some more important business to take care of.

CHAPTER 26

Three days ago
12:35 a.m.

THE PRIVATE WAITING ROOM in Florida Hospital was deserted except for the four friends who were seated together, silently passing the time, waiting for some word or update. Hawk looked across the room at the others. Juliette had arrived back in town and headed straight to the hospital after Hawk called her. Shep had been the first to arrive after Hawk, immediately after Hawk's call. Jonathan Carlson, the fourth member of the former staff of Celebration Community Church, had joined them. Along with Juliette and Shep, Jonathan had moved into a new role in the Disney Company when Hawk inherited its leadership role.

The current silence in the room had allowed them all time to piece together what had been happening behind the scenes over the past few days. Finally Shep broke the quiet to continue the conversation.

"So let me get this straight . . . Jon, you have been traveling the country, visiting medical centers for the past few days?" Shep leaned back and folded his arms as he asked.

"Yes," Jonathan affirmed.

"And you started all of this running around because Hawk interrupted your vacation while you were traveling?"

"Sort of." Jonathan hesitated.

Hawk inserted more information into the story. "Jonathan, Sally, and the kids were over at Disneyland Paris when we were attacked. After I found out Farren had been poisoned and there was no antidote available, I called him."

"He told me to keep Sally and the children as far away from Walt Disney World as possible. He let me know some of the things that were going on. It sounds like you've had your hands full." Jonathan seemed genuinely glad to be back among his friends. "I'm sorry I wasn't here to help."

Juliette leaned forward. "So, Sally and the kids are . . ."

"Safe in Paris and having a great vacation, on Hawk's dime I might add." Jonathan pointed at his boss.

"That should help. There are some days Sally just doesn't like me too much." Hawk smiled as he said it. He knew Sally loved him and they were family, but over the past few years, the changes they had all been through had placed Jonathan at risk. She didn't like that at all and had expressed it to him a number of times. "I'm glad I could pay for their vacation."

"But you didn't come straight home. You started making the tour of medical centers across the country?" Shep returned to the topic of where Jonathan had been.

"Yes, once again on Hawk's credit card. He contacted me and had the doctors send me all the information about this poison Reginald had used on Farren so we could see if someone, anywhere was working on any kind of cure." Jonathan closed his eyes, trying to recall all the places he had been. "Once I got back to the States, I started traveling. Hawk set up a private jet for me to use, and I went from one medical facility to the next. They would look at the poison's composition and see if they had anything that might help."

Over the past six years, Jonathan had secured his pilot's license, and for this project it had been essential. "It became apparent pretty fast that there was no ready-known cure, but as always, medical research facilities are always working on something." He opened his eyes and continued. "So I would visit one place, they would be familiar with a doctor or some work that another was doing, so I would head there, we would do some testing to see if we could evoke a reaction, and well . . . eventually I ended up in Minnesota."

"Minnesota?" Juliette she sat up a bit straighter.

"Yes, the University of Minnesota Medical Research Center. They have been working on an experimental antidote for torpid cyan-toxoid."

"Why?" Shep asked.

"They are doing some work in the field of biochemical research, trying to help victims of terrorist attacks. It's still an ongoing concern that poisons may be released and people infected with them, so they had developed a fast-acting antidote that is still in the experimental phase. They weren't ready to move the test to human subjects yet, because they would have to poison someone first—but they determined that this case presented a great opportunity to see if their antidote would work."

The four friends smiled at one another. They knew the rest; Jonathan had brought the antidote back.

"Not only did I bring back the antidote, but I brought three members of their research team back as well. It seems Dr. Grayson Hawkes gave them a very generous grant to continue their research and had enough clout with the medical team here to clear Farren Rales as test patient number one." Jonathan nodded toward Hawk.

"Wow, it pays to be important doesn't it?" Shep laughed as he spoke.

The doors opened, and Dr. Briggs Kuhn strode in. His face was beaming, and he motioned for the group to remain seated. He took a seat across from Hawk, and they all leaned in to hear his report.

"Farren Rales is going to be okay," the doctor announced. "The antidote is working, and we began to see results in less than five minutes. Amazing what the right medication can do. The team from the university is monitoring him, but it looks like he is going to be all right."

A collective sigh of relief, along with smiles and a few tears, came from the foursome.

"What about his injuries from getting thrown through the window?" Hawk asked.

"Well, as I told you before, they are serious . . . but he is stronger than you think. He will now be able to focus on recovering from those. It won't be an easy recovery exactly, but he should be fine. We will keep a close eye on him. He isn't ready for visitors yet, and the Minnesota team is still working with the experimental drug to make sure we get it right. But I wanted you to know, we are going to make it."

Dr. Kuhn stood up to leave. He reached across and shook Hawk's hand. "I have no idea how much this cost you or what you had to do to pull it off. You managed to bypass all the administrative entanglements of managed health care and research. But you did it—good for you, and great for Mr. Rales. He has a very good friend in you."

Dr. Kuhn left the room, once again leaving them alone. A quiet, hushed thankfulness filtered across the four of them, and each spent a few moments in silent gratitude before Shep once again cracked the quiet.

"And so, boss, this was your plan? The one you whispered to Farren, the one you told us about but wouldn't give us the details?"

"This was the plan." Hawk motioned toward Jonathan. "I thought since Jon wasn't even in town, it would be easier for him to do the hunting. I hoped perhaps it wouldn't be noticed, since he wasn't here to begin with. It turns out I was right."

"Not that it matters to you, I guess I am just curious—what did this cost?" Juliette asked.

"Yes." Hawk now leaned forward toward Jonathan. "How much *did* this cost?"

"Trust me, you don't want to know right now. The bills will be rolling in soon enough. And yes, I did keep receipts." Jonathan answered.

They laughed, the healthy laughter that only comes at the end of a crisis. They all knew there was still much to be done and that nothing was really over yet, but for a moment it was an oasis in what had been a very dry week with moments like this nowhere to be found.

Juliette moved them from the oasis back to the journey they were on. "And now you don't have to give Reginald Cambridge anything."

"Exactly . . . and I am looking forward to telling him that." Hawk smiled again. He took a deep breath, and it felt like his chest expanded more than it had for the last three days. Farren was going to get well. It was a very good day.

"How are you going to find Reginald to do that?" Jonathan asked.

"I don't know. He always seems to find me." Hawk rolled his eyes.

"Now we just have to make sure Farren stays safe and Reginald doesn't get another opportunity to get at him." Jonathan stated the obvious and necessary. "Is there a plan for that?"

"I hope so." A sound at the door made Hawk look up, and once more he smiled. "Speaking of a plan for that, here it is right now." He motioned to the door as Mitch Renner stepped inside.

They greeted one another, and Renner got right down to the business at hand.

"I imagine once Cambridge finds out his plan isn't working like he thought, he'll be tempted to make another run at Mr. Rales. As we have learned before, he is resilient and ruthless—"

"And not afraid to send someone into a hospital," Juliette finished. Hawk knew the assassination attempt on him was still fresh in her memory.

"Yes. Right now, as far as we know, Cambridge doesn't know what's happened yet. Hawk will let me know the moment he does. We have a fortress set up to guard him, so I think we will be fine."

"But Cambridge was able to infiltrate the Orlando Police Department earlier." Juliette voiced the concern of the group. "What's to keep him out of here?"

Renner raised his hand. "I know that we have a very capable and connected enemy in Cambridge. As soon as Rales is well enough, we will transfer him and the team of doctors working with him to a private, undisclosed location so he can recover and remain secure. For now, we're all on high alert. When Cambridge infiltrated the OPD, we didn't even know he was out of prison. This time we're watching for him."

They all looked toward Hawk, who simply nodded to confirm this was the plan he and Renner had created. Last time Rales was in danger, he'd been shot after assassins tried to kill Hawk. They'd protected him by faking his death, putting an end to any leverage someone could gain against Hawk by using him. But Reginald Cambridge understood how important Rales was, and they would not be able to fool him again. Hawk had confidence in the new plan he had devised along with Renner, but for it to work, Rales had to get healthy enough to be transported to a place where he could be kept safe.

"We'll be in touch." Renner stepped back and with a wave, left the four of them alone together once again.

"So what now?" Shep asked.

"Let's go home," Hawk suggested.

"That's it?" Jonathan crossed his legs. "No great adventure? No mystery to unravel? No puzzle to solve?"

"Sure, we have plenty of that to do." Hawk got to his feet with a wry grin. Exhaustion washed over him, and he wavered on his feet for a moment. "Tomorrow. For right now, Farren is going to make it, Reginald is still waiting for me to turn my findings over to him, and until he knows different, he thinks that is happening later today or tomorrow . . . whatever time it is." Hawk rubbed his eyes. "I feel like I haven't slept in forever, so for a few hours, I'm going to rest. We'll get together in the morning at the fire station about ten o'clock if you can be there."

They moved together to leave. A line of police officers was stationed along the corridor to make sure they were protected and safe. The lieutenant by the door greeted them and informed them they would all have escorts to their vehicles, which would be checked to make sure they were secure before they left.

Juliette slowed for a moment and spoke to Hawk. "I had a visit today from Homeland Security."

"Ah yes, that would have been Agent Batterson." Hawk waited for her to continue.

"I think we have a problem. She is aggressively trying to figure out why Homeland Security hasn't been given the lead on this investigation. She's frustrated that the sheriff's office isn't giving them the latitude they want and *furious* because Disney appears to be interfering with their investigation. She's read the reports, and it appears to her that a full-blown domestic terrorism situation has occurred, but for some reason McManus and you have been able to clamp down all information and all details. You are putting people at risk, as far as she's concerned, and she has zero tolerance for whatever game you think you are playing."

"Wow, that must have been some meeting." Hawk looked off toward the officers in the hallway. "I met her earlier today or yesterday."

"I heard. You weren't very cooperative. According to her, you are hiding something."

"You weren't able to give her enough information to satisfy her?" Hawk asked.

Juliette rolled her eyes. "It is kind of hard to explain explosive devices in all four theme parks, the sheriff's department tying to tackle it as an ordinary criminal offense, and an escaped prisoner who has blatantly taken responsibility for the act, and yet for some reason we don't want Homeland Security getting involved." Juliette smiled. "She doesn't understand it. I don't blame her. But I think if we don't get this figured out quickly, she will try to get the entire investigation under her control. Then we lose the relationship and the leeway the sheriff is giving you right now to do whatever it is you are trying to do."

"Then I guess we need to keep after it," Hawk said. He pushed up his sleeves as he said it. Homeland Security was a distraction that he had to shove into the background as easily as he shoved his shirtsleeves up his forearms. Things were finally looking better for them, and he couldn't allow Agent Batterson to slow him down.

"You promised me we were going to end this once and for all," Juliette reminded him.

"Yes, I did. And we will."

"But . . ." Juliette lowered her voice. She spoke softly, keeping her voice from bouncing off the hollow hospital corridor they walked through. "What are you going to do about Reginald? He is not going to be pleased when he hears about Farren. Maybe you should let Homeland Security loose on him."

"I'm not keeping anyone from going after Reginald." Hawk shrugged. His eyes narrowed in concern. "Cambridge has managed to escape and elude anyone who gets close to him. I'm not convinced that law enforcement, Homeland Security, or you and I could find him—he's almost a ghost."

"There has to be a way to stop him," Juliette said.

"I agree. I just don't know what it is."

"Someone needs to figure it out."

CHAPTER 27

Three days ago
2:32 a.m.

THE EARLY-MORNING WALK across Town Square was beautiful. Hawk allowed himself a moment to get lost in the glow of the lights twinkling around him and glanced down the length of Main Street, U.S.A. toward Cinderella Castle. Main Street embodied the American spirit and American dream. Walt Disney had envisioned it as a place where people were friendly, hard work was valued and rewarded, and most importantly, people shared dreams of a better life. This quest Walt Disney had created was about so much more than running the largest entertainment empire in the world. It was about making the world a better place, about touching and changing the world, and about being willing to do the hard work to make it happen.

Hawk continued to move past the streetlamps that illuminated the center of Town Square. The empty flagpole was the heart of this area. He glanced at it and smiled, remembering the flag retreat ceremony that happened each afternoon as the flag was lowered for the evening. It was a powerful reminder of the American spirit, embodied by the man this world had been named after. Walt Disney was certainly a dreamer and visionary, but that only was the tip of the complex and brilliant individual he was.

Hawk thought back to his conversation with Thomas Dudley. He had never realized that Walt Disney had been so influential in designing and redesigning the military and even the nature of warfare. His insights and guidance had been the starting point of a huge shift in how things were done, beginning with the telling of a powerful story. That kind of influence and responsibility was not to be taken lightly. Farren Rales had told Hawk on a number of occasions that what he had been entrusted with was so much more important than any of them realized. For the first time, Hawk was starting to realize why.

Stepping along the sidewalk past City Hall, he rounded the corner to his fire station apartment.

"Good morning." The voice startled him. "I thought you would never get here."

Hawk looked up the steps to his apartment and saw Agent Batterson, seated about halfway up, still dressed in the same crisp suit she had been wearing earlier.

"I told you we needed to talk later. I figured now was as good a time as any," Batterson said in a very even tone.

Hawk groaned inwardly. Every cell in his body was aching for rest. "I'm sorry, but it has been a long few days, and I really want to grab a few minutes of sleep."

"That is not very nice. I have been waiting here for some time, and now you don't want to talk again." Batterson shook her head. "I'm getting the impression you are trying to avoid me."

Hawk waited and pondered what to do next. She was blocking the path to his door. "If you wouldn't mind moving, I will talk with you tomorrow, okay?"

"I was wondering," Batterson said as she remained seated on the steps, "why it is, with all that has been going on over the past few days, there is no security anywhere near you, your apartment, or anywhere out here on the street?"

Hawk looked around and realized how deserted Town Square really was. Eerily quiet and still—the only two people anywhere to be found were Batterson and himself. He had almost forgotten his earlier conversation with Al. Apparently Al had honored his request and pulled back the security that had been hovering around Hawk the past few days.

"It's not real smart. I've seen your file. You aren't a very popular guy . . . among some people, anyway." Batterson tilted her head and paused before continuing. "Someone is always threating you or trying to hurt you, or others close to you. Funny thing is, the file is very light on details. Almost like someone is hiding things for you. And now, here you are again. There has been an attempted terrorist attack on the world's most popular vacation destination, and you, Grayson Hawkes, are the man who figured out how to stop it. That would make you a target in my mind. Yet I was able to march right in here and take a seat right outside your front door. Then you just wander across the street, lost in thought, and run right into me."

She wrinkled her nose. "And no one is out here to see it, to watch you, your apartment, or try to keep you safe." She rose to her feet. "That's odd, isn't it, Dr. Hawkes?"

"When you put it that way, I guess it does sound odd." Hawk smiled. She was right; he understood what she was thinking. But he also knew she had no idea how important unsupervised freedom was for him to be able to unravel the mysteries he was chasing.

"Then why don't you put it in a way that does make sense to me?" She placed her hands on her hips and stood her ground, still blocking him from easily walking up the steps. This conversation was not going to be over until she decided it was. Hawk allowed a wavering smile to briefly cross his face as he thought about how to respond when he heard a sound . . . a sound that didn't fit into the abandoned, late-night atmosphere around them.

Eyes widening, he stepped back and turned from the stairway, moving into Town Square. Batterson, noticing his puzzled look and perhaps sensing that something was wrong, moved down and off the steps into the street.

"What are you hearing?" she asked as she followed his gaze.

He stared up toward the Main Street Train Station. "Do you hear a train?"

They both listened deeply into the sounds of the night. The chugging of a train became louder and clearer.

"Yes," Batterson replied softly. "Do trains normally run this late at night?" Then correcting herself, "Or this early in the morning?"

"No, they don't." Hawk took a step toward the station as suddenly the train grew even louder. Was it speeding up?

Why was a train running at this time of the morning? There was no rational reason he could hang his thoughts upon. As he moved toward the station, his familiarity and love for trains revealed some things that caused him to stop in his own tracks. By the sound of the train he could tell it was moving very fast—too fast to be approaching the station. He would be able to catch a glimpse of it as it arrived, but it was moving way too fast to stop.

Then the train burst into view briefly before being obstructed by the massive building. There was something wrong. Hawk's mind tried to develop the image he had seen briefly before the engine and tender car disappeared behind the station. Had he seen flames?

The train emerged from the other side of the station, and this time he saw clearly flames bursting out of the tender car behind the red cab and red boiler jacket of the locomotive. The color pattern and large Diamond smoke stack told him that the train moving past the station, billowing smoke and fire, was Engine No. 1, the *Walter E. Disney.*

"That train is on fire," Batterson stated.

"And it didn't stop." Hawk started to move back toward his apartment. After a few quick steps he broke into a full run. Agent Jillian Batterson followed.

Together, they raced through the cast member entrance and behind the fire station where Hawk had parked the Harley. In on fluid motion he climbed aboard and with a glance realized that Batterson had every intention of going with him. He shook his head to tell her no, but she fired a look at him that told him there was nothing he could do to stop her.

Tilting his head, he gave her permission to climb aboard as he kicked the bike to life. The engine revved, and Hawk clicked the motorcycle into gear. The Harley jerked beneath him they roared out onto Main Street, U.S.A. Hawk mapped out their pathway in his mind. He couldn't get to the train station in Frontierland before the locomotive arrived; it was moving too fast and it was too far. He set the bike in the direction of the Fantasyland Station.

The lights of the shops on Main Street, U.S.A. were an indistinguishable blur as Hawk coaxed power out of the Harley, racing to the end of Main Street, U.S.A. and into the hub in front of Cinderella Castle. Leaning to the right, he guided the bike to the ramp that carried them up and inside the castle entrance. The engine echoed off the mosaic-covered walls of the castle's interior. The sound hurt his ears as it bounced off the brilliantly colored tiles. Before the noise became unbearable, the motorcycle flew out of the other side of the castle, lifting up slightly as it cleared the entrance. Jillian's grip tightened around his waist as she struggled for a moment to hang on.

Throwing his weight to the right, he moved the bike past the Seven Dwarf's Mine Train. Glancing at it brought back a memory: a day the attraction had lit on fire. Fireworks had landed on one of the buildings, and they'd had to get guests off the train and out of the attraction. The fire had been quickly extinguished, and the conversations and changes that followed had centered around keeping the guests safe. For a fleeting moment Hawk wondered if a simple explanation like fireworks going wonky could explain the locomotive being on fire. The thought quickly extinguished itself. With all that had been happening, there was no way this was just an accident.

The path moved to the left as they raced past the Barnstormer roller coaster and Hawk slid to stop at the entrance of the Fantasyland Train Station. Getting off the bike, he jumped over the gate of the entrance queue and moved over the fence onto the station platform. He could hear the train approaching quickly, though he couldn't yet see it. Batterson joined him on the platform and placed her hand on his shoulder.

"What now?" she said as she looked down the tracks.

The train came into view. The engine was coming straight toward them. Red and yellow flames flew out behind it, outlining it with a mesmerizing glow. It was moving even faster now than it was earlier, Hawk stepped to the end of the platform and jumped down the to the rocky track bed.

"You have a plan?" Batterson called.

"I think I'm going to have to catch a train," Hawk said as he waited for the train to arrive.

CHAPTER 28

Three days ago
3:32 a.m.

THE TRAIN THUNDERED TOWARD HIM, plumes of flame billowing out from behind the engine. Hawk stepped back far enough from the tracks to let the engine pass. As it drew closer, he started to run in the same direction the train was moving. If he mistimed the jump, he knew he faced the possibility of tumbling off and perhaps falling under the train itself. But he was willing to take the risk.

A locomotive, this Disney locomotive, could not be moving unless there was somebody inside the cab at the controls. There was no autopilot feature on these steam trains, so Hawk had to find out who was at the helm.

Batterson moved to the end of the platform and watched as the train streaked past. Hawk's legs pumped like pistons as he sprinted alongside the train. He was going to have to time his vault perfectly. He leapt. His foot hit the step of the cab as his hand grabbed the handrail. Tightening his grip, he felt his foot slide off the step. He hung off the side of the engine with only his right arm holding him on the train. His body slammed against the side, and he kicked his feet, trying to gain a foothold. The train jerked to the right into a slight turn on the track, and once again his body banged against the wall of the cab. This time he got a foot on the step and then placed the other one on the step above it. He grabbed the rail with his left hand, secure at last. He had made it, somehow. He sighed and offered a quick, silent prayer of thanks as he pulled himself up into the cab.

His eyes widened in horror as he looked at the controls at the front of the cab. Thomas Dudley lay in a heap on the floor, his arm strapped to the dead man's switch of the train, forcing it into the run position.

Dropping to his knees, Hawk shook his head as a vivid image, a reoccurring vision, flashed across his mind. He had found Kate Young with her hand secured to the fail-safe control in a monorail on the day she had been killed. He had saved her that day, only to hold her as she died a few minutes later.

Blinking through the misty memory, he struggled to free Thomas's arm. He did, and instantly the train began to slow in speed.

"Thomas, can you hear me?" Hawk asked as he reached up to throttle back some of the speed so he could apply the brakes. "Thomas, are you with me? Come on, talk to me."

Hawk applied the brake and heard the squeal of the brakes as they engaged. The train shuddered as it began to slow. Thomas Dudley stirred, and Hawk let out a sigh of relief that there had been a response. Gently leaning Thomas against the wall of the cab, he stepped up and brought the train to a stop. He looked up and back toward the tender car and saw the source of the flames: a fire blazed on the top covering of the car, flames dancing across its surface. Some sort of fire accelerant had been placed upon it. He had no idea what it might be, but the flame was beginning to burn out. It had been for show and, he feared, to get his attention. It had succeeded.

Putting aside those thoughts for a moment, he turned his focus back to Thomas Dudley, who was now struggling to sit up straighter on the floor of the cab.

"Take it easy, Thomas, it's going to be fine. I stopped the train," Hawk reassured him.

"She said you would get to me in time," Thomas whispered. His voice was cracked and strained.

"What? Who said?"

"Kiran. A beauty—and evil." Thomas patted Hawk on the arm as he assisted him to sit up straighter. "She said for me not to worry, that you would get to me in time before the train crashed or derailed. She was right."

"She was right." Hawk nodded. His throat had tightened at the mention of Kiran. He had trusted her once. Betrayal still stung.

"Kiran gave me a message for you," Thomas said.

"Of course she did."

"She wanted you to know that she is back and is very close. She said it was her job to get you on track." Thomas's eyes widened. "She is evil and crazy, Hawk. I think she wants to kill you."

"I imagine she does. She's tried before, but it doesn't usually go as she plans." Hawk inspected Thomas to see if he was injured. Looking for blood or visible injury, he saw none. Merely rumpled clothes and a ripped sleeve on the arm that had been strapped to the switch. "Are you hurt?"

"No, just a little shaken. She showed up at my door right after you left. I actually thought it was you. She burst in, kicked me, slapped me, and then I blacked out. I woke up in the trunk of a car. Don't know how much time had passed. She took me into the roundhouse and put me on the train. How does she know how to run a steam train?"

"She seems to have a lot of information about how Disney transportation works." Hawk lowered his head and shook it. "Kiran knows a great deal about park operations. She is dangerous, as you found out."

"She's caused you a lot of heartache. I'm sorry I couldn't fight her off." Thomas's voice trailed off.

Jillian Batterson arrived and stepped up into the cab of the train. Surveying the situation, she knelt down and began a quick examination of Thomas Dudley to see if he was injured. Hawk leaned back and gave her room. Her confidence surpassed his knowledge of what to do instantly.

"That was the craziest thing I have seen in a long time," Jillian said as she inspected Dudley. "You're lucky you weren't killed and didn't fall underneath the train."

"I don't believe in luck." Hawk watched her work.

"Really?" She paused, raised an eyebrow, then turned her attention back to Thomas. "Then whatever you believe in rescued you. That was insane. Who did this to you?" she asked Thomas.

"Who are you?" Dudley looked into her face.

"Agent Batterson, Homeland Security." She smiled at Dudley, whose eyes cut over to Hawk for confirmation. He nodded.

"It was Kiran Roberts," Thomas Dudley replied.

Batterson turned her head and looked at Hawk. "The same Kiran Roberts who tried to kill you more than once, tried to kill your girlfriend, kidnapped Juliette Keaton, and—"

"That's the one," Hawk confirmed. "No nightmare is complete without her."

"That's an interesting way to put it," Batterson said under her breath. She helped Thomas Dudley to his feet. "Let's get away from these flames, they are throwing off some heat. What do you say?"

Hawk slid to the other side and helped hoist Thomas up, and the two of them gently lowered him down the steps to the ground. Although unhurt,

Thomas was a little wobbly as they helped him to his feet. The train was sitting on the section of track between Tomorrowland and the Main Street Station. Security vehicles were starting to arrive, and members of the Reedy Creek Fire Department pulled up alongside of the road, trying to mobilize a team to get next to the train.

Once Hawk and Jillian had gotten far enough away from the train, they sat Thomas down in the grass, and he lay back as emergency personnel reached them.

Batterson turned her attention to Hawk, looking at him with her usual intensity—although this time her expression showed concern. "Are you really all right?" she asked.

"I think so."

"Your body was bouncing off the train pretty good when you went into that turn back there."

"I couldn't keep my feet on the step. Didn't wear my train-jumping shoes." He laughed.

Jillian laughed for the first time since he had met her. She shook her head and leaned back, seated on the grass as more and more rescue vehicles arrived. She looked back at Hawk and studied him for a moment.

"You're an extremely complicated individual. Not really what I expected," she admitted. "And you drive a motorcycle pretty well."

"It was an E-Ticket ride through the Magic Kingdom, wasn't it?" He laughed again.

"Is that a Disney thing?" She looked puzzled.

"Huh?"

"E-Ticket ride . . . is that a Disney thing? I don't know what that is, but if it is a Disney code word kinda thing, I don't know about it. I'm not really a Disney fan."

Why didn't that surprise him? "Never mind; no reason to explain it then." He looked back toward Thomas and the paramedic working with him. "Is he going to be fine?"

"I think so, nothing serious here." The man looked up at them. "Are you both all right?"

"All good here," Hawk answered.

A blueish hue from the moonlight cast shadows around them. The emergency lights of the rescue vehicles glowed in it as the dampness of the early morning refreshed him. Closing his eyes, he contemplated the reemergence of Kiran Roberts in his world. Reginald and Kiran had worked to ruin his world in the past, and now here they were again, together, to try to do it again.

Somehow he had known Kiran would show up. She always did. He had not seen her since he left her trapped on Tom Sawyer's Island in the Magic Kingdom. As she always did, she had somehow inexplicably managed to escape—from an island surrounded by law enforcement. Kiran hadn't been seen since, until now.

The relief of finding an antidote for Farren had been a welcome respite in the mayhem that surrounded him. Now, fresh battle lines were drawn.

A deputy stepped in front of them. "Sheriff McManus is on his way out here. He said to tell you he wanted to see you when he arrived."

Jillian turned her head toward Hawk. "You're a popular guy. It seems like everyone wants to talk with you."

CHAPTER 29

Three days ago
9:45 a.m.

HAWK ENDURED THE ENDLESS BARRAGE of questions from law enforcement until they at last came to an end. A part of him wished he could be more helpful. The return of Kiran Roberts was surprising, but at the same time, expected. Exactly how she fit into the scenario was the problem, but that had always been the problem with Kiran—she never seemed to fit. Manipulative and without any boundaries, she was on a relentless quest for power, riches, and control. Early on she had fooled him and tried to be a friend, perhaps more—but when he was able to step back and understand who she really was, she became more frightening to him than Reginald Cambridge had ever been.

Thomas was correct, and Hawk knew it; ultimately, Kiran's goal was to kill him. But until she could have the secrets she believed Hawk possessed, she would wait for the opportunity. Although he had managed to outwit her in their last encounter, the price had been way too high. Kiran had realized there was more Hawk needed to discover, and apparently she believed now was the time for him to find it. The opportunist she was could not let the moment pass, so she had injected herself into his world once again.

Cal McManus was frustrated and borderline furious that Hawk was refusing any law enforcement protection. Weary and unnerved by Kiran's return, Hawk found himself wishing the sheriff *could* figure out the mystery enveloping him, but at the same time, he knew he was the only one who could understand the cloaked conundrums Walt Disney had left for him.

His cell phone received a text message as he concluded his heated conversation with McManus. The message read, *The fire station—now!* The sender was unknown.

A chill raced across Hawk. It had to be from Reginald. Today was the deadline Cambridge had set up for him. Without mentioning it to McManus, he excused himself.

Making his way through the train station and heading for his apartment above the fire station, Hawk was troubled by the gnawing reality that even if he hadn't found a way to rescue Farren, he really didn't have anything he could have given to Cambridge that would have satisfied him. Sure, he could have turned over the kingdom key, the silver bars, the Mickey Mouse icon ring, Walt's personal diaries, and the Wernher von Braun notebook containing his space secrets. All of those items were priceless for certain. But it wouldn't be enough for Reginald—just like it wasn't enough for Hawk. There was still a missing piece, the piece the third Imagineer had been responsible for sharing, the one piece Hawk still had not managed to find. Reginald was not going to be happy. And even though he was not afraid of Cambridge, Hawk knew he was extremely dangerous and volatile.

He paused as he passed the flagpole on Main Street, U.S.A. Rocking on his feet, he looked up toward the second-story window of his apartment. All looked as it should, but for an instant Hawk wished he had not been so adamant about not needing security protection. He wouldn't mind Al Gann's people tailing him at the moment.

Exhaling sharply, he weaved through the crowds walking along the street, keeping his gaze down, careful to avoid eye contact. By the time guests recognized him, he had already moved past them. Reaching the bottom of the steps, he started climbing. In the early hours of the morning, Jillian Batterson had stopped him from ever making it up these steps. This time there was no one there to obstruct his path, and he reached the landing by his door. Grabbing the doorknob and taking out his key, he was not stunned to discover that the door was already unlocked.

He slowly allowed the door to open. Remaining on the landing, he leaned cautiously inside.

"Hello?"

Silence followed. He took one step across the threshold and paused. He didn't really know what he expected to happen, but the unlocked door, the quiet, and the tension he was already feeling kept him slow. He was sweating, and he rolled his shoulders as he stood in the doorway, forcing himself to relax and calm down. Still he heard nothing. He took another step. The board of the hardwood floor creaked slightly, the noise causing him to freeze in place as if the sound might bring whoever was in the apartment with him into view. Again, there was no sound except for his nervous breathing.

Moving slowly across his living room, he searched the apartment with his eyes. There was nothing out of place; everything was as he remembered leaving it. The room was deserted. He moved into the dining area and again found everything as it should be. Mentally telling himself to relax, he turned toward the kitchen and felt his breath catch in his chest.

Taking an involuntary step backward, he crashed into his dining room table as his eyes focused on the sight in front of him. With his posture rigid, muscles tensed, and internal alarms blaring with every heartbeat, he forced himself to take a breath.

Feeling his lungs expand and the oxygen replenishing his capacity to move, he took a small step forward, toward the shape stretched out on his kitchen floor. It was a body, facedown, with a pool of blood coming out from underneath it.

Hawk recognized the body immediately. Crouching down and placing a hand on its back, he felt for movement. There was none. He grabbed the shoulder and lifted it, turning the person over to check for a pulse. As the head turned, he looked into the face that confirmed his moment of recognition.

A massive stain had spread across the man's chest. Hawk reached in and felt for a pulse against his neck. There was nothing.

Gently he allowed the body to slide back to the original position he had found it in. Reginald Cambridge was dead.

 *Three days ago*
 10:45 a.m.

REGINALD CAMBRIDGE HAD BEEN STABBED in the chest with a knife. The medical examiner's initial examination had revealed that fact. The Orange County Sheriff's Department was searching diligently for the murder weapon but, as of yet, had not found it.

Hawk sat on the sofa of his apartment alongside Juliette, Jonathan, and Shep. They had all arrived, as agreed upon, at ten o'clock, when they discovered Hawk hovered over the body of Reginald. Calling McManus directly, Juliette reached him already on Disney property where Hawk had left him just a short time before, investigating the runaway train incident.

The small apartment was flooded with natural light streaming through the sheer curtain-covered window as more and more people crammed into the tiny space. Silently, the friends watched as law enforcement officers explored the apartment, scoured for clues, and secured the scene. An officer had come came over and asked the four if there was a place they could go and wait to be interviewed. Hawk nodded slowly, trying to think of a place. They needed to get out of the apartment so the officials could do their work. Juliette suggested a small office in the adjacent City Hall building. After a few minutes of discussion, the same officer who had made the request, a Lieutenant Raines, guided them down the steps, across the walkway, and into City Hall.

Hawk glanced out at Town Square. Half of it had been closed to guests entering the park. Along the security perimeter was a line of officers and Disney security personnel, keeping visitors far away from the crime scene. He dreaded moments when guests were forced out of areas of the resort. While he understood the need to keep them safe, their experience would forever be different because of what they could not do. He realized they needed to stay back, out of the way, but he felt horrible about it, because they would never be able to understand all that was happening in this moment.

Once inside City Hall, the four were seated in a small office, which was sparse and used as a general work space for anyone who might need it. A computer, telephone, and compact printer sat on the desk, with five chairs lining the walls of the room. Juliette took the seat behind the desk as Hawk, Shep, and Jonathan took chairs along the wall. As the deputy closed the door, they instantly began to speak in hushed tones.

"How long were you in the room?" Juliette asked.

"Just a few minutes."

"And what is the story about a train on fire and Kiran Roberts being back?" Shep asked. He hunched his shoulders as he spoke. He had been fooled badly by her once before, and the results had been catastrophic.

"It's true. Kiran sent a message to me by putting Thomas Dudley on a train, setting it on fire, and sending it around the Magic Kingdom railroad line. She was banking that I would get there in time. I was going to tell you all this morning, but I had just left there before I went home. That's how the sheriff arrived so quickly." Hawk shook his head. "Then I walked in and saw Reginald. I figured he was there to get the stuff he wanted me to turn over to him."

"Were you going to give him anything?" Jonathan raised his eyebrows.

"No." Hawk leaned back in the chair and crossed his arms. "But he didn't know that."

The door clicked and swung open, and a very tired Cal McManus walked in. Saying nothing, he closed the door behind him and sat down on the desk facing Hawk.

"All right." He ran his fingers through his hair. "Let me make sure I have this correct. You got a text as we finished talking, telling you to go to your apartment?"

"Right." Hawk nodded. He had already made a brief statement in the apartment.

"But you didn't bother to tell me about the text, and that you suspected it came from Reginald Cambridge?"

"No. I knew he wanted me to turn over the things he had asked for so he could give me a cure for the poison."

"The poison you'd already found a cure for?" Cal studied Hawk.

"Yes, but he didn't know that."

"But you felt it was best not to tell me that you were going to meet a man who is an escaped criminal, who has attempted to kill you in the past, and who was responsible for planting explosive devices threatening thousands of innocent people in the world's most popular vacation destination?" Cal slammed his palm down on the desk as his voice elevated. "Have you lost your mind?"

Hawk lowered his gaze and realized just how dumb that choice had been. It sounded even worse as he heard McManus say the words out loud for them all to hear.

"When was the last time you were in your apartment?" Cal asked, voice returning to his usual calm.

"Yesterday," Hawk answered.

"You haven't been home since yesterday?"

"No. When I tried to go home last night, I couldn't get in."

"Explain 'couldn't get in,'" McManus instructed.

"I had an encounter with Agent Batterson. She was waiting for me on the steps of the apartment. I was talking to her when we saw the train go by on fire, we chased it, and then . . . well, you know the rest."

"Homeland Security agent Jillian Batterson was at your apartment last night and wouldn't let you in?" Cal said slowly.

"Uh . . . yes. Like I said, she was waiting to talk with me and so waited at my apartment for me to get there. The train derailed our conversation."

"Hey boss, the train derailed your conversation . . ." Shep pointed out the unintentional play on words before Hawk cut him off with a glance.

McManus hesitated before continuing, and the room fell into silence for a few moments. Hawk glanced at his friends. All looked troubled and deep in thought.

Juliette gave word to their shared opinion. "This sounds like Kiran Roberts was in your apartment. Business as usual for her."

"Really?" Cal McManus asked. "Is that your opinion as you have investigated the crime, or is that statement based on some deep dark Disney secret that you have not shared with me?"

"I'm just saying it fits into the way she's operated in the past." Juliette leaned forward toward the sheriff. "You know it is."

"Kiran and Reginald are both bad news, and they wanted to hurt Hawk, and all of us, everyone close to him, and take control of the company," Jonathan joined in. "They and all the people they have worked with have shown they will do anything to get what they want. Maybe Kiran turned on Reginald. The last time they were both around, they didn't get along that well."

"Well, thanks for wrapping the case up for me." McManus allowed his voice to drip with sarcasm. "Now I can take the rest of the day off. All you need to do is show me what evidence you have."

"Evidence?" Jonathan asked.

"Sure. You make a compelling case, so what is your evidence?" McManus looked to each person in the room. "Because based on the evidence, your theory might be true . . . but then again, how do I know that Hawk didn't just kill Reginald when he came to meet him in the apartment? After all, Hawk could have told me he was going to meet one of the most wanted men in the country, but he didn't. Maybe he wanted to finish him."

McManus pushed a finger toward Hawk for emphasis. "That is what this is about, isn't it? Solving this great big secret you all keep and finishing it once and for all? Well, you finished Reginald."

"I didn't do anything to Reginald!" The words stung Hawk and had not been anticipated. He knew that at first glance it did look bad, that made sense. But he hadn't expected the accusation to come his way. "Like I told you, he was dead when I walked in."

"Right. Dead in your apartment on your kitchen floor, stabbed in the heart." McManus glared at Hawk. "Why didn't you tell me you were going to meet him?"

Hawk fell silent. His decision had been more than foolish, and he knew it. The quest to solve the mystery Walt left for him had at times blinded him before, and it had done so again. The bulk of the time his instincts were good and right, but this time they had failed him. "I didn't do it."

"Then if you didn't do it, maybe a federal Homeland Security agent did it. After all, she didn't let you go into your apartment, and she was trying to find Cambridge. Maybe she killed him in your kitchen to get him out of the way," McManus said. "At least we can place her at the scene of the crime, if I can believe your story."

Hawk opened his mouth to answer and then shut it again. He realized that Reginald's death had thrown an unexpected ripple through the mystery, and if anything, the story had become even more dangerous. Reginald was ruthless and would stop at nothing to get what he wanted. But now, someone had been able to stop Reginald. That could only mean there was a far more dangerous adversary lurking in Hawk's world.

McManus got up from the desk with a sneer and moved toward the door to the office. He grabbed the doorknob, paused, and then looked back at them all.

"Don't leave. I am sending down an interviewer, and I need all of your statements." He opened the door and again paused in the doorway. "Hawk, I have been very generous about giving you free rein to do whatever you are doing in this magical kingdom of yours. Now you will do what I tell you to do. Got it? Make sure you stay somewhere where I can find you."

The door slammed behind him.

Again, silence filtered across the office. Shep was the first to speak. Silence was never comfortable for him.

"So who stabbed Reginald?"

"I still think it was Kiran," Juliette said. "They knew each other, they are both our enemies. She could have gotten close enough to have done this to him, and we know she is back. She did it while you guys were all out cleaning up the train mess. It was the perfect distraction to let her do what she wanted."

"What do you think, Hawk?" Jonathan asked.

"Not sure." Hawk shrugged. "Juliette might be right. Kiran certainly could have done it. But Reginald was one tough guy. One of the toughest men I'd ever met." Hawk grew quieter. "At one point, we believed he was our friend."

All of them remembered their early days of transitioning from being a church staff to becoming the power players at Disney. Reginald Cambridge had been the head of Disney security and had spent endless hours with each of them in a variety of settings. They had done life together, and that closeness had allowed Cambridge to nearly destroy all of them.

"Why was Agent Batterson waiting to talk with you in the wee hours of the morning?" Jonathan asked.

"She surprised me," Hawk admitted. "I had been effectively finding ways to not talk to her, but I guess she decided eventually I had to go to the apartment. So there she was."

"What do you think she knows or doesn't know?" Shep asked.

"She's convinced we're all hiding things, I would guess, because for her what happened in the parks was pretty cut and dried. We had four different bombing attempts in our theme parks and a hate symbol prominently branded in Epcot." Hawk closed his eyes for a prolonged moment, opened them, and continued. "And for reasons she wants to understand, we don't seem to be panicked or reacting like we should be. She's not our enemy, but she thinks we're all pretty suspicious. Can't say I blame her."

"That's my take on her as well," Juliette said. "She understands that something is happening outside the ordinary. She doesn't know what, but she is suspicious of whatever it is we're doing."

"And now she has seen the handiwork of Kiran Roberts for herself," Shep pointed out.

"Hawk, before all of this craziness happened, last night at the hospital you wanted us to meet you at your apartment. You had something to tell us or show us?" Jonathan brought them back to the moment.

Hawk sighed. Last night already seemed like a lifetime away. "I wanted to catch you up on what I've found. Jon, while you were looking for an antidote, we have been finding clues and trying to unravel a mystery. I have one more clue. Thomas Dudley gave it to me. I was going to look at it with you all."

"You haven't read it yet?" Juliette asked, her voice halting in surprise.

"No. We've been busy."

"Well, what's the clue?" Shep leaned forward.

"Not now." Hawk tilted his head toward the door. "We're all waiting to give statements and answer questions for the police. This isn't the time."

On cue, the door opened and three uniformed deputies walked in. Hawk slumped back in his chair as they entered, convinced that he, Juliette, Shep, and Jonathan were in for a very long afternoon.

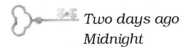 *Two days ago*
Midnight

SILENTLY HE WALKED ALONE, his footsteps echoing in the entryway. He moved through the lobby area with purpose in each step. The Iron Spike Room was tucked away inside the Villas at Wilderness Lodge. Officially named the Carolwood Pacific Room, it was a sitting and games room just off the entry lobby of the villas building, decorated in a rustic vintage railroad motif. Oversized soft leather chairs, benches for sitting, and an always burning fireplace complete with a one-of-a-kind railroad fire grate made the room inviting and comfortable.

It was one of Hawk's favorite places to go in the Walt Disney World Resort. Most guests never took the time to visit the space, even if they were staying in the Wilderness Lodge Resort, because there were too many other things to do and too many other entertainment selections demanding their time. As a result, this always quiet place was a refuge of sorts for Hawk. It also served to keep him connected at a deeper level with the life and legacy of Walt Disney.

Bypassing the first entrance to the room, Hawk walked to the second entrance, taking him past a glass display case loaded with railroad memorabilia. It was a train collector's gold mine and would catch the eye of anyone fascinated by trains. The case was located outside the Iron Spike Room in the lobby area, a sneak preview of what might be discovered if you took the time to venture inside. Behind the glass was a highly detailed model railroad engine, similar to the steam engines used in the Magic Kingdom. A rustic railroad lantern, an engineer and conductor's cap, a conductor's railroad timepiece, and an assortment of photographs, flyers, and tickets created a historic trip across years of riding the rails for any guest who wished to explore what was hiding behind the glass doors.

Hawk always slowed down and took a lingering look inside. Usually there was one item that would catch his interest or spark his imagination. He would study it, gaze a little longer than he expected, and walk away convinced he had never noticed that item before.

In the early hours of this morning, despite the fears and pressures hounding him, it happened once again. This time he focused on the conductor's watch and made the observation that it read twelve o'clock—the time it was right now. He studied it closer and could see that the watch was actually running and keeping accurate time. Who made sure the watch mechanism was wound each day, he wondered, and how long had that been someone's task? Had the watch always kept the right time, and he had never noticed it all these years until now?

A quick shake of the head and he moved into the far entrance of the Iron Spike Room and was instantly transported back in time. Rail-inspired artwork in the form of paintings hung on every wall in the room. Photos of trains and railroads all accented the railroad theme, but the most impressive item on display was the miniature train owned by Walt Disney.

Stepping across the room, he placed his hands on the glass case that housed the train cars and peered down inside. He imagined what it would have been like to actually ride this train, as some of the pictures in the room depicted, with Walt Disney himself as the engineer. Walt's love for trains was a well-known fact. Some historians believed that one of the reasons Walt built a theme park to begin with was to have a place to put a real working steam train, which of course he did. In 1950, prior to his creation of the Disneyland Park, Walt Disney had created a one-eighth-scale model live steam railroad at his family's Carolwood estate in the Holmby Hills area of Los Angeles. The Iron Spike Room featured two of the original freight cars built in the studio's machine shop by Roger Broggie for the Carolwood Pacific Railroad. Walt would entertain family and friends and allow the passengers to ride on the cars over 2,615 feet of track that ran throughout the five-acre property on Carolwood Drive. A few years earlier, Hawk had found a clue hidden in one of the cars displayed under protective glass.

Moving away from the train cars, he slowly worked his way around the room, losing himself in the wonder and fascination of vintage trains of a bygone era. Numerous photos of Walt and his adventures on trains dotted the walls, and a painting that captured the essence of Walt and his love for trains hung for guests to see as they connected with the stories. It was titled, *Walt's Magical Barn,* a painting by artist Bob Byerley created in 2001 in celebration of Walt Disney's one hundredth birthday. Hawk smiled at the painting. It featured Walt as most remembered him from his television appearances, wearing a pair of denim coveralls, working on a model train. The room was comfy, homey, and for Hawk, a refuge from the hectic pace of his life. Walt would have loved this space, he thought. Here, Hawk always felt more connected to the visionary who had indirectly chosen him to protect the world he had worked so hard to create.

This visit had been planned earlier that afternoon. Interviews and questions had taken the bulk of the day. His apartment on Main Street, U.S.A. was officially a crime scene, and until forensics had time to completely investigate, Hawk was not allowed back in it. By the time they had all been released, it was evening. Hawk had told everyone to go home, do what they needed to do, and then gather later that night, or morning as it were. The pace of the resorts slowed down, guests were settling in for the night, and a massive reset happened all over Walt Disney World after closing time. Night was the best time for Hawk to move freely through the resort, and it was also the best time for the friends to figure out what to do next.

Juliette, Shep, and Jonathan were already seated in the huge chairs in front of the fireplace. Their conversation was low and relaxed, and they had been eagerly waiting for Hawk to arrive.

He took a seat and sat back in the chair as he relaxed for just a brief moment. Closing his eyes, he refocused his thoughts beyond the craziness and stunning death of Reginald Cambridge. Although an enemy, Hawk felt a great sense of loss. Although Reginald's evil agenda had eventually surfaced and consumed him, Hawk had never forgotten the good qualities he'd seen in his one-time friend.

Over the hour that followed, Hawk told his trusted allies of the events that had happened over the last five days. Although they each knew certain portions, none of them except Hawk understood how they fit together. As he talked, he became painfully aware that even he didn't have the complete picture—but at least now, as a team, they could see a bigger picture. Perhaps all together they could solve this mystery.

"So the third Imagineer is named Press?" Jonathan interlocked his fingers and placed them below his chin as he spoke. "Do we know anything else about him?"

"Not much," Juliette answered. "Press may be a nickname, but I did a quick search after we got the name to see if I could find out more. I couldn't. I contacted the Disney Archivist department to see if they could come up with something, but I haven't heard back yet. Perhaps it was someone who worked at WED."

"What is WED?"

The female voice from the far end of the room startled them.

In the darkened nighttime lighting of the Iron Spike Room, someone emerged from the shadows. Jillian Batterson had been listening to their conversation. Hawk hadn't seen or heard her enter. How much she had heard or how long she had been there, he had no idea.

"I said, what is WED?" The federal agent repeated her question.

"Walter Elias Disney Enterprises. It was the creative dream company Walt created," Shep answered for the group. "Eventually it became known as Imagineering, and the people who worked there were called Imagineers."

"And so Press is an Imagineer, who has you on some magical mystery adventure to save Walt Disney World?"

Uninvited, Jillian joined the group and took a seat directly across from Hawk.

Hawk groaned inwardly. During the last hour, the group had unpacked and relived the events that had brought them to this point. Who knew how long she had been in here listening? She had obviously managed to slide into the room undetected, and between their conversation and what she had been able to discover on her own, she knew far more than he wished she knew.

"Something like that," Hawk answered her question.

"You guys intrigue me," Jillian said with no emotion. "From what I've been able to figure out, you're on some great quest to preserve some secret left years ago by Walt Disney, and to do it, you are willing to put thousands of guests at risk, interfere with criminal investigations, and become targets for ruthless perpetrators—and I am supposed to believe you are simply doing this for the legacy of a man who died in 1966? And so all you have to do is figure out where Walt Disney hid the pixie dust, and you will set the world right. Is that how it works?"

The four didn't answer. They realized how far-fetched and unbelievable their story really was. There were times as Hawk moved through the course of each day that even he had trouble believing it. The world he now lived in was full of heroes, villains, and as Jillian had called it, a quest. There was little point in explaining it. She was here with an agenda. He knew it. She just hadn't gotten to it yet.

"So am I right? Did I miss something? That's what you are up to?" Jillian Batterson looked from person to person, waiting for an answer.

"More or less," Shep responded.

"Which?" Batterson fired back quickly.

"Huh?"

"Which is it? Is it more or less of what you are up to?" Jillian again took a moment and looked at each of them. "I want an answer."

"No." Hawk sat back in the leather chair. Crossing his arms across his chest, his expression tightened. "We are not giving you an answer. We don't expect you to understand, and it really isn't your business." He sounded much ruder than he had intended, but he needed to push the conversation with her forward, and he desired to regain the moment that had been lost when she unexpectedly appeared.

"Really?" Jillian raised an eyebrow as she smiled slightly. "It's not my business and you don't want to tell me?"

"That's pretty much the way it is." Hawk leaned forward. "What do you want, and why are you here?"

Jillian Batterson sat back. Eyes widening and lips parting slightly, she allowed Hawk's response to fall across the space between them. Her smile was now gone, and her eyes locked in on Hawk with the same glaring intensity he had seen in their first meeting.

"I am here to investigate the possibility of terrorist activities and threats against your resort. But I arrived to discover that local and state law enforcement seemed to be steering me away from investigating. They also seem to have some unwritten and unexplainable rules about keeping their hands off of you and whatever this little game is that you are playing here. And while I am trying to figure out why no one but me is worried about bombs and thousands of people being hurt or worse in the vacation capital of the world, the person I believe to be the chief suspect ends up stabbed in your apartment." She pointed an accusatory finger toward Hawk. "So now someone has murdered my chief suspect, and you guys are more concerned with some Disney scavenger hunt than worrying about who is killing people in your theme park."

"Maybe *you* killed Reginald Cambridge." It was Shep who hurled the unexpected accusation.

Hawk cut his eyes toward Shep and struggled to keep a smile from spreading across his face. Jillian was going to react quickly to this, but he decided to let Shep work it out on his own, at least for a minute or two.

"I what?" Jillian's face flushed red.

"You were sitting on Hawk's apartment steps earlier that day, and you wouldn't let him go into his apartment. Maybe that was because you had killed Cambridge, and you didn't want Hawk to see. You would have been the last person at the apartment to have had the chance to do it as far as anyone knows." The words had come out fast, and Shep's voice raised in pitch just a little as he spouted them all out in one breath.

"Or maybe Hawk did it, or Jonathan, or Juliette, or maybe you did it, Shep," Jillian said in a soft voice with a harsh edge. "After all, you needed to work your way back into the good graces of Hawk after you sold out your friends to Kiran Roberts a few years ago. That didn't turn out so well, did it? So maybe killing Cambridge was your way of making things right." Her flinty eyes flashed.

"That's enough." Hawk was on his feet and stepping between the agent and Shep.

"You're right." Jillian was on her feet just as fast. She stepped boldly into Hawk's personal space, squaring off as if prepared to fight. "You know what I think? I think I should arrest all of you for obstructing a federal investigation."

Refocusing her attention on Shep by looking around Hawk, she pointed toward him. "I'll start with you."

The situation had disintegrated and then boiled over with startling speed. Hawk stepped slightly to his right, again blocking Jillian's view of Shep. Jonathan and Juliette were now on their feet as well, with a desire to help but lacking a course of action to deescalate matters.

"I asked you before, and I am asking again," Hawk said, holding his position and squaring his body toward her. "What do you want, and why are you here?"

Earlier when they had raced together to catch a runaway train, Hawk had sensed that Jillian desired to understand and get to the bottom of what was really happening. Perhaps it was just the shared experience, but for a moment he had thought that for her, this was no longer as simple as a straight federal investigation. Perhaps he had been wrong or misread her.

Jillian's jaw was set, and her chin was held high as she looked up at the taller man in front of her. She took a deep breath and exhaled loudly, calming herself slightly. Leaning forward, she almost spit the words, "Give me a good reason not to arrest all of you."

"Because," Hawk swallowed hard, "if you arrest us we won't be able to figure out what is really happening here. And the consequences of that might be far worse than anything you are trying to prevent already."

Hawk's statement silenced Jillian but also startled his friends, who stared at their boss intensely.

"Explain," Batterson said through clenched teeth.

"Yes," Juliette echoed faintly. "Do."

"I believe this secret we are trying to find has something to do with power and control that reaches far beyond the Disney entertainment empire. It was so important to Walt and Roy that they created an elaborate plan to protect it beyond their lifetimes, and there have been people, bad people, like Kiran and Reginald who were willing to wait for years and years to find it, take it, and control it for their own purposes . . . whatever it really is. Doesn't that tell you it isn't just about movies and parks? There's something bigger going on here. Something national, even international."

Hawk looked at Jillian as her eyes bore into his. He could see thoughts working behind her eyes as she processed the possibilities of what he had just suggested. Slowly he saw her start to relax. Her breathing slowed, and the intensity that had reached a flash point mere moments ago yielded to a calmer sense of purpose.

Taking a half-step back, she raised her palms in mock surrender. "Fine. How do you figure out what it is?"

"That's what we were working on when you decided to show up and interrupt us." Hawk smiled, trying to further diffuse the moment.

"Yeah. If you would have just kept quiet and left us alone, you could have eavesdropped and heard the whole thing," Shep quipped.

Jillian tilted her head and looked past Hawk toward Shep. Shep cowered back in his chair.

"Ignore him." Juliette rolled her eyes as she said it. "We do, all the time." She motioned for Jillian to have a seat. Juliette sat back down as did Jonathan. Batterson looked behind her, decided to accept the invitation, and took a chair next to Juliette.

As she was seated, Juliette offered softly, "Just for the official record, I know you didn't kill Cambridge. I believe Kiran did it."

Jillian smiled slightly and nodded. "So noted."

Hawk now stood alone in the center of the room. The faceoff was over, and it appeared that Agent Batterson was going to be an extra member of their team for a short time. He didn't like it—but then again, maybe her resolve and grit would come in handy. He hadn't formed a complete opinion of her yet. She was yet another unknown factor that he had to work with as he tried to keep moving forward. With a shrug, he returned to his seat, reached into his pocket, and produced the piece of paper that Thomas Dudley had removed from the book in his home with the promise that what was on it would keep him moving forward.

The typewritten words fit the same style as the previous clues. Holding out the paper, he read the clue for the first time with his friends and the federal agent.

Since the World began
this Disney gift
has Lit the way to Success and Happiness.

CHAPTER 32

Two days ago
3:45 a.m.

MULLING OVER CRYPTIC THOUGHTS, Hawk paced the perimeter of the Iron Spike Room before retreating to the Inglenook alcove around the corner. Another personal favorite, it was a hideaway where you could nestle on well-balanced rocking chairs in front of a roaring fire and relax. Knowing of these escapes within the Disney resorts had always allowed Hawk an extra bit of freedom to move unnoticed, although at this time of the morning, there was really no one moving about to see him.

Jonathan joined him and sat rocking in his own chair silently for a long time before speaking.

"Do you really think Agent Batterson was going to arrest us?" he said with a smile.

"I didn't, until Shep accused her of stabbing Reginald." Hawk tilted his head. "Then she got intense."

"So did you."

"Well, things were about to get out of hand."

"True . . . so was letting her in on what's going on the best decision?" Jonathan looked at the fire as he spoke.

"It was the only decision we had left." Hawk reflected. "She had already heard us talking, she was creeping around trying to find out anything she could, and I don't think she was going to go away and leave it alone. So we're stuck with her."

The two continued to rock when Shep called out from the other room.

"I have an idea, I think," Shep said.

Hawk and Jonathan left their rocking chairs rocking a steady, slowing rhythm behind them. Shep had set up his laptop and laid out a notepad with paper beside it. They were joined by Juliette and Jillian, who had been talking by the window near the cars from the Carolwood Pacific Railroad. All four of them huddled around Shep.

After initially reading the clue, the team had tried to brainstorm, but it seemed vaguer than the previous clues. Hawk had suggested the clues Press had been giving had all been focused in Epcot, but that had been as productive as they had gotten—and even that was a dead end, as far as they could tell. Epcot had not even existed when the Walt Disney World Resort was opened, and they had quickly agreed that must be the meaning of the phrase "since the world began." They'd bogged down after that. The last forty-five minutes had been spent sharing ideas out loud, but not of them had been enough to go anywhere with. Eventually the conversation had ceased, and everyone was drawn into pondering the meaning of the clue alone.

After a while, Jillian and Juliette had withdrawn to the far corner of the room and entered into a very quiet conversation about the big Disney mystery that had consumed their lives the past few years. Hawk knew as he saw them slip away to talk that of all the friends, Juliette would best be able to explain the way they had chosen to approach this. She was better at explaining the unexplainable than anyone else Hawk had ever seen—her job over the past few years had her doing it often—and there was not one person he trusted more. He had decided to stay out of the way and keep his mouth shut. If anyone could get Agent Batterson to relax and give them the room they needed, it was Juliette.

Hawk, on the other hand, was still working the clue . . . and one other item that continued to distract him. Who had killed Reginald Cambridge, and more importantly, why? Kiran was an easy answer, and Hawk knew she was more than capable. But Kiran was a master of manipulating people and situations for her own benefit. If Cambridge was forcing Hawk to find something for him, it was more of Kiran's style to swoop in when all the work was done and steal it for herself. By nature, she was a scavenger, not a predator. Greed had split her partnership with Reginald, but why would she eliminate someone she could use or might need later?

All of his ruminations made him realize something: he didn't believe she had done it. But that brought him back to the question that plagued him. Who killed Reginald?

Pondering that question had carried him to the fireside retreat where he and Jonathan had been talking before Shep summoned them all back together.

"I don't have much, but here's what I've been doing." Shep continued to tap keys as he spoke. "I've been searching Google for some connection, something in the key words that might help us."

"How did we live BG?" Hawk said with a slight smile.

"BG?" Jillian asked.

"Before Google," Juliette answered for Hawk.

"I used the words that were capitalized and tried to come up with a hit, any kind of hint or find that might help," Shep said.

"And?" Hawk leaned over his shoulder.

"The words *success, happiness,* and *lit* mean very little in sequence, so I changed *lit* to *light* and got nothing that sparked my mind. But then I started thinking about different words or types of light."

"Like a lamp, bulb, fire, flashlight, that kind of thing?" Jillian asked. "That's how I would have approached it."

"That's what I did, thanks for the affirmation," Shep said. "But still not a lot of things I found were helpful."

"But what happened?" Hawk was anticipating some good news.

"I kept playing with the words, and then I tried the word *lantern* with *happiness* and *success.*" Shep pointed at the screen. "And be happy, for I may have had success."

They all looked toward the screen at the images that were there. The screen was lined with small squares of row after row of pictures of lanterns. Although there were a wide variety of styles, to Hawk the bulk of the images looked distinctly Japanese.

"A toro lantern is a stone lantern used to illuminate the grounds of Buddhist temples, Shinto shrines, Japanese gardens, and other locations that are steeped in tradition. They have a hollowed-out top piece where a candle or oil lamp is placed to give light. The most famous of these lanterns are the several thousand lining the entry to Nara Prefecture's Kasuga Shrine." Shep sat back from the screen and allowed them to look at what he had found. "So does that help at all?"

The entire group, including Jillian, looked toward Hawk. He studied the pictures for a few moments and then let out a soft whistle. There was something . . .

Stepping away from the table, he walked over toward the window, trying to remember a story he had heard a long time ago in his many travels through the world of Disney history. He walked restlessly as he tried to reassemble details from a long un-thought-of morsel of gourmet history. A jolt fired in his mind, and all of the story lined up. He realized they might be on to finding the next clue. Turning to face the group, he found that they were all staring at him, waiting for him to share what he was thinking. He couldn't help grinning.

"A lot of the clues we've found through the years have connected us back in some way to the life and times of Walt and Roy Disney." Hawk looked toward Jillian as he said this. "Most of the time, we think of the secrets we are finding as Walt's . . . but Roy had secrets as well."

"Roy Disney was Walt's brother." Shep directed this fact toward Agent Batterson.

"I've got that," she snapped back at him.

Hawk shook his head at Shep, silently telling him to quit pushing his luck with the federal agent. "Roy had the unimaginable task of taming a Florida swamp and reforming it into a Magic Kingdom. He came out of retirement to tackle his brother's dream, and it became Roy's dream as well. Apparently, Emperor Hirohito of Japan was a huge fan of Disney. In 1975 he took an exclusive tour of Disneyland and was given a Mickey Mouse watch as a gift. On formal occasions, the emperor was known to wear this watch. It was one of his most cherished possessions. There was almost a national crisis in Japan in 1979 when the watch stopped ticking. The story was reported in *Time* magazine. Someone in the palace rushed it off to Tokyo to find a specialist in American timepieces. They discovered that the watch simply needed a new battery, and the crisis was averted."

Jonathan injected an observation. "But we've been thinking the clue was referring to the opening of the Magic Kingdom and the resort when it says 'since the world began,' right?"

"Yes, but we also have been focusing on Epcot, because that is where the other clues have been located," Hawk responded.

"But the dates are not making sense to me. The story you just told about Roy's friend the emperor of Japan happened in 1975 and 1979, years after the Magic Kingdom opened and Roy had passed away." Jonathan shrugged. "So all you have told us is that a Japanese emperor had a Mickey Mouse watch and was a friend of Roy's. Can you throw a little light on the story with, I dunno, a lamp or maybe a lantern for us?"

"Hang on." Hawk smiled as he continued the story. "When Walt Disney World opened in 1971, there were at least two Japanese companies exploring the possibility of opening a Disney theme park in Japan. Official talks with lawyers began in 1974, and they signed a contract in 1979. So the watch incident unfolded during the ongoing connection between Japan and Disney. The relationship between the company and the nation started years before that, and as a token of goodwill between Japan and Disney, Emperor Hirohito personally presented to Roy Disney, for the dedication of the Magic Kingdom in 1971, *a Japanese lantern to light the way to success and happiness.* It was a toro lantern."

"No way." Shep sat back in his chair, pleased with how the clue was making sense.

"How do you know that?" Jillian looked from Hawk to the others in the room. "That story, where did it come from? Who knows that kind of stuff?"

"Scary, isn't it?" Juliette offered a reassuring smile. "That's how his much cluttered brain works. If it's a Disney fact or some piece of obscure Disney trivia, he tends to know it. What really makes it interesting is that he'll usually take the trivia and find some deeper meaning."

"And most of the time there *is* a deeper meaning." Jonathan looked from the federal agent back to Hawk. "And so there is a toro lantern here on property?"

"As a matter of fact, there is." Hawk smiled triumphantly. "At Epcot. For nearly ten years the lantern was on display, without any signage telling people what it really was, at the Polynesian Resort. When Epcot opened the World Showcase with a Japanese pavilion, the stone lantern was moved there. It's still there at the entrance, across from the eighth-century pagoda inspired by the Horyuji Temple in Nara."

"'Since the world began' . . . the opening of Walt Disney World. 'This Disney gift,' which is a gift to Walt's brother Roy, from the emperor of Japan, 'has lit the way to success and happiness' because it is a toro lantern, and that is one of the things they are supposed to do." Jillian Batterson allowed herself to smile, impressed at how they had solved the clue. "And it's sitting out in the open somewhere inside Epcot?"

"You've got it." Juliette started to move toward the exit.

"So what happens now?" Jillian turned her question to Hawk.

"Simple. Now we go to Epcot and see what we can find."

Leaving Jillian to come along behind, he followed Juliette toward the doorway.

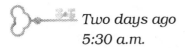 *Two days ago*
5:30 a.m.

HAWK GLANCED AT HIS WATCH as he and Jillian entered the area of Epcot's Japanese pavilion. It wouldn't be long before the sun rose over Walt Disney World and a new day full of fun and excitement for people from all over the planet would begin. The red torii gate in the lagoon welcomed guests to the pavilion. Similar to gates found throughout Japan, this particular torii gate was based upon the one that serves as the entrance to the Itsukushima Shrine on the Inland Sea. In Japanese design, the gates were originally conceived as perches for roosters to welcome the new day.

Hawk had kept the pair moving along the waterline, trying to stay in the shadows wherever possible as they navigated around the World Showcase Lagoon. Shep had remained behind, using the Iron Spike Room as their temporary command center. Juliette had securely nestled herself along the edge of the Victoria Gardens in the Canada pavilion, keeping watch for anyone or anything out of the ordinary that might pose a threat to what they were trying to do. Canada was the first pavilion anyone would enter coming from the main entrance and to the right.

Jonathan had mirrored the plan by moving to the left and hiding himself along the far side of Mexico's pyramid. The plan was simple and practical: if either saw anything that raised suspicion, they would alert Hawk.

Jillian had insisted that she was going with Hawk to search for the next clue. They both knew she wouldn't be much help when it came to Disney trivia, but she had other skills and would help any way she could.

The massive stone lantern that had been given to Roy Disney sat to the right hand side of the main entrance into the pavilion. No marker told the story of how this lantern had come to be placed where it was. A strategic decision years ago had suggested that although this was a part of Disney history, it was not a part of the Japanese history or story that the Imagineers were trying to tell in this pavilion.

Not only that, Hawk thought, but one of the Imagineers had known there would come a day when Hawk would need to find it. Once again, they had been able to keep something hidden in plain sight, in front of the eyes of thousands of people each day.

Stepping up into the soft green grass surrounding the lantern, Hawk felt his foot sink into the plush landscaping. The serenity of this pavilion with its nods to traditional Japanese culture was evident from the moment you entered. The trees, shrubs, and manicured turf provided a picturesque location for this very real piece of history to call home.

"What do we do?" Jillian whispered to Hawk as she surveyed the massive structure in front of them.

Hawk didn't answer as he made his way around the stone structure. To call it a lantern was misleading—it was more like a statue or monument, and most guests would conclude that as they glanced toward it on their way into the pavilion. Even Hawk had never really inspected the structure until now. He reached down to see if there was any place on its base that might contain a switch, a button, or some type of compartment where a clue or item might be placed. Jillian quickly picked up on his strategy and began to search the opposite side.

"Anything?" Hawk whispered as he stood up.

"No, nothing here," Jillian responded in a hushed tone.

Hawk reached up to the top of the lantern and worked his hands along the outer edge. Finding nothing along the cool gray stone, he now moved his hands inside the lantern . . . and discovered that there was a ledge hidden inside the upper portion of the lantern. He stepped back and looked at it closely. There was no way to see it from the perimeter of the lantern. This had to be discovered by touch alone. He moved his hand back inside the lantern and began to slide it along the ledge.

Jillian's eyes widened as she watched Hawk search. She stepped back to his side and leaned in, trying to see what he was doing. Suddenly Hawk's fingers ran across what felt like a piece of paper. Fingertip poking the edge of it, he placed a finger on top and slid it toward the edge of the ledge, allowing him to pinch it between his fingers. He looked at Jillian and smiled as he retrieved the discovery and pulled it out of the lantern, holding it up so they could both see. It was a small, note-sized envelope.

"That's it, right?" Jillian moved closer.

"Let's find out." Hawk flipped the envelope over in his hand and prepared to tear the end of it open.

His phone vibrated in his pocket, interrupting him. Tilting his chin down and frowning at the distraction, he saw the call was from Jonathan. He slid his finger across the screen and held the device to his ear.

"Hey Jon, what's going on?"

"You've got company headed your way." Jonathan's voice echoed softly. He was whispering. "Three armed visitors. Black uniforms, hoods covering their faces, they are definitely not cast members." There was an urgency in his voice.

"Got it, thanks." Hawk was stone-faced like the lantern as he ended the call and motioned for Jillian to follow him.

"What's wrong?"

"Three unexpected guests have just come through the Mexico pavilion headed our way."

"They're coming after us?" Jillian asked.

Hawk raised an eyebrow. "They're dressed in black, wearing hoods, and armed. They're not waiting for the attractions to open."

With Hawk leading the way, they headed the opposite direction around the World Showcase. Hawk knew the sheer size of the showcase gave them plenty of time to escape, and the three were a long way behind them, but he glanced back over his shoulder nervously anyway. This time instead of moving along the waterline, he chose to duck in and out of the entrances to the pavilions. If they had to find a hiding place from searching eyes, it would be easier in the pavilions.

Jillian kept up with ease as they jogged beyond the Morocco pavilion and into France. Most of the design of this pavilion took its inspiration from the city of Paris. During the period between 1850 and 1900, known by most as the Beautiful Age, Baron Haussmann was the master planner of the city, and he created the aesthetic design that made Paris one of the most recognized and beautiful cities in the world. The beauty translated into Epcot and allowed Hawk and Jillian arcade entrances, sidewalk cafes, and water fountains surrounded by gardens to navigate and hide behind as they moved.

"Who is after us? And when I say us, I really mean you?" Jillian breathed toward Hawk as they ducked behind a fountain and scurried around a sidewalk.

"I'm not sure. Someone who is working with Kiran. Maybe whoever killed Reginald. Maybe someone else." Hawk paused and thought. "In the past when someone has been after me, it hasn't been armed teams. At least, not that I am aware of."

"You have a very strange life here in Disneyland." Jillian shook her head.

"Walt Disney World," Hawk corrected.

"What?"

"You said Disneyland. Disneyland is in California, we are in Florida, so we are in Walt Disney World."

"Same thing." Jillian waved him off as she continued to follow him.

"I promise you, it is nothing close to the same thing." Hawk turned and slowed. The area just ahead would expose them to anyone who was watching, but they had to pass through if they were going to keep moving.

Just as he got ready to move out, his phone once again notified him there was a call coming in. This time it was Juliette. Like before, he slid his finger across the screen and waited.

"Hawk?" Juliette's voice came in a barely audible whisper.

"Yes, are you okay?"

"There is a team of three men heading toward you from Canada. They're headed into the United Kingdom pavilion right now. They are armed, they are wearing hoods, and they are dressed completely in black. Whatever you are doing, you need to hide." Her whispered voice was strained with tension.

"Got it." Hawk's eyes instantly turned to look in the other direction. "We've got more company," he told Jillian bluntly. "They're coming at us from both sides."

Hawk was already up and moving. No longer trying to hide in the shadows, he realized they were about to be trapped. With adversaries closing in from both sides, there was no way out of the Showcase . . . except one. Jillian followed him closely as he ran toward the United Kingdom.

"Are we running toward them?" Jillian's half-whisper as they sprinted was overly loud.

"They're coming both ways," Hawk restated. "We have to move."

"Move where?"

"Here." Hawk slowed as they crested the bridge between the France pavilion and the United Kingdom. The bridge was a replica of the pedestrian bridge Pont des Arts, which crosses over the Seine River. In the World Showcase it takes guests across a canal that connects the World Showcase

Lagoon with the International Gateway, a back entrance into Epcot accessible from Disney's Boardwalk Resort. The entrance was primarily used by guests staying at the resort or locals who took advantage of the lesser-known ways to travel into Epcot.

"What's here?" Jillian slowed to a stop on the bridge behind Hawk and strained her eyes in the dawn, scanning for the intruders.

"Let's go." Hawk stepped to the rail of the bridge.

"I asked before, where?"

"We're going to jump."

Jillian didn't react. Hawk turned to see that she had reached into her jacket and was holding her gun, leveling it back across the bridge toward anyone who might be headed their way.

"Seriously?" Hawk grabbed her arm and spun her toward him. "By my count there are at least six people, all armed, headed toward us. You have a handgun, and I'm sure you're good with it. But unless you think you are going to flash your Homeland Security badge and they are going to lay their weapons down, we are outgunned and in trouble here. You need to trust me and jump."

Jillian's gaze darted toward both sides of the bridge. She licked her lips, holstered her gun under her jacket, and nodded. Following Hawk's lead, she stepped over the rail, and they both paused, perched on the edge of the bridge. He tapped her on the arm and leaped.

A hollow sound surrounded him and filled his head as he submerged beneath the cool, dark water. Temporarily swallowed up in the slow-moving river, he pushed through the current away from where they had splashed into the wet escape. A quick kick brought him back to the surface, and he took a gulp of air and looked to his right as Jillian surfaced as well. Silently he reached out and touched her arm, motioning for her to follow him. The water wasn't terribly deep, but it was deep enough for boat traffic to navigate. They made their way to the edge of the canal and slowly began to swim, kick, and glide through the water. They stayed low, slowly drifting through the water. Floating, trying to remain unseen against the surface, keeping their bodies submerged with only their faces out of the dark water.

Sunlight was beginning to dance across the morning, and the reflection off the water gave them an additional layer of cover. As they swam, Hawk glanced back and saw three men run across the bridge toward the France pavilion. He felt a swell of gratitude and relief. That had been a narrow escape, even for them.

They silently swam along the canal connecting them to Crescent Lake, the waterway that gave Disney's Boardwalk Resort a waterfront to hug. Originally envisioned as a village across the water, the Boardwalk's friendly row of restaurants, shops, and galleries was a welcome sight as they swam their way to safety.

As the morning sun rose over the Walt Disney World Resort, Grayson Hawkes and Agent Jillian Batterson emerged from Crescent Lake along the white sandy shores of Disney's Beach Club Resort. They were wet, soggy, and safe for the moment. They slogged their way across the sand, which stuck to them as they moved.

"I forgot to ask you if you could swim." Hawk smiled at Jillian.

She laughed. "You think of asking that now?"

The moved up toward the lobby of the resort. Walking across the concrete pathways for guests, they left a drip trail along the sidewalk.

Hawk became aware that he was walking alone and turned to see that Jillian had stopped. She was gazing back toward Epcot in the distance. Securely hidden by trees, she could look back and know that no one could see her. Her hand rubbed her neck as she was lost in some thought, and then she turned to see Hawk looking back at her. Quickly she moved to rejoin him.

"What is it?" he asked.

"It's you. This thing you are doing . . . you are not what I expected, and this is bizarre. I have just been chased out of Epcot by six armed gunmen because you are on some sort of treasure hunt." Her voice trailed off as she looked at him. "What are you looking for?"

"I ask myself that question every day." He took her arm and gave it a slight tug for her to follow. "Welcome to my world."

CHAPTER 34

Two days ago
7:30 a.m.

HAWK WAITED AS JILLIAN TOOK a chair at the restaurant table, then slid down into one of the red chairs himself. Smiling wearily at Juliette, he waited for her to end her phone conversation. As he leaned forward on the table, he realized she was talking to Al Gann, who must have been giving her an update on the armed hunters who had been stalking him. She shook her head, her expression grim, and he knew that the gunmen had escaped.

Beaches and Cream was a fifties-style soda fountain that offered old-fashioned favorites, tucked near the pool of Disney's Beach Club Resort. Red vinyl booths lined one wall, with iron parlor chairs and tables in the center. Hawk, Juliette, Shep, Jonathan, and Jillian surrounded one of the round tables inside the deserted restaurant.

Flexing his influence, Hawk had secured this area as a private place for them to meet. There would be no guests inside until it opened at lunchtime, when the jukebox would begin to play, the grill would start sizzling, and the milkshake machines would whir as the place filled to overflowing. It was another hidden treasure within the resort. Hawk would often drop by for a six-cheese grilled cheese sandwich and tomato soup, his favorite menu selection here.

Borrowing some towels from the pool area, Hawk and Jillian had dried off as best they could, and then Hawk used one of the landlines from the resort to contact his friends. Each had arrived shortly thereafter, Juliette and Jonathan wearing their concern on their faces. Giving a mandate that would keep the dining room free of cast members for at least an hour, Hawk himself had managed to make coffee for the group. Shep was the last to arrive, and once he had loaded his mug with coffee, he joined the group.

"What made you decide to dive off the bridge?" Juliette asked Hawk as she sipped from her cup.

"Desperation." Hawk grinned. "Jon had called, so we were sneaking our way toward you, then you called . . . we were out of options."

"So you improvised?" Juliette used the cup to hide her smile.

"No." Hawk smiled wryly. "It was a well calculated, well thought-out plan. It gave us our best probability of success. After I took a few seconds to calculate it, I implemented it."

"Sure you did." Jillian laughed. "'Let's jump' was your big plan."

"It worked," Hawk countered with a grin. "You were going to have a shoot-out right there in the World Showcase."

"If they wanted a fight, I was going to give them a fight." She held up her hands. "That's all I'm saying."

"They didn't want a fight, they wanted you." Jonathan brought the group back the moment as he pointed at Hawk. "And whatever you found. You did find something, didn't you?"

"I did." Hawk took a very moist piece of paper out of his pocket and gently unfolded it.

Trying not to let it tear, he carefully flattened it, and Juliette dabbed it with a napkin to help it dry. He then moved his hand back, and each person read it silently.

Walt, Wernher, and Babson
Before his last days figured out
what It is, how It works, and how It may be controlled
it remains at the UT Archway

The coffee pot burped and hissed as the fresh pot Hawk had started finished. Shep opened up his electronic tablet and began touching the screen, trying to connect some words and phrases.

"Wernher?" Jillian asked. "As in Wernher von Braun?"

"Yes, he and Walt were old friends," Juliette answered before Hawk had the chance.

"Walt Disney and the main man of the American Space Program were friends?" Jillian asked. Was that a new note of respect in her eyes?

"Yes," Hawk answered. "It is amazing the influence Walt had. His friends and acquaintances were far more extensive than most people realize, because he was a man who was always pushing the limits of what had to be done so we could discover what could be. Wernher referred to Walt as a genius, one of the smartest men he had ever met."

Even as he said the words, Hawk's mind flashed to the work Wernher von Braun had entrusted to Walt Disney. Hawk had found the book inside the metal mountain of Space Mountain. The handwritten journal had been loaded with notes on things conspiracy theorists had wondered about for years. Wernher had given it to Walt as they visited together in 1965. Walt died before he could ever do anything with the information it contained, but he did manage to figure out how to keep it safe. It was one of the many secrets that had been entrusted to Hawk to preserve—and to figure out what to do with them, a responsibility Hawk considered almost sacred.

Hawk had taken some time off after Kate was killed. He had devoured the contents of the journal and read it over and over again. Some of it he understood, other parts were so technical that he could not get a handle on what they meant, and other sections were so startling in the ramifications of what might be created that it frightened him. Hawk had memorized every note Walt had written in the notebook in his very distinct penmanship. Scribbling in grease pencil, like he was marking a movie script, Walt had placed notes, thoughts, and additional remarks throughout like a commentary. He had also memorized the back page of the book, a handwritten note from Wernher von Braun to Walt Disney.

Walt, what you have here are things I don't think the world is ready for. I believe these discoveries can revolutionize what we know about energy and power, and in the right hands could accomplish great good. In the wrong hands, they could be used to control others. So I am placing them in your hands. I am hoping you can figure out how we can best use them, when we can share them, and who we can trust. Wernher.

And now suddenly, the names of Walt Disney and Wernher von Braun were a part of a clue again. But there was also an additional name, one Hawk had never heard before.

"Hawk . . ." Shep's voice came echoing through the reflection of his thoughts, dragging him back into the present. "Babson might be . . . no, *has* to be . . . Roger W. Babson."

Hawk shook his head. "Who is that?"

"As I am reading here," Shep pointed to the screen, "he is connected, loosely, to von Braun. No connection to Walt that I am aware of, though."

"Explain," Jillian said.

"Roger Babson founded something called the Gravity Research Foundation."

Jillian's eyes lit. "And Wernher von Braun was reported not only to have discovered a way to escape gravity using rocket propulsion but also to have found some ripple in how gravity works and some type of anti-gravity propulsion as well."

"Wow, you know your conspiracy theory." Hawk was impressed. "For years people have thought that von Braun had discovered something far greater than rocket propulsion."

"I have to know conspiracy theory, I'm Homeland Security," Agent Batterson replied. "There are a million nut jobs out there convinced of unseen forces, some unknown agenda, and some great plot to overthrow the world. It makes people do crazy things."

Hawk let her statement hang in the air. Time stood still, and then she locked eyes with his. Leaning forward across the table, she reached out and grabbed his hand as he tried to take another swig of coffee.

"Just what was Walt Disney hiding? Is this just about some nutty conspiracy theory, some freaky cartoon movie plot unfolding for real in Walt Disney's land?" Jillian frowned.

"That would be Walt Disney World," Shep corrected.

"I've got it, Junior," she snapped back. "Please tell me this is not a bunch of whacked-out conspiracy nuts who are trying to kill you and everyone else who gets in the way."

Hawk looked at her and shrugged. "You tell me."

"No, *you* tell *me*." She continued to keep her firm grip on his arm. "What exactly did Wernher von Braun share with Walt Disney? I think you know. What do you have that everyone wants?"

"I'm sorry, I'm not going to tell you." Hawk stared back at her, a bead of sweat starting to form along his hairline.

"Now we're back to obstruction charges." She tightened her grip on his arm. Her gaze was once again unrelenting and her tone intense. "Conspiracy nuts are some of the most dangerous people out there, because they aren't even connected to any rational cause. There is no reasonable way of figuring them out. What are you hiding that they want, Hawk?"

A tapping on the table caught everyone's attention. Juliette was tapping a fingernail on the tabletop, demanding they look back toward the clue. They all turned to her, and she caught eyes with both Hawk and Jillian.

"You can arrest Hawk later for obstruction. It will keep him out of trouble for a while. But for now, let's get back to the clue."

Jillian released her iron grip on Hawk's arm. She narrowed her eyes as she did, her look an unspoken reminder that they would pick this conversation back up again later. Hawk let out a breath he didn't know he'd been holding and turned back to the clue with gratitude for Juliette's rescue.

"This Babson guy was an interesting one. Apparently he dropped a bunch of money in the form of grants to colleges across the country that were doing research on how to control gravity," Shep said, sounding pleased that attention was back on him where it belonged.

"Control gravity?" Jonathan leaned back. "How do you do that? What goes up must come down. Right?"

"Well, according to this, Babson's foundation wanted to release the world from the confines of gravity. Each year, there has been a contest that gives prizes to some of the most brilliant scientists as they figure out space travel, how to manipulate time, quantum physics . . . some pretty heady stuff."

"And what does this have to do with the clue?" Hawk asked.

"The UT Archway," Shep said triumphantly. Everyone looked blankly at him, and he hurried to explain, "It's a road on the campus of the University of Tampa where the Gravity Research Foundation has placed a tombstone."

"What did they bury?" Hawk placed his cup down on the table.

"It is a memorial to gravity. The death of gravity as we know it."

"You have got to be kidding," Jillian said.

"The guy sounds like a nut," Juliette agreed.

"Nut or not," Hawk drew them back to the moment, "that is the next clue. I need to get to Tampa."

"I can get you there." Jonathan pushed his chair back and got to his feet. "I'll need about an hour."

"Great." Hawk nodded. "That gives me time to get ready. How many seats in the plane?"

"It will be a two-seater," Jon replied.

Hawk looked back across the table toward Jillian. She didn't look as put out as he expected.

"Don't worry about me. I have plenty to do now. For starters, I am getting ready to unleash a holy rain of fire on whoever tried to hunt us down this morning. I am going to be giving your friend the sheriff a call and catch them up on what happened."

She paused and ran her hand through her hair. "I am also going to tell him about this conspiracy nonsense you are caught up in. You should have told him. And if he knows and has been keeping it a secret, he has to give an account for that. Just don't get killed while you are gone."

"Your concern is heartwarming." Hawk smiled.

"This is not a game or a fairy tale you're living out, Hawk." Jillian wagged her finger at him. "You're resourceful and resilient, I will give you that. But there are some crazies out there who will do whatever they think is best to get what they want. And you are playing with them. That makes you as crazy as they are."

"I've been called worse." Hawk got to his feet. If she only knew how acquainted he was with the tactics of these "crazies." Sadness weighed on him for a moment, but he shook it off.

"You aren't kidding." Juliette smiled sweetly at him. "I, for one, am going to take a break from the chase. I am going to see if I can bring some order to the chaos of this company you are in charge of. Last time I checked, I had a few million dollars' worth of artwork here on sight that we are supposed to be getting ready to display."

"I forgot all about the art exhibit!" Hawk suddenly remembered.

Jillian shook her head. "A multimillion-dollar art exhibit . . . another prime target for thieves, nut jobs, terrorists, extortionists, and the everyday run-of-the-mill thug. You people just can't keep from opening up the doors for the lunatics to jump out of the clown car and come stumbling in."

"Jonathan, I'll be ready in an hour. In the meantime, I have someone I need to talk with." Hawk began to make his way to the door.

Juliette followed and caught him while another conversation broke out around the table. She leaned in close so no one could overhear.

"You know, Jillian may be on to something here." She glanced back toward the agent at the table. "This might be more out of control than we realize."

Hawk stubbornly set his jaw. "Nothing is any different than it was before, except now we are putting more pieces in this puzzle. I told you I was going to finish it this time. I *am* going to finish it." Hawk put his hand on her shoulder. "Don't worry. I will be safe."

"That makes me feel much better. You and playing it safe haven't been on speaking terms for years."

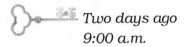 *Two days ago*
9:00 a.m.

THE LARGE REDDISH ORB, easily identifiable as the planet Mars, reminded Hawk of what an amazing and inspirational attraction Mission: SPACE really was. The otherworldly look of the planet was achieved by using a color-shifting paint that cost over $800 a gallon, making it some of the most valuable paint on Earth.

Leaning forward into his brisk walk, Hawk listened as the words of John F. Kennedy played in the courtyard: "We choose to go to the moon, not because it is easy but because it is hard." A quick glance at the giant replica of the moon reminded him of the risk and daring of explorers. The markers displaying all of the lunar landing locations never ceased to amaze him, and he wondered what it would be like to travel to a place that so few had ever set foot upon.

Moving inside the entrance area of the attraction, he found himself instantly immersed in the storytelling genius of Imagineering. He was walking inside the International Space Training Center. Words of greeting looped constantly in Italian, Russian, Chinese, and English. With a slight smile, he ducked out of the main thoroughfare into an area most guests would never see—a lounge created for special guests. This second-floor exclusive area featured cast members, refreshments, specially designed seating areas, and additional entertainment options from television, reading material, and electronic showcase pieces designed for the sponsor of the lounge.

Special lounges like this weren't uncommon inside Disney attractions. This one would let special guests view the waiting area of the ride through one set of windows and gave a spectacular view of Epcot through the windowed wall on the other side. Reaching the back of the room, he used his kingdom key to open an locked door and found himself in a hallway that ran the length of the attraction. His footsteps echoed off of the bland walls as he passed nondescript metal doors and approached the door at the far end of the hallway. Pausing and looking back down the hall behind him to see if had been followed, he knocked twice. The door quietly opened, and Hawk looked into the smiling face of Ollie Leslie.

Ollie was a long-time resident of the small apartment he kept on the second floor of Mission: SPACE. He had actually been a human clue, much like Thomas Dudley, with a story to tell entrusted to him by an Imagineer on behalf of Walt and Roy Disney. Ollie had proven to be an expert story-teller. He was so good at the craft, in fact, that Hawk had falsely believed at one point that he was actually the third Imagineer. Convinced now he was not, Hawk had nevertheless taken up Ollie's invitation to come and visit him here many times. Ollie had been given this place to dwell in the design of Epcot because of his expertise on space, space travel, and the possibilities of what might be in the future. He was a dreamer who understood the past and was able to apply its lessons to the future. It was a rare ability that most did not have.

The small living area centered on an oval area rug, with chairs and a small couch positioned atop it. A well-worn pair of television trays nearly bowed under the weight of the books, magazines, and a single computer monitor that were stacked on them. This was Ollie's home, office, and research center. Hawk had always found the stories that Ollie told him enlightening and challenging. He had come for another story this time.

"I hear tell that you've been very busy these days." Ollie took a seat on the sofa and motioned Hawk toward a chair. "The rumor mill says someone nearly blew up the theme parks and that something horrific has happened in the Magic Kingdom."

"The rumor mill?" Hawk smiled at his old friend. "Who's sharing and passing along those kind of rumors?"

"Oh, you know . . . I may be old, but I have my sources. Not that I plan on telling you who they are. That would take away the fun of having you wonder how I know what I know, now wouldn't it?" Ollie's grin announced that he was pleased with himself.

"I suppose it would." Hawk leaned back and sighed. "What can you tell me about a man named Roger Babson?"

"Ah, I knew there would come a day when you might ask me that." Ollie nodded his approval.

"You did?"

"Of course I did. Since I was the one who first introduced you to the connection between Wernher von Braun and Walt Disney, I always knew that at some point you would have to ask about Babson."

"Did the three know each other?"

"No, not really." Ollie closed his eyes before continuing. "Walt's only connection with Roger Babson would have been through Wernher. Wernher was very aware of Babson's work. They had some mutual friends, and they would have periodically bumped into one another at various places, conferences and such, and I am sure they corresponded."

"So what's his story?" Hawk leaned forward.

"Roger Babson had an enemy. Gravity. It was his lifelong nemesis. Roger had a sister who drowned as a teenager, and he blamed gravity for her death. He went on to become a millionaire businessman, and he founded a place called the Gravity Research Foundation to find a way to defeat it." Ollie locked his fingers together as he spoke.

"And the connection to Wernher von Braun was because, in the field of rocketry and developing engines to send things into outer space, von Braun was also an enemy of gravity. He was always trying to figure out how to defeat it," Hawk stated.

"Correct." Ollie looked at Hawk thoughtfully. "Many people believe the secrets that von Braun discovered were the key to defeating gravity once and for all."

Hawk sat back in the chair a bit uncomfortably. Ollie's statement told him that although Ollie had a sense of the bigness of the secret Wernher von Braun had shared with Walt Disney, he didn't know any details as to what it was. Hawk intended to keep things that way for Ollie's own well-being. He sometimes second-guessed his commitment to secrecy, but he couldn't put his friends at risk.

"And that relates to Babson how?" Hawk asked.

"Babson gave big dollar grants and stock to universities and colleges that were doing research on how to defeat and control gravity. It involved lots of physics, quantum physics, and awards where some of the best and brightest would submit papers and research to win prize money and have their work published in journals. So although he started with some very suspect methodology, he eventually went on to fund some pretty important research, and he helped give a forum to those who were trying to push the limits of what was known and understood." Ollie waited, allowing his words to sink in. "Babson provided over a dozen universities with memorials put up in exchange for the grants he gave their programs. They were to memorialize the demise of gravity."

"I'm getting ready to go find one." Hawk offered no more detail.

Ollie nodded—not surprised, but intent. "Then be very careful. It sounds like the rumors I have heard are true, and you are on a quest again."

"As always, I just don't know how it all fits together . . . yet."

"Well, you have always navigated it and figured it out. But can I give you some more help?"

"Please, by all means." Hawk again sat back.

"It's in the form of a story." Ollie laughed.

"I had no doubt." Hawk laughed as well.

"I don't know what you know. But I do know what I have told you before about Walt's old friend Wernher von Braun. Conspiracy theorists for years have believed and shared the stories that Wernher discovered something far greater than jet propulsion—that he stumbled across, researched, and figured out the secrets of anti-gravity propulsion and what it took to power it." Ollie's square face radiated a gentleness that rippled across the deep lines of age that gave it character. Those lines thinned as he smiled briefly, then continued.

"Some believe that Wernher von Braun understood this power and not only knew it but feared it. He knew that the world was not ready for it. There were some, he knew after his years in Nazi Germany, who could effectively dominate the entire world if they could control it. That is how great his discoveries were." Ollie squinted his eyes for a moment before continuing. "At least, that is what conspiracy theorists say. It can't be true, because it is too far-fetched. Right?"

"Right." Hawk was emotionless.

"But if I were you, I would be trying to figure out what all of this had to do with Walt Disney. And I have to tell you, I have no idea. But I have a *theory*. Not a conspiracy theory, just a theory based on enough fact to keep me curious. You want to hear it?"

Hawk sat up a little straighter. He hadn't expected this. "Of course."

"I thought you might. And maybe, my theory might just help you out a little bit. The more you know, the better you might be able to understand the enemy and stop them." Ollie smiled and rubbed his hands together. "So here goes. Let me tell you something I have always wondered about." His eyes sparkled just a bit with a hint of excitement. "You well know that Epcot was Walt Disney's ulti-mate dream. The Experimental Prototype Community of Tomorrow was going to be Walt's crowning achievement. The theme park of today is built on some of those ideas, but it's nothing like the world Walt envisioned."

Hawk nodded, and Ollie went on.

"What you don't know is that Walt Disney believed firmly that Epcot would succeed and that the cutting-edge technology to make it work would come from American industry. The year he died, he spent a great deal of time and effort meeting with technology giants to pitch them his Epcot concept and see if they would jump in and participate. Two different com-panies, Westinghouse and General Electric, were some of the most intrigu-ing to Walt."

"Why were they so intriguing?" Hawk spoke in a hushed tone, as if someone might overhear what Ollie said next. Curiosity was coursing through him.

"Walt gave each company a presentation on Epcot and then was given a tour of the company's research and development labs. Real top-secret, state-of-the-art stuff to be sure. He saw cutting-edge laser technologies, and at Westinghouse, he was shown something called the Skybus, which was at that time an automated transportation system. Walt was impressed and wanted to take the concept and develop it to be used at Epcot."

"That is fascinating, but . . ." Hawk was intrigued but not making the connection that Ollie was trying to get him to make.

"Don't rob me of the fun of my story." Ollie folded his hands across his lap. "Walt spoke with each of the companies with the intent of getting them to help him build better cities, the city he was dreaming of, the Disney world of tomorrow. He gave them blueprints, concept art, and enough detail to intrigue them. They gave Walt a sneak preview at what they were doing as well. But Walt was doing more than just seeing if they were interested in helping build Epcot."

"What else was he doing?"

"He was auditioning them." Ollie once again grinned. He knew Hawk wouldn't understand yet.

"For what?"

"To see if they were ready to be a part of developing Epcot. I think Walt knew a lot more about how to build the city than they did. He was looking for people he could trust with the technology he was already developing at

WED and see if they were ready to take it to another level." Ollie's expression turned very serious. "Of course, that is only a theory, my theory based on what I know about Walt, his friendship with great innovators, and what I believe Wernher von Braun had discovered."

Hawk frowned, trying to put together what Ollie was saying. "You think Walt Disney was developing state-of-the-art technologies beyond what he was using in his theme parks and the World's Fairs, so he could do something that would revolutionize the way people lived . . . in cities . . . like Epcot?" Hawk tilted his head.

"Why not?"

"How revolutionary was the technology he was working on?"

"So revolutionary that he had to create a plan to protect it, had to choose the right people to share it with, and had to decide whether or not the world was ready for it." Ollie sighed. "It is something far bigger than most could ever imagine."

"You couldn't keep that a secret. If he had been doing that at WED, someone would know." Hawk paused. "Wouldn't they?"

"Walt thought of WED as his backyard laboratory, a workshop away from work. He knew his ideas were far too abstract for most investors to understand, and WED Enterprises allowed him to develop his ideas to a point where people would begin to recognize the potential. He was using WED to develop a number of things. When Walt died in 1966, Roy hadn't even been in the WED building for years. He had no idea of all that was going on there. Then WED was acquired by Walt Disney Productions, and Roy caught a glimpse of how big his brother's vision really was. He realized just how important it was to protect the Disney legacy and all the secrets Walt was responsible for. So there was a plan locked into place. The decision was made to preserve what Walt had been doing, and they reworked the way everything was structured. Without Walt, there was no WED. Roy made the necessary changes. When Walt Disney Productions was rebranded into the Walt Disney Company in 1987, WED Enterprises became Walt Disney Imagineering."

"That is a big theory." Hawk thought about all he had just heard.

"And if it is right, how valuable are the secrets Walt was working on? How much would someone spend to get them? How far or to what extremes would someone go to control them? If these secrets were as big as I believe they were . . . why wouldn't someone use them to do whatever they wanted to?" Ollie held his head high. "Those are the kind of secrets worth dying for."

CHAPTER 36

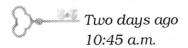 *Two days ago*
10:45 a.m.

THE TWO-SEATER PIPER TOMAHAWK descended through the ominous skies of the Central Florida morning. Built back in the 1980s, this classic airplane was one of Jonathan's favorites and had been one of his first purchases after he got his pilot's license. Hawk had pressed his skill set into service on a number of occasions, taking full advantage of Jonathan's hobby. He was always happy to offer assistance.

The flight had been bumpy, the light plane jostled by the threatening storminess of the Florida morning. The airfield in Kissimmee they'd flown out of cautioned them to delay their flight until the storm cell had passed. Hawk had insisted they didn't have the time, and Jonathan was confident the weather would hold until they made it to their destination.

As the plane leapt and dropped, Hawk remained silent, almost not noticing. He was replaying the conversation with Ollie. Ollie's theory made a lot of sense, but Ollie was suggesting something far beyond the notes Hawk possessed. The journal entries for both Walt and Wernher had been sketches, drawings, thoughts, and formulas. There was nothing in the journals to suggest that either man had figured out a way to actually create the things they had theorized about.

The plane suddenly dropped, and Hawk looked out the window and saw an airstrip come into sight below.

Nearly ninety miles southwest of Disney World, Jonathan safely landed the plane in the city of Tampa. Taxiing down the runway and stashing the plane safely in a hangar, they sprinted across the tarmac into the small office, where they picked up the rental car they had reserved. Thunder clapped across the sky as they sped out of the airport.

Accelerating the car west on Kennedy Boulevard, they raced across the bridge toward downtown. Taking a sharp right, they found themselves on the campus of the University of Tampa, a beautiful campus tucked away in the large city. Their car disappeared into a different world, lush and green, secluded from the hustle and bustle of Tampa. Jonathan and Hawk discussed which way they needed to go when Hawk looked out the window and saw the sign marked University Avenue. The directions he'd been able to track down were sketchy at best. There was not a lot of information available about the memorial.

"I knew we weren't lost," said Hawk in jest.

"But we haven't found what we're looking for, yet," Jonathan replied dubiously.

They drove straight down University Avenue toward the back of the campus as the road took a slight bend to the left.

"Are you sure you know where we're going?" Jon peered out the window at the unfamiliar sights. The administrative buildings, unmarked roadways, and driveways made navigation tougher than both had anticipated. The shallow canyon of buildings disoriented them as they looked for a landmark that would be helpful.

"We're supposed to be going to the library." Hawk continued to search for a directional sign that might help them on their way.

Light rain dotted the windshield. Hawk fumbled trying to find the wiper switch. After a few tries the blades of the wipers stretched across the window, allowing them to see clearly.

"Hey, don't miss that STOP sign," Jonathan said, pointing out the windshield.

Hawk, who had been looking out the driver's-side window, had almost missed it. "I see it!" Hawk said louder than he intended as his foot slammed on the brakes.

The car screeched to a halt, the slick pavement adding an additional moment of hesitation before it stopped. Both the driver and the passenger were shoved toward the dashboard for a moment before they rocked back into their seats.

"Nice stop," smirked Jonathan.

"Just like I planned it," said Hawk.

As the car idled at the stop sign, both looked out the window to orient themselves to their surroundings. Hawk pointed to a sign on their right that read "MacDonald-Kelce Library." Jonathan followed his gaze. The crosswalk had placed them very close to where they had been trying to go.

"Like I told you. I planned it this way." Hawk smiled as he continued to explore his surroundings through the windows of the car.

"What is it we are looking for again?" asked Jonathan.

On the left end of the crosswalk was a gated parking lot and a sign that read "UT Archway Lane."

"I think what we're looking for is right over there," Hawk pointed toward the parking lot.

"Where?"

"There!" Hawk got out and closed the door behind him.

Jonathan opened his door and spoke to Hawk across the roof of the car. "Are you leaving the car here in the middle of the street?"

"Why not?" Hawk said, motioning for Jonathan to follow. "We'll only be here for a minute . . . I hope."

Jonathan shook his head and moved around the car, falling in step with Hawk as they crossed the street. The slight drizzle created a cool mist that was surprisingly refreshing. The last few days had been long, Hawk was tired and fatigued, but he knew he didn't have time to stop. They stepped up onto the curb, passed the corner of the lot, and there, next to the street, found what they were looking for.

"There it is." Hawk picked up his pace. They ducked under a tree and came to a stop.

The pair stood in front of a gray-etched tombstone standing in plain sight. Waist-high, it looked like something you might see in the queue line to the Haunted Mansion. It was big enough for someone to hide behind it and never be seen. That thought crossed his mind as they approached it, but as they got closer it disappeared in the excitement of finding it. Hawk read the words out loud for both of them as they stared at it.

"This monument has been erected in 1965 by the Gravity Research Foundation—Roger W. Babson Founder. It is to remind students of the blessings forthcoming when science determines what gravity is, how it works, and how it may be controlled."

Jonathan let out a whistle as Hawk finished reading it. "Well, that certainly does fit in with the clue." "What it is, how it works, and how it may be controlled."

Hawk shook his head. "Roger Babson really did create a tombstone for the death of gravity. You can't make this stuff up!"

"This thing is huge." Jon walked to the side of the stone and reached out to touch it.

"For someone who thought gravity was his enemy, he sure decided to place a rock so big that it couldn't be moved." Hawk shook his head. "Thanks to gravity."

"So what now? What are we looking for?"

"I'm not sure," Hawk admitted. "Just look closely."

Both men examined the monument. Detailed scales of justice were engraved into the top. The tombstone sat in a soft, grassy area and probably went unnoticed by most of the people who traveled up and down the street. As Hawk moved to the back of the marker, he stepped across a tree branch that obstructed his path and view. Now behind the tombstone, he looked over the smooth granite marker for anything that might give him a hint of what he was searching for.

"I have something, I think," he said from behind the tombstone. Jon joined him immediately. Hawk took his finger and traced something on the lower right-hand side of the gravestone.

"What is that?" Jonathan peered in over Hawk's shoulder.

"I don't know. But it's something . . . or maybe nothing." Hawk moved his hand so Jonathan could see clearly. "There are numbers: 759.13. Do those numbers mean anything to you?"

"No, they seem random."

"But they are here, on the gravestone, and they're the only thing that seem like they don't belong." Hawk placed a hand on the top of the stone and stood up.

"You mean the only thing out of the ordinary besides a tombstone commemorating the demise of gravity?" Jonathan said.

"Something like that." Hawk smiled and noticed the rain had quit falling for the time being. "But what do the numbers mean? 759.13 has to stand for something."

"A combination or code?" Jon asked.

"Perhaps, but what kind?"

"A location or reference number, maybe."

Hawk looked back toward the automobile sitting in the deserted street. He had left the wipers on and could see them scraping across the now clean windshield. He gazed around and took a good look at the campus surrounding them. Smooth landscaping, the crosswalk, some students entering the building across the way. The massive building was brick accented in white, with spires reaching upward. He reread the name of the building, Macdonald-Kelce Library, in black letters across the roof line. He pointed toward it.

"Maybe what we're looking for is in there," he said, trying to sound more confident than he really was at the moment.

"You think?" Jonathan shrugged. "Let's go find out. But first we might want to get the car out of the street and park in a parking lot somewhere."

Hawk looked back at the car and groaned. A University of Tampa security officer had pulled a patrol car in behind their rental vehicle. Both he and Jonathan made their way toward the car as the officer got out to meet them.

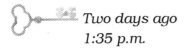 *Two days ago*
1:35 p.m.

NOW HOLDING A TRAFFIC CITATION as a souvenir from the University of Tampa, Hawk and Jonathan parked their car and headed inside the MacDonald-Kelce Library. The words *Create-Innovate-Learn-Inspire* greeting them on a banner as they walked inside the spacious building. An information desk was their first stop.

The young lady behind the counter greeted them warmly. "Hi, how can help you?" she asked. Her name tag identified her as Sue.

"We're looking for a book, we think." Hawk stammered as he said it.

"Well, then . . ." Sue nodded, looking amused. "This would be the place to find one, since we are a library after all. What book are you looking for?"

"I'm not exactly sure," Hawk said.

"Okay then." Sue smiled. "There are a lot of books here, so I will try to help you figure out what you want to look for if you can tell me something about it."

"I think this will help." Hawk reached over the counter, grabbed a notepad, and jotted down the numbers 759.13. He then spun the paper around so Sue could read it.

"Does that help?" Hawk asked, anticipating a positive response.

"Not sure, maybe." Sue looked at the number and back at Hawk. "Hmmm . . ."

"I thought maybe it was a reference number for a book."

"I agree." Sue looked at it again. "I'm not a librarian, I just work the information desk to help get students started in the right direction. I do most of my research online and use the electronic resources in the library. But if you go back to our reference desk, they can help you I'm sure."

Sue pointed across the lobby toward the far end of the area. There was a desk marked "Reference" with two people staffing it.

"Okay, thanks." Hawk grabbed the note he had written, and they turned to head that direction.

"Good luck," Sue offered.

As Jonathan and Hawk moved across the tiled floor, Jonathan leaned in and spoke in a hushed library tone.

"What if it's not a reference number?"

"Then we go back out and look at the tombstone again for whatever it is we missed."

"Can I help you?" Stan, the reference manager, as identified by his name tag, greeted them.

"Yes, I am looking for this." Hawk placed the note on the counter.

"Ah. . . yes, that would be a book on the arts." Stan turned toward his computer.

"The arts?" Hawk leaned on the counter, sure Stan must be mistaken. "Don't you mean science?" It had to be some sort of reference book on gravity—didn't it?

"No, sciences are listed in the 500–599 range of the Dewey Decimal classification system. If this is a valid number, then you're in the 700–799 range, which is of course, the arts." Stan paused, took off his glasses, and rubbed his eyes. He placed them back on the end of his nose and leaned closer to the screen to read carefully what was written before him. "That's odd."

"Odd?" Hawk tried to read the screen but the angle wasn't good, so he couldn't see what Stan was reacting to.

"Hmm . . . I'll be right back," Stan said as he stepped away from the counter and disappeared behind racks of books into a part of the reference section that Hawk couldn't see from his vantage point.

Hawk leaned against the counter and looked back toward the information desk. Sue glanced toward them and smiled as she waved. Both men returned the wave. Jonathan drifted away from the counter and stood at the windows overlooking the entrance area. Nonchalantly he spoke over his shoulder.

"It's starting to rain again."

"Shhh," the other person behind the counter across from Hawk scolded.

Hawk rolled his eyes toward Jon, and they exchanged a quick smile. Hawk made his way over to a lounge area at the side of the lobby. He sat down and glanced at his watch. It seemed like Stan had been gone a long time, but Hawk didn't have a frame of reference to go by. He hadn't checked the time when they arrived.

Hawk noticed Jonathan was pacing along the line of plate glass windows. Looking back toward Hawk, Jonathan stopped and turned his palms upright, gesturing his wondering at the delay. Hawk shrugged his shoulders. But still they waited.

Ten more minutes passed, then another ten. Hawk finally felt like he had to ask where Stan had gone, so he made his way back to the reference counter. As he arrived, he noticed that the shusher had also managed to slip away, and during the wait, Hawk had missed his departure. Thinking he would ask Sue, he turned to look back across the large lobby toward the information desk and discovered it was empty as well. Looking around the room, he saw that he and Jonathan were the only people here.

"Is it just me, or does this library feel deserted all of a sudden?" Hawk spoke, his voice booming across the tile floor much more loudly than he'd anticipated.

"Yes, I noticed the same thing. And what happened to Stan?" Jon said.

"I'm here." Stan emerged from behind a floor to ceiling bookshelf.

Hawk stepped back to the counter to meet him. Stan carried a large manila envelope in his hand. He placed it on the counter and pushed it across the wooden surface toward Hawk.

"I believe this is for you," he said.

Hawk looked down at the envelope, too surprised to answer. It was sealed and had "759.13" written on the front of it in big black numbers. He picked up the package and flipped it over. There were no markings on the back, just the front.

"I had trouble finding it," Stan admitted. "My reference screen informed me the book was on permanent reserve and had been pulled off the shelf for the exclusive use of the owner. The notation also said that if the owner came to reference the work, it should be turned over without question. The owner, according to the logged information, would request the work by the Dewey Decimal reference number and not by the title. Which of course, I have no way of knowing, since it has been removed from our active system." Stan lowered his voice as he said this. It dripped of disapproval and disappointment.

"When was this instruction dated?" Hawk asked curiously.

"1982." Stan said. "Other than that, I have no other information, except for the fact that the package is yours and belongs to you. I assume you know what it is."

"Yes, thank you." It wasn't exactly a lie. Hawk didn't know what the package contained, but he did know it was the next piece of the elusive puzzle he was trying to piece together. He also knew that 1982 was the date Epcot opened. He wondered if this particular clue had been put in place at the same time the clues within Epcot had been created.

Placing the package under his arm, he was bursting with curiosity to know what was inside. He moved quickly toward the front doors but slowed when he noticed the look of concern on Jonathan's face as he approached. Jonathan was standing at the front windows looking out across the entrance-way. He now turned back toward Hawk and began moving to meet him.

"We're not going out that way," he said.

"Why not?"

"An SUV just pulled up and three men got out. Dressed in black, looking like they are wearing some sort of riot gear just like our friends in the World Showcase last night. They have to be coming for you." Both men looked toward the front doors as Hawk's mind raced.

"Go and get the car. Meet me around the back of the library," Hawk said as he pushed Jonathan back toward where Stan had come from earlier.

"And you?"

"I'll buy you some time." The words weren't even out of Hawk's mouth before he was sprinting toward a curved staircase that wound its way over the tops of book shelves to the second floor. He had reached the first landing when he heard someone yell for him to stop from below.

He had no intention of stopping.

Emerging onto the second floor, he saw tall, sturdy rows of bookshelves, lined with colorful books, standing at attention like soldiers lining the length of this level. He raced down the center aisle and then cut to his left to race down a tighter row of books. If anyone was following him, he intended to make himself hard to find.

Leaving the shelves, he passed through a series of small cubicle workstations, where students were working on whatever research materials had brought them to the library. He heard the sharp pop of what sounded like a shot being fired behind him and saw the splatter of paper in the air. Screams suddenly filled the workstations as students dove under chairs, startled by the sudden activity exploding around them. Tiny flakes of parchment fluttered to the ground, and Hawk assumed the bullet had hit the row of books next to him. Ducking his head, he cut down another row of shelves. Maybe he could lose whoever it was in the maze of books.

Hearing voices, he tried to gauge where his attackers might be and decided to try something he had seen work in old adventure films. He paused at the shelf closest to the wall and looked up to see if it was anchored to the ceiling or was free standing. It was free standing. Perfect.

Bracing his back against the brick wall, he placed his feet firmly on the shelf in the middle of the rack and pushed with all of his strength. Legs straining, he felt the shelf give just a little and then rock back toward him. This time he shoved against it with all the strength he could muster and saw the massive shelf lean and then begin to fall away from him. The result was exactly what he had hoped for. Like an oversized set of dominos, the first shelf fell into the second, which fell into the third, starting the chain reaction of distraction he had hoped for. No one had been standing in this line of shelves as he passed, and he prayed no one other than his pursuers would get hurt or trapped.

Hawk raced away from the ongoing avalanche of books coming off of shelves and the thuds of each shelf hitting another as it fell. The emergency staircase was right behind the door before him, and he hit it hard. It flung open, and he took the flight of steps in leaps to the bottom. Repositioning the package under his arm, he carried it like a football and braced himself to burst the final door. He hit it and stumbled out onto a sidewalk behind the library.

At that moment the rental car, with Jonathan at the wheel, came around the corner and drove down the sidewalk toward him. The car slowed, the door opened, and Hawk jumped inside. Swinging the door shut behind him, he looked back at the emergency exit. No one else emerged. Jonathan swung the car back around to University Avenue and pushed the accelerator to the floor heading for the airport.

Hawk's phone rang in his pocket and he looked to see the caller ID read "Al Gann." He glanced back to see if they were being followed and answered the phone with, "Al, I need some help."

"What have you done?" Al's voice came through the receiver.

"Nothing, but I have some type of attack team after me and Jonathan."

"Where are you?"

"Tampa."

The line was silent for a moment before Al spoke again.

"You aren't at the resort?"

"No, I said I'm in Tampa." Hawk relaxed a bit as the car found its way back to the interstate.

"You need to get back here. Agent Batterson has spent the last few hours talking with Sheriff McManus and has the entire department worked up about some conspiracy theory and terrorist group being after you and getting ready to attack the resort. McManus wants to see you now and wants you put under protective custody. I'm supposed to be picking you up right now."

"Well, that is not going to happen," Hawk stated. His stomach churned, and he momentarily regretted allowing Batterson to join them, but he'd had no choice. "I have some very professional, very aggressive people chasing me right now. I saw them last night at Epcot and now they're here. I need you to figure out who they might be, but I also need you to make sure Juliette and Shep are safe."

"I'll check on them and see if I can figure out who is after you."

"I also want to know how they found me in Tampa. Nobody really knew where I was except people I trust. I'll give you a call when I get back."

"How long will it take you to get back?"

"Not sure. We're flying."

"In this weather?" Al's voice was grave. "We are having a horrible storm here near the resort. The airports are shut down or rerouting traffic."

"I'll call you when we're close," Hawk assured him and hung up.

Hawk ended the call and saw what Al had been talking about. Although he wasn't looking at a radar, the angry sky that had been throwing rain at them was a solid mass of dark clouds. Not only was there a storm over the greater Orlando area, apparently the same storm cell had extended its tentacles of turbulence across the state.

As the rain hit the window, Jonathan said next to him, "It is going to be a rough flight back home."

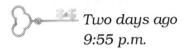 *Two days ago*
9:55 p.m.

THE STORM WAS MUCH MORE INTENSE than either of them had real-ized, and it took them a few hours to finally have enough of a break in the weather to leave Tampa. Even then, they found themselves soaring into cer-tain and severe turbulence.

Hawk had waited until they got into the Piper Tomahawk before rip-ping open the 759.13 envelope. Dumping the contents into his lap, he looked at the oversized book that now sat before him. A sudden coldness hit at his core. He did a double take, rubbed his eyes, and wondered what this surprising edition might contain. He was not sure what he had expected, but it certainly was not what he now had in his possession. It was a coffee-table style book, thick, loaded with pages—455 of them, according to the page numbers in the volume. The title was simple: *Norman Rockwell, 322 Magazine Covers.*

Hawk flipped through the pages quickly. The book was loaded with the cover art the famous artist had done for the *Saturday Evening Post.* The magazine and Rockwell's art were forever connected in American history. This book however, was not a reprinting of the covers; instead it was a reprinting of the works of art themselves.

As the plane banked to the right and they entered a line of low-hanging storm clouds, Jonathan glanced over as Hawk flipped through the book in the dim light from the control panel.

"We went to Tampa, found a tombstone saying good-bye to gravity, and then got shot at for a book of Norman Rockwell prints? You have to admit, even in your world, this is a little stranger than normal." The plane jolted to the left as Jon spoke.

The ride instantly became rougher, and it felt like they were riding a roller coaster as the plane rose and dipped, giving them the sensation of free falling. Only this ride was for real and not a thrill ride. They had taken another dangerous, calculated risk by trying to get back. Even now, Hawk worried that they might have made a mistake.

"You're thinking we might have made a wrong move, aren't you?" Jon tried to lighten the moment. "Well, we probably did. But it's too late now. According to the radar, we're surrounded. The only thing we can do is ride it out and go through the storm."

Jonathan handed Hawk his cell phone, which featured an open app that showed them exactly where they were and the weather they were now facing. "Our biggest problem is where to land. I can guarantee you they've closed the airport in Kissimmee. If we come in and land anyway, we're going to have a whole lot of questions and paperwork to fill out."

The plane shuddered again, and Hawk felt himself grabbing the seat to stabilize himself. Instinctively he tightened his already tight seat belt. There were worse things than paperwork, he thought. Hawk allowed himself to smile as he said a silent prayer. They were headed back home in a storm, the new owners of a book they didn't know what to do with, with no place to land. It was all a typical Grayson Hawkes kind of day.

That thought gave him an idea.

"I know what to do," he said loudly enough to be heard over the storm. He had always told Jonathan that flying in these small planes was like flying in a soda can. Right now, it felt like the soda can was about to be recycled. He tried to keep his voice calm and stay focused on the plan. "Let's land at Disney World."

"What? Where?" Jonathan did not take his eyes off the control gauges.

"At the STOL outside the Magic Kingdom."

"Is it clear? It hasn't been used in years, has it?" Jon glanced toward Hawk. In the late 1960s and into the 1970s there had been an effort to eliminate the ever-growing traffic problems in major America cities. Short Take-Off and Landing, or STOL, was the solution, or so some thought. The plan was to build a national network of STOLports to provide inter-city regional transportation that could move people more effectively. Small aircraft would be able to fly in and out of these small airports and help people miss traffic jams by taking short trips on commuter airlines. Florida was to be a pioneer in this project, with twenty different STOLports between Central Florida and South Florida. Walt Disney World had stepped to the forefront of the project, but their port was the only one ever actually constructed. Fuel costs, the ability of small commuter airlines to find and hold their markets, the construction and expansion of the Orlando International Airport . . . all had worked against the plan. As Epcot was connected to the Transportation and Ticket Center by a monorail line, the STOLport was eventually retired.

"Well, not for planes, but it's still there," Hawk said, still talking a little too loudly. Most guests had driven down World Drive, headed toward the Wilderness Lodge or the Contemporary Resort, and seen it on the right-hand side of the road without knowing what it was. "It still looks like an airport runway. And it's clear—I banned using it as a staging and storage area, because it just looks bad for guests to see stuff sitting there."

Jon's forehead wrinkled. "So why haven't we used it before?"

"The monorail line runs dangerously close to the airport runway. That's going to make the landing tricky."

"That and the storm," Jonathan added. "I think *tricky* is putting too nice of a spin on it."

Hawk forced down a fresh surge of nerves. "I need to reconnect with Al and make sure everything is all right. I told him I would call him back." Hawk picked up his phone, grateful for the distraction.

"You should have coverage from here. If you don't it's going to be because of the storm, not because of the plane."

Al answered on the first ring and didn't say hello. "Are you all right?" Al's voice crackled through the phone connection.

"Yes, we're almost home."

"Are you flying in the storm?" Al's voice cut out for a minute, then came back. "It is terrible outside."

"Is everyone okay?"

"Fine. I have checked on everyone, and they are safe and sound."

"Good, thanks," Hawk said, relieved.

"Hawk, I have done some digging to see who was after you in Tampa and how they found you. Here's the best I could find out. You and Jonathan flew down there and rented a car, right?"

"Yes," Hawk said.

"You went to the University of Tampa." Al's voice again cut out but Hawk was able to fill in the gaps. "The university police department . . . ran the tags on your car. . . . ran your license, and . . . traffic ticket."

"Yes, but the officer was very nice." Hawk tapped his pocket where he had stashed the ticket.

Al's voice came through more clearly this time. "But when your name got tagged through the DMV, someone out there who is watching found out where you were. Only a select few knew where you were, right? You didn't tell me, so I can't really protect you. But when someone wants to find you bad enough, they usually can."

Hawk took the scolding without protest. He still felt bad about how he had dealt with Al earlier, but he was confident they would work through it. Al was a great guy and a good friend. But for now, Hawk still needed enough freedom to finish the mystery.

"Thanks for figuring out what happened. Now if you could just figure out who it was," Hawk said.

"Working on it. Give me some time." Al paused. "How are you flying in this weather? I bet the airport is closed. Let me see if I can get someone to open it up for you and make sure the lights are on."

"Not necessary. We're landing at Walt Disney World on the STOL. We should be there soon," Hawk said.

Al's voice betrayed disbelief. "You are landing at the Magic Kingdom?"

"Yes, the old airstrip."

"Doesn't it have a monorail track running across it?"

"Not across it, right next to it," Hawk corrected. "Talk to you soon."

He ended the call. He was going to have a lot of making up to do to Al when this was all over. The plane rocked side to side and then once again dropped inside a pocket of air, leaving Hawk's stomach behind. Jonathan was sweating and working hard to hold the plane level. Finally he broke the noise of the cockpit. "Are you sure that landing at the STOL is a good idea? I don't have a better one, but I'm not so sure it's smart."

Hawk swallowed his nausea. "Can you do it?"

"I'm not sure. It's night, there are no lights, we are in a storm . . . we're going to be landing blind. We need a better plan."

"I don't have one." Hawk thought for a moment. "If Al were to open up the Kissimmee airport for us, it would create so much attention and take so much time, I'm afraid it would alert whoever was after us in Tampa that we're back. After all, they figured out that we rented a car from an airport; they have to know where we would return. If you can pull this off, Jon, this is the best way to get back undetected."

The plane creaked as it was jostled about. The turbulence felt like it would shake the little plane into pieces. Hawk felt Jonathan begin to descend and could see the lights of the resort in the distance. In just a few moments they were passing over the nighttime vision of Cinderella Castle and Space Mountain shining through the rain.

"They sure look pretty at night. It would be easier if we could land on Main Street, U.S.A. At least there we would have some lights," Jonathan said, concerned.

Hawk perked up. "Could you do that?"

"No, not wide enough. Just making an observation."

Hawk looked out the window. He could see what Jonathan was talking about. The area where they needed to land was dangerously dark, with only some ambient light thrown toward it from the parking lot and World Drive. It was not an understatement to say they would be landing on a wing and a prayer.

Jonathan banked the plane through the rain as lightning lit up the night sky. Hawk wondered if the lightning would help them find the landing strip better if it kept flashing around them like it was now. The plane dipped, and Hawk could see as he glanced at the controls that Jonathan was lining the plane up to make his approach.

"You can do this, Jon," Hawk said confidently as he stared out the front window at the rain-streaked nose of the plane.

As they descended, a gust of wind felt as if it would flip the plane over. Both men let out a gasp as the plane came level again. Lower and lower through the driving rain and stormy skies, the plane drew closer to the ground. Jonathan was going to have to drop the plane over the top of a monorail track and then get it down to the ground fast enough to hit the runway. It wouldn't have been an easy maneuver on a clear day, much less a stormy night.

The plane eased across the Epcot monorail line, and its nose severely dipped down. Hawk felt Jon pull it back up as he fought to keep the plane under control. He caught a quick glimpse of a long concrete runway as the lightning flashed across the sky once again. The wheels of the airplane touched the ground, skipped up for a moment, then touched down once more. Jonathan exhaled loudly, and Hawk took that as a sign that they were going to be fine.

Before he could start breathing easy, the plane violently veered to the right and twisted, and then Hawk felt the world around him go upside down. The plane had struck something on the runway. It catapulted through the air, tumbling over and over, giving the two passengers a ride like tumbling inside a dryer.

Scraping, metal-bending sounds echoed in Hawk's ears. He felt himself flung from side to side with only his seat belt anchoring him in place. Then everything stopped, and the world fell silent.

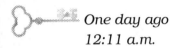 *One day ago*
12:11 a.m.

HAWK BECAME AWARE of a light flashing across his closed eyelids. Slowly cracking them open, the flashing became more intense, and he became aware of the blue lights of a law enforcement vehicle as well as the red and white emergency lights of the fire department.

He was lying on the pavement. A paramedic bent over him, and he vaguely heard the words "be still" echo somewhere in the background as he turned his head to survey the scene around him.

Jonathan was on the ground near him. Hawk could see people working on him and realized with a lump in his throat that Jon was moving. That had to be a good sign. He looked beyond the clump of people huddled around Jonathan and could see the crumpled airplane. It really did look like a crunched soda can. A strap on the plane was stretched taut and connected to the tow bar on a car with flashing lights on top. It looked like a Sheriff's Department SUV. Turning his head even more, he looked back onto the runway they had traveled down. There it was—a massive railroad crosstie sitting on the runway. That had to have been what they hit.

Jonathan had told Hawk many times that the only real danger they were ever in when it came to the plane was if there was something they couldn't see on the runway—something that would cause them to flip. After that, who knew what could happen. Now they knew. The wave of pain that shot through Hawk's back hurt more than he could process but reminded him that he was still alive and that was a miracle. If Jonathan was all right, there would be a tomorrow. They could second-guess themselves about the landing into their old age.

"Hey, are you still with us?" Juliette knelt down over Hawk, and her hand touched his face.

"I'm here." Hawk tried to smile, but it hurt. "How is Jon?"

"Like you, tough and ornery. He is going to make it just fine. Both of you are cut up and a bit bruised," Juliette said.

"You hit something on the runway." Al Gann leaned in over Hawk. "It flipped you over like you were in a tornado. After we talked I started to head over this way. I saw you guys dip down, but then boom . . . it all fell apart. I used a strap to flip the plane over and drag you both out."

"Al had you both out of the plane and was taking care of you when the ambulances arrived," Juliette added.

"I'm gonna check on Jonathan," Al said and pushed himself away.

Hawk felt himself being sat up by the paramedics. One of them said in his ear, "Take it slow, take your time. You are going to be sore for a while."

"Thanks." Hawk steadied himself on the shoulder of the paramedic.

Shep arrived, racing across the airstrip. "Are you guys okay?"

"They're fine," Juliette said. She looked back at Hawk. "They're both too hardheaded to get hurt too badly."

Shep instantly drifted off to check on Jonathan. As he did, the paramedics gave Hawk another look-over and made the decision to take Jonathan to the hospital to check out a bump on his forehead more closely, although they assured an anxious Shep that they were pretty sure it was fine.

Hawk moved gingerly to where Jonathan was being placed on a stretcher, and they briefly shook hands and managed a whispered conversation before he was placed in an ambulance.

"We almost made it." Jon winced as he smiled weakly.

"You did a good job getting us down. It was a perfect landing . . . almost." Hawk returned the smile.

"Why was that thing on the runway?" Jon's expression grew dark. "I thought you said it was clear."

"It was supposed to be." Flashing lights danced across Hawk's face as he glanced back down the runway. "I have no idea why it was there."

"Kinda random, if you ask me." Jon said softly. "But we already know that with you, nothing is ever really random."

Hawk nodded in agreement. He knew Jonathan was right.

"Figure out what's in that book." Jon swallowed hard.

A paramedic approached Hawk and suggested that he could ride and get checked out as well. This had already been discussed and Hawk had stubbornly refused.

"Well, was it worth it? Did you find whatever you were after?" Al asked as he returned to Hawk and helped him toward Juliette's car.

"Yes, I did, as a matter of fact."

"And what was that?" Al said as he held the door open for Hawk.

"You know better than that," Hawk said with a sigh.

"Yes, the conspiracy theory that you are chasing that never dies. Although tonight it almost killed you," Al said.

"What almost killed me was that log sitting in the runway." Hawk motioned to the wooden crosspiece still sitting ajar where they had hit it.

"Where are you taking him?" Al asked Juliette.

"Well . . . I'm not sure." She hesitated.

"I'm going to my office," Hawk said. "I don't have access to my apartment yet, and I need a place to rest for a few minutes and figure out what I'm going to do next. And," he added for Al's benefit, "you know where I am, so you can keep an eye on me."

"Great idea." Al winked at Hawk, clearly thankful for the change in attitude.

"Hey, hold on." Hawk stepped away from the car and on wobbly legs made his way back across the crowded runway. Stepping around security vehicles, sheriff's department cars, and rescue trucks, he made his way to the twisted airplane still connected by an industrial-strength towing strap to Al's bumper.

Reaching inside the plane, he grabbed the oversized book he had carried back from Tampa. Tucking it under his arm, he slowly made his way back to Juliette's car under the watchful and puzzled gaze of both Al and Juliette. On arriving, he held the book out to Juliette.

"I didn't want to leave it here."

"What is it, and why are you giving it to me?" Juliette looked at the heavy book in her hands.

"I picked it up for you while I was gone. I figured that since you're working with art these days, you might want it," Hawk answered.

"Uh, okay . . . thanks," Juliette said, clearly confused as she tossed the book into the back seat.

Hawk nodded with a slight smile. Why he'd been given the book and what he was supposed to find in it was still a mystery, but he was not about to leave it in the wreckage of the Piper Tomahawk for anyone else to find.

Seated in the passenger seat of Juliette's car, Hawk watched as the ambulance pulled away with Jonathan in the back. The paramedics had assured him the trip to the hospital was just precautionary.

As Juliette turned her car onto World Drive and headed toward the Contemporary Resort, Hawk closed his eyes and replayed the events of the last hour. The storm, the descent, seeing the obstruction on the runway with no time to react or miss it, and then the sickening, endless tumbling of the plane when the world faded to black for a few minutes. The trip had not ended as planned, and he had no idea what the next step might be.

The answers, he was sure, were somewhere in the book. All he had to do was figure them out.

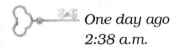 *One day ago*
2:38 a.m.

HAWK'S BODY BEGIN TO ACHE in earnest as the elevator doors opened and he and Juliette made their way to his office in the Bay Lake Towers. They had been silent on the drive, and the silence continued until they were safely inside the exclusive private suite of offices. As soon as the doors were secured, Juliette asked the question she had been wondering about since they left the STOL.

"What is this book you brought me?" She sat the heavy book down on the table in the conference room area. "What is it really?"

"I didn't really get it for you," Hawk admitted. "I just needed a good reason to go and pull it out of the wreckage."

"Because this is what you found in Tampa, right?" Juliette flipped open the book and began to thumb through the pages.

"Exactly." Hawk lowered himself carefully into one of the conference room chairs next to her at the table and looked over at the book as she examined it.

"The Norman Rockwell Museum has given us a number of pieces on loan for the art show." Juliette looked at page after page. "I'm sure most of the works they shipped down are somewhere in this book. You know there are over 450 pages in this book? It weighs a ton. No wonder the airplane flipped; it was out of balance because of this book!"

Hawk chuckled, but he was too tired and sore to quip back.

"What made you think you should use the old abandoned airstrip?"

Hawk shifted uncomfortably, trying to take pressure off his bruised tailbone. "The other airports were shut down because of the storm. Any of them with any type of monitoring would have diverted us, rerouted us, and not let us land. The STOL was the only airstrip I had any control over. So we decided to use it." Hawk rubbed his chin. "It would have worked, if it hadn't been for the railroad tie in the runway. The funny thing is, the company isn't storing anything on the runway anymore. I thought it looked bad for our guests as they came down World Drive, so we had cleaned it up. It should have been clear."

"What are you saying?" Juliette stopped looking at the book.

"I am saying, how did that obstruction get on the runway?"

"You think someone placed it there?"

"Of course they did. The real question is did they do it on purpose? And why?" Hawk looked at her as Shep entered the room.

Armed with his laptop, he had entered the secured office using his own personal code. Now he took a seat across from them and set up to get to work.

"So what are we doing?" Shep looked at them and toward the book on the table.

"This is what we found." Hawk tapped his fingers on the book. "This is what someone tried to stop me from finding by sending an attack squad into the library. The tombstone led us to this."

Hawk spent a few minutes catching his friends up on the adventures he and Jonathan had experienced in Tampa. He told the story completely, including the flight back through the storm, the conversation with Al, and the crash landing that had brought them back to the office with the book.

"Wow, that's some day." Shep pursed his lips.

"So now we have to figure out what Norman Rockwell has to do with the secrets of Walt Disney," Hawk finished.

On cue, Shep started tapping on the keyboard. The clicking of the keys was the only sound in the room, and Hawk felt himself grow wearier. The post-adrenaline crash, the stiffness in his joints from the jarring of the accident, and the lack of sleep over the past week suddenly tumbled on top of one another in the security of his office and the comfort and familiarity of being with friends. He allowed his eyes to close for just a moment.

"Who knew?" Shep exclaimed.

"Knew?" Juliette looked toward Shep. Hawk blinked his way back into the moment and leaned forward in his seat. He'd fallen asleep for a moment. Resting his arms on the table, he looked across to Shep, struggling to clear his mind.

"What did you find? Tell me about Rockwell and Disney," Hawk said.

"Rockwell's obituary in *Time* magazine when he passed away in 1978 read, 'Rockwell shared with Walt Disney the extraordinary distinction of being one of two artists familiar to nearly everyone in the US, rich or poor, black or white, museum goer or not, illiterate or PhD.'

"That's a testimony to both Walt and Rockwell, but I guess people forget how influential Norman Rockwell was. He is one of the great artists of all time. A genius." Juliette's voice rang with admiration.

"And a friend of Walt Disney's?" Hawk anticipated the answer.

"Of course. As we have found out, Walt seemed to have lots of very special and talented friends." Shep was scrolling through information as he spoke. "Rockwell painted one of Walt's favorite paintings, it seems. Back in 1942, President Franklin D. Roosevelt gave a speech about the 'Four Freedoms' everyone should have: freedom from fear, freedom from want, freedom of speech, and freedom of worship. Norman Rockwell painted these Four Freedoms in four separate covers for *The Saturday Evening Post*. They impressed Walt so much that he wrote him a letter. He told him, "I thought your Four Freedoms were great. I especially loved *Freedom of Worship* and the composition and symbolism expressed in it."

"I've never heard that story before." Hawk sank into thought, trying to figure out how this might be important to what they were trying to unravel.

"Well, there's more. If you aren't familiar with that, then you probably haven't heard this either." Shep read for a moment and then continued, "Walt was traveling with Lillian, her sister Hazel, and Hazel's husband, Bill. They were traveling in New England and grabbed a bite to eat in a little tea room. The restaurant had pictures done by Norman Rockwell all over the place as decoration. Apparently Walt says to the waitress, 'Doesn't Rockwell live near here?' Next thing you know the waitress is not only telling him that Rockwell lives about three miles from the tea room but gives Walt directions as to how to get there."

"And Walt went to meet him," Juliette said.

"You're jumping ahead in the story." Shep glanced up from the screen toward her. Going back to the screen, he continued, "The travelers made their way to his home and knocked on the front door. Someone who worked there, lived there, or some family member answered. Walt said he was there to see Norman Rockwell. The person told him the artist was at work and couldn't be disturbed. Walt laughed and told the person to go and tell him that Walt Disney was there to visit. The guardian of the door said no and told Walt he would give him a message but they needed to leave. He told Walt good-bye and closed the door."

"So what happened next? There's no way that Walt just left and went away." Hawk was intrigued.

"Of course not." Shep smiled. "While everyone else went back to the car, Walt wandered around the back of the house and out to the smaller house on the property that Norman used as an art studio. He knocked on the door, Norman answered and instantly recognized Walt, and then, of course, Norman invited them all in and they spent the rest of the afternoon visiting. They became very good friends, close. So close that Rockwell did portraits of Walt's daughters."

"I had no idea!" Hawk said. He looked back toward the book. Once again, Juliette was flipping through its pages.

"So Rockwell was a good friend of Walt Disney's. They knew each other very well. And you were left a book years ago, back when Epcot opened, full of Rockwell paintings. It was left at the library by someone who knew that one day, someday, someone would come to pick it up. Why?" Juliette recapped and asked the question of the hour as she continued to look through the book.

"There is more," Shep said. "*The Saturday Evening Post* and Norman Rockwell are American institutions. Rockwell did over three hundred covers for the magazine."

"At least 322." Juliette smiled as she pointed to the cover of the book. "Norman Rockwell, 322 Magazine Covers."

"At least," Shep sighed. "In one of Rockwell's paintings, *Shuffleton's Barbershop,* which appeared on the cover of the *Post,* April 29, 1950, there's a shelf with comic books in the lower left-hand corner. Rockwell often worked using photographs. Well, he had apparently snapped a shot of an actual comic on a shelf: *Walt Disney's Comics and Stories,* issue No. 111. It was published by Dell in December of 1949. The cover is Donald Duck leaning over a fence with an amused look on his face as he watches his nephews, Huey, Dewey and Louie, trying to give a hairy, sad-faced brown dog a perm using rollers."

"Maybe that's in here." Juliette flipped through the pages and suddenly stopped. "Hawk, did you see this?"

Hawk leaned over as she reached into the book and pick up a piece of paper the size of a bookmark. She glanced up and him and read it silently.

Juliette placed the slip of paper on top of the book and slid it over toward him. He reached down and picked it up the slip of paper.

"No, I didn't see this," he responded.

"What? Didn't see what?" Shep looked up over his keyboard.

"I didn't see the clue we were looking for."

Hawk turned the note for Shep to read for himself.

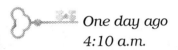 *One day ago*
4:10 a.m.

SHEP READ THE CLUE, NODDED, and then looked up at Hawk for some explanation. Hawk touched the base of his neck for a moment and then shrugged. He didn't have one.

The clue was on a rectangular piece of paper that looked like a bookmark. It was typed, as were the other clues he had found from Press the Imagineer to this point. But this one, Hawk realized, had been typed and hidden years before he was ever selected to be the protector of Walt's secrets. He read the clue aloud, and his voice trembled just a little. He was finally getting close to solving this mystery forever.

759.13
Find the Rockwell that he
put Walt in
bring it and meet me
In Progress City

"So you are supposed to find a painting and take it to Progress City," Juliette said. "Don't you think it's rather convenient that we just happen to have works of art coming in from all over the world for the art show at Epcot? Including works by Rockwell?"

"Yes, it is convenient," Hawk agreed. "Or maybe the announcement of the art show was what prompted Press to decide this was the time, the best time to give me the clue."

Juliette pondered this as did Hawk, right after he said it. He had been immersed in this world of Disney mystery so long now that he realized very little happened by accident. He chose to look at his role in the world of Disney as part of a massive story that Walt and Roy had begun to tell in their lifetimes that continued until this day.

"Do we have the painting?" he asked abruptly.

"What painting?" Juliette responded.

"The one Shep mentioned, the one you saw in the book?"

"The odds of that are . . ."

"Just as great as the odds that we don't. Show me the picture in the book."

Juliette flipped through the pages, trying to remember where she had seen the picture that Shep had mentioned. "I didn't notice any comic book in it, but I remember the painting because it was a barbershop, at night—it reminded me of a place I used to go with my grandfather."

Hawk waited impatiently. Juliette paused. She had found it. Placing her finger on the page, she turned the book where Hawk could see it. Shep had been tapping on the keyboard again as Juliette searched for the picture. As Hawk looked closely at it, Shep read a description he had found from some online source.

"*Shuffleton's Barbershop* appeared on the cover of *The Saturday Evening Post* on April 29, 1950. The painting is considered by many to be one of Norman Rockwell's finest and most enduring works. On no other work did he lavish more attention to detail. The interior of the barbershop was created using dozens of photographs as points of reference to make sure there was nothing that did not fit the world Rockwell was trying to recreate. The light from the back room where the band is playing, along with the embers from the potbellied stove, lend a certain warmth to the entire composition. The window sash that strikes across the foreground lets the viewer know that we have just happened by this scene captured in time by accident. We are merely passing by."

"It's beautiful." Hawk had never seen the painting before. It looked like so many vintage Rockwell creations, yet he understood why it was considered one of the artist's best. Rockwell had managed to recreate a moment in history that everyone could connect with. The items resting on the shelf to the right—the fishing rod, the fishing basket, the cap, the rifle all nestled in their resting places, revealing the barber's love for the outdoors. The broom, having been used to clean the shop at the end of the day, now leaned against the doorjamb. A towel hung over the edge of the classic barber's chair, and a rack of reading material could be seen through the window.

Hawk moved his face closer to the page and surveyed the cover of the comic book on the bottom of the rack, on the right hand side. He could make out the image of Donald Duck—and another figure, making him chuckle. Shep had been right on the mark.

"Find the Rockwell that he put Walt in." Hawk looked up from studying the picture. "This has to be it. The clue references the Dewey Decimal number of the Rockwell book that was waiting for me. This picture is one where Rockwell took a work of Walt's art and put it in his—so he put Walt in it. Not only that, but the Imagineer chose to give the secret to the clue with a Dewey Decimal number, and the image of the Disney comic has Donald Duck's nephew, Dewey, on it. This is it. So do we have the painting for real?"

"I don't know, but we can find out." Juliette was already up and moving across the room. Crossing the hall at a jogger's pace, she ran to her office and accessed the network to see what she could find. Hawk and Shep followed. By the time they got there, she was smiling and had turned the monitor around for them to see.

"It's here as part of the exhibit," she said with satisfaction.

"No way could that be an accident. This has to be it," Hawk said for the third time, trying to reassure himself. He fidgeted and licked his lips in anticipation of seeing the portrait in person.

"Let's go find it." Juliette was once again up and moving. Hawk and Shep walked briskly to keep up.

"Where are we going? " Hawk said as they entered the elevator and the doors slid shut.

"Next door. We are staging and prepping the exhibit in one of the ballrooms at the Contemporary. As a matter of fact, we're going to have a private viewing before we move the works to be put on display at Epcot. The plan is to cycle the works in and out through the arts festival so that on any given day, a guest will see something different. Didn't you read the brief I sent you on this?"

"Um, well, no," Hawk admitted. "I knew you were on it and could handle it. I had no doubt you had a great plan."

Shep saw the brilliance of the plan. "But by rotating the works of art, the guests will keep coming back to see what else is on display."

"It also helps us keep them secure. We don't ever have all the paintings in one place, and there is no way thieves could know where everything is at." The elevator doors opened, and they moved across the breezeway connecting the Bay Lake Towers with the Contemporary Resort. The stillness of the predawn hour gave them an uninterrupted walk. The covered walkway gave them a view of a now clear sky. The storm that had threatened to swallow up the airplane hours ago had completely disappeared.

"Do you really think anyone would try to steal them?" Hawk asked.

"Seriously?" Juliette laughed at the simplicity of the question in light of all they had seen, all they had experienced, and all that happened over the past week.

Exiting the breezeway, Hawk looked up into the massive mural that climbed the tower of the futuristic resort. The Grand Canyon Concourse they now moved through was surrounded by rows of guest suites lining floor after floor, each clearly visible from the base of the canyon. On the other side was a monorail station that connected the resort to the Magic Kingdom, the Grand Floridian, and the Polynesian resort hotel. The uniqueness of the Contemporary was that the monorail track actually ran in and through interior of the resort. Its design was streamlined down to the décor. Most didn't realize that when the Contemporary was originally conceived, guests were supposed to be able to walk from the Magic Kingdom's Tomorrowland directly into the hotel. It was a vision of what the future might look like. Disney's Contemporary Resort was an icon of Walt Disney World, strongly influenced by Walt Disney's own vision. It was the resort that Roy made sure was ready in 1971, upon the opening of the Magic Kingdom.

At this time of the morning there were no guests and no cast members moving about, with the exception of the early morning crew prepping the resort for the start of the morning. They moved to a private elevator, where Juliette produced a master key and inserted it into the lock, summoning the elevator to their level. She used the same key to activate the touch pad allowing her to choose the floor they were heading to.

The elevator doors closed, and Hawk leaned against the handrail. He heard the squeak of the passenger car as it lifted toward their destination. His senses were in overdrive. He tried to slow his breathing but found he couldn't wait to see the portrait. A soft ding echoed around them, and the door quietly slid open. Once again they were on the move, briskly walking across the plush carpet of the resort, their shoes sinking into the softness as they arrived at the doors of the ballroom. Two security guards stood sentry outside. Juliette flashed her name tag, and they stepped away from the door with a nod. Using her key, she unlocked the door. The three moved inside, and she locked it behind them.

Hawk stopped in his tracks as he gazed upon row after row of portraits and other works of art. At first glance, he noticed paintings that were not done by Rockwell; this exhibit featured art that had either influenced Walt Disney or had been somehow meaningful to him personally. He caught his breath as he realized for the first time what a huge project and exhibit Juliette had been piecing together.

Strategic lighting illuminated each featured work, and a small bench in front of each piece gave viewers a seat where they could study the work. There was a large amount of space between paintings, and Hawk realized it was to prevent a viewer from being able to clearly see any other work except the one he or she was looking at. The smell of lavender drifted across the room. Where was that coming from? Juliette glanced at him as he took a deep breath.

"We're pumping the scent of lavender into the room. It's common in galleries," she explained. "According to my master list, the painting is over here."

Following Juliette, the three moved through the displays, made a right turn, and came to a stop at the end of the line of paintings. Hawk smiled. They were now looking through the window into Shuffelton's barbershop. The print in the book had not done the painting justice. The detail was exquisite, the colors were warm and inviting, and as he gazed at the portrait, Hawk felt like he was stepping back in time, standing at the barbershop window, complete with a cracked pane of glass in the lower right-hand corner.

"There it is: *Shuffelton's Barbershop* by Norman Rockwell, Donald Duck comic book and all." Juliette waved a hand toward the painting.

"Great. Can I have it?" Hawk asked.

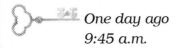 *One day ago*
9:45 a.m.

ON THE GROUND BELOW THE MOVING beltway leading up to its track, the Tomorrowland Transit Authority PeopleMover overlooked a long line of guests waiting to ride. The TTA was a powerful representation of Tomorrowland as a land on the move. In the layers of backstory created for this section of the Magic Kingdom, the TTA served as the primary means of travel from the hoverburbs outside of Tomorrowland into the city. Walt Disney saw the future as a fast-paced, constantly changing and always improving way of life. His was a vision loaded with promise and potential, and in many ways the TTA attraction captured the essence of that idea. Linear induction powered the ride vehicles, 533 electromagnets sending out a carefully timed sequence of pulses that pushed and pulled the train forward along the track. The uniqueness of the attraction vehicle was that it had no moving parts. So shutdowns were rare.

The guests in the Magic Kingdom on this day were experiencing one of those rare downtimes for the attraction. The cause was not a mechanical breakdown or a technological glitch: rather, Grayson Hawkes had given the word to shut down the attraction as the Magic Kingdom opened. As a result, the always moving ride was motionless, and the attraction was free not only of guests but of cast members as well.

Hawk emerged from the offstage edge of Tomorrowland carrying the large oversized carrying case that housed the Rockwell painting. *Shuffelton's Barbershop* was worth a sizeable amount, and the original inside the case was irreplaceable. Juliette had informed him as he packed it up that they were now in violation of more rules, mandates, and contract agreements than she could recount for him. Hawk had gotten the message, understood her concern, and in the end, as usually occurred, she agreed with his plan.

The guests passing by noticed him, and some spoke up as he moved. Thankfully, he didn't have far to go. From behind the Buzz Lightyear Space Ranger Spin, it was a short walk across the street to the ramp for the Tomorrowland Transit Authority.

Leaning forward on the now stopped rubber conveyer belt that normally carried people up to the second story of Tomorrowland, Hawk slowly and carefully moved upward to arrive at the normally busy loading area. It wasn't the first time he'd been inside the attraction when it wasn't running. That was one part of the clue he'd understood immediately: he knew exactly where Progress City was.

He moved past the stopped blue transportation vehicles and along the 4,574 foot track toward the interior corridor where the ride vehicles would pass Progress City. The model city was originally located in the post-show area of the Carousel of Progress in Disneyland in California. In 1975, the Carousel of Progress and half of the model made their way to Walt Disney World to make Tomorrowland their permanent residence. With the creation of Epcot well underway, it was believed that this would be a better home for the model inspired by Walt. It served as a preview of coming attractions as the company tried to get people to embrace Walt's futuristic concepts. Many of those would become part of the Epcot design. His vision of the world of tomorrow could now be seen by everyone who took this trip.

Hawk walked through the darkened tunnel along the TTA route and looked behind the glass of an enclosure at the model city that stretched out over twenty feet long and ten feet deep. It was massive in size, as was Walt's dream of the future.

He stopped, alone in the dark. What now? He was here, and he had done what the clue told him to do. This had to be it, and he had to be right. At least he thought he was.

Hawk stood for nearly an hour, turning periodically as he thought he heard a noise coming from one end of the tunnel or the other. Each time it was just background noises coming from the busy world of Tomorrowland below. He sat down on the concrete floor in front of the window to Progress City. The coolness of the wall penetrated his shirt and felt relaxing against his back, which was still sore from the airplane crash. He pushed his head back against the wall and closed his eyes. How long had it been since he really had time to sleep? He didn't know, or couldn't remember. That could only mean it had been too long.

It seemed like he had just blinked for a second when he heard a voice say, "Do you remember what the original name of this attraction was?"

Hawk opened and closed his eyes and realized he had dozed off in the shade of the tunnel. A cool breeze was blowing through, and it had lulled him into a few minutes of rest that he now fought to push away.

"What?" he asked groggily as he turned toward the source of the question.

"I can come back later if I am disturbing you," the voice said.

"No." Hawk struggled to his feet. "That's not necessary. I just closed my eyes."

"I imagine you've had a busy few days," the voice said gently.

Hawk looked into the shadow of the tunnel and saw an elderly gentleman resting against a walking cane, standing at the other end of the tunnel. His heart picked up its pace.

He had found him.

"Are you Press the Imagineer?" Hawk said and took a step toward him.

"That is one of the names I have been known by," the man said. "I am Preston Child. I am an old friend of the Disney brothers and some of Walt's nine old men." Press smiled faintly in the dim light. "I was just a little over twenty years old when I first met Walt. It was in the 1950s, and I got a job in the studios doing whatever I could do. After hours I would wander around, seeing what everyone else was doing. I wanted to be an animator, so I would see what the guys were working on. Late one night as I was puttering around I was caught by Walt himself." Press laughed. "He was doing the same thing I was, just checking out what was going on."

The old man paused for a moment. "I thought I was going to get fired right there on the spot, but Walt put his arm around me and let me walk with him through the animation department. For the next few hours he asked me all about my life, my background, and what I wanted to be. It was a night I will never forget."

"I can only imagine," Hawk said.

"I was still afraid that I would get to work the next day and find out I had been fired. Walt did have a little bit of a fiery side to him, after all."

"I've heard that." Hawk nodded.

"Instead, I found out I had been promoted and was to report to work at. . . oh, yes, I asked you a question earlier. Do you know what the Tomorrowland Transit Authority PeopleMover used to be called?"

Hawk smiled. "The WEDway People Mover was what it was called when it opened in 1975."

"That's right." Press said with a lift to his voice. "And what does WED stand for?"

"Walter Elias Disney. Walt's initials."

"You are good, Dr. Grayson Hawkes. Just like I have always heard." Press leaned heavily on his cane. "Apparently my fellow Imagineers selected you very well. And now, you have brought me something."

A warmth radiated through him as he felt like years of work were about to suddenly fall into place, and he would finally understand what he had been doing. Hawk glanced at the oversized case beside him. "Yes, but can I ask you something?"

"Sure."

"Why now?"

"Ah, that is a great question. The answer is not complicated. It is simple, really: because I am getting old. I have been waiting for a signal to let me know it was time. I have not been able to stay as connected to the happenings around Walt Disney World as I used to be able to do, so I had to wait. For years, I have monitored a window in the Magic Kingdom waiting for a sign. Then all of the sudden, there it was. So I knew it was time."

"Why have you been so disconnected?" He lifted his chin as he spoke, this man was somehow different than Farren and George. Hawk reached over and tightened his grip on the carrying case with the portrait inside.

"Like I said before: because I am old. The older you get, Dr. Hawkes, the harder it is to do all the things you like to do. I used to be involved around here every day. Then I retired. I had some family who worked for the company, and they used to keep me in the information stream of what was going on each day. You know, make me feel like I was still a part of it, but a few years back they retired, and then . . . well, all I could do was wait."

"Then you saw the signal and sent me on a quest to find what you had to give me." Hawk said.

"Yes. The clues had been designed and ready for years. I worked a great deal in designing Epcot's World Showcase. It was Walt's dream, you know . . . Epcot. So I always felt like I was in some way completing the work I started way back in the days I worked for WED in California. Oh, yes . . ." Press shook his head. "I was in the middle of telling you the story about me. I found out that I had been promoted and was now a part of WED

Enterprises. Later we were called Imagineers. I came to Florida with the team that helped create the Magic Kingdom and Epcot."

Hawk watched as the man paused to catch his breath. Doing the math quickly in his head, Hawk realized the Imagineer standing in front of him had to be over ninety years old. Press had certainly seen a lot of changes through the years as he had transitioned from the west coast to the east as the world of Disney expanded.

"Now I just have to know something." Press lifted his hand with a raised finger. "Was one of the Imagineers Walt chose for this special assignment Farren Rales?"

"Yes, it was." The question surprised Hawk, but it reminded him that Farren had always said he didn't know who was a part of Walt and Roy's elaborate plan. It only made sense that Press wouldn't be aware either.

"Ah, that is great. I always suspected it. I'll bet he was the one who was in charge of selecting you. Right?"

"Right. I am a good friend of Farren's," Hawk told him. Hawk allowed his mind to whir and wonder if the two had been friends, whether they had merely been acquaintances, or whether they had remained close through the years.

"Oh, he is still alive then . . . wonderful. I have not heard of him for a number of years now. So glad he is still with us." Press's face seemed to beam in the shadow of the tunnel. "Now you must tell me: who was the other Imagineer who was a part of our legacy team?"

Hawk opened his mouth to respond, then paused. He wanted to answer, but at the same time, he had just met Preston Child—and if he had learned anything in this journey, it was that nothing was ever as it appeared.

Even as he hesitated, he glimpsed movement behind Press and leaned forward to see what it was. Hawk stared in horror as a knife blade reflected a glimmer of light in the tunnel and was quickly, sleekly pushed up against Preston's throat.

The old man jerked back, his cane tumbled to the concrete floor with a clank, and he was being pulled backward and supported by an arm around his chest while the other held the blade to his throat.

"The name of the other Imagineer would be George Colmes," said a female voice behind Press.

"Oh my." Press turned his head to see who had grabbed him. A relaxed smile crossed his face. "Easy now. I am just an old man."

"Don't say anything else and you won't get hurt." Kiran Roberts's face broke into a broad smile as she looked down the tunnel toward Hawk.

"Kiran, let him go." Hawk took another step toward Press. "This is not going to do you any good." His adrenaline was racing, and yet . . . something about this still wasn't as it seemed.

"It is so good to see you, Hawk. I have missed you so much, and I am sure you have missed me." Kiran tilted her head so she could see him better. "Do you think about me a lot? I know I think about you, nearly every single day. You look good. Life treating you good?"

"Kiran, your problem is with me. Not him." Hawk took another step toward them, keeping his eyes on Kiran, desperate for a way to distract her. "Why not put the knife down, and let's take a look at what I have in the case."

Kiran Roberts was capable of anything. Hawk was convinced of that. She was unstable and totally unpredictable except in her lust for the secrets left behind by Walt Disney. She had proven there was nothing she wouldn't do to attain them.

"I told you, but you didn't believe me." Kiran laughed. "I told you I had the third Imagineer."

"You told him what?" Press now said over his shoulder. "What is going on here? Cut out this foolishness and let me go, right now."

"Don't move and you won't get hurt," Kiran said in his ear.

"Press, just stay still and do what she tells you," Hawk said as he took another step closer.

"Listen, sweetheart," Kiran nearly purred at him. "I see you trying to come over here and see me up close and personal, but you need to quit moving or this is going to turn out badly. And we both know how awful I can make your life, don't we?"

Hawk stopped moving. In an instant his mind flashed back to all the memories he had collected with Kiran. He remembered when he had believed they were friends. He relieved moments when she had helped him find those first clues that Farren had hidden from him. He then recalled how she had tried to kill both Kate and himself. The painful reality of how he had allowed her to manipulate and play him hurt deeply. Each memory and moment flew across his brain, and he was reminded again just how dangerous she was.

"Now here's what is going to happen. You are going to set down the case and walk back out of the tunnel and exit the attraction," Kiran said with a smile. "If you do what I ask, we all will live happily ever after."

"Let me give you another option." The voice came from over Hawk's shoulder, startling them all.

Hawk turned to see that another figure had moved into the tunnel. He instantly recognized the toned athletic form that emerged from the shadows behind him. Gun drawn and leveled toward Press and Kiran, Agent Jillian Batterson stepped up beside him.

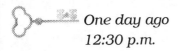 *One day ago*
12:30 p.m.

JILLIAN STOOD WITH HER WEAPON aimed directly at Kiran. Her hand was steady, and Hawk noticed her breathing was slow. If the situation felt tense to her, she did not give any indication. Hawk anxiously shifted his weight.

"Hmm . . . you have a new friend, it appears." Kiran's smile disappeared. "I'm jealous, Hawk."

Jillian cut her eyes quickly to Hawk before returning her glare back to Kiran. "Here is your other option. Actually, it is your only option. You are going to drop the knife, step away from the kind old man, and step to the side so I don't shoot you between your crazy eyes."

"Crazy eyes?" Kiran laughed. "I am a lot of things, but crazy isn't one of them."

"I've read your file. Actually, crazy is at the top of your list . . . you are bat-out-of-the-belfry crazy." Jillian stepped in front of Hawk. "Drop the knife."

"Relax." The old Imagineer turned his head toward Kiran. "Stay calm. Don't do anything rash here." He turned back toward Hawk and Batterson. "There is no need for violence; nothing bad needs to happen here."

"You're right." Jillian's grip remained steady, and the handgun did not move. "I am trying to make sure nothing bad happens here."

"Listen to what she says," Press said to Kiran. "Drop the knife; they don't understand."

"Understand what?" Hawk stepped up and stood next to Jillian. His hand firmly gripped the protective case holding the painting.

"You don't understand that my granddaughter would never hurt me. She loves me." Press said to Hawk.

"Your what?" Jillian turned her head to Hawk for confirmation.

Hawk felt his jaw drop slightly. His *granddaughter?*

Suddenly the old man fell forward. The blur of motion shielded Kiran as she disappeared into the shadows behind him. Jillian had taken her eyes off of Kiran just long enough to stare at Press in surprise at the startling news—and in that moment, Kiran had done what she always managed to do. She had grabbed the moment of surprise and turned it into her moment to manage. She was gone. Her footsteps echoed down the tunnel back toward them.

"Check on the old man!" Jillian yelled as she raced off into the darkness after Kiran. Hawk rushed forward and leaned over Press. Kiran had shoved him forward, causing him to stumble. The push hadn't been violent—instead it was a well-placed move that used the old Imagineer as a shield so she could gain the few seconds she needed to extract herself from the situation. It had worked.

Carefully setting the case on the concrete, Hawk knelt down and faced Press. He placed a hand gently on his shoulder and helped him slowly straighten back up. When Press was mostly up, Hawk reached over and retrieved the fallen cane. He placed it in the old man's hand, and Walt's old friend used it to stabilize himself in a seated position on the concrete.

"I'm fine." Press coughed as he tried to laugh. "Just a little startled. Give me a second to catch my breath."

Hawk waited and watched the man closely. He tried to read his face as Press relaxed and regained his composure. He noticed that Press's cheeks flushed a bit, and his bony fingers were turning white as he gripped the cane. Hawk sensed he was embarrassed—but he had questions too. He heard himself ask the first one. The sound of his voice was weaker than he had intended.

"Kiran is your granddaughter?"

"Yes, yes . . . she is my only grandchild. Her mom, Nancy, is my daughter." Press responded.

"Nancy Alport?" Hawk had wondered what had happened to her.

Nancy had worked for Farren Rales for years and was his assistant when Hawk first met the Imagineer. When Rales retired from working day to day with the company, Hawk had brought Nancy on staff with him. She had managed his new office and helped him during the early transition days as he became the CCA of the Disney Company. During his battle with Reginald Cambridge, Nancy had mysteriously disappeared. They'd discovered that she was the person responsible for allowing Hawk's enemies to track him at all times, but the sheriff's department had never found her, and she had dropped off the grid. She hadn't been seen for years.

Kiran had dropped the bombshell of Nancy's relation to her, stunning Hawk and explaining that Nancy had realized long ago that Farren was the keeper of some great mystery Walt Disney had designed. Nancy had told the stories to her daughter, and as a pair they believed that one day, Farren might choose Kiran to be the one to share those secrets with. The selection of Dr. Grayson Hawkes, the former pastor of the Celebration Community Church, had changed all of their plans. Now, in the matter of a just a few minutes, all of the pieces of mystery had become interlocked in the person of Preston Child, the third Imagineer.

Press, thankfully, seemed perfectly willing to talk. "Nancy worked for the company for a number of years. I helped her get a job with Farren Rales. After she started to work with him, she would occasionally share stories of how Farren was working, and I began to suspect that maybe, just maybe, he might be a part of Walt and Roy's legacy team. She also told me about you. How you and Farren had become friends, how he met with you and your church staff to teach you about how to tell a great story. Nancy also said that you and Farren had grown very close. After you became the head of the company, I realized that you were indeed the chosen one."

"Where is Nancy these days?" Hawk asked, trying to sound as casual as possible. His mind was spinning through a cyclone of scenarios trying to make this situation make some sense.

"Gone." Press coughed again. He looked downward. "A few years ago she just left. She never said good-bye—just up and left. Kiran and I haven't heard from her since. I have been worried. Fathers never stop worrying, and I just don't understand what happened. Did you fire her?"

Hawk felt a pang for the old man and answered truthfully. "No, she did the same to me that she did to you. One day she just left. She offered no explanation; she just didn't show up one day." The explanation had been offered by Kiran. There was a part of Hawk that believed Kiran knew exactly where her mother was.

Press looked into Hawk's eyes. His own were tired, bloodshot, and rimmed with tears. "What was this about? Why did my granddaughter just put a knife against my throat?" His voice cracked.

Hawk read his expression. The old man's bony hand wiped his forehead, and he waited for an answer. Was he really surprised, or was he too part of this elaborate scheme to steal the secrets of the kingdom? Hawk decided to only share as much as he felt comfortable with, leaving plenty of room for him to eventually figure out how Preston Child fit into the bigger picture.

"Your granddaughter is an interesting woman," he said in a pastoral tone. "She is not what or who you think she is, I'm sorry to say."

"What does that mean?" Press sounded surprised and defensive.

"She wants to have for herself whatever it is that Walt Disney chose you to protect."

"Whatever it is?" The old Imagineer's voice grew sharper. "You don't know what it is yet?"

"No. You told me to bring you a painting, so I brought it. You have to tell me what it means." Hawk said it more defensively than he had intended.

"I don't know what it means! I just know that you need it." Press tried to get to his feet with the help of the cane. His voice was laced with feistiness that bordered on frustration. "Once you see it, you should know what to do with it."

Hawk tried to help him, but the man struggled to be independent and do it alone. Hawk used his hands to guide him with support more than actually help him. Finally, Press was back on his feet and standing on his own power.

Press straightened himself into a dignified posture and then began moving down the tunnel. "I am supposed to give you this piece of the plan. I was told years ago that if I were to give you the one thing you needed, you would have everything else to work it out."

Hawk moved next to him. Without discussing it, they made their way back toward the main entrance. As they stepped out of the tunnel onto the covered PeopleMover track, the heat of the day chased away the last remnants of shade and relief provided by the tunnel. In the light, Hawk saw the deep lines crossing the Imagineer's face. He saw how slowly he moved and sensed a tiredness in the man that only comes after years of living.

"My granddaughter is a good girl. She is a lot like her mother. They both seemed to enjoy working for the Disney Company until you arrived. Perhaps you aren't the man Farren believed you to be." Press kept pulling away every time Hawk reached over to help him navigate the second-story walkway. "And now, after all these years, you don't know what to do with the clue I have given you."

Hawk said nothing to defend himself. He didn't know what to say. Rubbing his forehead with his fingertips, he tried to reengage his mind into what he had missed when he looked at the painting. A heaviness bore down on him as he realized he had no idea what do with the newest clue. As Hawk and Press slowly and painstakingly entered the boarding area, Hawk spotted Jillian Batterson walking up the motionless ramp. Jacket opened, sweat causing her blouse to stick to her body, she was breathing hard as she stepped onto the platform. Before she could say anything, Hawk knew with a sinking feeling in his gut that Kiran had gotten away.

"You didn't catch her." Hawk stated the obvious.

"No, I didn't." Jillian nearly spit out the words. "She just disappeared somehow."

"She knows all the access points for the attraction. Every stairwell, every emergency exit, I guarantee it." Hawk looked around as if he might catch a glimpse of her below. "Kiran knows her way around the resort as well as anyone I know. She was a tour guide, she worked behind the scenes, her grandfather was an Imagineer, and her mother worked for one." Even as he spoke, Hawk realized that in Kiran, whether he wanted to admit it or not, he had an adversary with enough knowledge of the resort to maneuver just as well as he could. Or maybe even better.

Jillian reached over and placed a hand on Preston's arm. With Jillian guiding him toward the ramp, they slowly began to make their way down. Hawk followed, carefully watching their progress as they descended down into Tomorrowland.

"Mr. Child," Jillian said to Press as they arrived at the bottom of the ramp, "I really need to talk with you and figure out a little more about what is going on. The sheriff has been looking for your daughter and granddaughter. I am sure they will want some help."

"If you want to take him over to my office, you can talk with him there, it's comfortable, he can relax." Hawk offered.

"That works." Jillian guided Press toward Buzz Lightyear's Space Ranger Spin.

"Hold up," Hawk called after her. As she turned, he whispered in her ear, "Thanks for showing up when you did. Your timing was perfect."

She smiled. "You're in a mess, Grayson Hawkes. Even Jiminy Crockett couldn't help you."

"Huh?"

"Isn't he a Disney character?" Jillian blinked.

"Well, yes, sort of. Davy Crockett was a real person Walt Disney made a series of movies about. You know, the raccoon skin cap and all . . . and then Jiminy Cricket is well, a cricket." Hawk shrugged. "But Jiminy Crockett is not a Disney character."

"I don't care." Jillian turned again to leave. "I had your back; you're welcome." As she guided Preston away, she muttered under her breath loudly enough for Hawk to hear, "Disney geeks."

Hawk found himself smiling as he watched them walk away. Still holding the carrying case in his hand, it dawned on him that he was now standing all alone, in full view of the guests, with a painting worth over a half-million dollars in his hand. He wanted to get someplace where he could examine the painting with some privacy. That Press hadn't given him any new information was a blow. Press had apparently just wanted to see the painting and perhaps hear what Hawk knew about it. The revelation that the Imagineer didn't know what the clue meant forced the mystery back upon Hawk. He would have to restudy the painting and look for something he had somehow missed before.

Hawk's phone dinged, notifying him that he had a text message. Finding it in his pocket, he touched his finger to the touch screen and read the message from Shep: *Bring painting to Seven Dwarfs Mine Train, loading area.*

Wrinkling his forehead, Hawk reread the message. Why would Shep . . .

A sinking feeling in his stomach told him something was wrong.

He touched the call back icon and listened as the call went to Shep's phone and instantly sent him to voicemail. As the beep sounded, Hawk hesitated and then left a message.

"I got your text, wanted to see what's up. On my way over now from Tomorrowland."

CHAPTER 44

One Day Ago
4:18 p.m.

HAWK QUICKLY MADE HIS WAY TOWARD Fantasyland. The futuristic, sleek lines of Tomorrowland gave way to the brick walls and towers of the castle surrounding the whimsical world of fairy tales and princesses. As he turned the corner next to the brightly colored spinning teacups, he saw instantly that there was no line for the roller-coaster attraction. That was highly unusual and could only mean it was closed temporarily. But there was no scheduled closure for this day, so something was going on.

Hawk increased his pace as he stepped beyond the entrance gates and began to wind his way through the queue line toward the area where guests would board the mine train. Walt Disney World's Seven Dwarfs Mine Train was considered by some Disney fans to be the most beautiful attraction in the history of the Magic Kingdom. The mountain that provided its home formed the heart of Fantasyland. The mine train rolled through a lush forest, rocketed past intricately detailed rockwork, and rumbled through a gem mine worked by the dwarfs, made famous by Walt Disney's first feature-length film, 1937's *Snow White and the Seven Dwarfs*. The vehicles resembled hand-carved wooden carts.

What most guests didn't take the time to realize was that this attraction was actually a prequel to the no-longer-in-existence Snow White's Scary Adventures. The conclusion of the ride pulled up next to the dwarfs' cottage, where all could see Snow White dancing with some of the dwarfs in a delightful scene from the film. But if guests glanced quickly, they would also glimpse the Wicked Witch at the cottage door, cackling, with the poisoned apple in her basket. All the fun has just been a precursor to the real danger about to unfold. In the long-gone original attraction, guests followed the film version of the story, where Snow White was stalked and poisoned by the witch. None of that mattered in this attraction. It was the fun that happened as the danger lurked just outside the door that the Imagineers created for guests to experience.

A sense of foreboding caused Hawk to stop in his tracks for a moment. He wondered if danger was lurking for him beyond what he could see. He had no idea what was going on. But urgency drove him inside.

Holding the carrying case closely by his side, he wound his way inside the cool cavern of the mine, headed toward the area where guests would load and unload on the mine train. The footprints of various forest creatures, as well as sticks, stones, and acorns, were embedded in the earthen walkway that carried him closer and closer to the main entrance. The waiting area wound around a couple of blind curves, creating the illusion of being inside a mine and opening into a cavern that served as the loading and unloading area of the ride. In the final series of switchbacks, guests could get a great preview of the train itself, people climbing on board, and the train leaving the take-off area. Faux wooden gates, timbers and braces were imbedded in and around the rock walls, making it look as if the cavern was secure but had taken years to carve out and make usable. As soon as he rounded the curve, he realized that something was dreadfully wrong.

Standing across from him, on the other side of the mine train itself, separated from him by wooden loading doors, ropes, pylons, the track, and the train were two women—both watching his every step as he approached. The shapely woman standing directly behind the mine train was dressed in a full-length black jacket that nearly touched the ground. A smirk written across her face, hands on her hips, she waited for Hawk to get closer. He recognized her instantly. It was Nancy Alport. To his right, also within the barrier of loading doors and train track, was Kiran Roberts. She was standing behind the control panel of the ride mechanism, hands placed on both sides of it, leaning slightly forward with a broad smile lighting up her face.

"Well, well, well," Nancy spoke first. "If it isn't my old boss."

Hawk tried to hide his surprise at seeing her. "Nancy, I want you to know that I somehow missed your resignation letter. I just assumed you weren't ever coming back to work."

"Witty like always. You know, that's what I liked about you. Your sense of humor. You were always a little irreverent, which was so odd with you being a reverend and all . . . but you always had this unshakable streak that wanted to do the right thing. You were impossible to work with. So I quit." Nancy smiled as she said it. "I haven't missed you a bit."

"I met your dad. He seems like a very nice man." Hawk cleared his throat as he spoke.

"That's what I hear. He is a saint, somewhat misguided, incredibly loyal to his promise to Walt, and so naïve as to how the world works."

"So he really doesn't know about the way you and your daughter like to do things?"

"The way we like to do things?" Kiran spoke up. Her voice was a little heated. "My mother and I only want to do the best things and claim what is rightfully ours. Which, of course, is why you are here."

"If it's rightfully yours, why bother stealing it?" Hawk asked. Hawk searched quickly for some sign of Shep, but he couldn't see anything.

Nancy crossed her arms. "I worked for old man Rales for a lot of years. I realized that he was an Imagineer like my dad, that Walt had given him some great secret to take care of. And like my dad, he was incredibly loyal to Walt and Roy."

"That's why Walt chose them," Hawk said.

"Don't even attempt to lecture me about either of them." Nancy cut him off.

"I wasn't going to lecture; I was just making a point." Hawk said.

"Give him enough time and he'll start preaching," Kiran said smugly.

Nancy ignored her too. "Rales was getting older, my father was getting older, and the time was coming to pass along the secrets of the great Walt Disney. I was a loyal company person, my daughter was a loyal Disney employee and expert on the company. Destiny would have us be the ones chosen to inherit the riches of all that Walt left behind with the Imagineers." Nancy smiled as she remembered the past. "Then you came along. The storyteller in you intrigued Rales. He grew to think of you as the son he never had, and then the next thing you know, you become the head of the company. It was painfully obvious that he gave you the secrets of Walt, and the rest of the things you needed to know were not too far behind."

"I did my best to stay close to you." Kiran leaned against the ride controls. "I could have been by your side, Hawk. Together we could have taken the world of Walt to an entirely different level. But you just weren't willing to share and play nice. So we couldn't trust you anymore to do the right thing."

"So you decided to do whatever it took to steal what Walt left behind?" Hawk knew the answer, but he stalled and tried to comprehend where Shep might be.

"My father has always called it Walt Disney's legacy. That is what we are after. It's what we are entitled to and you are not deserving of." Nancy stepped closer to the train car that sat in place along the track and extended her hand. "So reach over the fence, place the painting on the ground, and leave. Now!"

"You don't really think I'm going to do that, do you?"

"She was hoping you would, Sweetheart. I knew better." Kiran picked up something from the control panel and threw it toward Hawk.

It flipped through the air, and he could tell it was a cell phone. Watching it come straight toward him, he let go of the painting, reached up, and caught the flying phone, cradling it in both hands as he did.

"Great catch," Kiran said, pleased. "Now look at the pictures."

Hawk realized as he turned the phone over in his hand that it belonged to Shep. Touching the photo icon, he instantly saw what Kiran and Nancy intended for him to see. It was a picture of Shep, bound, gagged, and tied to a familiar roller-coaster track. The color, the style, and the details alerted him instantly that Shep was here—he was tied up somewhere on the track of the Seven Dwarf's Mine Train. He looked up, eyes widening, toward Kiran and Nancy.

"Well, Mom . . . I think he figured it out," Kiran said to Nancy.

"Then I will tell you again," Nancy said, her voice cold. "Give me the painting, but this time you are going to toss it over to me, and then you can go and help your friend. If you don't, I am afraid that Shep will probably not survive." Nancy looked to her daughter, who reached down and pushed the green plunger button on the control panel.

Hawk watched in horror as the mine train streaked out of the loading area with a squeal that echoed off the rock walls. Then the room fell silent for a moment that seemed just as deafening.

"Toss her the painting, and I will push the stop button." Kiran held the control up, teasing Hawk by almost pushing the red plunger that would stop the ride. "If you don't . . . well, you know. The ride lasts less than two minutes. You don't know where our old buddy Shep is tied up, so maybe he has less than ninety seconds. We are standing here talking and wasting his time, so you might have a minute to end this and save him." Her expression narrowed. "Toss the painting and I stop the ride. If not, I can promise you—you will never get over the fence and across the track to us in time to do it. Because to be honest with you, I would love the chance to stop you."

As she finished, Kiran pulled out the same knife she had held to her grandfather a short time ago and gently placed it on the ride controls.

"Is that the same knife you used to get Reginald Cambridge out of your way?" Hawk nodded his head toward the weapon.

Kiran laughed. "Reginald was a useful tool for me. He was great for keeping you occupied, for creating mayhem, and he had a mean streak. It was much better and easier for me to have him around."

"So why did you kill him?"

"I didn't kill him. If you haven't figured it out yet, genius, there are more people than just me trying to get Walt's legacy. You have someone out there after it who is far more dangerous than me." Kiran laughed again.

"Shep is running out of time." Nancy smiled. It was an evil, malicious grin.

But she was right.

Hawk swung the case and lofted it across the track. It clattered to the ground at Nancy's feet. She bent down and retrieved it, cracked open the case to peek inside, and then closed it.

"Good choice." She turned with the case in her hand and nodded to Kiran.

Hesitating another moment with her hand just above the red plunger, Kiran looked at him, winked, and then pushed it. The emergency stop alarm sounded, and immediately Kiran and her mother raced out of the exit area and were gone.

Hawk jumped across the loading safety fence, leapt across the track to the side where Kiran and Nancy had been, and ran to the control panel. The lights flashed a warning that the ride had been stopped, and he could see that there was only one mine train currently on the track. It had been stopped inside the mine area of the sequence.

Deciding to work his way from the back of the track forward, Hawk moved out and began to walk along the track from the exit area. He slowly navigated the track, making sure he did not slip and fall through the openings of the metal rails. He was guessing Shep was somewhere near the end of the ride, perhaps near the dwarfs' cottage. He carefully made his way along the track and realized that here, in this area, he was out of the line of sight of any theme park guest. You had to be on the ride to see this portion of it. He moved quicker, certain that he was getting close. Rounding the corner, he saw Shep, firmly secured to the track with a series of ropes. The gag in his mouth was tied so tightly that he couldn't speak. Shep's eyes widened as he saw Hawk come around the bend, Hawk quickly released his mouth from the gag and went to work on the ropes.

"Those two women were waiting for me at the Contemporary Resort. They drove up next to me. The older lady I didn't know was Nancy Alport called me over to the car, and then the next thing I know I got hit with some kind of electrical jolt. I am so sorry, Hawk. I guess it was a Taser of some kind. It dropped me. Kiran kicked me and then they hoisted me into the car."

Hawk just shook his head as he worked on the ropes, relief flooding his body at the sound of his friend's voice. "It's okay, Shep. How did you get here?"

"They hit me with the shocky thing a second time and blindfolded me. They put me on some kind of cart. A golf cart or work cart or something and drove me here. They tied me up and dragged me across the track before tying me down. They told me that if you didn't get here in time, they would let me get run over by a mine train."

"How long have you been here?" Hawk continued to unknot the ropes.

"Since before the Magic Kingdom opened this morning."

Hawk put the timeline together in his head. Shep had been the insurance policy Kiran had put into place in case he didn't turn over the painting in the PeopleMover. They had somehow managed to set up for the attraction to be closed, taken Shep's phone, and waited for the events of the morning to play out. They had managed to stay a step ahead of him all day.

"Did you give them the painting?" Shep asked as he was finally freed. He rubbed his hands to get circulation moving in them once again.

"Yes, I had to give it to them. I had to find you." Hawk smiled at his friend.

"Thanks, like I said, I'm sorry."

"You have nothing to be sorry about." Hawk responded . . . and then he heard something.

Holding his head up and straining to listen, he heard the whine and felt the vibration in the track they were both seated on. Grabbing Shep, he tugged at his friend's stiff, clumsy form—Shep had been there so long he wasn't yet able to move very well. Hawk pulled him off the track just as the mine train car roared around the corner, swaying toward them, and then zoomed past where they had just been.

The breeze from the passing train blew their hair. Shep looked with wide eyes at the passing train and then at Hawk. Both realized that if they had been on the track, they could have been hurt or killed.

"Glad you made it in time." Shep patted his friend on the shoulder.

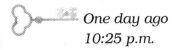 *One day ago*
10:25 p.m.

LOOKING OUT OVER THE MAGIC KINGDOM from the conference room in the Bay Lake Tower office, Hawk watched the finale of the nighttime fireworks spectacular. As the last sparkle of light disappeared into the darkness of the sky, leaving behind its smoky remains, Hawk felt as if his opportunity to save Walt's secret had disappeared like the lights. Like the painting with Nancy and Kiran. Lost in this thoughts, he didn't hear Juliette take a seat in the chair behind him. He was startled as she spoke.

"I am going to give you grief for losing an incredibly valuable painting later. Right now, I'm just glad that you're fine and that you pulled Shep off the train track."

"Is he okay?" Hawk turned in his seat to face her.

"Sure, just a little shook up. I think the jolts of electricity surging through him probably did him good." Juliette smiled as she said it.

Hawk returned the smile, and then it faded. "I knew it had to be a trap, but I went anyway. The text message was way too odd . . . but I had to go."

"Of course you did. What else could you have done?"

The two sat at the table as the lights of the Magic Kingdom at night painted an enchanted background for the nightmare scenario they had been living through. After waiting for a few moments trying to organize his thoughts, Hawk realized he was stuck. He had no idea where Kiran and Nancy might be. He had no idea what was on the painting that was supposed to be the next clue or how it could help him figure out the puzzle he had been pursuing. There was nowhere to go, no action to take, and nothing more that he could think of.

"You have a very confused Imagineer in your office right now." Juliette reached over and patted Hawk on the arm.

"Has he been helpful?"

"Not from what I've overheard." Juliette glanced back. "Jillian Batterson is pretty impressive. She has been talking with him, getting information. She's managed to very gently move him along. She knows a great deal about this legacy that Walt Disney has left for you to find, although she knows nothing about what it really is . . . because Preston Child, George Colmes, and Farren Rales only worked on a need-to-know basis." Juliette looked at Hawk with tired eyes. "Walt Disney knew what he was doing. He was brilliant, and this secret or legacy or whatever, is huge. Whatever it is you know or are supposed to know, it's so much bigger than we ever dreamed a few years ago."

"But apparently I need the painting to figure it all out or put the pieces together. And I have managed to lose it." Hawk sighed.

"Like I said, we can talk about you losing the painting later, but for now you need to figure out how to get it back." Juliette rubbed the back of her neck.

A gentle knock against the doorframe of the open door drew their attention. Jillian stood there waiting for them to look her way. She rested a hand against the doorframe and leaned against it. She too looked tired.

"How are you doing Hawk?" Jillian asked, concerned.

"I'm okay. And you?"

"Good, thanks for asking." She straightened up in the doorway. "I'd like to know if it's all right if we let Preston chill here for the night. I don't want to have to send him home and put him into a protective custody situation. I think we can keep him safer here for now."

"Did he really not know that his daughter and granddaughter were working so hard to steal what he was trying to protect?" Juliette asked.

"That's his story," Jillian answered.

"You believe him?" Hawk leaned forward in his chair.

"So far, I would say . . . yes, I think he's telling the truth." Jillian sighed. "But I have a lot of other things I want to talk with him about. His story is absolutely fascinating." She looked directly at Hawk. "And then, later, I have some more questions for you that I would like you to answer for me." She raised an eyebrow as she said it.

"I always try to be helpful."

"Sure you do." She turned to go back across the hallway. "I am going to set him up to stay in one of the office suites. I've got the sheriff's department in line to provide security."

"Let me help get him settled." Juliette pushed back from the conference room table and stood. "Follow me, and I'll show you where he can get some sleep for the night."

Hawk watched as Juliette moved out of the room. Jillian followed her, and as she left, she glanced back over her shoulder, once more making eye contact with Hawk. Her gaze was penetrating. It seemed if she was trying to unravel and understand the complexities of his world in a single look. Just as quickly, she turned away and moved into the other office.

Hawk turned back toward the window and looked out over the Magic Kingdom. The lights of Cinderella Castle glowed against a black sky. The brilliant white design of Space Mountain and the twinkling lights of the entrance to the theme park invited guests to enter a world where dreams really could come true. As bleak and confusing as things seemed, there were some things that offered hope. Jonathan was going to be all right; the nasty bump on his head was nothing serious, and they were going to be letting him out of the hospital soon. Hawk had found Shep in time. The sheriff's department had taken him home and were going to be keeping an eye on him. Farren was getting stronger each day and was expected to make a complete recovery. The mysterious third Imagineer had been found. He was real. That was a relief to Hawk personally, because there had been some days when he believed he never would find him.

Meanwhile, old enemies had returned. Kiran Roberts and Nancy Alport had continued to surprise him and once again had become a threat to what he had been entrusted with. Now that they had the painting, he had to figure out how to get it back, and he couldn't do that until he figured out how to find them. Hawk rubbed his temples with the tips of his fingers and thought again about Reginald Cambridge. By his own admission, Reginald had been the one who had threatened Hawk by planning the series of potential attacks throughout the resort. Now he was dead. Kiran had denied killing him and suggested there were other enemies that Hawk should be worried about. But who? Kiran and Reginald had always been the villains at the top of Hawk's list. Nancy Alport was up there as well, but if Kiran hadn't been responsible for killing Reginald, it meant there was someone else out there. And Hawk had no idea who.

He shook his head to clear it and reminded himself that Kiran couldn't be trusted. She always spoke in partial truths and was the queen of manipulation.

She would twist and turn every situation into a pretzel that she could use to her own advantage.

Hawk stood and stepped over to the window, allowing his forehead to touch the glass. The glow of the lights flicked across his face as he continued to think. He had to recover the painting. He had to have it to figure out the next piece of the mystery, and he had to keep his promise to finish this battle once and for all.

His phone emitted a notification ding, letting him know he had a text message. It was the first time he had checked his phone since the text from Shep's phone earlier in the day. Taking it and sliding his index finger across the screen, he cradled it in his hand and read the screen. He lowered his brow as he focused on the words glowing in the message.

You have messed up and lost what you needed most—today your world will end—it begins as I send it into orbit.

Hawk looked around the room. He was still alone. The sound of voices he had heard a few minutes ago had faded into silence, and he realized that Juliette and Jillian were probably busy getting Preston the accommodations he needed for the night. He looked at the screen and read the words again. The message was from an unknown caller . . . and it was written like a clue. Hawk's mind instantly began to decipher the meaning of the message. In quick bursts of thought, a series of ideas raced through his mind. He had messed up and lost the painting. That was indeed what he thought he needed most. Whoever had sent this knew he had lost the painting. Today the world, his world, would end. This threat was both personal and had the ripple effect of threatening the entire resort. The world Walt had created was now his to run, manage, and lead. He understood better than anyone else that he was the keeper of the kingdom. He was the one who possessed the key to it all. But the end of the text, the last line . . . it was an opening. That was either on purpose or by accident, he wasn't sure which. It begins as I send it— meaning the world that Hawk was in charge of—into orbit.

Raising his head and looking back toward the Magic Kingdom, Hawk took in the sight of the massive and majestic Space Mountain, and behind it, the lights of the Astro Orbiter. Into orbit.

Hawk turned and moved quickly out into the hallway. It was empty, and he slowed once again, listening for any sounds. Hearing no voices, he headed into the hall and turned to his left. He decided to take the stairwell down instead of the elevator. He hoped he was wrong, dreaded that he was right. There was going to be an attack on the Magic Kingdom and he knew where it was going to begin. Or so he thought.

Racing down the stairs, he opened the door and dashed through the lobby. A sheriff's department officer saw him emerge from the stairwell and came toward him. "Get in touch with Sheriff McManus," Hawk called out to him, not slowing his steps. "Have him call me."

The deputy looked alarmed. "What else can I do to help?" he asked.

"Just get in touch with the sheriff!" Hawk yelled over his shoulder as he moved into the darkness of the early morning. His heart pounded in his chest as he raced across the parking lot and down the red brick walkway from the Contemporary Resort toward the Magic Kingdom. Veering off the path, he went down a sidewalk, through a hedge-lined gateway, and into a service area he knew would take him to the off-stage area of Tomorrowland.

It was now after midnight. The Magic Kingdom was closed, and only a very small number of people were still in the area. Grabbing a maintenance cast member, he pulled him aside and told him to find his lead supervisor. "On my instruction, I want all your personnel out of Tomorrowland immediately. Do you understand?"

The seriousness of the task sent the young man running to share the information, and Hawk pushed his way through the backstage doors and into the guest area. He focused his eyes toward the center of the themed area and ran toward the elevator of the Astro Orbiter.

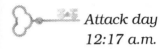 *Attack day*
12:17 a.m.

TWO METALLIC DOORS CLOSED WITH A SOFT CLICK, and the elevator began its rapid three-story ascent to the top of the Astro Orbiter. The ride up to the attraction's loading platform would only take a few moments, but as the doors shut and the floor beneath him began to vibrate, Hawk knew he had made an error. On a normal night in the Magic Kingdom, guests rode the elevator skyward along the gantry and were deposited into the boarding area of the Astro Orbiter.

The genesis of Hawk's mistake was in assuming this night was normal.

In recent years, Hawk had refurbished the galactic attraction—the visual centerpiece of Tomorrowland—so that now, not only did the twelve rockets rotate around the ornate ironwork of the center tower, but the planets also swirled around the outside. The proximity of the twirling planets and moons spinning around the open-air rockets while they rotated in the opposite direction created the illusion of speed at a dizzying height. To enhance the illusion even more, each guest would have to ride up one of two elevators along the launchpad gantry to board their starship. He had been passionate about the remodel and redesign. There had been extensive coverage of it in the press.

Hawk had stepped inside the elevator marked "Lift B to Rocket Platform" and pushed the button that would take him to the top of Rocket Tower Plaza. But a hitch in the upward movement of the car gave way to a sudden jerk, and then the lift squeaked to a halt between the second and third levels. The ride had lasted just a few moments, but it was long enough for Hawk to realize he had stepped into a trap. The unplanned stop could have been a random malfunction, yet somehow he knew this was not the case. In his rushed attempt to reach the Astro Orbiter, he had ignored what should have been obvious.

The message had been designed to taunt him, scare him, intimidate him, and also bait him into coming to the attraction. Whoever had texted it to him knew him well enough to know that he would impulsively and instinctively head toward the danger that lurked out there. Although he had sounded the alarm and let the sheriff know something was going on, although he had tried to clear the area of all cast members, he had still stepped onto the elevator.

It had been a mistake.

Reflexively he pressed the control buttons, but the elevator wouldn't budge. The lights flickered and then went to black. For a few brief seconds, Hawk was swallowed up by darkness until an emergency light fought through the inkiness and cast an eerie jade glow across the interior. Hawk took advantage of the illumination to start looking for a way out. The ominous sensation of being trapped inside a closed box threatened to cloud his clarity in searching for an escape.

An explosion jarred the elevator car violently, and the gantry shuddered, driving Hawk against the floor. His ears ringing from the deafening blast, he placed a steadying hand along the wall and willed himself back to his feet. The elevator swayed. Through the ringing he heard what sounded like a hiss of steam. A surge of smoke filled the cabin of the elevator, and waves of overheated air rushed into his lungs, causing him to gasp. The temperature inside the elevator was rapidly rising, and Hawk willed his eyes to see through the smoke.

His brain screamed at him to find a way out. Now on his feet, he began mentally replaying the loop of memory he had created moments before. There was an escape hatch on the roof of the elevator. He had seen it. All he had to do now was find it. He had been in situations more dangerous than this; he just had to orient himself and get out while he was still able to think through the fog of smoke that threatened to smother him. Stretching out his arms, he jumped up off the floor and hit the roof. He had guessed correctly; the escape hatch retracted at his touch. Through the blinding haze, he felt his way along the wall and grasped the handrail. He lifted his foot up onto it and launched himself, his fists blasting through the escape panel. Grabbing one side of it, he gripped it tightly, swung his body away from the wall, and pulled himself up.

Thick smoke raced upward through the opening, hungrily searching for an escape, and Hawk envisioned himself riding up it toward safety. With both hands gripping the edge of the opened hatch, he pulled his body up in the billowing plumes of smoke through the opening.

He was holding his breath, halfway through the hole, when a second explosion ripped through the elevator shaft, lifting the car and tossing it back and forth like a pinball trapped between two bumpers. The violent movement tore his hands away from their precious grip on hope, and he was flung like a ragdoll through the air. His body, now covered in slick sweat, thundered onto the bottom of the car. The four-sided metallic fist that trapped him retightened its grip.

Overhead, glowing orange flames peeked through the crawling smoke. Hot sparks rained down through the opening, and a searing pain in the back of his throat prevented him from crying out for help.

The moment he had pressed the button on the elevator, he had made a serious miscalculation. A mistake. This was his fault. He had failed, and this time they had finally beaten him. His chest heavy, and struggling to find his next breath, Hawk closed his eyes as the heat inside the furnace he was trapped in engulfed him.

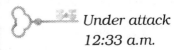 *Under attack*
12:33 a.m.

"GET UP!"

The penetrating heat jarred his body in wave after wave of pain.

"Get up!"

Hawk coughed and heard the roar of the fire around the elevator car.

"Get up!"

He blinked his eyes wide open, yet saw nothing but darkness. Where was he? It was hot, way too hot. The heat was overpowering, and it hurt. His vision couldn't penetrate the darkness around him. Was it smoke? His mind fought to clear a path through the haze of the past few moments. He was lying on the floor of an elevator that threatened to cook him. Flat on his back, face turned upward, he looked into an unclear future. And then the voice.

"Hawk, get up!"

Another cough seemed to clear some of the cloudiness in his head. He heard himself gasping, trying to get air. More coughing, and then from the swirling smoke around him the voice was heard once more.

"Hawk, get on your feet. I can't do this alone."

Hawk rolled to his side. The floor of the elevator felt as if it would sear him if he remained any longer. Pulling up to his knees, he steadied himself as best he could and looked upward toward the escape hatch in the ceiling. That must be where the voice was coming from. The temperature seemed to rise with every breath he struggled to take.

In one push, he rose to his feet. As he did, he saw something cutting through the smoke. An outstretched hand.

"Hawk, take my hand. I'll pull you up the best I can. But you are going to have to grab the opening and help me. I can't get you through the hatch alone."

He couldn't think clearly enough to know who was talking to him, but he knew enough to obey. He reached up and placed his hand inside the hand of his rescuer. He felt the strong grip close around his as he latched on.

"On the count of three, jump up. And grab the side of the opening. One ... two ... three!"

Hawk jumped into the air. The hand he was holding on to pulled him up. The extra force propelled him toward the escape hatch. Hand wildly searching for something to take hold of, he found the side and locked his fingers on it. Now suspended in the air, one hand holding the side of the opening and the other firmly held in place by his rescuer, he kicked his legs and slowly pulled himself up through the opening. He took in a refreshing gulp of air. It wasn't clean air—there was way too much smoke swirling around him—but it was more oxygen than he'd had while trapped inside the fiery box of death below.

Leaning on the roof of the elevator, he felt himself being dragged upward the rest of the way to stand on his feet. His rescuer had not released her grip. Hawk looked into the face of Jillian Batterson.

"I thought I'd lost you for a minute." She smiled, breathing hard, her hair strewn across her face. "You're alive."

"Well toasted, but alive." Hawk returned the smile. "Thanks."

"Don't thank me yet." She turned and looked around the elevator shaft they now occupied. "We aren't out of the pressure cooker yet."

"Follow me." Hawk tapped her on the shoulder. He pointed to an access doorway on the opposite side of the elevator passage. "This is the one the electricians use. It should be unlocked and get us outside the gantry."

Stepping across the roof of the elevator, they moved toward the door. Hawk took a quick glance around and could see the explosion had happened inside the other elevator. The blast radius had rattled the entire gantry, nearly destroyed his elevator car, and started fires inside Rocket Tower Plaza. As they pushed on the door, it opened.

"I wish I'd known this was here. I climbed up this hot mess looking for you," Jillian said as they stepped through the hatch.

They climbed down the ladder inside. The rungs were hot, almost too hot to hold on to, but they didn't grip them long. Downward they climbed, through the rising heat, until they stepped through the access door on the ground level. Stumbling out onto the pavement, they headed toward the open area of Tomorrowland. Hawk and Jillian took in deep breaths as they watched fire and rescue personnel racing into the area. Disney Security and Orange County Sheriff's Department deputies also flooded the area.

"What were you thinking?" Jillian said as she gulped more fresh air.

"I got a text saying I'd messed up and lost what I needed most. Today my world was going to end, and it would begin as it was sent into orbit. I figured there must be an explosive device on the Astro Orbiter, so I was coming to find it." Hawk took in lungful after lungful of air as he spoke. He winced at how foolish he sounded. Why had he tried to do this alone—again?

"Well, you did find it." Jillian offered the understatement of the day.

"How did you find me?"

"We were in Bay Lake Towers tucking in Preston Child for the night when Juliette got a call telling her a news report had just been leaked that said Tomorrowland in the Magic Kingdom had been attacked." Jillian breathed deeply, then continued. "So we raced back to your office to see what might be going on. You were gone. Then I got a call from the sheriff's department saying you had moved into Tomorrowland and cleared all cast members, alerted the sheriff's department . . . and that was it. Which meant you were already here, right in the middle of it all." She again paused to catch her breath. "Juliette has the entire resort on crisis alert. I came here to see what you were into. As I got here I heard the explosion, saw the fire, and guessed that if you were anywhere, you had to be in the elevator. I guessed right."

"I'm glad you did."

"You are fairly predictable. If there is trouble, you seem to be right smack in the middle of it." Jillian lay back on the concrete.

To his surprise, Hawk realized he owed her a lot.

The ground rumbled as another explosive wave raced across Tomorrowland. The noise was loud, and the sound of alarms, hollering, and the cracking of concrete drew their attention to the source of the noise. The Interplanetary Convention Center building was on fire. On the other side of Tomorrowland, Hawk could see the emergency teams scrambling to respond.

"That's explosion number three." Jillian sat up. "We're still under attack."

"Number three of how many?" Hawk looked across the expanse of Tomorrowland.

"That is the question. We can't stay here."

Hawk didn't respond. He was looking back over his shoulder toward the attraction behind him. The gleaming white Space Mountain stood stoically and majestically in the midst of the chaos unfolding around it. Jillian turned to see where Hawk was looking.

"What is it? What are you doing?" She glanced from the attraction back to him.

"I have to do something." He turned and got to his feet.

She reached up and grabbed him by the arm, turning him back toward her.

"You aren't going in there." She pointed toward the mountain. "There might be an explosive device in there as well. Tomorrowland is under attack."

"I know, but I have to risk it. There is something in there I have to save."

"Nothing is that important."

"This is. It's part of why all of this is happening."

They stood in the moment facing one another. Hawk had always taught and lived that each moment was an intersection. Every moment was the place where all of the experiences of your past had brought you to, and at every moment, your next step would take you into your future. What you did in the moment, in that intersection, would either create momentum that would change your life and possibly the world forever, or would squander it, and you would remain stuck in the intersection. He knew the future depended on his moving forward, now, in this moment.

To his surprise, Jillian seemed to know that too.

"Do what you have to do and get back out here." She leaned forward so he could hear her over the increasing noise of rescue vehicles pouring into the area. "I didn't save you from one blast so you could be destroyed in another."

"I'll be fast." Hawk turned and ran toward the gleaming mountain in front of him.

Moving into the entrance area of the attraction, he ran up and down the winding pathways that guests would wait in. He jumped over guardrails and over retaining barriers that allowed him to skip past the usual sights seen by visitors. Stepping back into the deep recesses of the operational area, he wished he had time to turn all the lights on inside the attraction. It was dark, even darker than normal because the stars and meteors that were usually projected were nowhere to be seen with the attraction shut completely down and abandoned.

Hawk shook his head in disbelief at what he was about to do. He was going to climb up into Space Mountain for the second time in less than a week. The first time he was looking for a bomb.

This time he was looking for the reason there might be another one.

As he began making his way up, his strategy was one he knew well. He had mapped it out carefully a number of times before. He would use the access ramps and ascend the track area of the ride. At the top, there was an emergency maintenance landing connected by a small staircase and ladder system that would take him to the very peak of the attraction's interior. Hawk had discovered this years before in studying the drawings of the attraction. He had traveled it a few times since. This portal was where he was headed right now.

It took time in the dark, but he found the series of ladders and, rung over rung, began making his way to the top of the mountain. The narrow landing allowed him to unlock the security lock that would access the roof. He opened it up and found himself looking up into the nighttime Florida sky.

Space Mountain rose 183 feet into the Disney skyline. Illuminated with bright white spotlights, the glowing pearl of Tomorrowland was inspirational, one of the most recognizable landmarks in the Magic Kingdom. The iconic structure had a rocket-shaped spire that protruded from the top, and beyond the view of any guest, the spire contained a compartment at its base that served as a place to store various assorted tools, parts, and wiring. It was never used and was most often ignored. Hawk had found it a few years ago and repurposed it into a secure, weatherproofed hiding place for treasures he had found in his journey to protect the world of Disney. Here he had placed the personal journal and notes that Wernher von Braun had entrusted to Walt, along with the notes Walt had added.

He reached the compartment, aware with every moment that he didn't have much time. He inserted the kingdom key into the specially designed lock he had fabricated in the search and design warehouse and removed the small carrying case that housed the journal.

Quickly returning the lock and securing the hiding place, he turned to go back through the hatch when the next explosion rocked Tomorrowland. This one came from deep inside Space Mountain. The building shuddered, and Hawk was thrown backward as the blast rippled through the interior of the building.

He had been tossed back across the metallic roof, and as he tightly gripped the case, he wondered if he could go back the way he came. The explosion had occurred inside the attraction and he was now on top of it— above the damage and above the inevitable fire that had started below.

He cautiously moved back toward the hatch to look down into the interior of the mountain. Where it had been dark earlier, it was glowing with a red crimson that seemed to pulse into view then disappear. Wisps of smoke came up through the hatch looking for a place to escape, and Hawk felt a sinking feeling knowing he was going to have to descend into the danger lurking below.

Then the fifth explosion occurred, this one from deep inside Space Mountain as well. Instinctively Hawk pulled himself back from the opening, and as he did, smoke billowed out, angrily looking for open air. The mountain rumbled below him; the opening spewed smoke like a volcano. Space Mountain had erupted, and something horrible had happened inside of it. Hawk was trapped on the top of the mountain.

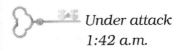 *Under attack*
1:42 a.m.

HAWK STOOD ATOP SPACE MOUNTAIN and looked out over Tomorrowland. The land was on fire. After the five explosions that had already taken place, the rescue personnel and responders were rapidly pulling back, not sure if another was coming or where it might be coming from. It was a long way down to the ground, and he was trapped. Surveying the damage, he saw waves of smoke coming from the Astro Orbiter and the Interplanetary Convention Center, along with the smoke smoldering up from below him inside the mountain. He flexed his fingers into fists; anger rose within him like the smoke racing into the nighttime sky. He had to move. Hawk jumped down off his perch to a more secure plateau about six feet below.

The distinctive look of Space Mountain came from the design of a Disney legend named John Hench. The original drawings of the mountain were what most people expected: concrete beams spaced inside the building to hold up the roof structure. It was Hench's idea to move the beams to the outside. This meant the inside was smooth, and with star fields, planets, and meteors projected against it, would create the illusion of space. The massive beams on the exterior also helped give the illusion of greater height. As the beams grew closer together near the top of the mountain, the forced perspective made the attraction seem even more impressive in sheer size. The exterior beams formed huge oversized spaces that resembled gigantic gutters running down the building from the top to the bottom. Hawk had always been impressed with the design; as were so many things in Walt Disney World, it was genius.

But now, breathing deeply, looking for an escape, he realized for the first time in all the years he had been viewing Space Mountain that each giant gutter resembled a massive slide.

The night breeze blew through his mop of hair as he glanced toward the ground where people scrambled for safety, anticipating the next attack. He knew what he had to do. It was his only chance of escape from Space Mountain.

Hawk took a step and leaned back. For a moment he felt he was in freefall, and then he hit the back of the mountain. His body slid downward, gaining speed with each foot he traveled. There was nothing below him to slow his descent, nothing he could hold on to, to somehow control his speed. Gravity forced him snugly up against the exterior of the mountain, and as he slid downward, faster and faster, he struggled to keep the angle of his body turned feet first.

With each second that ticked by he gained more speed, and he feared the pain to come, when he hit the bottom of the mountain. With bone-jarring speed, his feet connected with the ring that ran around the base of the mountain, ten feet above the ground. He struck it, and his momentum carried him forward over the edge. He fell toward the ground below, striking it with a tuck and roll. Somehow as he rolled away from the base of the mountain, he realized he was able to move, it didn't hurt as badly as he thought, and he was on the ground.

"Wow! You are certifiably insane!" Jillian raced over to help him to his feet. "That had to be one of the craziest things I have ever seen!"

"Kind of like riding a big slide in a water park," Hawk said as he did a quick inventory of limbs and other body parts. As far as he could tell, he wasn't hurt. He still held the journal case in his hand.

"Except there was no water, no safety design, and nothing safe to land in." Jillian glanced back up to where he had started his slide. "Other than that, it was easy, right?"

"Exactly."

"Hawk, there have been at least five explosions. The two in the tower that trapped you, one in the building on the other side of Tomorrowland, and at least two inside the mountain. We can't keep emergency people in the area until we're sure that's all there are going to be." Jillian began to guide him toward where he had first entered Tomorrowland. "The sheriff and I have ordered everyone to pull back until we can come in with some certainty that the blasts have stopped."

As they ran toward the access area, Hawk slowed his pace, began to jog, and then came to a stop. He turned back to look at the smoldering Tomorrowland that stretched out in front of his vision. Jillian realized he was no longer with her and turned back to see where he was. She grabbed his arm and held it firmly, tugging him back in the direction they had been heading.

"Hawk, I said we needed to get out of here and pull back," Jillian said in his ear.

"No, there are not going to be any more explosions. Whoever did this made their statement." Hawk stood his ground and continued to gaze over the futuristic landscape.

"I don't follow you."

"Whoever did this was making a statement." Hawk pointed toward the center of Tomorrowland. "They wanted to kill me because I had lost what I need to preserve Walt Disney's legacy. So they baited me into a trap and blew it up. They attacked the visual centerpiece of Tomorrowland. The convention center is the main gathering place and entrance to Tomorrowland, so they attacked that. They also attacked the symbol and most recognizable landmark of Tomorrowland. Effectively, they attacked and destroyed the future as Walt envisioned it here. Whoever did this has sent a message that they are going to control the future. That is what this is about. It's what it has always been about."

Hawk began to move back toward the center of Tomorrowland. With bold strides he moved out in the open where he could be seen.

"What are you doing?"

He looked back at her, eyes blazing. "I'm letting whoever did this know they messed up. They didn't destroy me, so they didn't destroy the future Walt envisioned. I may have lost the painting, but I didn't lose anything else, and *they* have failed." Hawk was looking around the area as he got closer to the flames in Rocket Tower Plaza. His eyes searched through the isolated themed land for a glimpse of someone, anyone who didn't belong there.

"This is not some silly game! This is a terrorist attack."

"No, not the kind you deal with." Hawk turned to face her. The glow of the flames reflected off their faces. "This isn't some zealot with some misguided cause. The explosions aren't random just to see how much damage they can do; this is a very carefully calculated plan to get something they want. They were banking on the hope that someone close to me would step up after my death and give them what they want. When I had the painting, the last piece of the puzzle, and lost it, I all of a sudden became expendable. All the pieces are now in play. They don't need me anymore."

"I don't know, Hawk. That seems like a stretch." Jillian shook her head but listened intently, trying to understand.

"I may have lost the last piece." Hawk finally smiled. "For the time being. But I will get it back. And I still have all of the other pieces to figure it out. And I am not dead."

"Not yet." Jillian tightened her grip on his arm. "You can't stand out here."

"Yes, I can." Hawk pulled away from her. "Just wait. My guess is someone watching us right now. They are watching their fireworks show, and they have now seen me and figured out they missed. They are recalculating."

Jillian and Hawk stood near the flaming gantry as rescue workers, watching from a safe distance, began to make their way back into Tomorrowland. There had been no other explosions, and the CCA of the company was standing right in the middle of the mayhem. Cueing off of his lead, they began to work to restore order and extinguish the flames that had ignited after each explosion.

Hawk raised the journal case in the air and slowly turned in a circle so it could be seen.

"Come on!" he yelled into the early morning sky. "You have to have this! You want this, come and get it!"

"Stop it." Jillian looked about as she watched Hawk scream at anyone who might want to listen. "It has been a long few days, you're tired, and this is a little nuts. I don't think you're reading this situation right."

His phone startled them both, causing them to jump as it began to ring. They exchanged a puzzled glance, and Hawk pulled the phone out of his pocket. Looking down at the screen, he smiled.

"Who is it?" Jillian leaned in to look at the touch screen.

"Unknown caller." Hawk looked at her, eyes widened with anticipation. "I'm guessing it's the same person who texted me to come here earlier."

Hawk answered the phone and placed the call on speaker so Jillian could hear. They leaned in, as a male voice came from the speaker sounding hollow and distant.

"I am very impressed, Grayson Hawkes. You don't seem to want to die."

"You just aren't very good at what you do. You have managed to make quite a mess, but you still haven't managed to get what you want." Hawk's eyes darted about as he talked, looking into the distance. Whoever was on the other end of this call had been close enough to see him just a few moments ago.

"You make me laugh. I am good at what I do—ask Reginald Cambridge." The voice paused. "Oh, wait, you can't because I killed him. And you are next. But since you have managed to delay that, I want you to bring me the case you pulled off the top of Space Mountain."

Hawk smiled. His instincts had been right. Whoever this person was—and as hard as he was trying he couldn't place the voice—had been watching the entire show unfold from some safe location.

"What do I get if I bring it to you? What's in it for me?" Hawk continued his visual search through Tomorrowland.

"You get to live," snickered the voice through the speaker. "I won't destroy the rest of your beloved theme park, I will leave your friends alone, and I will disappear forever. Bring me the case in one hour."

"Where?" Hawk waited for the answer.

"Your apartment, the fire station on Main Street, U.S.A."

Hawk hesitated a moment. He hadn't been inside his apartment since it became a crime scene, and he hadn't been given an all-clear from the sheriff's department to return. Why would this person want to meet there? Did they want to return to the place they had stabbed Cambridge? Was there some other reason they would risk meeting in a heavily guarded crime scene? It made no sense.

"No, we aren't going to meet there." Hawk said into the phone.

Jillian turned her face to look closely at him. She raised an eyebrow slightly, in a glance asking what he might be doing. He shook his head and looked back toward the now-silent phone in his hand between them.

"Did you hear me? I said I am not going to meet you there." Hawk repeated his defiance.

"Where do you want to meet?" The voice was now more cautious, speaking in a slow and steady tone.

"Cinderella Suite inside Cinderella Castle. Be there in one hour." Hawk slid his finger across the screen and ended the call.

"What are you thinking?" Jillian looked into his eyes as she asked the question.

Hawk set his jaw. "I am changing the way we are playing his game. We're going to throw him off just a little bit. I'm going to end this, and I'm going to try to take some control back. This isn't a terrorist. This is a thief. Whoever it is has an agenda and wants whatever secret Walt Disney left. Now let's see how bad they want it."

"Why the castle?" She glanced toward the castle, its spire visible in the distance.

"Because as soon as this mystery man comes up to Cinderella Suite, he's trapped. You coordinate with McManus and hide people all around the castle. There are only two entrances to the castle and the suite itself. Cover them. If this guy is greedy enough to show up, he's stuck."

"And the way I figure it, you are stuck there as well. So you become a hostage and he uses you as his E-ticket out," Jillian said.

Hawk grinned. "Good try with the Disney reference, but that didn't really make sense. Still, I appreciate the effort."

"Disney nerd," she said. "How do you make sure you aren't killed or taken hostage?"

"It's a risk, to be sure." Hawk smiled again. "But I know another way out. You just have to make sure you don't let whoever this is slip away."

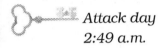 *Attack day*
2:49 a.m.

HAWK PURPOSEFULLY MADE HIS WAY TOWARD his carefully selected destination. The early morning streets of the Magic Kingdom were deserted as he searched them cautiously. His senses were on heightened alert anticipating what would happen in the next few minutes. Each shadow was glanced at; he wanted to make no mistakes. He absorbed every sight and sound as he kept on pace and on task, heading toward Fantasyland. His choice of the Cinderella Suite was on purpose.

Old-style luxury collided with digital-age technology in the Renaissance-styled Cinderella Suite high within the walls of Cinderella Castle. Created as part of an anniversary promotion, the suite was one of the most exclusive places to visit in all of the Magic Kingdom. While on very rare occasions some special guests might get the chance to stay there, more often than not, the suite remained empty. This night was no exception.

Hawk had started toward the castle as soon as the phone call ended. He took the short walk from Tomorrowland, exiting past the Tomorrowland Speedway, cutting around the Mad Tea Party, and walking along the edges of the shops and attractions on the border of Fantasyland. Eventually he wound his way over to Sir Mickey's, a gift shop directly behind Cinderella Castle. Stepping inside for a few brief minutes, he watched and waited to see if there was any noticeable activity along the rear portion of the castle. He had purposely waited for Jillian to coordinate with the sheriff's department and Disney security, allowing them to put in whatever surveillance they felt they could while remaining out of sight.

Once Jillian arrived at Sir Mickey's, as they had agreed, she would stay there as close as possible to the castle. Quickly setting up a table and her cell phone along the window ledge where she could see the archway leading into the castle, she motioned to Hawk that it was time to move.

Hawk had stepped inside and made a quick detour that he told no one else about, then made his way to the private elevator that opened into the foyer adorned with original movie art and a display case holding the legendary glass slipper. The once-upon-a-dream suite featured bathroom sinks that looked like washbasins, faucets that resembled hand pumps, and a cut-stone floor that made even the washroom a designer's dream. He stood at the sink and splashed cold water on his face while he waited.

Hawk paced the suite, listening for the soft whirring sound of the elevator opening in the foyer. Rubbing his arms and glancing around the room, he tried to calm the anxiety bubbling inside of him. He had a plan, but he recognized that within it there were so many unknown possibilities where it could go horribly wrong. Juliette often accused him of making most things up on the fly. This was one of those times. His cell phone vibrated. He retrieved it from his pocket and looked down at the screen. It was a text message from Jillian.

All quiet out here—no one has come in or come out.

Hawk glanced at his watch. His appointment was late. Tapping his finger on the screen, he began to touch back a message when he heard the elevator moving. Pausing, he quickly deleted the message he had started and immediately typed out, *There is someone coming up to the suite in the elevator right now.*

Pressing send, he moved across the room so he would have a good view of the elevator doors as they opened in just a moment. His phone vibrated again. He had gotten a text back from Jillian.

That is impossible. The only people near the castle are with us—the good guys—law enforcement.

Shaking his head, he again quickly typed back.

The elevator is here—someone has to be inside—someone is coming to the suite.

A soft ding signaled the arrival of the elevator. The doors silently slid open, and Hawk watched as the person inside stepped out. Slowly walking into view, he looked at Hawk and smiled.

"Unbelievable," Hawk said as he tilted his head. "It's you."

The familiar face didn't smile. "Yes, it's me."

"I haven't seen you in . . . how long has it been?" Hawk asked.

"Years, actually. I think the last time I saw you, we were in Tony's Town Square Restaurant. You were not having a very good day, if I remember correctly."

Hawk was trying hard to mask his surprise. It had been years since he had seen this man. Jim Masters had been the partner of Kiran Roberts when Hawk was first given the kingdom key by Farren Rales. The last time Hawk saw him was in the restaurant, and he had simply disappeared—much like Nancy. In the years that followed, his whereabouts had remained unknown. Until now.

It wasn't hard to see how Jim had managed to get up here without discovery. He was dressed in an Orange County deputy sheriff's uniform. Anyone who didn't know him already would never know that of all the things he was, he was not a law enforcement officer. Jillian hadn't reported any unusual activity outside of the castle because Masters had moved in to provide cover for Hawk along with the security detail.

"So where have you been all of this time?" Hawk watched closely as Masters moved into the suite and took a seat in one of the chairs in the sitting area.

"Oh, I've been around." Masters smiled. "But I have been very close to you the entire time. Watching and waiting as you stumbled and bumbled around. I figured eventually you would figure out what Walt Disney had hidden. I just didn't think it would take years."

"Good thing you're so patient." Hawk said with no emotion.

"Good thing." Masters nodded toward him. "Now I believe you are here to give me the carrying case in your hand."

"And when I do . . ."

"I'll keep my word. I won't destroy your beloved theme park, I will leave your friends alone, and I will disappear again. All you have to do is give me the case." Masters held out his hand, still smiling.

Hawk returned his smile. "Somehow, I just don't trust you."

"I don't blame you," laughed Masters. He lowered his hand. "Let me tell you what you want to know. I have been working with Kiran and Reginald all these years. I was the silent partner for both of them, although they never knew I was working with the other. So I always knew what Kiran was up to. She is after the Disney empire—the power, the prestige, the fame, the fortune, and the glory that goes along with it all. She's driven by greed."

Masters shrugged his shoulders. "I can deal with that. I can even understand it. But Reginald is driven by something else, or I should say *was* driven by something else."

"You killed Reginald?" Hawk interrupted his story.

"Yes, I killed Reginald. His boneheaded play to poison Farren Rales was crass, crude, and uncalled-for. Once he got out of prison, he was way too impulsive. I guessed there was no way you would ever turn over what he wanted, although you wanted to save Rales. But the secret is worth dying for; you had proved that already. So I showed up at your apartment when he was waiting for you and took care of him. His usefulness to me was done."

"And once I give you this journal, my usefulness to you is done as well." Hawk hefted the case and then returned it to his side. "So you will kill me too."

"Yes, I could. I have already tried. To be honest, you made me angry." Masters got to his feet and stepped toward Hawk. "I haven't liked you since we had our little scuffle in Liberty Square a few years back. When you just handed over the painting to Kiran and her mother, that was the last straw for me. I decided you had lost your desire to see this thing through. So I decided to declare war on your Disney World here. But hey, you surprised me. You survived and then raced right off to get me what I needed."

"So you decided to change direction and just let me turn it over to you after all?"

"I assume by now you have had enough. I have already proved that I can destroy this entire resort if I want to. And if you mess with me or mess this up, I will. Trust me when I tell you that." Masters's face grew menacing. He slowly reached for the service revolver on his hip. Unfastening the safety strap holding the revolver in the holster, he held out his other hand, palm up. "So give me the case, Hawk."

Hawk took a step closer to him and held out the case, then suddenly drew it back. Masters pulled the pistol out of the holster and leveled it at him.

"What are you doing?" Masters growled.

"Just a question, really," Hawk stepped away and moved toward the window, "Since Kiran has the painting and that really messed up your master plan. This journal doesn't really help you. You need the painting. But it doesn't sound like you are working that well with Kiran right now. What are you going to do about that?"

"I don't think that should concern you." Masters smiled as he continued to aim the gun toward Hawk. "Kiran and I are close, very close. I think she will give me what I want."

"You never did tell me the rest. What is it that you want?" Hawk asked. Casually taking a seat, he realized that this situation might fall apart very quickly, but his curiosity, his desire to completely understand what was driving Masters and even Reginald continued to bother him.

Masters sneered. "That has been your problem. The old preacher in you wants answers that are simple and easy. You are always trying to understand and make sense of things that are hard to explain, and then you tell people to just have faith and it will be all right. You just don't realize how big this whole Disney secret is. You never have. That is your fatal flaw."

"The choices you make, make you," Hawk replied. "You have chosen to be what you are."

"And what do you think I am?"

"You? Just a common criminal. You will do whatever it takes to get whatever you want. It doesn't matter who or what gets destroyed along the way." Hawk got back on his feet.

Masters's face darkened. "Now I am insulted, Hawkes. I am a lot of things, but I am not common. Give me the case." He stepped toward Hawk and tore the case from his hand.

As Masters opened the case, Hawk eased his way toward the elevator and waited for the reaction he knew was coming.

"There is nothing in this!" Masters turned toward him.

Hawk laughed. "Of course there isn't. You didn't think I was just going to walk in here and hand it over? I needed to know who you were and what we were doing."

The man's face went red. "What we're doing? What I'm doing is getting ready to kill you!"

"If you do, you will never get the journal. And right now you are *so* close." Hawk pressed the button on the elevator.

"What do you mean?" Masters covered the distance between them and pressed the pistol against Hawk's temple.

He tried not to show his fear. He took a deep breath and felt himself swallow hard. If his plan was going to work, he had to hold his nerves together for just a few more minutes.

"I mean I brought the journal to the castle. It just isn't in this room." Hawk pushed back against Masters and shoved him away.

Even as he did, he braced himself. He didn't know if Masters was going to shoot and bring his big play to an abrupt end or whether he had intrigued him enough to string him along a little bit further. His hastily prepared plan wasn't good, but it might be good enough.

"I'm listening," Masters said.

Some of the tension in Hawk's muscles released. "Follow me. It's in another part of the castle."

Right on cue, the elevator doors opened, and Hawk stepped inside. Cautiously, Jim Masters followed him in. As the doors closed, Masters backed against the side wall of the elevator and kept his gun leveled at Hawk. Hawk's heart was hammering in his chest. He had Masters doing exactly what he'd hoped he would do.

The elevator descended back to the ground floor, the doors opened, and Masters motioned Hawk out with the gun. Feeling the weapon pressed up against his back, Hawk moved out of the elevator and across the massive breezeway of the castle. Eyes darting back and forth, he saw no one else in the area. That was according to plan. Pushing their way through an unmarked door, the pair entered another hallway that led to a gray set of concrete stairs.

"I'm following you," Masters said as they moved upward.

The stairwell led up into one of the spires of the castle. Like walking up into a lighthouse, the stairs began to twist and spiral up in front of them until they came to another door. Turning the handle and stepping out, they walked out onto a landing atop one of the highest towers of the castle. The Magic Kingdom stretched out below them in the clear early morning. They were on the same level as the Cinderella Suite but were now outside the rooms, in an area that was inaccessible to guests.

"Now what?" Masters snapped. For these last few moments he had not been in control, which was Hawk's plan. He had hoped by changing the meeting place Masters had wanted, he could swing the element of surprise back in his direction. Now that Hawk knew the identity of his antagonist, he realized how brilliantly evil Masters had been. Working in the background, patiently, for years leading up to this moment . . . his patience and planning made him a scary adversary. Still, Hawk had managed to throw him off his game just a little bit, and that little bit might be all he needed. He hoped.

Hawk moved around the landing and stopped. He motioned to the edge of the balcony. Hooked on a decorative metal post was a brightly colored Walt Disney World souvenir shopping bag.

"There it is," Hawk said. "The journal is inside."

"If it's not, you are dead." Masters shoved him out of the way and moved to collect the bag.

As Masters headed for the ledge, Hawk stepped back and began to retreat toward the doorway. He already knew the reaction that would follow would not be good. This was where his plan could shatter into pieces. With Masters just outside of the line of sight of the doorway, Hawk opened the door and slammed it loudly, but he didn't step through it to the stairwell. Instead he moved the opposite direction, making his way around the opposite side of the spire. A moment later he heard Masters yell out in rage.

He had opened the bag.

Hawk had picked up an empty notebook and wrapped it at Sir Mickey's before he came into the castle. He had hidden the real journal on one of the shelves inside the gift shop. Now he could only hope and pray the angry Jim Masters would chase him down the stairwell for a few precious minutes before he realized Hawk wasn't there.

This was the part of his plan that was a lot sketchier than he was comfortable with. Standing on the balcony along the spire, he reached down and picked up the equipment he had carefully hidden when he detoured on his way to the Cinderella Suite earlier. He stepped into the canvas-strapped harness and quickly cinched down the buckles and straps. Grabbing his phone, he texted a message to Jillian.

In stairway 3—Jim Masters—in uniform—the bad guy.

Hawk moved quickly and carefully along the edge of the tower as it curved toward the front of Cinderella Castle. A majestic view of Main Street, U.S.A. stretched out in front of him as he looked toward the train station. To his left, Tomorrowland was still smoldering, with the flashing of emergency lights dancing inside the smoke where it rose into the darkness of the predawn morning.

"Hawk!" The voice of Jim Masters echoed through the air, and Hawk heard the opening of the stairwell door as Jim thundered through. This was the moment he had been waiting for. How long would it take for Masters to realize that Hawk hadn't run down the stairs but was still on the landing? The answer to that question would come soon enough. But until it did, he had to be ready to do what he'd never dreamed he would.

CHAPTER 50

Attack day
5:18 a.m.

HAWK HAD DONE THE MATH AND KNEW his plan might not work. He weighed nearly 185 pounds, and he could only hope there was enough of a cushion built into the structure to support him. With the urgency of one chased, he took hold of the very long metal ladder secured against the side of the castle spire. He placed his foot on the lowest rung and began to climb, quickly going from handhold to handhold, moving upward without looking down. He focused on the ladder and the climb itself. At the top would be a tiny landing, with room enough for two people to stand on. The height would be dizzying. The landing was near the highest point of the castle, and that was his destination.

In the distance below him he heard a door open and assumed that Jim Masters had returned to search the landing below. With a renewed sense of urgency, Hawk continued upward and pulled himself up onto the small landing. Glancing below, he could see Masters circling the balcony. He fought the urge to close his eyes at the dizzying height. Masters had not yet looked up, but he would, and Hawk was sure he would follow.

"Hawk!" Masters's voice came from the level below.

Hawk took a deep breath. He had been seen. This plan to escape and trap his enemy had seemed better when he was thinking about it. Now that it was time to execute it, he was not so confident.

He stood on the platform high atop Cinderella Castle and looked above his head at the taut metal wire that stretched from the spire across the open sky toward Tomorrowland. This was the famous zip line Tinkerbell used each night to make her flight, signaling the beginning of the late-night fireworks spectacular. In the dark, highlighted with a spotlight, the Tinkerbell cast member would fly through the nighttime sky in a battery-powered costume decorated by twinkle lights. Hawk had been up in the castle one other time and watched the process take place.

As usual, Hawk had noticed details. He remembered that the line was designed to carry a weight of 135 pounds. That was the weight of the cast member, the harness, the costume, and the battery that powered the costume. On a show night, there would be a cast member to help Tinkerbell hook herself to the line after getting in the harness and then shove her down the zip line to create the dramatic flight across the sky. In the dark, it was an amazing moment. YouTube was loaded with videos of the event, captured by guests who marveled in disbelief that Tinkerbell was really flying from the castle.

Hawk could only trust that the extra weight he would be putting on the line would not make it snap. The line itself was strong enough to support the weight. The real stress points would be at the connections that pulled the line taut both on the castle and in the landing area atop the Plaza Restaurant complex below. Hawk remembered one night when he had watched this part of the show from the castle. Tinkerbell had gotten stuck on the line, the spotlight was cut, and he had watched as the cast member pulled herself hand over fist along the line to the landing area. He was informed that happened at least once a month, but that was the nature of the high-wire stunt.

In the best version of this plan, the cavalry would arrive and grab the villain before Hawk had to fly down the zip line. But as of yet, there was no rescue arriving. This wasn't a fairy tale, and there wasn't a magical ending in sight. He realized as he hooked the clip and tugged on the attachment to see if it was secure that he was really getting ready to fly across the Magic Kingdom sky. Looking down, he saw that Jim Masters was at the bottom of the ladder, trying to figure out what Hawk was doing. From Jim's view it might appear that Hawk was trapped and perhaps baiting him to come up.

Masters began to climb the ladder. The time had arrived.

Cinderella Castle stands 189 feet tall. It is visible from the Ticket and Transportation Center two miles away. The coat of arms proudly displayed at the front and back entrances of the castle is the Disney family crest, signifying the castle as the icon of the Magic Kingdom. Now Hawk was about to do the unthinkable—jump off of it. He looked down one more time and saw Masters climbing up toward him.

Then he took a deep breath and pushed himself out into the air.

Hawk felt the line give as his weight was fully supported on it. He sailed through the air, flying across the expanse of the hub in front of the castle, high above the Magic Kingdom. He glanced back and saw that Masters had stopped climbing and was watching as Hawk flew away. Uniformed officers were streaming around the landing toward the base of the ladder. *Where were they a few minutes earlier, before I jumped?*

Soaring across the skyline in the early morning of the Magic Kingdom, for just a moment Hawk lost himself in the flight. Lights twinkled below, and the magical land he was entrusted to keep stretched out below him, a wonderland waiting to be discovered. The breeze was exhilarating. But just as quickly, he realized his added weight on the line was actually causing him to travel faster than the cast member might during the normal evening show. Soaring was one thing. Stopping was another.

Racing across the zip line, he continued to pick up speed, and the thought occurred to him that he wasn't sure how he was supposed to stop at the other end. When Tinkerbell would travel, there was a cast member to catch her and help unhook her at the other end of the trip. There was no one waiting to help him. Hawk looked down the line as he flew toward the top of the Plaza Restaurant. He held out his arms and tried to swing his body so he could use his legs to absorb the sudden stop that he knew was imminent.

Before he could prepare himself, he slammed up against the landing point. His body rattled as his forward motion suddenly ceased. The line bobbed at the sudden stop and he bounced backward for a moment before coming to a complete halt. Now reaching up above him, he used the release hook and disconnected himself from the wire. The slight drop plunked him back down on the top of the building, and he looked back to the top of the castle. He could see Jim Masters being led across the balcony by what had to be at least a dozen sheriff's department deputies—at least, that's what it looked like. With Masters wearing a uniform, it was a little tough to see what was really going on from a distance.

His cell phone vibrated in his pocket, and he reached down to see who it was. Jillian Batterson's name appeared on the screen. He slid his finger to answer it.

"Hello."

"You are insane." Jillian laughed as she said it.

"I'm fine, thanks for asking." Hawk smiled.

"Oh, I am certain there is something wrong with you. Actually, there is a whole lot wrong with you, Grayson Hawkes."

"I appreciate your concern."

"We've got him. Jim Masters is now in custody." Jillian laughed again. "Look across at the castle."

Hawk looked back to the balcony where he had just been once again. The security teams were gone, and one lone figure stood there waving. Even from this distance he could see it was Jillian.

"You are just as out of control as Juliette told me you were," Jillian said.

"Juliette said that about me?"

"Yes, and a lot of other things as well." She paused. "So Masters is our bad guy?"

"Yes. He admitted he killed Reginald and that he is your terrorist," Hawk said. His head rocked back slightly as he glanced heavenward. A gentle wave of relief washed over him, and he inhaled deeply, held it, and let the breath out slowly. He felt like the danger might finally be over. "Like everyone else, he was after the Disney secrets."

"And of course he didn't get them."

"Of course not." Hawk smiled. "Masters stalked me for years. He was working with both Cambridge and Kiran Roberts. He was playing them against each other, or so goes his story. But he's the one behind the madness we have been going through this past week."

"You will testify to all of that on the record, I assume. And I promise you, we will get the truth out of him and make sure." Jillian's voice grew serious. "So what was it like?"

Hawk blinked. "Pardon?"

"What was it like to fly across the Magic Kingdom?"

He nearly laughed at the unexpected question. "To tell you the truth, I enjoyed it for a half-second. But I do know this: we are going to give Tinkerbell a raise, immediately."

"McManus has a team coming to get you right now. Stay put. I'll see you later," Jillian said. "I've got some work to do now that we have Masters."

The call ended, and Hawk watched her move around the balcony out of sight. He realized as she left how glad he was that she was actually here. As he watched her leave he realized how much could change in such a short time. Life never slows down and it never stops moving. The door behind him opened, and a stream of deputies accompanied by Disney security flooded out onto the roof. Cal McManus stepped out from behind them, a big smile across his broad face.

"Well, how are you?" Cal grabbed Hawk's hand and shook it. Placing a hand on his shoulder, he leaned in and whispered, "Good job. Now this can all finally end, right?"

"Yes sir." Hawk returned the smile and realized that for the first time in a long time, there really was an end in sight. "The loose end is Kiran Roberts. She has a painting I think we need to get back."

"Wait a minute." A voice from behind Hawk caught his attention. He turned and saw Al Gann step up and stand next to Sheriff McManus. He was beaming. "Your loose end isn't loose. Your new friend Preston Child has been very helpful. He gave us his address, and we did a bit of surveillance work at his house. Believe it or not, his daughter and granddaughter showed up to see if they could find any more stuff the old Imagineer might have stashed that would help them figure out what to do with the painting. Being greedy will get you every time. We have them both in custody."

"And the painting?" Hawk asked hopefully.

"We have it as well. They had stashed it in the back of Nancy's minivan." Al patted his friend on the back. "Are you okay?" He looked back toward Cinderella Castle and the zip line. "That is an interesting way to get out of the castle."

"I'm good. Thanks," Hawk said as he embraced his friend.

McManus turned and walked with Hawk, once again placing a firm hand on his shoulder. "Your apartment is clear and cleaned. We got word to your staff, and they unleashed a maintenance crew inside. We kept the place under guard while they did. You can go back to your apartment whenever you like." McManus stopped and turned toward Hawk. "We have some cleanup to do here in the Magic Kingdom. It is closed today, right?"

"Yes. We need to make sure Masters hasn't left us any more explosions."

"Good. We're thinking the same way." McManus sounded thoughtful. "It's a mess over there in Tomorrowland. It's going to be closed for some time."

"Then we will have to rebuild the future." Hawk sighed. In all the excitement, he had momentarily forgotten the massive damage that Masters had managed to do to the Magic Kingdom. There would be a lot to clean up, a lot to explain, and a lot of questions to answer. Juliette had her job cut out for her. Maybe Hawk would even help this time.

But first, he had to do a little shopping.

As Hawk followed McManus back into the hub of the Magic Kingdom, heading for Sir Mickey's and the journal that waited for him on the shelf, the sun was beginning to rise. The new day brought new hope with it. All the villains were in custody, all the pieces of the puzzle had finally been found, and when he got the painting back, it was possible that all the pieces would click together at last and he would finally understand what Walt had been trying to protect.

There was a lot of work to be done, but at least they could start without the threat of someone trying to steal it all away. It was the beginning of a very good new day.

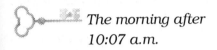 *The morning after*
10:07 a.m.

FARREN RALES SAT IN A FAUX LEATHER RECLINER in the high-rise tower of the Florida Hospital. The old man looked less feeble than when Hawk had last seen him, and his color had returned. He was expected to make a complete recovery. Hawk sat on the sofa, catching Farren up on all that had transpired while he was at death's door.

"It sounds like you have had quite an adventure." Rales looked over the edge of his glasses toward his friend. "And you are not hurt?"

Hawk smiled. "No. I'm tired but relieved that it's over. We have a lot of work to do in the Magic Kingdom. We're going over every inch of it to make sure Masters didn't leave any more surprises hidden for us. But we are getting there."

"And so you have the painting?" Rales repeated the question he had asked when Hawk first showed up in his hospital room to visit.

"Yes, I told you so. I almost have it, actually . . . the sheriff's department confiscated it when they arrested Kiran and Nancy." Hawk laughed. "I know that putting all the pieces together to this mystery Walt left behind has taken a lot of years. Now all I have to do for all of us is connect the pieces. So I'm going to wait to study the painting until you're better and can do it with me."

"No." Rales's expression grew serious. "You need to finish solving the puzzle right away. Don't wait for me. You are the chosen one to become the keeper of Walt's secrets. You have to understand them completely to preserve his legacy. You don't need to be waiting around for me to be released so we can do it together."

"Okay." Hawk sat back on the sofa, surprised at the reaction. "I'll look at it later today. The sheriff's department is returning it to us later this afternoon."

"Good." Farren relaxed in his chair and tilted his head back. "Then you should have enough time."

"Enough time?"

"Yes, enough time to finish." Farren's eyes brightened as he refocused on Hawk.

Hawk struggled to understand what Rales was trying to say. They had been waiting years for all this to come together. What was the urgency now?

Farren sat back. "I knew there was a painting or picture that you ultimately had to find. I had no idea it was a Norman Rockwell painting. *Shuffleton's Barbershop* was an ingenious choice. I never knew about the comic book hidden in the corner. I would have guessed the painting you needed would be *Freedom to Worship*. That was Walt's favorite from the *Four Freedoms* series that Rockwell painted. The whole series resonated with Walt, but he loved that one most. But . . . like everyone else, I only know what I need to know." He paused. "And the one more thing that you need to know."

Hawk furrowed his brow as the words sank in. "There is one more thing I need to know?"

"Yes. You have to be able to look at the painting."

"I will, closely. I will get to see it later when the sheriff—"

"No, no, no." Farren held out his hand to stop Hawk from talking. "Give me my cell phone."

Hawk looked about the room and saw the phone sitting on the rolling tray that played host to meals, medicine, and reading material for patients. There was Rales's smartphone resting on it. Hawk retrieved it and handed it to his friend. Rales hit the screen with a finger and punched in a passcode, and Hawk watched as he started scrolling through photographs.

"Did you know that Walt Disney wore glasses?" Rales asked as he scrolled.

"No, he didn't." Hawk thought for a moment. "I have never seen any photo or read anywhere that Walt had eye trouble."

Farren looked up at him for a moment with a reproving glance. "Like everyone else, when you age your eyesight starts to fail. He was not photographed in them, so according to the historical record, Walt Disney didn't wear glasses."

"I never knew that." Hawk leaned forward as Farren continued to search his phone.

"Like I said, Walt never wanted to be photographed in his glasses. But if he didn't know the photo was being taken, there were a few times he was caught wearing them."

Rales turned his phone and showed a candid photo of Walt on the screen. It was a recapture of an image taken years before, long before the world had ever heard of cell phones or digital media. It was a vintage black-and-white photograph of an older Walt Disney, seated in a director's chair and wearing a suit as he marked up a thick script with his famous grease pen. Perched on the edge of his nose as he looked down and read were a pair of reading glasses.

"Who knew?" Hawk sat back and looked at Farren.

"I did." Farren smiled. "And now you do as well. You need to know everything you can about Walt, my boy."

"Well . . . thanks for letting me know."

"You need those glasses so you can look at the painting like Walt looked at the painting." Farren waited for Hawk to process what he had just said.

Hawk thought about it for a moment. "A hidden message in the painting?"

"Something like that. I guess." Farren rubbed his chin. "I don't know what is in the painting. That is not my story to tell you. Like always, I can only share what I know when you are ready. And now you're ready to know this: you need those glasses."

"And you have them?"

"I know where they are." Farren slowly allowed a smile to creep up from the corner of his mouth.

"Wait a minute . . . you mean," Hawk wrinkled his nose, "I have to go find them?"

"Well, I couldn't just keep them lying around. They're way too valuable. Most people never even knew Walt had glasses." Farren laughed at Hawk's surprise. "All you have to do is go get them."

"Another puzzle?" Hawk rubbed his eyes. "Are you going to send me out to unravel another mystery?"

"No, not really. This one will be much easier." Rales pondered a moment as if trying to decide how difficult to make what he was about to say next. "Go and find Sorcerer Mickey in Tomorrowland. Once you do, just look above the fire." He sat back and folded his hands. "Then you will have the glasses and can really look at the painting."

"Okay..." Hawk said with a bit of confusion.

Hawk's relief at finally having all the pieces of the puzzle melted away. He already had a good idea where Farren was sending him, but he was now wondering if there would ever be an end to all of the mystery. It seemed as quickly as one chapter of the story closed, another one began.

"Don't make this difficult. Like everything else, these things are so valuable that you just can't leave them out where they can be easily found. This time, you know what you are looking for. Find Walt Disney's eyeglasses so you can see like Walt."

CHAPTER 52

The day after
12:07 p.m.

"Go find Sorcerer Mickey in Tomorrowland; look above the fire." Hawk repeated the clue Farren had given him to Juliette as they walked past the barricades into Tomorrowland.

A phone call to Sheriff McManus had gained him the all-clear to enter the area that had been rocked by Masters's explosions the day before. Isolated, empty, and now strangely calm, the land almost seemed as though the destruction of the day before hadn't happened. The reports said otherwise. Most of the extensive damage was out of sight, as the explosive devices had been hidden inside building structures. The exception was the gantry of the Astro Orbiter. The structure was leaning and visibly damaged and charred from the dual blasts that had shaken it while Hawk was inside.

"You are very fortunate you weren't killed," Juliette said as she followed his gaze toward the warped metal structure.

"Juliette, remember I promised you that this time we would finish this thing? That finally we would unravel whatever it was that Walt Disney had left behind for us?" Hawk looked at her as they made their way toward the Carousel of Progress. She was family to him. Juliette had stood beside and believed in him, even when others would have been tempted to walk or run away. He could never tell her how grateful he was, but he intended to keep his promise to finally find the answers they had been seeking for such a long time.

"Yes."

"Have you wondered what will happen once we have done it? I mean, once we have solved it once and for all? What do we do then?" Hawk asked.

She thought as they walked. Together they moved up the ramp through the turnstiles. Juliette said nothing until they arrived at the doors of the attraction.

"I suppose that once you know what it really is, what the legacy of Walt Disney is, then you will lead the company forward with that knowledge. While one chapter of all of our lives comes to an end, another one begins, and each day will be a new page, a new story, a new adventure to discover." She shrugged.

"That was deep." Hawk smiled. He recognized her words.

"I heard some preacher say that back in the day." Juliette smiled back. "Seems like years ago."

"It has been years," Hawk agreed. Although he might not have said them in years, he smiled inwardly knowing how recently he had just thought the exact same thoughts. "Let's go in."

Using a master key that allowed him to override the controls, Hawk bypassed the normal way to enter the attraction. The doors popped open and released with a click, and the two stepped inside the theater.

"Why are we here?" Juliette watched Hawk move to the cast member controls to start the attraction.

"To find the last piece of the puzzle," Hawk said as the beginning sequence started to play. The lights dimmed as the narration started. But Hawk held a lever that started the theater rotating around the stage. Created originally for the World's Fair in the sixties, this attraction was the longest running show in the history of theater. Hawk knew from previous experience that for maintenance and during emergencies, the normal operating format could be changed. He planned on moving quickly through each scene until they had rotated into the finale of the show. The ride moved through time while it moved through seasons. Eventually it ended with an American family sharing moments during Christmas in a near-future setting.

Hawk slowed the progress of the carousel as it reached the final scene, and it stopped. The show sequence played as if the theater were full of guests. Hawk jumped to the stage and reached back to give Juliette a hand up. With a quick leap and a step, she joined him in the midst of an audio-animatronic family waiting on Christmas dinner, enjoying presents, and talking about life as it was and the progress and hope of the future.

Hawk rolled his shoulders and neck. He was stiff from the wear and tear of the past week but was anxious to find what Farren had sent him to collect. He turned to face Juliette, ignoring the family scene playing out around them.

"Farren said to find Sorcerer Mickey in Tomorrowland." He pointed to the wall at a painting that hung between the living room and the kitchen area. "What does that look like to you?"

Juliette stood in front of the living room set piece and squinted up at it. She turned to Hawk with her mouth slightly open in amazement.

"Sorcerer Mickey." She pointed at it. "It's a modern-art style version of the scene from *Fantasia*."

"Yep, it sure is. Most people have taken this ride over and over and never seen it. In some ways it's one of the best Hidden Mickey's in all of the resort. Farren said to find him and then look above the fire."

Juliette turned and smiled. The fireplace was on the opposite wall. Garland and lights decorated the mantle. An artificial fire gave the scene a cozy, warm feeling, even in the summer. She quickly moved to the fireplace and looked along the top of the mantle. There was nothing there. Hawk joined her and then reached down to check the stockings hung along the front edge of the fireplace mantle. Juliette did the same and then interrupted his search.

"Hawk," she said as she reached inside a brightly decorated Christmas stocking. "Look."

She removed her hand, and her fingers were delicately holding a pair of glasses. She gently placed them in Hawk's outstretched hand.

"There they are."

Hawk looked at them and turned them over in his grasp. He was bouncing slightly on his toes, excitement unexpectedly overwhelming him. This was it—the last piece of the puzzle. He was holding it in his hand. Juliette reached over and placed her hand on his forearm. Her eyes sparkled with eagerness that mirrored his.

"Let's go look at a painting," she said.

When Juliette and Hawk arrived back at Bay Lake Tower, the team he had requested was already there: Shep; Jonathan, with bandaged head, fresh from his hospital observation; and Preston Child. Jillian was supposed to have been there but had been detained and was still at the sheriff's office. As they moved into the conference room there were a few quick greetings and then Juliette disappeared momentarily. She returned carrying the case with the Normal Rockwell painting inside. They all stood around the table as she carefully opened the case. Hawk reached over to help her.

"No, I've got it. Last time you touched this, you lost it," Juliette scolded him.

"That was Shep's fault. He managed to go and get himself kidnapped, and someone had to ransom him."

"Don't blame me. These are all people I met through you, boss," Shep retorted.

The mood was light with anticipation and camaraderie. They watched Juliette remove the painting and place it on the table. They all leaned in, smiling, except for Press. He had gotten out of his seat to get a good look at the painting as the case was opened.

"It's beautiful. It feels like I'm really there," Jon said as he looked into the window of *Shuffleton's Barbershop.*

"Cool," Shep muttered as he looked toward Hawk.

Hawk studied the picture and looked closely at the corner where the Disney comic book had been placed in the painting. Reaching into his pocket, he pulled out the glasses. Placing them carefully on his nose, he glanced up to see both Shep and Jon staring at him.

"When did you start wearing glasses?" Shep asked, puzzled.

"I didn't know your eyesight had gotten bad," Jon added. Hawk chuckled. He would explain later. For right now, he wanted to see what he was supposed to find.

"I haven't started wearing glasses, and my eyes are fine," he answered. Amid their murmurs of surprise, he got down closer to the painting and placed his face next to it as he studied.

"Well?" Juliette asked.

"What is this?" the voice of Preston Child interrupted them.

They all simultaneously looked at the old Imagineer. His question seemed rather odd and out of place.

"Pardon?" Juliette responded pleasantly.

"I said, what is this?" The older man looked at Hawk as he spoke in an uncertain tone that trailed off at the end.

"This is *Shuffelton's Barbershop,*" Hawk said. "The Norman Rockwell painting. You said 'find the Rockwell that he put Walt in' and bring it to you. The artist added the Disney comic in the rack of reading material. He put Disney in the picture."

The room fell silent as Preston looked at each one of them. He cleared his throat as he sat down in the chair to the side of the table. Waving his hand toward the picture in front of them, he said curtly, "This is not the painting."

CHAPTER 53

The day after
2:45 p.m.

"WHAT DO YOU MEAN THIS IS NOT THE PAINTING?" Hawk asked with a stunned grimace.

"I mean," Preston looked at Hawk with a glare, "this is not the painting. I think I was pretty clear when I said it a moment ago. So I will say it again. You have the wrong painting."

Hawk looked blankly at the old Imagineer and then back to the painting. His brain replayed the sequence of events and information they had discovered that led them to this work of art. The past few years had found Hawk and company tracking down many obscure clues, connecting dots to seemingly random items, and finding meaning and purpose in the slightest detail. There had been a number of times he had guessed and made assumptions with a leap of faith. He realized and understood that. Their success had been uncanny, but they had been right so often that the possibility they could be wrong this time had been nowhere on his radar.

"Um . . ." Hawk began. "It's not the right painting, but you know which painting it really is . . . right?"

"Of course I do." Press sat back in his chair, obviously disappointed, and crossed his arms across his chest. "How did you blow the clue? Perhaps you aren't as good at this as I thought."

Hawk narrowed his eyes, trying to discern whether he was hearing anger or frustration in the old man's voice. He could understand if there was anger. Press had discovered that his very own daughter and granddaughter had been conspiring to undercut him and steal a secret he had been entrusted to protect years before. He loved them, he trusted them, and he hadn't had time to process everything and what it meant for his relationships. When you added the element of the betrayal being completely unexpected, there was no way Press was ready to embrace the people in the room with him as trusted friends. They were, after all, the people who had exposed his family for the scoundrels they really were.

And if he was frustrated, well, Hawk could understand that as well. This discovery had been years in the making. Now they were finally at the moment where perhaps they would finally have some answers . . . and they had the wrong painting. None of the Imagineers who had been a part of Walt and Roy's master plan had been promised that they would ever completely understand how it all fit together or what it was really all about. George had been killed before they had the answers. Press knew some of what had happened but no one had had time to paint the entire picture for him. Farren seemed to be the real mover and shaker of the talented storytelling trio, but by his own admission, he only knew certain parts of the narrative. To his credit, he was content with that and took satisfaction in fulfilling his role. It was Hawk who was expected to put it all together.

This time, his ability to unravel the mystery had failed.

Preston surveyed the room, reached across the table, and grabbed a notepad and a pen that were sitting in a stack of work materials shoved off to the side. He scribbled something and then twirled the pad around on the tabletop and slid it toward Hawk. Hawk grabbed it and turned it up to see what Press had written on it.

Scrawled in shaky handwriting, the note said, "Grayson Hawkes—If Rockwell put him in a picture but he didn't paint him into it—how else could he put him in it? Think about it, make me a fan again! Press."

Hawk read and reread the lines. Looking over at the Imagineer, he could see Preston was waiting for him to figure it out.

Then he understood. They had made the mystery of the painting way too complex and tried to find something far deeper than they needed to find. If he was reading this new clue right, it was as simple as the words on the page . . . literally. The answer he was looking for was right there on the notepad.

"He put Walt in the picture by writing his name on it. He autographed a painting for Walt Disney didn't he?" Hawk pointed at the personalized message Preston had just written out for him.

"Are you asking me if that is the answer, or are you telling me that is the answer?"

Hawk smiled with relief. "I'm telling you. There is a Norman Rockwell painting out there that the artist personalized for Walt Disney."

"I'll bet it's one of the paintings of Walt's daughters that he had Rockwell create," Shep said. "I read about the two paintings Walt had him do when I was researching the Disney-Rockwell connection."

"No, that wasn't it. But a good guess." Press placed his hands on the table. "Yes, there is a painting by Norman Rockwell that he personalized for Walt Disney. That is the painting you are looking for."

"The painting is called *Girl Reading the Post*," Juliette chimed in. "It's an original oil and is inscribed, 'To Walt Disney, one of the really great artists, from an admirer, Norman Rockwell.'" Juliette paused. "I saw it when the art was unpacked. I had to arrange to get this particular portrait directly from the Rockwell Museum. That's how I know so much about it."

"That's the one." Preston smiled at the team. "*The Saturday Evening Post* ran the cover in 1941. It depicts a coming-of-age schoolgirl in bobby socks, saddle shoes, and a plaid skirt with her face hidden, engrossed in a fictitious issue of *The Saturday Evening Post*, whose cover features a head shot of a beautiful model the girl reading hopes to become."

Hawk listened closely. Preston was unpacking a story he had waited years to tell. It was as if he was exhaling a breath he had been bursting to let loose. "The demand to see the real face of the model Rockwell had used with her face hidden behind the cover was so great that the magazine later printed a photo of her in a similar pose but looking around the side of an issue with the Rockwell painting on the cover. Her name was Millicent Mattison. It was great fun and one of his most engaging works ever."

"So how did Walt end up with it?" Hawk asked, intrigued.

"Well, Rockwell really liked Disney. They became such good friends that he offered Walt the original art of any of the *Saturday Evening Post* covers he still had. Rockwell invited Walt to come to his studio to pick out the cover of his choice, but Walt was swamped as usual and couldn't make the connection to do it. So he sent a man named Clyde Forsythe, an artist friend of both Rockwell and Disney, to make the choice. He chose *Girl Reading the Post*, and then Rockwell signed it, or in other words, put 'Walt Disney' into the picture or onto the picture permanently. He wrote 'To Walt Disney, one of the really great artists, from an admirer, Norman Rockwell.' Just like Juliette just said."

Press paused and then thought of something else. "Walt wrote to Rockwell to say thanks and told him, 'I can't begin to thank you enough.' He went on to say that the entire staff had been traipsing up to his office to look at it. 'They love it,' he wrote, 'and my team is convinced that you are some sort of god."

"That's pretty high praise," Hawk said.

"In appreciation with the note, Walt sent Rockwell a set of ceramic figurines featuring characters from *Pinocchio, Bambi,* and *Fantasia*." Preston looked off into the distance as if revisiting the memory and the place where it had originated. "The *Post* cover and the portraits of Walt's girls were on the wall of Walt's office for over two decades. After Walt passed away, the painting was moved to the Disney Archives and then to the offices of Retlaw Enterprises. I know, because I was the one who moved it each time."

"So where is the painting now?" Hawk asked.

"The family gave it on a permanent loan to the Norman Rockwell Museum. They believed it belonged there. But I want you to know something, Hawk. I fought against that move. The painting does not belong there; it belongs where it is safe within the Disney Company. It belongs with you. So you have to find it and figure out how to get it in your possession. No matter how much it costs, it is worth it. You have to have it."

"Why is it worth so much?" Hawk ran a hand through his hair, pondering what to do next.

"I have no idea, but I do know that it is. It *needs* to be in your care and possession." Press said this so strongly that his voice went hoarse, and he coughed through the end of the sentence.

"Well." Juliette moved next to Hawk. "I can't help you with securing the painting as your very own property. But I do know where it is. It is actually here. Like I said before, it's part of the art exhibit. It's over in the ballroom where this one was." She pointed to the barbershop painting on the table and smiled.

"I'll follow you. Let's go look at the painting." Hawk motioned toward the door.

CHAPTER 54

The day after
3:33 p.m.

HAWK AND JULIETTE EMERGED FROM THE CONFERENCE room and nearly bumped into Jillian Batterson, who was on her way in. An awkward dance to avoid each other and prevent a human collision in the hallway was successful and they faced each other.

"Sorry to interrupt you. You two look like you are headed somewhere in a hurry, but I need a minute if I could have one." Jillian's face was serious.

Hawk opened his mouth to object, then closed it again. He owed Jillian more than a minute. Motioning for them to enter his private office, he led the way then closed the door behind them and motioned for everyone to take a seat. Jillian wasted no time. "I don't know how to tell you this." She interlocked her fingers and looked at her hands for a moment, then released the grip and took a deep breath. "I know the general consensus is that everything is all wrapped up and we have rounded up the bad guys, solved the crisis, and put everything right with the world. Or in this case, with Disney World." She smiled briefly, then continued. "I don't think anyone is going to back me up on this. I talked with Sheriff McManus about it . . ."

"Talked with Cal about what?" Hawk said softly and leaned forward. He felt himself cringe as his eyes narrowed slightly. He was preparing for some bad news. Jillian was serious, and she had earned his trust. If she was bothered by something, then he knew he was going to be bothered by the same thing.

"The sheriff said it was a theory, but without proof, there was nothing actionable he could do. He reminded me of what I just said; we have the perpetrators in custody, we have rounded up all of the people we know are involved, and we will unravel this." Jillian looked from Hawk to Juliette and back to Hawk.

"That's all good, right?" Juliette questioned.

Jillian nodded agreement. It *was* good. Until this moment, Hawk had been feeling like he could catch his breath for the first time in years. But as he saw Jillian hesitate again, then shift in her seat, he felt a bead of sweat form along his forehead.

"It is good," Jillian agreed.

"But?" Hawk pushed her to keep talking.

"I don't think it's really over."

The words hung in the air like a loaded raincloud. Hawk looked to Juliette and shrugged. "Think about what just happened. We're in Tomorrowland and in the midst of an attack, Masters calls you and demands a meeting. You wisely change the original location and give us time to set the trap that is going to catch him. We cover every entrance, we have the place under the most extensive security possible. There was no way he was going to get out and escape us." Jillian looked to Hawk as she spoke.

"And he didn't. We got him. It worked like we planned." Hawk nodded.

"Almost. We got him . . . but the real question is how did he get in?"

"What?"

"How did he get in to begin with?"

"He was wearing a deputy sheriff uniform. So I assume he moved in with the security detail." Hawk tilted his head.

"Exactly," Jillian said. "That's my point. He was in uniform and close to you the entire time. He was in Tomorrowland so he knew you didn't die. He saw you climb out of Space Mountain, he placed the call, and then he was able to move with the security detail to Cinderella Castle. At each step of the way, no one thought for a moment that hey, we don't know who this guy is, why is he here, what is he doing?"

"Right, he was wearing a uniform," Juliette restated.

"But that's not enough. To work these details, no one shows up who isn't connected to the team. They know somebody. They aren't isolated. There's only one way Masters would have known what was going on. He had help."

Jillian waited half a second, then went on. "Masters had to have help on the inside. Someone was feeding him information, letting him know what was going on with you and whatever you were doing. That's how he got the uniform. It's probably how Cambridge was able to infiltrate the Orlando Police Department. Someone with some clout, some access to information, has been helping Jim Masters. We have Masters, sure . . . but we don't have whoever has been helping him. That person is still out there, somewhere."

Hawk felt himself deflate. He had done the inventory, and all of his enemies of the past few years were now where they were supposed to be. They were captured or killed and most importantly, all accounted for. He'd never even considered that there might be another, someone he'd never identified as an enemy. But as soon as she said it, he knew she was right. She had to be right. There had to be someone else.

"So the question is, who is left?" Jillian asked. "And what are they capable of? What is their next move?"

Juliette was now staring at him, wanting to know what Hawk was thinking. He simply nodded at her. It was his signal that he agreed with Jillian.

"So what do we do?" Juliette asked. She sounded as deflated as Hawk felt.

"We have to fish them out. Stop them before they have a chance to do anything else," Hawk said.

"I agree," Jillian said, relieved they had listened. "We have to get ahead of them and be proactive. But the sheriff doesn't think I'm right. We won't get any help."

"Well, maybe we can get enough help to do this," Hawk said as he got to his feet.

"What are we going to do?" Juliette asked him as she followed his cue and stood.

"It is time to do what I promised you I would do. It is time to finish this thing," Hawk said.

"How?" Juliette smoothed her dress getting ready to do whatever was needed.

"Jillian, do you happen to be carrying a stun gun or Taser?" Hawk held out his hand.

Jillian raised an eyebrow. Slowly, methodically, she opened up her black blazer, reached inside the coat to her waist, and unclipped a small black box. She handed it to Hawk and said, "What do you need this for?"

"How about getting me a boat?" Hawk looked toward Juliette.

"A boat?" Jillian stood to join them. "What are you going to do with a boat? What are you up to?"

Hawk just smiled.

CHAPTER 55

The day after
4:45 p.m.

THE DISNEY WATERCRAFT BOUNCED ACROSS THE WATER, Hawk at the wheel. Al Gann rode beside him. On the way out of his office at Bay Lake Towers, Hawk had put a number of things in motion simultaneously. With both Juliette and Jillian jumping in to move things forward, Hawk had made a quick call asking Al Gann to meet him at the dock area of the Contemporary Resort. Juliette had arranged to have a boat ready for him—a security boat, much faster than guest boats and designed for cast members keeping the Disney waterway system safe.

Hawk had made sure he was very conspicuous as he moved out of the towers, across the bridge into the Contemporary, through the lobby, down the escalators, and out the door. A number of guests had recognized him and waved. A couple stopped him for a picture and brief conversation. Hawk took each moment in stride. He was deliberately giving off the appearance that all was now okay in Walt Disney World, and he wanted to be seen by anyone who desired to take the time to look.

With a cool breeze off the water in his face, Hawk navigated the boat to a place he had been a few years before—Discovery Island. With a long history, from being an animal refuge and sanctuary through a number of short-lived tourist experiences to becoming extinct and unnecessary with the opening of Disney's Animal Kingdom, the island now was off-limits to everyone. It was rarely visited. When it was, it was always for a specific purpose. As nature often would do, the island was now flourishing with wildlife.

Hawk had made a startling discovery the night he was here previously. He wanted to revisit it now.

When the powers that be had abandoned the island and closed it down, they had literally abandoned it. Cages, storage units, buildings, and the remnants of directional signs and props littered the island. The power had never been shut off, and in many ways it looked like something terrible had occurred that caused all human activity on the island to simply cease. The wildlife had been left with complete freedom to roam any and every area of the island. In the middle of the night, it was a place where an active imagination could see a horror movie unfolding. In the afternoon sunlight, Hawk knew it would be a far different experience.

Al had met him at the dock, full of questions as they loaded themselves into the boat. Hawk had been vague; he hadn't wanted any cast members to overhear. Now that they were on the water and taking the short jaunt across Bay Lake, they would be docking in just a few minutes and making their way onto the island . . . and he didn't have to worry about anyone overhearing.

"I wanted you to come with me. Now that Masters is in custody, I'm going to round up all the pieces of this Walt Disney mystery so I can put them all together," Hawk said over the sound of the engine as he slowed and they eased up to the dock.

Al jumped out of the boat and tied it off. He made sure Hawk got out safely and then fell in behind him as Hawk began to push back the branches of tree limbs that had overgrown the fading remnants of any pathways that remained. Hawk remembered that parts were so overgrown that it was extremely difficult to navigate through. It was even worse than he remembered it. Struggling to remember in the daylight what he had found on a dark, stormy night, he slowly led Al deeper into the heart of the island. The noise of the birds calling all around them was deafening as they broke into a small patch of clearing with a few buildings in front of them.

"What is this place, Hawk?" Al asked from behind him.

"It is what's left of Discovery Island. I was here once in the middle of the night, and it was scary. When Disney shut it down, they just abandoned it. Now the only thing that happens here is an occasional boat will dock . . . usually a security boat. The place is off-limits. There is no real plan to do anything with it."

As he spoke, Hawk opened the door of the old building and cut on the lights. Inside the musty building were dilapidated signs and some brochures, remnants of the island's days as a tourist experience. Dirty old desks, cabinets, and shelves were lined with all sorts of reminders of a time gone by. Hawk stepped over to an old filing cabinet and tugged on the door. It was locked.

"Do you have the key?" Al said as he watched Hawk struggle with the drawer.

"Yes, I do." Hawk turned and reached into his pocket, retrieving the kingdom key that Farren Rales had given him years before. It was attached to a long metal chain that was connected to something inside his pocket. He held it up so Al could see it.

"This is the key that started it all. A key created by Walt Disney that has opened more things than I could ever imagine. In some ways it was the key to his entire kingdom, his entire world, and it changed my world forever."

"That is some key." Al smiled and eyed the key as Hawk spoke about it.

"The funny thing about a key is that it's amazing what it can unlock," Hawk said.

"What do you mean?"

"Well, this key is unique because it unlocks so many doors," Hawk continued. "But you know what else? It also unlocks things you would never imagine."

"Like what?"

"Well, for example. It can unlock what people think, what makes them tick, what they really want." Hawk smiled as he turned the key over in his hand.

"Say what?" Al laughed. "That sounds like a fairy tale. Like that's a magic key."

"It isn't magic, but it does unlock amazing things."

"Sounds like it," Al agreed.

"Sometimes it has unlocked things I didn't want to find," Hawk said and shook his head.

"Really?" Al stepped closer to Hawk, concerned. "What have you found?"

Hawk kept his voice steady. "I have found that someone who I thought was a friend wasn't really a friend at all. I have found out that the only reason they were close to me was to take for themselves what I had been finding. And I discovered that they would do anything they could to have those things for their own." Hawk now stared at Al, who retreated back to where he had originally been standing.

"Who are you talking about, Hawk?"

"Oh, I think we both know that, don't we, Al?" Hawk sat on top of the desk. "What I want to know is why you did it."

Al swallowed hard, pursed his lips, then broke into a huge grin. "How long have you known?"

Hawk's heart sank. A small part of him had hoped he was wrong—that this conversation would turn out very different. Al's reaction had confirmed what he feared. "Not long."

"Well, I always knew you would figure it out. You have proven to be relentless in your ability to solve puzzles and mysteries. I had planned on you being dead so you and I would never have to have this conversation."

Al moved over and sat down opposite Hawk on another desk. "So what do you think happens now?"

"That depends on you."

"Really? Why is that?"

Hawk watched Al closely. Taking in every move his friend-turned-enemy made, every sense he had was on high alert. There was a part of him that just didn't want to believe that Al had been working against him, but he had to suspend that disbelief or this could end badly. "Because you can tell me why you did it, tell me you are sorry, and then we will leave and you will turn yourself into the authorities." Hawk stopped himself and held up his hand. "But wait, you are an authority. So we will probably go right to the sheriff himself, and you can turn yourself in to him."

"That is what you think is going to happen?" Al laughed out loud. "Let me tell you what is really going to happen. You are going to give me that key and everything else you have found. I may or may not kill you, though I probably will, and then I will move on with my life."

"If you are going to kill me anyway, why would I give you anything?" Hawk shifted on the desk slightly.

"Because if you don't I will also kill Shep, Jon, Jon's family, Juliette, Tim, and their family as well. I know everyone you know. You give it to me, your death is a terrible accident. We never figure out what happened to you, and they all get to live. The power of life and death is in your hands. You can save the ones you love this time, Hawk. You can save your new family. You get a second chance, since you couldn't save your family the first time." Al smirked.

Hawk's eyes narrowed. "Wow, that is some offer. You know, Al . . . it took me a while. You had me fooled for a long time."

Al smiled as he listened. He was enjoying the conversation.

"Years ago, when I thought that Reginald Cambridge was a friend . . . it was right after Masters and Kiran escaped in Tony's on Main Street . . .

Cambridge said he had a friend in the sheriff's department. But interestingly enough, all the bad guys found a way to slip away. Almost like they had someone helping them. They all managed to stay one step ahead of ever being caught."

"Hmm. That is interesting," Al said smugly.

"And if I remember correctly, you joined the church in Celebration about the same time I started meeting with Farren Rales."

"You were much better at preaching than you have been at running the Disney Company."

"I have heard some people say that." Hawk cleared his throat. "But you were always close to me. You ended up in charge of my security. You showed up in a helicopter on the night I fought with Reginald on top of Spaceship Earth, and then amazingly, I was attacked by a helicopter on board a train with George Colmes . . . and you were the only one who knew I was there with him." Hawk got up from the desk. "Then there was the time I had Kiran Roberts locked away on Tom Sawyer's Island. An island surrounded by water, and she was a woman who couldn't swim. But somehow, she managed to get away. Because of course, she had help."

"I have been busy." Al was clearly pleased with himself.

"You were with Reginald when he attacked me and Farren at the ice cream shop. You helped Reginald infiltrate the Orlando Police Department and Jim Masters do the same with the Orange County Sheriff's department. And you were always close enough to me to get a steady stream of information."

"Until this week." Al stopped Hawk's monologue. "This week you decided that you wanted no more help, which meant I had to shift gears. You actually cost me some money this week. I had to start hiring some mercenaries to track you down. And surprisingly, you managed to keep giving them the slip. As long as I had you convinced there were a number of different groups after you, you were so distracted you never would suspect me. You have to give me credit; it was a full-time job keeping Reginald, Jim, Kiran, and Nancy at each other's throats and chasing you. But I always knew the day would come that you might figure it out."

"So you were the mastermind behind it all?" Hawk stood in the center of the room.

"Yes, I was. Are you impressed?"

"That isn't the word I would use."

"Come now, don't be that way. You have to give me some sort of credit for brilliantly playing you and your friends." Al watched Hawk warily but remained seated on the desk. "But now the real question is, have you figured out why I did it?"

Hawk stared at him. That was the question he couldn't answer—the one thing he *hadn't* figured out. As soon as Jillian had suggested someone on the inside was manipulating the situation, Hawk had known it was Al. He had suspected him at various points through the years of trying to know too much, of wanting to be on the inside track for information. Hawk had even felt guilty at times for not allowing him to know more than he was willing to share. Jillian's insight made the whole picture come clear.

Except for the why. That was still a mystery.

"You haven't figured it out yet. Well, I just have to tell you, because it wouldn't be fair to let you die without knowing the truth."

Al reached down and unclipped the safety strap on his gun belt. "Prior to World War II, Walt Disney was sent on a goodwill tour of South America at the request of the US government, which was concerned about pushing back the growing Nazi sympathies in the region. During the war, Disney produced some short films lampooning the Nazis, such as *Education for Death, Reason vs Emotion,* and *Der Führer's Face,* as well as the feature-length film *Victory through Air Power,* which advocated the use of strategic bombing to help defeat the Axis powers. I suspect you know all about it. This film so impressed world leaders that a Walt Disney cartoon reshaped the United States military, and he inspired countless soldiers and sailors to fight the Nazis through the training films the studio produced. I probably never told you that my grandfather fought in that war too. . . for Nazi Germany."

In all his puzzling, that was one motive Hawk had never suspected. "So you did all this because Walt Disney didn't like the Nazis?"

"No, of course not." Al rested his hand on the handle of the gun. "But after the war, Wernher von Braun came to find a new home in the United States and went to work for the US government. He brought with him secrets, things he had learned, and became an American and a friend of Walt's. You see, Wernher was a product of an environment that was aiming toward global domination, and he didn't have the stomach for it. So once he came to America, he made some discoveries on top of what he took from Germany and figured out how to do it. He realized his discoveries could actually give someone or some nation that power to dominate and rule the world. He gave those secrets to Walt Disney, but Walt died before he ever did anything with them. So he has passed them along to you. And you are about to give them to me."

"Because you are a Nazi? A modern-day terrorist who is chasing a self-seeking ideology that will destroy anything that gets in the way because you think you are superior to everyone else?" Hawk tried not to let his face convey the shock he felt.

"I am superior," Al said. "And whoever knows the secrets of von Braun and Disney will rule the world, because they will have limitless power. And that someone will be me."

Al now pulled the gun out of the holster. "So hand me the key, and let's round up the rest of the trinkets and secrets you have found these past few years."

"Then you will kill me."

"Yes, then I will kill you." Al flicked his wrist and motioned with the gun for Hawk to give him the key.

Hawk slowly held out the key and passed it over to Al. It was still connected to the long chain that disappeared into Hawk's pocket.

"What kind of keychain do you have it attached to? Give it to me." Al curled his lip.

Hawk reached into his pocket and let his fingers close around the black box Jillian had given him earlier. He had the chain wrapped around the Taser, and the other end was now connected to the key Al held. He removed the box from his pocket and saw the brief look of confusion on Al's face just before he pressed the trigger.

The electric jolt from the stunning mechanism arced and sent an electrical charge down the length of the thin metallic key chain and through the key in Al's hand. With a yell, Al dropped the key and recoiled. Hawk moved quickly, and in one motion he had unwound the keychain from the stun box. He pressed the Taser against Al's gun arm. Another jolt of electricity coursed through Al, causing him to drop the revolver. He fell to his knees.

Hawk pressed the Taser against his neck and fired it once again. This time Al screamed as he slumped to the ground. Hawk scrambled to find the gun, only to realize Al had fallen on top of it.

That was not part of the plan.

He turned and pressed against the doors that opened into the wild, untamed tangle of Discovery Island. Running at full sprint, Hawk retraced his steps back toward the dock where they had left the boat. The miniature Taser he had borrowed from Jillian was powerful enough to slow Al Gann down, but wouldn't incapacitate him for long. He hoped his head start was enough and that when Al gave chase, he wouldn't remember the best path back to the dock.

Hawk pushed himself, pumping his legs hard and crashing through the low-hanging tree limbs. He was not going to be stopped. His mind replayed what he had just heard Al say. His grandfather had been in Nazi Germany, and Al himself was convinced that Disney's secrets would give him a chance to achieve the global domination Hitler had wanted. Greed and corruption can make you think crazy thoughts—although Hawk knew from some of the notes that Wernher had left for Walt that he had tapped into something so big it had frightened him. For that reason, he had never shared it.

Could Al be right? Were Walt Disney's secrets big enough to alter the entire world?

Breaking through the trees, Hawk spotted the dock in the clearing next to the water's edge. He raced across the path and down the dock, untied the boat, and fired up the engine. Realizing he'd been holding his breath, he finally exhaled as he pulled away from the dock and the boat moved back out onto the depths of Bay Lake.

It was then Al emerged from the trees on the path. He locked eyes with Hawk and leveled his gun at him. He fired off the first shot, and it ricocheted off the pole holding the canopy above Hawk's head. Hawk ducked down behind the console, startled by a voice cracking through a nearby bullhorn.

"Al Gann—the island is surrounded. You are surrounded. Drop your weapon, place your hands on your head, and drop to your knees."

Hawk surveyed the water around him. Disney security boats lined the edge of the island. Aboard the boats were law enforcement officers from Orange County, the Orlando Police, and the Kissimmee Police departments.

That part of the plan had worked.

Al looked both ways and then refocused his sights on Hawk. Once again leveling his gun toward Hawk, he stood in the clearing as if trying to decide whether to fire. Then as if in slow motion, he sank to his knees and tossed the pistol out in front of him.

Multiple boats hit the dock simultaneously, and law enforcement swarmed the beach. The quickly but carefully constructed plan had worked just as he, Juliette, and Jillian had designed it.

The threat was finally over.

CHAPTER 56

The day after
10:00 p.m.

HAWK SAT ALONE IN HIS OFFICE. On his desk was the Norman Rockwell painting *Girl Reading the Post*, with the personalization Rockwell had added for Walt Disney. Hawk had made sure no one was around to see what he was about to do.

After his showdown with Al, he had been jarred into the reality that what he might find was far bigger than he had ever dared to think. Perhaps it was still better for no one to know what was on the painting. At least until he had the chance to see it first. With a screwdriver, he carefully opened the frame, releasing the painting from the structure surrounding it. As he worked, Hawk replayed what he had learned that brought him to this moment.

The conspiracy theories that Wernher von Braun had discovered the secrets of anti-gravity propulsion were so far out there and the stuff of science fiction that they had long been dismissed. After all, there was a space race going on when this school of thought first cropped up, and Americans were still working to get their first rocket into orbit.

But based on what Wernher had given to Walt Disney in his journals and notes, the idea was not as far-fetched as many believed. Because of what von Braun had witnessed in Nazi Germany, he realized how easily power and control of power could be corrupted and misused in the wrong hands. According to his own notes, he had what might be the greatest discovery ever made, but the world was not ready for it—so the world could not know about it. Wernher himself did some things that perpetuated the conspiracy angle in order to cleverly mask what he had really discovered.

But von Braun believed and had openly called Walt Disney a genius, clearly one of the most brilliant men he had ever met. He loved Walt's love of America. He knew that Walt had been instrumental in helping defeat the

Nazis through the use of storytelling and vision. He also watched as Disney took a stand against communism in the years that followed. Wernher knew Walt was an American patriot and far more than just an entertainer. It was Walt's brilliance that allowed Wernher to trust Walt enough to give him this secret. At the time, Walt was actively trying to develop his city of the future, the city of tomorrow, and he was doing so with a vision and passion that Wernher believed could put the discoveries he had made to good use and advance them, ultimately using them to make the world a better place by developing them for good and not evil. Hawk could tell from the notes Walt had added to the Wernher von Braun journals that Disney was aggressively trying to develop and use some of these technologies to make Epcot, the Experimental Prototype Community of Tomorrow, a reality—not the theme park as people knew it today, but the real actual working city that Walt explained in the Florida Project film before his death.

Over the past few days, as Hawk had once again been given the chance to come face-to-face with the creative brilliance of Walt Disney, he realized that as Walt was visiting and checking out American business partners to help him at Epcot, he was also screening what they were doing in research and development. He was actually looking for someone to share the secrets with—Wernher's secrets, the discoveries that had to be hidden from the evil powers in the world—so they could use them to move forward exponentially in their ability to create the future.

According to the notes, Walt was working with his designers and Imagineers at WED Enterprises to develop von Braun's ideas and concepts into something very real, very workable, and capable of revolutionizing the world. By his own writing, some of the ideas were too advanced for the times, but that hadn't stopped the Imagineers from trying to execute the concepts into something real.

And now there was this painting. One that had been protected as a personal possession of Walt Disney and moved about after his death so that no one could find it.

One that held the last of the answers he was looking for.

Releasing the painting, Hawk flipped it over and examined it. It was an original oil painting, the colors rich and vibrant, and it was beautiful—but it was just a painting. The back was a white, blank canvas, with no real distinguishable markings except the expected signs of creation, framing, and aging.

Carefully placing the painting face down on his desk, Hawk removed the eyeglasses that had belonged to Walt from his pocket and placed them on his face. As soon as he did, some markings and a diagram appeared on the back of the canvas.

He removed the glasses, and the markings and drawing disappeared. Repeating the process, he felt his heartbeat quicken, and he looked more closely at what was a schematic drawing of a device, labeled very simply "prototype."

There were notes on the side. He read them. According to the notes, it was called the Anti-Gravity Auxiliary Propulsion Energy unit. Scribbled in the distinctive Walt Disney handwriting he saw the words "the power to change the world—AGAPE."

Hawk smiled. As a preacher he knew the real meaning of *agape,* and it had nothing to do with anti-gravity but everything to do with power. It was the kind of love people discovered when they met God. *Agape* is a Greek word for love. And love could indeed change the world. He wondered if Walt had done that, labeled this drawing with that phrase, on purpose, to give it a dual meaning.

That wasn't a question he could answer—but the reality of what he was looking at was beginning to sink in. This was a schematic for a machine that literally had the power to revolutionize the world. Not only as a source of energy, but it could also be used in weaponry. Whoever controlled it—if it really worked, and Hawk was sure it would—would have the knowledge that could harness the power to change the world.

He found he was holding his breath, as the weight settled on his shoulders. None of the Imagineers had really understood what they had been protecting. They simply knew it was Walt's legacy. A legacy greater than he would leave behind for his family. They knew, or at least felt, that it had to be protected and used wisely or terrible things could happen. Hawk reflected on the awful things that had already come to pass, as people had tried to steal this design and gain the knowledge for their own. No wonder Press had been so insistent on Hawk keeping this painting and caring for it himself.

But now, what would Hawk do with it?

Sweating, he quickly began to put the picture back in the frame. He had seen what he needed to see, and realized that he had much more to learn, much more to research, and much more to do—starting immediately. He had to protect this secret with the same tenacity with which Walt and Roy

Disney had protected it. Their instincts had been correct. Only the right hands could develop and use this technology and make it a reality. In the wrong hands, it would be catastrophic. Now it was in Hawk's hands . . . what would he do?

This secret had the potential to help shape and change the world for the better. But that was the same challenge Wernher von Braun and Walt Disney had faced. Knowing how to best use this knowledge and power and the wisdom to do it at the right time in the right way would make all of the difference in the world.

Until he knew that, it was his turn to keep it secret.

Turning the picture back over, he secured it rightly in the frame as it had been. The drawings and notes on the picture were what made it truly valuable, but the eyeglasses Walt had developed to make it visible were now just as important as the key. In some ways they were a key in their own right, one that unlocked the end of the mystery. A mystery and secret that were now his responsibility.

Because he was the one who had been given the key to the kingdom.

CHAPTER 57

Four months later

"**WALT DISNEY ONCE SAID THAT PEOPLE SORT** of live in the dark about things. They think the future is closed to them, that everything has been done. It isn't true. There are still many avenues waiting to be explored."

Grayson Hawkes paused as he spoke and allowed the words to filter across the thousands of people listening . . . and into his own thoughts as well. It was true; there was still so much to figure out and discover.

"This land is a vista into a world of wondrous ideas, signifying man's achievements. . . a step into the future, with predictions of constructive things to come. Tomorrow offers new frontiers in science, adventure, and ideals; the challenge of tomorrow and the hope for a peaceful world. Walt Disney believed in all of these things and tried to create a land where people would be inspired to chase and pursue those dreams and make them a reality. He called it Tomorrowland."

Hawk paused to look over the crowds. "As most of you are aware, four months ago there was an attempt to wipe out and destroy the future. To turn our tomorrows into a memory, to corrupt our dreams and turn them into nightmares. But the future is not easily destroyed, and dreams worth chasing never die. Today we are excited to reopen the newly imagined Tomorrowland for all of you. Now, most are aware that as we were attacked, considerable damage was done to this land. But you are about to discover that we have not simply repaired and remodeled; we have redreamed and reimagined a world that goes far beyond anything we have ever tried before, one that keeps Walt's vision of the future alive. Due to the extremely talented and sacrificial efforts of our cast and team here at Walt Disney World, we are opening two months ahead of what we had anticipated being able to do. We worked around the clock each day to do it, but we did it. So for all of those who are willing to chase dreams, I invite you to step into and create the future in the new Tomorrowland."

Hawk stepped back to thunderous applause and with an exaggeratedly large pair of scissors cut the ceremonial ribbon that opened the pathway for people to begin streaming into Tomorrowland. The company had indeed done what many thought to be impossible. Four months after the attack, the land had been redesigned, reimagined, and rebuilt with a fresh look that was bold and something Hawk had been working on since he found the notes in Walt's personal journal years before.

Rocket Tower Plaza had been completely changed. The Astro Orbiter had a fresher more futuristic look. The Tomorrowland Transit Authority had a much more visible presence, with an enhanced Progress City now on display with elements that had been brought in from the Disney Archives. Space Mountain had some added décor, updating the quick view of space passengers got as they rocketed through the cosmos. The Interplanetary Science and Convention Center had sustained considerable damage, but the building interior had been gutted and an entirely new space exploration attraction, designed by Walt years ago, now had a home and a life inside Tomorrowland. While many of the additions were already well into development before the attack, the pace was accelerated by the work done after it.

"You did a good job here, Hawk." Juliette placed a hand on Hawk's shoulder as he stood on the temporary stage area that had been set up for the event, and she watched the guests enter. Hawk listened to their initial reactions and knew they were excited to once again enter this guest-favorite area. With the reopening of Tomorrowland two months ahead of schedule, the new look of the world of the future had been kept under tight wrap, and people were anxious to see what they had created. Hawk knew they wouldn't be disappointed.

"No, *we* did a good job." Hawk gave Juliette a hug. He looked fondly at his loyal friend. He knew he had made her life difficult . . . again. She had skillfully navigated the information flow in the days following the attack in a way that was both truthful and tactful. Not giving away anything the public couldn't know but sharing more than they *needed* to know had kept Walt Disney World moving forward, and the attacks hadn't become the public relations disaster they might have been. Somehow, in the midst of it, the story of how Hawk had helped to save the day had enhanced his image and status in the eyes of the public even more.

"Thank you." Juliette stepped back, and there were tears in her eyes.

"You're welcome. For what?"

"You kept your promise. You finished it this time." Juliette smiled.

"Again, we finished it this time." Hawk tilted his head back and felt the sunshine warm his skin. He looked back at Juliette. "You're welcome."

It had been a long and amazing journey. Just as the new world of the future was opening with the bright hopes and dreams of tomorrow, Hawk felt a sense of enthusiasm. The battle was over. There were great things ahead.

"Juliette, did the kids get to come?" he asked, as he scanned the crowd.

"Yes, by now they're probably on Space Mountain." She looked but did not see her children in the people moving past.

"Tell them to come and see me before they leave if they get the chance," Hawk said, turning to leave.

"Sure." Juliette raised an eyebrow and gave him a what-are-you-up-to look that he had seen many times. "Everything okay?"

"Just perfect. Thanks."

Hawk stepped off into the steady stream of guests who were moving past the stage. As he did, he felt a hand grab him firmly by the arm. Looking back, he found Jillian Batterson at the end of the hand. He leaned back and allowed her to pull him out of the crowd.

"Where do you think you are going?" She leaned in to be heard over the people surrounding them.

"I'm going home."

"To the fire station in the City Square?" Jillian looked around at the crowd surging through the area.

"I think you mean Town Square on Main Street, U.S.A.."

"Sure, Disney dude, that's exactly what I mean." She shook her head. "Like I told you, I am not a Disney nerd like you."

"Yes, but you are the new head of security for the company. So you need to get better at it."

In the months that followed the investigation, Hawk had approached Jillian about taking a job with the Disney Company. She loved her job with Homeland Security, but was intrigued with the opportunity to protect an entire world. Hawk had also told her some of the things he had discovered about the legacy of Walt Disney. Convinced that his discoveries could have a global impact, she had agreed to step into the world of Disney and was tasked with the responsibility of keeping Hawk safe and secure. They'd had some good moments and some bad moments together up to this point. But both believed they could make it work and that she was the best fit for the role. Besides, Hawk had discovered that he enjoyed having her around.

"I will make sure you get home safe." She tugged at his arm, and they began to make their way through the crowd. "So how does it feel?" Jillian said as they walked.

"How does what feel?"

"To know that this time we got the bad guys." She continued to guide him along the line of shops on Main Street, U.S.A.

Hawk leaned in and spoke into her ear so she could hear him above the background noise of the park. "It feels good. I'm glad you showed up when you did, and I'm glad you decided to stay."

"You're welcome," she said. "I hate to admit it. But there is something about this place that is just . . ." Jillian hesitated, looking for the right word.

"Magical?"

"Yes, that's it . . . magical." Jillian smiled.

Hawk looked at his home, Walt Disney World, and had to agree. It truly was a magical place. Just like Walt Disney dreamed it would be.

HERE WE ARE . . . TOGETHER WE HAVE TAKEN another journey behind the scenes into a world that is magical, exciting, fascinating, and always fresh and new. Walt Disney World is a place where on any given day you can discover something you have never seen before, find some amazing hidden detail, or experience some precious moment that becomes a memory you will never forget. This is the fourth time we have traveled with Grayson Hawkes and company into the world of Walt Disney, and as a writer I can't express to you how honored and humbled I am that you have chosen to come with me on the adventure.

In a day and age when there are so many things demanding our time, to realize that you have taken your most precious commodity—time—and chosen to spend it flipping through the pages of this story along with me leaves me speechless. Thank you so much. Through the years I have received letters from people from all over the world talking about the books, finding some of the hidden treasures within its pages, discovering that something they thought was fiction actually existed. The notes are always so nice and encouraging. That is why these stories and this series has continued into this latest installment.

Like so many of you, I am a huge Disney fan. I know it is not a perfect place as I walk into Walt Disney World, but it may be as close to perfect as any place you will ever visit. I am always amazed at what I find, what I see, and how my experiences not only entertain but inspire me. In some ways, I hope that the stories of Hawk in the world of Disney have done some of that for you.

The more I discover about him, the more intrigued I become with the life, history, and legacy of the man Walt Disney. He was so much more than just an entertainer. He was a visionary, a leader, a pioneer, a risk-taker, an explorer, and a man whose courage compelled him not to quit when others might have. The people Walt knew, his friends, the connections he had with others were nothing short of phenomenal. Those relationships would make some great stories in and of themselves. (Of course, I have introduced some of those very real relationships into the fictional world we have created.)

And so here we are. The four-story arc we began together has come to an end. So what happens next? That is a great question. A moment is the intersection between the past and the future. What we do in any given moment sets the direction for what is going to happen next, so I suppose anything could happen. That is the beauty and miracle of a moment. Time will tell what happens to Hawk and friends. But let me encourage you, as you are reading these words in this moment, to make a choice to embrace life to the fullest, chase your dreams, unleash your creativity, and become the best version of you . . . the version you were created and destined to be.

Again, thanks for spending this time with me. I look forward to our next adventure together—whenever and wherever it may take us.

Jeff Dixon

The following resources were invaluable in understanding the background, history, operation, and attractions within Walt Disney World.

Broggie, Michael. *Walt Disney's Railroad Story.* Virginia Beach, Virginia: Donning Company Publishers, 2012.

Canemaker, John. *Walt Disney's Nine Old Men & the Art of Animation.* New York: Hyperion, 2001.

Crawford, Michael. *The Progress City Primer.* Orlando : Progress City Press, 2015.

Emerson, Chad Denver (editor). *Four Decades of Magic: Celebrating the First Forty Years of Disney World.* United States of America: Ayefour Publishing, 2011.

Gabler, Neal. *Walt Disney: Triumph of the American Imagination.* New York: Knopf, 2006.

Ghez, Didier. *Disney's Grand Tour.* United States of America: Theme Park Press, 2013.

Ghez, Didier, editor. Homer Brightman. *Life in the House of the Mouse.* United States of America: Theme Park Press, 2014.

Gordan, Bruce and Jeff Kurtti. *Walt Disney World: Then, Now and Forever.* New York: Disney Editions, 2008.

Green, Katherine and Richard. *The Man Behind the Magic: The Story of Walt Disney.* New York: Viking, 1991.

Hench, John. *Designing Disney: Imagineering and the Art of the Show.* New York: Disney Editions, 2003.

Imagineers. *Walt Disney Imagineering: A Behind the Dreams Look at Making the Magic.* New York: Hyperion, 1996.

Imagineers. *The Imagineering Field Guide to the Magic Kingdom at Walt Disney World.* New York: Disney Editions, 2005.

Jackson, Kathy Merlock and Mark West (editors). *Disneyland and Culture.* Jefferson, North Carolina: McFarland and Company, 2011.

Korkis, Jim. *The Vault of Walt.* United States of America: Ayefour Publishing, 2010.

———. *The Vault of Walt Volume 5.* United States of America: Theme Park Press, 2016.

Kurtti, Jeff. *Imagineering Legends and the Genesis of the Disney Theme Park.* New York: Disney Editions, 2008.

Marling, Karal Ann. *Designing Disney's Theme Parks.* New York: Flammarion, 1997.

Miller, Diane Disney and Pete Martin. *The Story of Walt Disney.* New York: Holt, 1957.

Moran, Christian. *Great Big Beautiful Tomorrow—Walt Disney and Technology.* United States of America : Theme Park Press, 2015.

Neary, Kevin and David Smith. *The Ultimate Disney Trivia Book.* New York: Hyperion, 1992.

———. *The Ultimate Disney Trivia Book 2.* New York: Hyperion, 1994.

———. *The Ultimate Disney Trivia Book 3.* New York: Hyperion, 1997.

———. *The Ultimate Disney Trivia Book 4*. New York: Disney Editions, 2000.

Pedersen, R. A. *The Epcot Explorer's Encyclopedia*. Florida, USA: Encyclopedia Press, 2011.

Pierce, Todd James. *Three Years in Wonderland—The Disney Brothers, CV Wood, and the Making of the Great American Theme Park*. Jackson, Mississippi: University of Mississippi Press, 2016.

Ridgeway, Charles. *Spinning Disney's World: Memories of a Magic Kingdom Press Agent*. Branford, CT: Intrepid Traveler, 2007.

Smith, Dave. *Disney Trivia from the Vault*. New York: Disney Editions, 2013.

———. *Disney Facts Revealed*. New York: Disney Editions, 2016.

———. *Disney A to Z: the Official Encyclopedia*. New York: Hyperion, 1996; updated 1998, 2006.

Smith, Dave and Steven Clark. *Disney: The First 100 Years*. New York: Hyperion, 1999; Disney Editions, updated 2002.

Thomas, Bob. *The Art of Animation*. New York: Simon & Schuster, 1958.

———. *Walt Disney: An American Original*. New York: Simon & Schuster, 1976.

———. *Building a Company; Roy O. Disney and the Creation of an Entertainment Empire*. New York: Hyperion, 1998.

Thomas, Frank and Ollie Johnston. *The Illusion of Life: Disney Animation*. New York: Hyperion, 1995.

Vennes, Susan. *The Hidden Magic of Walt Disney World: Over 600 secrets of the Magic Kingdom, Epcot, Disney's Hollywood Studios, and Animal Kingdom*. Avon, MA: Adams Media, 2009.

Walt Disney World Explorer CD-ROM. Burbank, CA: Disney Interactive, 1996.

Websites

These are *a few* of the author's favorite Disney news and fan sites that helped provide information and resources beyond the printed page.

Inside the Magic w/ Ricky Brigante, http://www.distantcreations.com.

Jim Hill Media, http://www.jimhillmedia.com.

Disney Pal, http://www.disney-pal.com.

Passport to Dreams Old and New, http://www.passport2dreams.blogspot.com.

Resort Information, http://www.mouseplanet.com.

Disney History Institute, http://www.disneyhistoryinstitute.com.

DIS, http://www.wdwinfo.com.

Walt Disney World News, http://www.wdwmagic.com.

THE KNOCK ON THE DOOR OF THE APARTMENT above the fire station shook Hawk from his casual watching of people moving up and down Main Street, U.S.A. Heading across the room to the door, he opened it and saw Tim and Juliette's two teenagers standing there with big smiles.

"Hey, Uncle Hawk!" said Jason, the oldest of the pair. Now in high school, he gave Hawk a hug, breezed past him, and headed for the kitchen to find something to eat.

"Hi." Beth followed her brother inside. She was two years younger and just finishing middle school. "The new Tomorrowland was awesome. It's great to think about the future. Mom said you wanted to see us."

Hawk walked inside with Beth and invited her to sit down at the table. Once Jason had gotten something to drink, he joined the pair, and they sat together for a few moments. The kids had spent a lot of time with their Uncle Hawk. He was family, and they always seemed to love being around him. Over the past few years, his new role at Disney had changed all of their lives, and they had discovered a whole new world of things to do and explore.

"Thanks for coming over. I have something I want to give you." Hawk got up from the table, walked into the living room, opened a drawer in the desk, and pulled out a square black box. He tossed it into the air and caught it in the same hand, then made his way back to the table. He placed it on the wooden surface and slid it over so it rested between them.

"What is it?" Beth asked.

"Open it." Hawk grinned as they hurriedly obeyed.

They pulled back the lid on the box and gazed inside.

"Whoa." Jason's eyes widened and his mouth opened in stunned surprise.

"They are beautiful." Beth's eyes too were wide with wonder.

"What do they do?" Jason asked.

"What are they for?" Beth quickly followed.

"Ah, that is the fun of it," Hawk said, watching them examine his gift. "That is what you have to do. Figure out what they do and what they are for. Then you will really understand how valuable the gift is . . ."

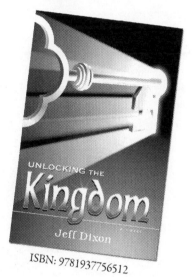